Advance praise for BORN AGAIN

"Kelly Kerney's ⸺ :alism,
and one very a ⸺ ruggle
is funny, touch ⸺ ally is
born again, an ⸺ too."
⸺ *e East*

"Read Kelly Ke ⸺ story
illuminating Cl ⸺

⸺ *Garbo*

"Melanie comp⸺ ⸺ e her
congregation, a ⸺ hy—
until she begins ⸺ men-
talist Christians ⸺ —in
an uncertain wc ⸺
—S ⸺ *tland*

KELLY KERNEY

BORN
AGAIN

A HARVEST ORIGINAL ⊂×✕⊃ HARCOURT, INC.

Orlando   Austin   New York   San Diego   Toronto   London

www.HarcourtBooks.com

Library of Congress Cataloging-in-Publication Data
Kerney, Kelly A.
Born again/Kelly Kerney.
p.   cm.
"A Harvest Original."
Summary: While surreptitiously reading Darwin's "Origin of the Species,"
hoping to prove it wrong, fourteen-year-old Mel, a "Jesus freak," uncovers
a family secret that changes her views on her family, her church and,
most vitally, her assumptions about God and science.
[1. Christian life—Fiction.   2. Evolution—Fiction.   3. Family problems—Fiction.
4. Schools—Fiction.   5. Indiana—Fiction.]   I. Title.
PZ7.K457875Bor   2006
[Fic]—dc22   2005034607
ISBN-13: 978-0-15-603145-5   ISBN-10: 0-15-603145-0

Text set in Bembo
Designed by April Ward

Printed in the United States of America
First edition
A C E G I K J H F D B

FOR ANTHONY WALTON

"Now the Lord God had planted a garden in the east, in Eden; and there he put the man he had formed. And the Lord God made all kinds of trees grow out of the ground—trees that were pleasing to the eye and good for food. In the middle of the garden were the tree of life and the tree of the knowledge of good and evil."

—Genesis 2:8–9, New International Version

"Thus, in the light of the science of evolutionary biology which Darwin founded, man is seen not just as a part of nature, but as a very peculiar and indeed unique part. In his person the evolutionary process has become conscious of itself, and he alone is capable of leading it on to realizations of possibility."

—Sir Julian Huxley, in
his introduction to the Mentor edition
of *The Origin of Species* (1958)

CHOOSE LIFE,
YOUR MOTHER DID

The "Morality Check" abstinence rally was silent, everyone waiting for me to finish my pledge, but somehow I had forgotten the words. I had practiced for weeks these three simple sentences, but now, squinting in the spotlight at the crowded gymnasium, the last one escaped me. Something about intimacy and God. I improvised.

"And in pledging my purity, I promise to be intimate with no one but God."

Silence. And then applause. Pastor Lyle ushered me away from the microphone and to the side of the stage. Squinting out into the audience, I tried to locate my parents, but it was impossible to see individuals. These hundreds of people blended together into a vague gray mass that reminded me of a sleeping animal—a twitch somewhere, a noise every now and then, but still a single entity.

I stood in the shadows of the stage, watching Tessa Goodman make her pledge. She said it flawlessly, and she annunciated the last sentence like the punch line of some joke: "And in pledging my purity, I promise to be intimate with no one until I am joined with my husband in holy matrimony by God."

She took Pastor Lyle's arm, and I watched them walk over to me. She was smiling and her eyes were set about an inch to the left of my head. *Bitch,* I said to myself, but immediately repented. Pastor Lyle gave me a disappointed look as if he'd heard my thoughts. Why, I wondered, did that word pop into my head just now? I repented again, biting the inside of my cheek until it bled, to show God I meant it.

I had no idea how I had forgotten that last sentence, but I figured I got it close enough. I just forgot the marriage part, but everyone knew that anyway. Still, I was baffled. My memory was impeccable. I was the county Bible Quiz Champion. I could recite entire chapters of the Bible on command. And Tessa Goodman was no better than an idiot.

I watched all eleven of the girls recite their pledges. I had been first, for some reason that Pastor Lyle never made clear, although I had a good guess. He knew I was special, that I, above all these silly girls, would take a pledge to God seriously. When I was a baby, Pastor Lyle had prophesied over me, had told my parents that I was destined to do great works for God. These other girls just wanted to prance around onstage in pretty dresses.

They all looked elegant in the spotlight, and I watched Pastor Lyle escort each of them to a line next to me. It was like a beauty pageant, watching them in their new dresses. But I knew I didn't look like this. I was wearing a dress that was too big in the chest, that fell at an awkward length above my ankles. I ended up in one of my sister's old dresses, which had been white and puffy on her years ago, but on me was dingy and deflated, like old curtains. I looked down at myself, realizing for the first time that abstinence for me was not a choice but my destiny.

After we were all lined up, the spotlight found Pastor Lyle, leaving us in darkness. He was standing behind the podium, looking out at the audience. I could see the back of his body and his profile. Millions of dust particles swirled through the light that surrounded him, as if his intention to speak were enough to disrupt the tranquillity of things. He didn't even clear his throat before he started.

"Our nation's youth are under attack," he said in a somber voice that was just loud enough to reach the people in the back. "Our youth"—he thrust an accusing finger backwards at us girls without looking—"are precious to God. God has a plan for them. And I can tell you that plan does not involve AIDS, pregnancy, sterility, poverty, alcohol abuse, cervical cancer, and death." The audience jumped to life, clapping and yelling as Pastor Lyle put his hands out, as if to say he was just getting started. "Satan has infiltrated our culture and overtaken the media." He stopped to let this one sink in.

"Before a child in this country turns eighteen, she will have seen ninety thousand instances of premarital relations without consequences. This," he yelled, banging a fist on the podium, "this is what I mean when I say our youth are under attack."

There was more cheering. I was fourteen years old. How much premarital sex had I been exposed to already? The math quickly jumbled in my head. I tried to recall the last instance of premarital sex I had seen on television. Last week at my best friend Beth's house, I had seen a movie where two unmarried real-estate agents had sex. They were horizontal and rolling around in someone else's bed, yelling each other's names like curse words. Then he bit her shoulder. Afterward they lay there, the sheets pulled up to their armpits, talking about the tricks they used to sell houses. Essential oils on the lightbulbs, a baseball mitt left on the porch. There were no consequences at all. They seemed pretty pleased with themselves. I stared at the back of Pastor Lyle, watching his knees bobbing in excitement as he wound himself up for whatever he was going to say next. It was incredible to watch the Spirit move through him—his legs were working like crazy, but the upper half of him didn't move.

"God's plan for our children does not involve suicide and abortion. God's plan involves a man and woman, brought together under Him, to be made into one flesh. God made sex," he said, letting that word come out of his mouth like a puff of smoke. He paused to savor it, and I thought I would fall over right there onstage.

I had never heard Pastor Lyle say that word before, and now it lingered there, in the air in front of me, just asking me to breathe. I resisted the urge and began picking at a hangnail that I had worked almost all the way down to my knuckle.

"Man and woman were created by God to complement each other. They were made to be together. Men need sexual fulfillment, recreation, physical attraction, admiration, and domestic support. Women need affection, conversation, honesty, financial support, and family commitment. Men and women," he said again, "are meant to be together." He scanned the audience, as if daring anyone to oppose him. "And so God created sex, but He created it with boundaries. When it occurs within these boundaries, sex is"—he paused to choose his word—"awesome."

I couldn't hold my breath any longer and let it out with a small sigh as I tried to imagine Pastor Lyle having awesome sex with his wife. They were horizontal, wrapped up in sheets, biting each other's shoulders. I wondered if it was a sin to picture married people having sex. I repeated my pledge over in my head, just to make sure God knew I was sincere.

"But sex outside the boundary of marriage is terribly, terribly destructive."

I imagined the roof falling in on those sexy TV real-estate agents, their feet sticking out from under the rubble on the bed.

"But these girls," he said, pointing again at us. "These girls have been educated in resisting temptation. They have learned that the only way to resist the attack of the enemy is through Bible study, participating in the Church, and reading wholesome books that strengthen their faith." The crowd loved this one. As they clapped, I thought about *Wuthering Heights,* if Pastor Lyle would consider that one wholesome.

"These girls have made a commitment to preserve their bodies in the name of Christ. They have signed a contract with Him."

Pastor Lyle walked toward me, bringing the spotlight with him.

As he fiddled in his pocket, his blond hair fell just to his eyes, and he flipped it back with a nonchalance that made me bite the sore spot in my cheek. With his huge tan hands, he struck a match. He got on one knee in front of me and lit the pale cold candle I'd been gripping in my sweaty fist for the past half hour. My wick caught immediately in a large flame that sent wax dripping down the side and onto the paper shield. I turned to light Tessa's, and for a terrible second I considered letting mine tip so it would pour hot wax on her hand.

The crowd burst out in a delayed applause after all the candles were lit. We were then herded to some chairs behind the podium, where a high school girl was already standing, adjusting the microphone. The applause dwindled and the girl cleared her throat.

"I wish I had known two years ago that there were girls who were willing to stand up for themselves, for the sanctity of their bodies. If I had known, my life would be different today." She paused to take a breath. "I am a teen mother." The girl seemed shaken, as if the fact just occurred to her. "My name is Brenda Trickett." Another pause. The crowd was utterly silent as she composed herself. I could not see her face but stared at the back of her head. Her long dark hair and skinny legs could have been mine.

"Just two years ago, I was an ordinary girl. I was in the eighth grade, and I liked to go to the movies with my friends and ride my bike. But since I had Tucker, I can no longer do any of these things. I spend all day with my baby to make sure he doesn't put things in his mouth. My friends tell me about all these cute boys they've met, but I can't hang out with them. It's so lonely. I can't even get a boyfriend." She sniffed in the microphone, and it sounded like the roof caving in. "But I love my baby," she clarified. "I wouldn't trade him for anything. I just wish—" She stopped, and I watched her lift her right foot and scratch her left calf with it. "I just wish I would have waited until I was married."

She stepped away from the podium. A few people instinctively applauded but quickly stopped. I didn't know what I was supposed to do. This girl had ruined her life. No boy would ever respect her. She was destined to be alone her entire life because we hadn't reached her in time.

I looked down at my hands and realized that I was still holding my candle. It was burning furiously, as if it were consuming something much greater than the wick. I looked down the row and saw that the other girls had blown out their candles and put them under their seats. I looked again at my candle and noticed that there was a puddle of wax between my feet. What was I supposed to do? Pastor Lyle hadn't actually told us what the significance of the candle was, but I had thought it was supposed to represent the fires of lust. I had decided that we were supposed to let the candle burn all the way until it extinguished itself. That it represented the fires of lust being squelched in us. But now, I thought, maybe that isn't what it was supposed to mean. The candle was about two inches from my hands. If I blew it out, that might reverse the pledge. I tried to think what exactly a blown-out candle was a symbol for.

As I went through the possibilities, I tried to look attentive. I set my eyes on the next speaker—a man who had AIDS. He was so angry, he said, when he found out he had it that he wanted to sleep with as many girls as possible to give it to them. I had read about people like him in my booklet. They were everywhere, and the fact that this guy looked like a hundred men I knew didn't surprise me at all. I tightened my grip on the candle, deciding that I wouldn't blow it out.

By now the other girls had noticed my candle. They leaned forward, staring at me as if I had lit myself on fire with it. Not willing to meet their eyes, I looked down at my hands, at the fires of lust that were getting dangerously close to burning me. I will endure it, I told myself. I will put my trust in God and He won't let me be burned, just like Shadrach, Meshach, and Abednego. I was a child of God.

I heard some other people shifting around onstage, but I didn't look at them. In order to gather my strength, I had focused on the basketball hoop that hovered over the podium like a misplaced halo. I focused on the shape of it—a perfect orange circle—as I waited for God's protection. At just the time I imagined the fire burning through the paper shield and settling into my palm, I noticed Pastor Lyle standing over me. He had taken off his suit coat, and I could see the mystifying shape of his chest underneath his white shirt. Before I could say anything, he bent over and blew my candle out.

After the rally my parents found me near the drinking fountain. Standing under those stage lights for an hour, I felt as if every drop of moisture had been cooked from my body. I had been taking a long drink, and when I finally resurfaced, there was my father's face, right in mine.

"How's my Born-Again Child?" he asked, already hugging me. I had no choice but to wipe my mouth on his shirt. Over his shoulder I could see my mother, standing across the hall with her feet together. She held her big red purse in front of her with both hands. She was a small woman, but this huge purse made her look even smaller, almost like a child. I could smell her chemical perfume as if she were right next to me. She smiled across the distance between us.

"So this is the beginning of your adult life," my father lamented into my hair. "How about we get some ice cream."

Dad insisted I try the Peanut Butter Blast Sundae, even though it cost five dollars. The boy working the counter seemed annoyed that I had ordered the most complicated item on the menu, but my parents didn't notice. As he battled with the frozen block of peanut butter ice cream, they just kept talking to him.

"We just came from the abstinence rally," my father said to the boy, who must have been sixteen and was not handsome in the least.

"Too bad you had to work, or you could have gone. It was really powerful."

The boy nodded.

"My girl here pledged her life to God." Dad pointed at me. "She made an oath. There was a ceremony and everything," he said.

I took pleasure in that moment, in the fact that this boy now knew I was never going to sleep with him.

"She's going far in life," Dad said, leaning over the counter, demanding his attention.

The boy squinted down at me, making me remember how homely I must have looked. I shifted in the too-big dress while he studied me, as if he really had to try hard at imagining my success.

"Ask her anything about the Bible," my mother said to him. "Ask her anything and she'll tell you. I'm not kidding."

The boy just nodded, not taking the suggestion seriously until my father slapped his wallet on the counter and said, "Go on, ask her. If you stump her, I'll give you ten dollars."

This got the boy's attention, and mine. This almost sounded like betting. My mother made a small noise in the back of her throat, probably thinking the same thing I was. But my father seemed up to it; he was just beaming, tapping a beat on the counter.

The boy stopped scooping, looked at the ceiling for a good one, but all he could come up with was "What's the order of the books of the Bible?"

Of course, I was a bit disappointed with such an easy question. This boy definitely did not go to church. I wonder if he'd ever even read the Bible before. He looked miserable, like someone who hated the path he had chosen for his life. This is the type of person Dad would usually invite to church with us.

I recited the sixty-six books in order, switching Habakkuk and Zephaniah, just for fun, just to see if the boy would even notice. But all he said was "wow," handing the crooked tower of ice cream over to me. Dad didn't even catch the mistake.

Walking back to the table, I asked my father if what he did was betting. "Mel," he said, "betting involves chance. And there was no chance you'd miss any question that kid came up with. I have complete faith in you. So no, it wasn't a bet. There was no chance I was going to lose that ten dollars. It was yours, anyway." He handed me the ten, told me to save it.

Suddenly, I felt guilty for having shown off. My father had put his faith in me, and I had given in to vanity. Technically, that ten dollars was no longer mine. It belonged to the boy. But I couldn't bring myself to say anything. If I did, my father would realize what I had done. And what I had done had made him a gambler.

My mother didn't get ice cream, just watched me and Dad eat ours. Dad hurried through his, and then just sat back and watched me, a smile on his face, ice cream in his beard.

A few other people from church showed up at the ice-cream shop, including the McBrides, who had all been at the rally. The McBrides had four children, all under the age of eight. It occurred to me for the first time that the McBrides must have had sex at least four times in eight years. They seemed young, definitely a lot younger than my parents. Possibly too young to be married for eight years.

Mr. McBride sat next to us, while his wife stood at the counter with the children, who were all yelling their orders at the boy behind the counter. I found myself watching her, trying to determine her exact age.

"Good rally," Mr. McBride said to us, ignoring the chaos his children were creating up front. He was right next to me, the long hair of his arms brushing my hand as he adjusted his chair. "Melanie, you're a good example. I'm telling you, I'm scared for my kids. I mean, being out in the world every day, seeing what my kids see, I feel powerless, you know? It's like everyone and everything in this world wants them to fail." He was speaking mainly to my parents now. "You wouldn't believe what I saw the other day, coming out of the Food Lion. I'm not kidding, I really saw these teenagers in a car—there must have been seven of them packed in there—emptying cans of Reddi-wip out the windows and into the parking lot. You know what they do with those, don't you? There was just this huge pile of whipped cream right there in the parking lot, for anyone to slip on."

My parents were shaking their heads. I had no idea what deviant kids did with whipped cream, but I was not going to ask. It sounded sexual.

Mr. McBride then put a hand on my shoulder. "But I look at your girl and my hope is restored. I think maybe things will turn out okay for them."

My parents nodded and everyone was suddenly looking at me. I smiled, stared down into my ice cream, noticing all the whipped cream the boy had put on it, like some kind of obscene gesture. Feeling myself blush, I scraped it off with my spoon.

I was lucky, I knew, to be in a family that cared about what happened to me. And I was lucky to be in a church that took an interest in my well-being. Too many churches were what Pastor Lyle liked to call "Sunday churches." They just cared about their members on Sunday and vice versa. These people would do whatever they wanted for the rest of the week and still call themselves Christians. They could drink and fornicate and slowly destroy themselves and their families, and the church wouldn't do a thing to help. Religion, Pastor Lyle always said, should never be passive. Satan is active. Sin and temptation and the vices of the world are all active. How can we be passive when Satan is actively recruiting?

All the McBrides were now at the table, the kids scooting chairs in between us. They were all staring at me as they stuffed ice cream into their already-sticky faces. They'd miss their mouths with their spoons, getting chocolate sauce all over themselves, but still they wouldn't take their eyes off me, like I was some sort of celebrity or something. As I watched them eat, I pushed my sundae aside, not able to finish it. If I went to a Sunday church, things might be different for me now, I realized. I might have four little kids; I might be like Brenda Trickett. She was probably raised Lutheran or Presbyterian.

When we got home, I ran to my room to take off that horrid dress. I threw it in a corner, where it landed stiffly—almost upright—against the wall like shed skin. I stared at it a moment, wondering the mathematical chances of something like that happening. It was one in a million, I was sure.

Sitting on my bed in my underwear, I flipped through the abstinence booklet Pastor Lyle had given me. There were quizzes and exercises and a list of things to say to boys who were trying to tempt me. I read over this list, wondering if I would ever have to use it.

"We don't have to do it," I read in a stern voice. "Let's go get pizza instead."

I didn't like that one very much.

I looked down the list, trying to find one I could see myself saying, and saw it near the bottom. I stood up, adjusted my underwear, pointed a stern finger at the wall, and said, "Unhand me. My body is a temple of the Holy Ghost, and no one but my husband is authorized to enter."

I liked that one. It reminded me of something Catherine in *Wuthering Heights* would say. I repeated it, imagining Pastor Lyle lighting my candle, down on one knee in front of me. His arms would circle my waist as he moved in to bite my shoulder, and I'd give that line right back to him.

I realized then that when I read *Wuthering Heights,* I imagined that Heathcliff looked just like Pastor Lyle. I wondered if this was a sin, imagining him in a book like that. It wasn't a banned book, at least not according to my *Surviving a Secular Classroom* booklet, which had been given to me a few years ago by Pastor Perle, the children's pastor, when the church school closed and all us kids were forced into public school. In the back there was a list of books that contradicted the Word of God, books that public schools liked to try to make kids read. If I was assigned any of these books, the booklet said to tell my parents immediately. There were also tips on respectfully arguing religious points with secular teachers and how to endure the inevitable ridicule from other students. I had never had to use this booklet before, although I had almost referred to it last year, when my seventh-grade science teacher had said that the world was billions of years old. This clearly contradicted the Bible, but I did not know what I'd say to argue. There wasn't even really a scripture to quote for that one. And so I had sat at my desk, trying to open myself up to the Holy Spirit. I remembered the booklet said to do that, that there have been children who were filled with the Spirit at these times and come up with arguments that made their teachers immediately repent. And so I sat there through the entire lesson, waiting to be filled, but it never happened.

I had never planned on reading *Wuthering Heights* until a few weeks ago, when Mr. Vogel, the principal, called me down to his office. I had been chosen to receive a scholarship for the summer academic camp. "Congratulations," he said. "This is the beginning of the rest of your life." And I believed that it was. I suddenly felt very important, like I had a big responsibility. I thanked him and said, "Yes, I accept." He gave me a bunch of forms for my parents to sign, told me to return them by the end of the week.

I didn't realize until I got home that the readings for the academic camp included a lot of books that were on the blasphemy list: Sagan, Vonnegut, Shakespeare, and Charles Darwin. Darwin's *The Origin of Species* was allotted the number-one spot on the blasphemy list. It was also number one on the required reading list for the biology section.

I ended up forging the permission slip that listed the required readings. I had struggled all week with the decision, trying to convince myself that this was too important an opportunity to pass up. The camp didn't start until school ended, so I had a little while to decide what I was going to do. I told my parents about the camp, saying that it was an extension of my regular schoolwork, meaning we would be doing more in-depth studies of the books they had already approved at the beginning of the year. So they had no idea what I'd be reading. And I knew that if I showed them the reading list, they wouldn't let me go at all. I figured there had to be a better way. I could come up with a way to avoid the readings and still attend. Forging the permission slip just bought me some time to come up with a plan.

But it had been weeks and nothing had come to me yet. I had almost finished reading all the books that weren't banned. I was already over halfway through *Wuthering Heights,* which was required for the literature section. After that I had nothing left. I had to make a decision soon.

I took the *Surviving a Secular Classroom* booklet out of my desk drawer and stared at the list of blasphemous books, wondering if I could just skim them. I flipped to the middle of the booklet to look over the section on how to deal with evolution. "Just ask your teacher," it said, "how evolution can exist alongside the second law of thermodynamics." It went into a brief description of this law, how it says that everything moves toward chaos, that everything eventually breaks down that way. "How then," it said, "could things be constantly deteriorating and evolving at the same time?" I stopped a moment to consider this. It was a good argument, I decided. But then I wondered if this law contradicted the Bible, too. God's order is supposed to preside over everything; how could the world be ordered and deteriorating at the same time? Unless God's order was deterioration, but that didn't sound right, either. Why would the Church want to disprove evolution by using another law that contradicted our faith?

I was supposed to go to my best friend's house tomorrow to get Darwin. Her parents owned a copy, and I figured it couldn't hurt to look it over, just to see how wrong it was. Beth said she hadn't read it, but it was sitting in her garage. And I couldn't put it off any longer. Camp was starting in a month. So I made a deal with God. I told him that if I could just get the book and look it over so I could get by at camp, then I would convert Beth. Beth's family was Methodist, which was about the same as having no religion at all.

I had known for a while that Beth wasn't saved, but I had been reluctant to approach her about it. The Bible said that believers shouldn't yoke themselves with unbelievers. I was afraid that if Beth rejected my attempts to tell her about God, then I would have to stop being friends with her. Beth was smart, smarter than me. And my parents had warned me about arguing religion with people who are smart. "They make fancy arguments," they said, "and try to trick you with facts. Be careful." I had no idea if Beth would do this, but so far I had not been willing to risk it. If she was unsaved because she hadn't heard the Good News, that was one thing. But if I tried to tell her and she rejected it, she was an adamant unbeliever. If that happened, I wouldn't have a single friend left at school.

But now, with my current dilemma, I knew I had to make this deal with God. If He forgave me for taking Darwin home to skim it, then I would confront Beth with His message. I would begin to work on her tomorrow, when I went to pick up the book. The abstinence rally had inspired me, and I felt ready to do it.

I spent Saturday morning practicing for my encounter with Beth. In my *Surviving a Secular Classroom* booklet, there was a section on confronting unbelievers. There was a list of questions to put to them, questions that would make them see the error of secular thinking. I chose a few questions that I thought were particularly convincing:

1. Without a personal God, how are you anything but the co-incidental, purposeless excrement of nature, spinning through the blackness of space for a fraction of a second before your life is extinguished into eternal nothingness?

2. In a world without absolute morals, what's to distinguish Hitler from Pat Robertson?

3. If there is no life after death, then what's the use in morality at all? What's to stop us from killing and torturing each other?

4. In a universe without God, how are humans different from a pile of maggots or a mud pit full of pigs?

5. How do art, love, music, compassion, family, and relationships mean anything if the world doesn't matter? And where do these things come from if we are just a bunch of simple molecules?

6. Can you explain how absolutely no Bible prophecy has ever failed? David, in Psalms, predicted Jesus' death in the New Testament, before the New Testament was even written! The prophet Micah, in his book, predicted the birth town of Jesus seven hundred years beforehand. And in the book of Isaiah, Isaiah predicted the birth of Jesus seven hundred years before it occurred.

7. Are you able to live consistently with your present worldview?

8. Isn't it arrogant to think that great men, like George Washington, were misled in their faith? Would you be so bold as to accuse the Founding Fathers and the Declaration of Independence of being wrong in saying "All men . . . are endowed by *their Creator* . . ."?

At the bottom was a tip for arguing your faith: "It is interesting to note that most people who argue against Christianity and the validity of the Bible are only parroting what they've heard from other people. Whenever they give an argument, you should ask them to give specific examples. Most of the time, they will not know what to say."

I highlighted this, along with the eight questions I chose to put to Beth. I practiced these questions in front of the mirror, saying them over and over until I didn't need the book anymore.

∝ ⋉

The Basses' house was a single story on Juniper Drive, right next to a lumberyard, about fifteen minutes from my house. I once counted the distance on the bus. Every school day, fifteen minutes and forty-five seconds of sitting alone.

When Mom pulled into the driveway, she said that she and Dad would be back before play practice to pick me up. They were in a play at church that was going to open in a month. I nodded, dreading the awkward silence of my mother trying to decide how to say good-bye. She never kissed and rarely touched anyone. She never even held Dad's hand anymore and insisted on wearing yellow rubber gloves around the house. But now she placed a hand on my wrist, roughly petting me.

"Bye, sweetie."

"Bye, Mom." Her skin was dry, scaly. Her long fingernails, almost reptilian, reminded me of claws.

Beth's mom and dad, the Methodists, answered the door and told me that Beth was in her room. I walked unattended to the back of the house. No matter where you were in that house, you could always hear the sound of power saws, the air around the house being ripped into long shreds, like peeling wallpaper. Because of the noise, there was always music playing, usually the Beatles, her mom's favorite band. The Beatles scared me. Their nonsensical lyrics, I thought, might have some subconscious influence on me. Pastor Lyle was always talking about the subconscious influence of rock music.

I hurried through the house, squeezing my backpack to my chest. This backpack and I were inseparable, and for good reasons.

There was no homework inside, like my parents thought. They were always commenting on how studious I was, such a hard worker, always lugging around this backpack, almost filled to capacity. Right now it held *Wuthering Heights,* a blue lighter I had found in the school parking lot, my booklet on surviving in a secular classroom, *A Boy's Manual on Sexual Maturation* (a blue booklet that was given to all fifth-grade boys—I got a pink one, but I traded it with Tim Warrens for his blue one), and a Janet Jackson tape that Beth had loaned me that I had tried to listen to backwards but ended up breaking. It would carry out *The Origin of Species.* The mere fact that her dad owned the book confirmed everything I believed about the Methodist Church.

Beth was waiting for me in her bedroom, sitting on the carpet with a big smile on her face. "Close the door and lock it."

I did what she said and sat next to her on the floor, trying to think of a good way to ask my first question. Beth was short, like me, with a perfect bowl of dark red hair that curved just under her chin. Although we were both fourteen, we looked about ten. She was covered in freckles and had round gold glasses that were too big for her face. I adjusted myself on the carpet to look her right in the eyes but found myself staring at my reflection in her glasses instead.

"If there's no life after death, then what's the use in morality at all?" I asked her. "What's to stop us from killing and torturing each other?"

She gave me a look like I was talking in a foreign language.

"I was just thinking," I said, but then couldn't come up with anything else.

"Are you wearing underwear?" she asked me. She maintained a serious expression that demanded a serious answer.

"Of course."

"I'm going to need them."

I noticed then that she was holding a pair of scissors. She used the blade to point to the Frederick's of Hollywood catalog splayed out in front of us. On one page was a picture of a man in his underwear and a woman in hers. I wondered if this was one of the ninety thousand instances of premarital relations I would witness in my childhood. I squinted to see if they were wearing wedding rings.

"Do you find yourself living consistently with your present worldview?" I asked her.

"Yes," she said, after a moment's consideration.

This was not the answer I had been expecting. I stared at the fornicators, trying to remember the other questions.

"Not that," Beth said. "That." She pointed to the opposite page. There was a whole row of women's bottoms, round and tan, covered by nothing more than colorful strings that disappeared into their cracks. All colors, a rainbow of indecency right there in front of me. I wondered if this was a sin, looking at women's bottoms, but I couldn't not look. I had never seen anything like this in my life. I tried to be objective, to understand why anyone would want to wear anything like this, but the logic escaped me. They looked uncomfortable, silly, obscene. But still, there was something appealing in the small colored triangles resting right above their bottoms, something intimate in the compactness. From that moment on, my understanding of women's underwear was changed forever. There was a secret sexy world that lurked beneath the simplest pair of jeans and sweatpants I encountered daily. Even my teachers, as fat and used as they looked, could be sporting scandalous strings of silk that contained their haunches like strings around a pot roast. But not my mother. Never my mother, with her army of cotton underwear pinned to the clothesline, billowing in the backyard like a line of American flags.

My underwear was a bit baggy to fashion into a thong, but Beth did her best, cutting the fabric up to the elastic until it looked like a well-chewed cat toy. I just sat next to her, hands on my lap, not saying or doing anything, hoping that God would consider me only an innocent bystander in all of this. I resisted the urge to bite my nails, which would be an immediate admission of guilt. I had tried,

I told myself, to talk to her about religion. God must know I had tried. But she had stumped me. I would have to study more.

When Beth had finished cutting my underwear, she demanded that I try them on. It did not take much convincing. I slipped my jeans off, kicking them into a corner of the room. I hid behind her closet door as I wriggled into my new lingerie, which started to fray as I pulled it over my hip bones. Stepping out for Beth to see, I turned around in the full-length mirror on her wall. She applauded as I turned around to inspect the back, squinting away the uneven lines until I could only see the neat magenta triangle poised over my tailbone.

With only a few turns, the fabric had already worked its way into discomfort. I reached back to pull it in place.

"You'll get used to it, I think. Just don't think about it." She handed me my jeans, and I put them back on, careful not to rip my new underwear any more.

Next we worked on a pair of her underwear. This time we both cut them, taking turns and measuring the best we could with a straight ruler. "We're definitely getting better at this." Beth giggled, turning in the mirror to admire our work.

This was how we spent the day. I felt so guilty about not fulfilling my promise to God that I didn't take Darwin home. Instead, while Beth was cutting even more of her underwear, I read the first chapter. But I didn't let myself read it too closely. I wrote down some words to look up and copied some quotes, thinking that I could compose a journal entry with this sparse information. The assignment sheet for the biology section said I had to keep a journal as I read Darwin. I had the idea that by keeping the book at Beth's, I could swing it without compromising my morals or my promise to God.

When my parents came to pick me up at six, they were already in partial costume for play practice. Dad asked what Beth and I did all afternoon. For me, lying had become a necessity. Although I struggled with it at first, I soon realized that if I just asked God for forgiveness every night, the sin would be erased from my record. The first thing I learned in church was that we were all sinners, and so, after a while, I decided that I wasn't going to argue with that basic law or live in denial. The second thing I learned was that God always forgave you if you just asked. And so for the latter part of my childhood, I lived comfortably within the safe space of these laws, abusing God's trust and wondering if He'd ever call me out on it, if I would ever cash in my last token.

"We just studied. We have a science test on Monday."

Father nodded, pleased at my answer. Actually, we didn't have a science test on Monday, but that didn't matter. My parents stopped concerning themselves with my schoolwork a few years back, other than speaking with my English and science teachers at the beginning of every year, just to make sure I wouldn't be reading anything that conflicted with our faith, like Darwin or J. D. Salinger. I just brought home the report cards for them to sign. My father always bragged to his friends at work that I had never gotten a B in my life. This was untrue. In second-grade music class I got a B– because Mrs. Whitner found out that I lip-synched our entire Christmas concert. Jason Redlow told her, and I admitted it because I had not yet discovered the loophole for lying that would allow me to navigate around the unrealistic demands of adults while still maintaining a spot for myself in Heaven.

"What's the test on?" Dad glanced back at me through the rearview mirror. I could see the swirled mess of his stage makeup, black streaks that looked demonic despite his smile.

"Microscope identification. All the parts and what they do." This came out of my mouth like shards of glass. I squirmed in my seat, trying to swallow the lie. Something was wrong. I was terribly uncomfortable all of a sudden. I shifted again, this time feeling my thong riding up even more, making my entire body tense. That was it. This feeling, like God watching me, becoming more and more unbearable. The scratchy edges of elastic rubbing against my skin, each time I moved, making me conscious of every single action. Sitting back, crossing my legs, leaning my head against the window. I was infected with an intense self-consciousness, like God's eyes were following me. I was going to Hell.

Dad nodded again. "The play's coming along great. Your mom makes a beautiful angel." Mom, who had been quiet the entire ride, giggled from the passenger seat as he elbowed her. She turned her head in profile so I could see the sparkly makeup on her cheeks. She leaned toward him in a rush of affection but did not touch him. She then turned her head back to silence, looking out onto the houses. I closed my eyes and tried to clench my body into complete stillness.

><

SATURDAY, JUNE 1, 7:30 P.M.
CHAPTER I: *Variation Under Domestication*

Darwin says traits are passed on from parent to child, making it possible for people to control the physical traits of animals. Some traits, he says, don't show up right away but appear at the same time in the lives of the parent and the offspring: "At whatever period of life a peculiarity first appears, it tends to reappear in the offspring at a corresponding age, though sometimes earlier." Don't know what this really has to do with "evolution"—how people develop from monkeys.

I'm not really sure about this whole inheritance thing since I know a lot of people who don't look like their parents at all. I think it is right for animals, but humans are different. 1 Corinthians 15:39 tells us that animals and people are different; it says, "All flesh is not the same: Men have one kind of flesh, animals have another, birds another and fish another." Men are different from animals, so even if something like inheritance happens with animals, that doesn't mean it happens with people. I think we are more complicated than that. In the Bible there are lots of kids who aren't like their parents. Like Eli's sons, Korah's sons, and the Prodigal Son. In Psalm 58:3 it says about rebellious children: "Even from birth the wicked go astray; from the womb they are wayward and speak lies." I think this is pretty obvious, that some children are just born different from their parents. If Darwin is going to base his whole evolution theory on the fact that all offspring are just like their parents, I think he's on shaky ground, especially when he starts trying to convince us that people come from monkeys.

Darwin uses a lot of big words when he doesn't really need to. I know about people who do this. They just want to confuse you and to make you agree with them because you get too tired to keep up. I am looking up whatever words I don't understand. Here are some major ones that I need to remember:

Definitions:

variability—a tendency to vary within a species.

monstrosities—a considerable deviation of structure, generally injurious, or not useful to the species.

deviation—something that is different from the majority.

structure—When Darwin talks about "structure," he means the general population of a species.

rogues—plants that are deviations from the structure.

correlation—relationship.

aboriginal—existing from the beginning. Beginning of what? Time, I guess. Or Darwin's idea of time.

anomaly—something contrary to the general rule; a monstrosity, a rogue, a deviation.

That evening my sister came home with a busted lip and a bruise around her eye the size of a grapefruit, on account of the guy she liked to call her boyfriend. The boyfriend she also liked to call the father of her child. Caitlyn was about six months old, screaming like a teapot. She had bruises, too, bands of blue wrapped around her baby-fat arms that had almost faded by the time Kyle stumbled through the front door, carrying Caitlyn in one arm and about eight loads of dirty laundry in the other. I was reading *Wuthering Heights* at the kitchen table when I heard her struggling with the door. She hadn't called in almost two months and didn't bother to let us know she was coming home.

When I saw her standing there at the bottom of the front stairs, what struck me as odd was not the blood crusted on her chin, but how absurdly small Caitlyn made her look. Kyle was about five foot three inches tall and a hundred pounds with change in her pockets—and now the thought of her squeezing that fat baby out of her made me wince. She could barely hold her and had to thrust her hip out about a foot to the side and carry her head almost perpendicular to her body in order to manage her.

"Hey," I said, looking down from the top of the stairs and not moving to help her.

"Mom and Dad's car's gone," she said matter-of-factly.

"They're at church tonight. Play practice. They'll be back at ten."

"Thank-fucking-God." She hoisted the laundry bag over her shoulder and went downstairs to throw a load in.

Our house was by no means large. It was a split-level, with two sets of stairs at the front door, one leading to the basement (my brother's territory) and the other leading up to the rest of the house. There was a living room and a kitchen, which were separated only by a waist-high partition. A short hallway led to three bedrooms and a bathroom. Somehow, in this small space, Kyle managed to avoid me those two hours we were alone together. Not a word between us. She walked deliberately around the house, like a champion boxer with her face all mashed up and her head held high. I continued reading at the kitchen table to stay out of her way. I stared at the pages, flipping them occasionally, while I held my sister in my periphery, her determined walk skirting the edge of comprehension, telling me I shouldn't give her a second thought. What, I wondered, was I supposed to do here? She hadn't even washed the blood off her face. I wondered if she had forgotten it was there. Maybe the point of this was that she didn't look half as bad as Lance. I tried to imagine my sister fighting back, her manicured nails clawing at his eyes. But I knew my sister. And I knew that if I so much as looked her straight in the face, she would completely deflate me with some remark or with that acidic silence of hers. So I continued staring at my book as she rearranged the furniture in her old bedroom, lugging storage boxes to the garage and stealing furniture from the rest of the house. When I heard her struggling with something on the stairs, something slipping from her grip and falling down the stairs—her cursing—I knew I couldn't help her.

I didn't know much about Lance, other than the fact that he was raised Jehovah's Witness by his parents in Missouri. When he was in high school, he got into some kind of trouble and was shipped here to Indiana to live with his uncle and attend school. Which was where he met my sister. I knew even less about their relationship. They moved to Fort Wayne after Kyle graduated from high school, to live in sin. My parents found out pretty quickly, but I guess his parents still hadn't caught on. They didn't even know about Caitlyn, since they checked up on him through the local chapter of Fort Wayne Jehovah's Witnesses. Kyle once told me that whenever they showed up to talk to Lance, she had to hide in the bedroom and try to keep Caitlyn quiet.

When Mom and Dad got home from play practice, the first thing they heard was Caitlyn crying. Dad, with some shadows of black makeup still smeared on his face, went running up the stairs with a big smile. Mom stayed at the bottom of the stairs, wiping the dirt off her feet and yelling at Dad to please take his shoes off.

Still trying to bury myself in my book, I listened to his footsteps down the hall, and then silence. Mom, in her socks, walked after him. Her scream caused a light to flick on at the Hewitts' house across the street.

Finally, I gave up on *Wuthering Heights* for the night. I left the light on in the kitchen and crept down the hallway, hiding the book under my shirt. Even though it was not on the list of blasphemous books, I still couldn't bring myself to tell my parents I was reading it. The book had been getting sexier, and I had a suspicion that it probably should be on the list.

Through my bedroom wall, I could hear Mom and Dad whispering, and Kyle trying to keep herself from crying. Without making any noise, I got dressed for bed. I had forgotten about my thong and had been wearing it all evening. Beth was right, you do get used to it. But the idea of getting used to a thing like that frightened me. I took it off and buried it at the bottom of my hamper, telling myself I would throw it away in the garbage can outside as soon as I could.

I prayed for a full hour before I finally let myself sleep. I wasn't exactly sure what I should be praying for. Should I ask for Lance to be brought to justice? For my sister's face to heal? For God to stop punishing her for being a backslider? There was no doubt she was a backslider. She had engaged in premarital sex. Beyond that, instead of repenting for it, she seemed to revel in it. She was living out of wedlock with Lance, and she made no apologies to anyone for her behavior. She acted like she was accountable to no one but herself, an attitude that I knew eventually made people very unhappy. Like Catholics and rock stars. And Kyle was now proof of that. She had been sliding by all this time, but now her sins had caught up with her. And still I prayed for her. Even though I knew she would never pray for me and would even yell at me if she knew I was praying for her. But that was what being a Christian was about—caring for people who would just as soon spit in your face. And so I prayed, and between these prayers I found myself repeating my abstinence pledge.

I slept well that night, despite the goings-on in the next room. I dreamed of P.J. Larkey, a boy in my eighth-grade algebra class who had never said a word to me, or anyone else as far as I'd noticed, all year. He was shy, with light brown hair and good teeth. In my dream he was sitting in front of the class while Mrs. Richards, my English teacher, was talking about compounded interest. I was wearing a red wool dress, one exactly like my mother's in the picture hanging in our hallway. I wasn't born yet when it was taken, but she was very thin, looking like my sister, maybe even an older version of me, and holding a pudgy, ungrateful Jared up to the monkey cage at the zoo. The dress was very short on her, but in my dream it was down to my shins and would not stop itching me. I kept scratching and scratching, all over with my fingernails, which weren't long enough to do any good. I had chewed them all off. All the other kids in the class were pretty much faceless, sitting quietly and listening to Mrs. Richards talking and moving her hands. The itching kept getting worse, but no one seemed to notice me squirming and pulling at the dress, trying to take it off. Being naked in front of everyone was somehow not as horrifying as keeping this dress on, and so I started to slip an arm out, but the fit was too tight. It got stuck somewhere in between. Right then, in the middle of all this, P.J. got up and walked over to me. I tried to get my arm back into the dress, but it wouldn't budge. I was stuck. P.J. grabbed the fabric and started pulling it over my head to get it off. I tried to shake him away. I told him we didn't have to do this, that we could go get pizza instead, but that didn't work. In the dream I knew there was something else I was supposed to say, something that would stop him, but I couldn't remember what it was.

It was early, six in the morning, when I woke up. The air in the house was cool, still tinged with darkness, a brownish pink. No one was awake yet, so I went to the bathroom without flushing the toilet. In the hallway I paused to look at the photograph of my mother and Jared at the zoo. My mother always wore dresses, but this dress was short and tight, nothing she would have let me or Kyle wear. Her thick, unruly eyebrows were slightly lifted, trying to be sexy. This was before Mom started waxing her eyebrows off completely and drawing them on instead. In the picture's background was a monkey—a chimpanzee, I think—with a face and ears that were eerily human. He looked like he was sneaking up on them, although I knew that he was behind glass. This glass, though, didn't give a single reflection or scratch, making it seem as if that monkey could reach them, reach out and touch them if he wanted. But Mom had her back to him, confident that the glass was indeed there, smiling at the camera. I had never seen my mother smile like this. This picture was taken when she still went to zoos and parties and amusement parks. When she could just walk outside on a whim, without the strict but cryptic schedule she now imposed on herself. Back then you didn't have to tell her weeks beforehand if you needed her to pick you up from school; she didn't cry if she had to make an unexpected run to the grocery store, insisting that she couldn't make time even though she had nothing to do, as far as I could tell, other than pace around the house and watch twelve hours of television. When I would look at old red-tinted photos like this and see her on Ferris wheels and in pools, as if she'd just jumped in without a second thought, her happiness was utterly baffling to me. By the time I started to make appearances in the pictures, when the pictures in the album started to have more realistic colors, she no longer looked like this. She was either standing off to the side with no expression or wasn't in the picture at all.

I crawled back in bed to think. I liked to do this, to think whatever I wanted at hours like these, with no one to interrupt. Not even God, I imagined, would be up now listening to my thoughts. And so I thought of P.J. and what I would finally say to him on the last day of school, how I would tell him that I loved him. Maybe he would go to the end-of-the-year dance with me. I couldn't imagine he had a girlfriend, but then again I knew that if he had working ears, he would never want anything to do with me. My reputation as a Jesus Freak had followed me for two years, ever since I tried to organize the "Prayer Around the Pole" during the first week of my seventh-grade year. I handed out flyers, trying to convince people to show up to school a half hour early, hold hands around the flagpole out front, and pray for God to be with us all day, for Him to guide and protect us as we studied and witnessed to other students.

No one came to the Prayer Around the Pole except for this very large boy named Vince, who wore all black and had a safety pin stuck through his ear. Not even Beth showed up, claiming that she had overslept that day. And so it was just me and this Vince. He smelled like cough drops. But still, to be inclusive and to show that God loves everyone, I prayed with him. I'm sure it was a sight, the two of us holding hands around the pole, while everyone else sat in the parking lot smoking and waiting for the bell to ring. I remember I asked Vince if there was anything in particular he wanted to pray for, and he said yes, his mother was in the hospital with a brain tumor and not expected to live. He didn't even cry but told me with a dry-eyed matter-of-factness I found disturbing. So we prayed, and afterward I told him that I would keep praying for his mother every day. He thanked me, still no sign of emotion, and disappeared inside the school. I never found out what happened to his mother and never saw Vince again. I think he was an eighth grader.

I didn't know if P.J. even knew about the Prayer Around the Pole, but it didn't matter. Even if he did ask me to the end-of-the-year dance, I would never be able to go. Our church was a notorious nondancing establishment. They protested proms and homecomings because the dancing nowadays "encouraged indecent behavior." They even went as far as to provide an alternative prom for high school kids when my sister was a junior: a formal spaghetti dinner with balloons, but no music. My parents made my sister go, even though her boyfriend at the time refused. So Kyle went to the spaghetti dinner with an eager Brody Arthur, our neighbor, who ditched his prom date for the chance to take Kyle to the nondance.

The only dancing members of the Church ever did was the kind inspired by the Holy Spirit. Pentecostal Revivalist Born-Again Christians like to jump up and down, speak in tongues, and fall over, in that order. Every Sunday grown men and women gyrate to the influence of the Spirit. People sweat and holler while Pastor Lyle paces up and down the stage. Sometimes these spectacles seem more indecent than any secular dancing I'd ever seen, especially when my mother starts getting all worked up, panting and sweating through her Sunday dress.

No one woke Kyle up for church that morning, which I didn't think was fair, but I was a little thankful, too. I hated to admit it and I knew it was vain, but I didn't want people to see my sister. She hadn't been to church in over a year, and if people saw her like that, carrying a baby around with no wedding ring on and a black eye, people might begin to think things about me, too. I couldn't afford that. Being persecuted at school for my faith was only bearable because I knew that at church I was admired and respected. At least they knew and recognized the work I was doing for God. I had brought two Bible Quiz Championship titles to the Church, and everyone there knew it. But now that could all change. People said I looked just like Kyle. A little younger, of course. I never saw the resemblance, but either way, I didn't want people to get us confused.

Jared was supposed to come to church every Sunday, too, but when Dad went downstairs to wake him, he wasn't there. Our older brother, who lived in the basement at the age of twenty-one, had real life experience. He had been a pretty good student in high school and was recruited by the Air Force to become a pilot. Somehow, having never flown before in his life, he knew this was what he wanted to do. But a week before he was supposed to leave, he failed a surprise drug test. After that, he moved to Chicago and joined an anarchist club. But being an anarchist in an expensive city was difficult, he said. Soon, he ran out of money and was up to his ears in debt. There was no choice but for him to come home. He now exercised free rein over the basement and said "Fuck you" on a daily basis to my mother, when she questioned the music or the smoke that drifted up through the vents.

Jared didn't pay rent. My parents told him that he could stay for free as long as he went to church with us every Sunday. He could never manage to be home on Sunday mornings, though. He worked at the Lynxx chemical plant, the night shift. He was a nocturnal creature by nature anyway, so it suited him.

Church service started at ten in the morning, but Sunday school started at nine. I was in the junior high classroom with about twenty other kids, kids I had known all my life and didn't get along with: Tessa Goodman, who was always done up in lace and ruffles; Jessica Cowley, a girl who had flunked two grades and liked to pick her nose in public; and Joe Levine, who would sneak into the women's restroom and listen to girls pee.

There were Bible characters drawn on the walls of the classroom and paper crosses dangling from the ceiling. Bumper stickers covered the only window with inspirational messages—CHOOSE LIFE, YOUR MOTHER DID—all over the glass, blocking out the sun and any view of the surrounding forest.

Our teacher, Mr. Polinski, was now trying to get our attention, standing in front of the classroom, doing nothing. He had also been my teacher when I was seven and still asked questions. When our dog had run away, I had asked him whether God allowed pets into Heaven. I remember the crease of concern that had gathered right between his eyes, the way he seemed to be searching for an answer or the proper way to give me the answer. No, he finally said, pets cannot get into Heaven. When he saw how upset this made me, he reassured me that *he* was going to be there.

Now looking at the way he was scrawling on the chalkboard in that important handwriting of his, pleased at the silence he instilled in us, I realized that I didn't like a lot of these people who were supposedly going to Heaven, especially Mr. Polinski. How would I feel being in Heaven with all these people who annoyed me so much? With Mandy Perle, who was such a goody-two-shoes that she told on me last week when I skipped Sunday school to go in the woods behind the Church to read about Heathcliff digging up Catherine. How he kissed her dead body all over, possessed with passion that none of these people would ever understand.

Despite these distractions, I could not help but think of Kyle, waking to an empty house, shuffling through the hall in a T-shirt and an old pair of Lance's boxers. I never really realized it until now, but as I was reading *Wuthering Heights,* I decided that Catherine looked just like her. Kyle was beautiful, ghostly pale skin that revealed the intricate network of purple and blue veins in her wrists and neck, like faint bruises from a past she could not remember. Thin and fragile looking, I imagined her, wandering through the house, exploring the walls and doorways with her manicured fingers. Like a ghost. Like Catherine haunting the halls of Wuthering Heights. Helpless and confused. But by the time we would get home, she'd have her makeup on to conceal her bruised face, her hair done up in some new way. She'd be sitting on the couch watching television, not saying anything to any of us.

"Who brought their Bible and *Study Guide* today?" Mr. Polinski had his hands on his hips, standing next to the chalkboard, which read: "Critical Thinking and the Bible."

We all raised our hands.

"Good, now everyone come up and get a highlighter and a pen and a workbook."

After we were all sitting down again, armed with our books and supplies, Mr. Polinski gave us our assignment. We always had assignments in the junior high classroom, which I preferred to listening to some Bible stories and singing stupid songs. All that stuff was for the elementary kids. In this classroom we challenged ourselves and our faith with articles from the *Evangelical Warrior* and our *Teen Study Guide*. We wrote papers from *God's World* encyclopedias and analyzed Bible verses. I could lose myself in this work for days.

Once I got started on an assignment, it was easy to ignore the rest of the kids. Unless one of them forgot their Bible or *Study Guide* and I had to share with them. But thankfully, I was alone today. No one was going to come between me and God and my important work.

Today's exercise in the *Teen Study Guide*—part 2 of the "Critical Thinking and the Bible" chapter—focused on matching arguments point for point and referencing your source. There was a list of misguided opinions in column 1 and a list of Bible verses in column 2. We were supposed to match the proper argument to each criticism and write the full answer in our workbooks. And then we were supposed to look those verses up in the Bible to check our source. The first ones were easy to match:

Question: There are lots of religions that teach love and compassion. If I practiced one of those religions, is that bad? What's the difference if I answer to Buddha instead of Jesus as long as I'm a good person?

Answer: "If anyone teaches false doctrines and does not agree to the sound instruction of our Lord Jesus Christ and to godly teaching, he is conceited and understands nothing. He has an unhealthy interest in controversies and quarrels about words that result in envy, strife, malicious talk, evil suspicions" (1 Timothy 6:3–4).

Question: How are we expected to know that God exists without seeing Him? How can we be punished for not knowing what we cannot see?

Answer: "For since the creation of the world God's invisible qualities—His eternal power and divine nature—have been clearly seen, being understood from what has been made, so that men are without excuse" (Romans 1:20).

I worked through them quickly, having just enough time to get them done before class let out. The other kids would have to finish at home. On the last question, I paired up the only remaining question and answer.

Question: You can't take the Bible literally because it has been translated so much. Since so many people have changed it, isn't it impossible to know the truth?

Answer: "All Scripture is God-breathed and is useful for teaching, rebuking, correcting and training in righteousness" (2 Timothy 3:16).

I read this last one over, wondering if I had messed up one of the other answers. Of course, it was right. The Bible was God-breathed. And it was useful for teaching and such. But was it proper to quote the Bible to prove the validity of the Bible? The process seemed a bit off, although I couldn't exactly come up with the reason. Before I could think it through completely, Mr. Polinski dismissed us. I drew a faint question mark in the margin and handed in my workbook.

The adult service started right after Sunday School. The sanctuary was filled with at least five hundred people buzzing under ceiling fans, greeting each other, and making room for the older children who were filtering in from various entrances. The ceiling was high, stretched into a dome of at least fifty feet. But even now it barely seemed enough to contain these enthusiastic church members.

The sanctuary was newly renovated, with gray carpets and pews that were covered in a scratchy dark purple material that made us girls who weren't allowed to wear panty hose yet squirm all through the sermon. Mom and Dad had recently decided that I couldn't wear panty hose until I was fifteen, even though Kyle had worn them at thirteen. But despite the restrictions on makeup, panty hose, phone calls from boys, and any movie rated above PG, in the Church's eyes I had become an adult on my thirteenth birthday, when I graduated from Superchurch and was allowed to attend the adult sermons. I had attended my first one just over a year ago, the weekend of my thirteenth birthday. I was glad to leave Superchurch behind, with its baby games and oversimplified sermons. I was also glad to get away from the bus kids.

We called them the bus kids because they came to church on a sky blue bus that my father had helped paint a few years before. The church members had given money to start the Outreach Ministry, which was basically this bus driving around the slums of Slow Rapids to pick up kids whose parents worked at Lynxx or the coal stations and didn't come to church. There were about fifty bus kids in all, and they all sat on the left side of the gymnasium, usually talking all during the Message and getting in fights. And then there were the normal kids whose parents came to church. We all sat on the right side of the gymnasium, afraid of the bus kids.

When I was ten, something strange happened to me in Superchurch that I still cannot explain. It was a normal Sunday, with the bus kids on the left side of the gymnasium and us normal kids on the right, being quiet and listening to Pastor Perle's lecture on the evils of secular music—the giggles from the left side buzzing around us like flies we had grown to ignore. I remember I was sitting next to Tessa Goodman, unwillingly. Her dress was laid out carefully to flow over the folding chair. She was wearing gloves. Looking at her calm, obedient face, the way it ignored me even though she knew I was looking at her, something went terribly wrong. Without thinking, I stood up in the middle of Pastor Perle's sermon and yelled the name of my brother's favorite band, Def Leppard. Tessa Goodman almost fell out of her chair, finally looking at me and giving me a face like I had just denounced God. I smiled at her.

After that stunt I was ostracized from both sides of the gymnasium. I was worse than a bus kid now. I was a backslider. Everyone could forgive the bus kids for being terrible because they didn't know any better, but I had known exactly what I was doing.

I was sentenced to meet with Pastor Perle every evening for two weeks, where he informed me of the subconscious influence of back masking. I would have to sit in his office, listening to tapes of Michael Jackson's "Beat It" played backwards, which said: "I do believe it was Satan in me." A song that went "Another one bites the dust" was actually saying, "It's fun to smoke marijuana." And to my surprise, I discovered that the lyrics "Wake up" when played backwards meant "Fuck you."

But now I was safe in adult church, where no one seemed to know about the Superchurch incident, where there were no bus kids. No matter how old they got, they never left Superchurch, which was a relief. Now I got to hear the Word of God from Pastor Lyle. I didn't have anyone to sit with during adult church since both my parents were in the choir, so I usually chose to sit in the back, near newcomers I didn't recognize. But this Sunday my father found me before the service started. He was leading a guy named Len, who he introduced to me as one of his coworkers at the phone company. I had heard about Len before. He was recently divorced and had tried to kill himself about six months ago. Dad did not know that I knew this; I had overheard him telling Mother about it. But I remembered. I had always wondered what someone who had tried to kill himself looked like, and I guess this Len was it. He was very skinny and tall and looked about my father's age, although he had less hair. His posture was curved, making him look like a semicolon, his head perched on top and leading his entire body as he stood behind my father.

"Melanie, is it all right if Len sits with you during the service? This is his first time."

"Sure," I said, even though I really felt like sitting by myself today. But my father and I had this silent agreement. Whenever he brought new people to church, I was supposed to sit with them so they didn't feel alone. Mom and Dad and the rest of the choir were up onstage for the whole service.

"Good," Dad said. "Len, this is my daughter Melanie."

Len smiled and nodded at me from over my father's shoulder. "Hi," he said. He reached his hand out to shake and I took it. His fingers were large and warm and reminded me of death.

"Hi, Len," I said. "Let's go find a place to sit."

I had sat with many strangers through sermons in the past year. Every couple of weeks, my father would bring a guest that I was supposed to keep company. Coworkers, waitresses, Jehovah's Witnesses who had knocked on our door; once I even sat with a homeless man named Bart who had surprised me by not smelling terrible. Dad met him at the mall last winter, and he came to church only once. At the end of the service, he thanked me for sitting with him, and when I asked him if he'd come again, he said probably not, he was moving to Georgia next week. I wasn't sure how a homeless man could move to another state, but I didn't ask any questions. When I said I hoped he found a nice church down in Georgia, he said he was an atheist in warm weather.

Len and I sat down in the middle of section 14, with a few minutes left before the service started. We were right below the twenty-foot aluminum cross that hung from the ceiling, suspended at a generous angle so if you looked up you could see the entire thing in all of its shining glory. Len was just sitting there, staring up at it as if it could fall on us at any moment. I, too, looked up at the cross, hoping for inspiration. I was used to making conversation with complete strangers in situations like this, but the fact that this guy had tried to kill himself made me a little more nervous than usual. I didn't want to say anything to put him over the edge, but I couldn't help but wonder how he had tried to do it.

I turned in the pew to face him. "So how are you *doing*?" I asked, not as casual as I would have liked.

He gave me a questioning look and said, "All right." His hands were smooshed between his knees. I stared at them a moment, trying to see his wrists.

"So do you go to any other church around here?" I asked, and he immediately shook his head. His neck and ears looked sunburned and painful.

"No. I haven't been to church since I was married," he said with a nonchalance that startled me. Not the voice at all of someone who was contemplating killing himself.

"That's too bad," I said, just as the choir pranced in through the back exits. This was my chance to say something meaningful that might turn his life around and make him see things differently. "Church isn't only for special occasions. God'll be a part of your life only as much as you are willing to be a part of His. That's why a lot of marriages fail, because people think that getting married in a church is enough. But having a relationship with God is like the glue. A marriage is not a bond between two people, but three." I stopped talking suddenly, realizing that I'd been shouting this at him over the music. He was just staring back at me, his lips pressed tightly together.

"Yeah, three," he said finally, nodding. "That sounds about right."

I smiled at Len, glad that this concept came so easily for him. He smiled back and turned to listen to the choir.

This first half hour of the service was all singing, with my dad leading the choir and the congregation in songs that sounded more like war calls than worship. My dad had a beautiful singing voice. Whenever he sang "Amazing Grace," I had to try my best not to cry. But in church the choir never really sang slow songs. They liked to sing songs that were full of the Holy Spirit, as Mother liked to say. There were tambourines shaking all through the pews, and on-stage there were electric guitars, bongos, a drum set, a keyboard, trumpets, and a saxophone. There used to be an organ, but it was ripped out years ago to make room for the baptismal pool.

During the song portion, I liked to watch the congregation get all stirred up by the drum solos. The most modest of women would start jumping up and down in the aisles, their heavy chests swinging shamelessly under thin cotton dresses. My favorite was Mrs. Lovejoy, an old lady who would walk slowly and carefully to her pew, just to start running up and down the aisles with her tambourine a few minutes later. She would skip and yell, grabbing complete strangers to dance with her. I tried to imagine how Beth would see all of this if I ever brought her to church. Would she just stand there, looking terrified, or would she think this was much more fun than Methodist church and start dancing, too?

Today they started by singing "Blow the Trumpet in Zion," a fast song that got everyone clapping right away. I could see Len out of the corner of my eye, moving slightly to the music and trying to clap along, but he couldn't keep a beat. He was about a second behind everyone else but didn't seem to notice. I made exaggerated movements with my hands as I clapped, to try to help him out, but it didn't work. He had absolutely no rhythm.

I always clapped and sang in church but never danced. Even when my body wanted to. The music had a way of making you forget yourself, and I would always catch my leg bouncing or my hips swaying, just in time. Even though everyone else was doing it, I would have been embarrassed. There was something sexual in it all, something that made me blush whenever I would look up onstage and see my mother, her breasts bouncing and her face all sweaty and shiny in the lights, yelling and stretching her arms toward Heaven.

After the singing was done, Pastor Lyle strode up to the altar, a dark-stained wood podium that hid the entire lower two-thirds of his body. Other churches called it a pulpit, but here it was an altar. I guess it looked like one. It certainly was big enough to lay a human body out across it. It had a sheath of white fabric spread out over the top of it at the moment, spilling over the edge like the hem of a dress. The body of a virgin, I thought, as Pastor Lyle took his time opening his Bible. I placed my Bible on my lap, ready to open it to whatever chapter he was going to read from.

Pastor Lyle always began here, behind the altar, calmly sipping his bottomless glass of water. Slowly, he'd work himself into a level of excitement that sent him pacing at all angles, jumping and skipping to topics as horrifying as the reign of the Antichrist. He always wore sneakers, even with his suits, he said, to be physically prepared to do God's work whenever or wherever it was required. I didn't know if his duty to Christ ever involved jumping fences and chasing down sinners in the streets, but I liked to think that it did. Pastor Lyle was from New York City, so anything was possible. He had even gone to college and earned a degree in hospitality.

Today's sermon was on the "Providential Destiny of America." Pastor Lyle stared out at us for a moment, and then said those words real slow, as if they were decreed by God. He was excited by this sermon, I could tell. He had to stop for breath before continuing.

"Everything that happens in the world happens for a reason," he said, and then stepped back, to let us think about it.

I considered this for a moment, wondered what the reason was for Kyle coming home, for Lance beating her up. But I knew God's plans were too big to understand. But still, I felt better thinking about it in this way. God had a plan for Kyle, and it was now set in motion.

"Some people will tell you that history isn't ordered, that it's nothing but the collection of hard, unrelated facts. But I can tell you that there's order to everything when you turn to the Bible."

Everyone in the congregation said "amen."

"His plan for you, and you"—he pointed out people in the audience, not even close to me and Len. "His plan for everyone is clear; His plan for *nations* is clear." He ran his hands over the altar, leaning into it with his whole body.

"History'll tell you that God's direction is westward. Christianity started in the Middle East but moved west, to better places. It didn't go south to Africa or east to Asia. It went west. Am I right?" He looked out at us for confirmation, seeing head nods crest over the audience like a powerful wave. "History *tells us* that Christianity grew in Europe, was corrupted by the Catholics, and then moved west again, to America. Here"—he pointed to his own feet—"is where Christianity has been perfected. And now we've got to do our part to continue God's plan." His hands were kneading the altar ledge as he worked himself up for the next step in logic.

"God has blessed America with prosperity so that we can spread the Good News around the world. Our *duty* is to continue the march west, to bring Christianity to Asia and the Middle East. And only when that is done will Christ return to take us home." He looked up at the ceiling fans, contemplating home.

"Everything that happened in the world happened to establish America as the Beacon of Freedom. During the Revolutionary, Civil, and world wars, God performed many miracles to make sure that we would win. We've come so far, and now we've got to finish the job. We've got missionaries all around the world, trying to bring about God's Will, but there's still work to do." He stopped and pointed to someone in the audience. "You have work to do. There are still millions of unbelievers in our own country. How, my brothers and sisters, can America fulfill its Providential Destiny if we are not united under one faith? The True Faith? I know," he said, sweeping his finger across the room to include all of us. "I know that each and every one of you knows someone who has not been saved. And this is where *you* fit into God's plan."

I immediately thought of Beth. God planned this sermon just for me, I knew. God had told Pastor Lyle that there was someone who desperately needed this message. Someone who needed encouragement to reach a friend. It was for me. It was all for me.

Pastor Lyle continued, stepping out from behind the altar and showing us the rest of his body. "Now I know that there is someone out there struggling to bring the message to a loved one." I felt my heart beating in my throat. "And God wants me to tell you that He's on your side. He's going to give you the strength to reach your loved one this week."

After Pastor Lyle ran his voice down into a strained whisper, he stepped off the stage and let the ushers take up the collection. When the gold plate passed into my hands, I put in the ten dollars Dad had given me, to repent for my vanity and to thank God for helping me to witness to Beth. Len didn't give any money but stared a moment at the ten dollars that I put in before passing the plate to the people next to us.

Everyone in the sanctuary was talking and mingling during the ten minutes it took for those plates to make it all the way around. But I didn't know what else to say to Len. I just sat there, staring down at my Bible, which had remained closed on my lap during the entire sermon.

When we got home at around two, Kyle was watching television on the couch with Caitlyn. The phone was ringing.

"Don't answer that," she said, as I moved to pick up the receiver. Her face was red, her eyes set on the car commercial playing across the screen. Her lip was swollen on one side and her right eye was puffy, layered with makeup but still tinted green like an old penny. Her hair was styled carefully, shoulder length, and curled. Mine hung to my waist, too long and thick to do anything with. I stood a moment to admire hers now, the way she had curls piled on top of her head. She was beautiful even with her fat lip. She was wearing perfume.

I walked over to sit by her, wanting to say something useful, but my father's voice came up from right behind me and stopped me in my tracks.

"C'mon, Mel. I want to take you out to lunch. Just you and me. How about we go to Werstyn's?" He didn't even wait for me to answer, just pulled me away from my sister and toward the front door.

Werstyn's diner was typical, with booths and tables and a counter where old men liked to eat by themselves. The plastic upholstery of our booth looked as if it had been slashed with knives.

Dad was twisting at his black beard, which had started to turn gray before the thick hair on his head. He always did this when he was trying to be casual. I had never seen him without a full beard, outside of old photos where he was usually shirtless and standing next to Mom, who was impossibly skinny. He kept twisting and pulling at his beard like this, staring at the table until he decided what he wanted to say.

"So how's Beth?"

For some reason, Dad always liked to ask me about Beth. "Fine," I said, wishing he'd just come out with it.

"Are you excited about the play? It's at the end of the month, you know."

I nodded. My parents' play at church was an annual tradition. All church members were supposed to bring an unsaved friend or family member. And at that moment, the truth came to me. God wanted me to take Beth to the play to be saved. She could hear the message there, and I wouldn't have to do anything. No one could argue with the play—it was so powerful that even the most adamant unbelievers were moved by it. This was the help God promised me in Pastor Lyle's sermon. He knew I couldn't do it on my own, so He was going to reach Beth through the play.

"You should bring Beth to the play, I think," my dad said.

I nodded again, resisting the urge to yell "hallelujah" right there in the middle of the diner. "Yeah," I said. "Can I go over to her house today and invite her?" I couldn't believe how easy this was going to be.

My father smiled at me, probably thinking that I was going to fulfill my Providential Destiny. I was a part of God's plan.

We ate through a long silence, filled by solemn murmurs from the other tables and the cheerful interjections of the cash register. As I ate, I just kept thinking of Beth, how after she got saved, then I'd see to it that she was baptized. She'd told me once that she was baptized as a baby, but I knew that didn't count. It had to be a choice. I got baptized when I was thirteen. I had taken classes and learned exactly what it meant. I would teach all of that to Beth. I'd tell her how fun it was. I remembered watching Pastor Lyle pull himself through the baptismal pool in his famous Hawaiian shorts and T-shirt. Him standing there, waist-deep in water, as I waded out to him, holding my chin just above the waterline. And then soaking-wet Pastor Lyle put his arms around me and said something from the Bible. What, I couldn't remember, but then he asked if I was willing to walk in the path of Christ. "Yes," I said, "I would do anything for Him." And with that, he dipped me into the cool blue water.

After finishing his lunch, Dad cleared his throat and went for his coffee. I could still tell he wanted to say something. He hadn't brought me all the way here to talk about Beth. My father wasn't a man of many words, although he used to be when I was younger. He was still affectionate, but his thoughts now seemed to be overshadowed by something both singular and vague. He had become pensive.

"Thanks for sitting with Len today," he said.

"It was nothing. He's nice."

Dad nodded, and I asked, "Do you think he's going to come again?"

"I don't know," he said. "Maybe. Maybe if he felt something today." He looked around the restaurant, as if he had misplaced something.

I didn't think Len was moved by Pastor Lyle's sermon. At the end of the service at altar call, when Pastor Lyle asked for anyone who was unsaved to come up to the front and repent, Len didn't even seem to be considering it. I asked him if he'd like to go up, if he'd like me to go up with him, but he said no, he was fine, thanks. I wanted to say that obviously he wasn't fine and obviously his present worldview was not working out for him. But of course, I didn't.

"Your sister's going to be staying with us for a while." Dad said this into his coffee cup, which was paused under his chin. He did not take a sip.

People were bustling in and out, a lot of flannel shirts, even though it was June. I watched them, unsure of what he expected of me. This was why he brought me here, to talk about Kyle. But now, after stating that simple fact, it was as if he had absolutely nothing more to say about it. I was just about to say something, anything to save him from this, but then he cleared his throat.

"I think you're old enough now to see the lesson in this," he said, still not looking at me. "You're going to be making your own decisions soon, and you have to learn that there are consequences. Everything you do one day will have consequences, good or bad. Just remember that. You have made promises, and I know you intend on keeping them now, but things get tough and you might start to see things differently. Just remember," he said again. "Remember how you feel right now, remember this time in your life, before things get muddled and complicated. Right now, you can see everything clearly. Right now, good decisions are easy to make."

I nodded, trying to imagine myself five years from now, wondering how I could ever see things differently. Wondering how I could ever be like my sister. Did my father really think I was capable of sins like that? Hadn't I made a pledge to God? Was I the only person who took something like that seriously?

"But your sister's an adult now," he said. "She has to make decisions for herself, and there's nothing we can really do for her anymore, other than show her that she has our support."

I nodded again, but still he would not look at me. It was strange to see him like this, hunched over his coffee mug, just staring down at his blank plate, intimidated by a fourteen-year-old girl. I considered leaning in to touch him, but, as if he could feel it coming, he sat back again, out of reach. His eyes were dry, his fingers tapping nervously against his mug.

With his eyes still set somewhere between us, he said, "She'll start making the right decisions if she's confident," and then he took a hurried sip of coffee, as if washing the words right back down.

On the way home, we drove through downtown Slow Rapids. I watched the shops, the empty trains slowing just parallel to the road. Coal shipping used to be our big business, but it was now on the decline. A steel factory had gone up just outside of town a few years ago, so our boats shipped more steel than coal these days. We also had the Lynxx chemical plant, right near Clearwater Park, where my family used to go to the beach and swim in Lake Michigan. Beth's uncle worked at the Lynxx plant. He had gone to college and was one of the few Lynxx workers who wore a pocket protector instead of a white jumpsuit. My brother wore the white jumpsuit and said he'd let me use his gas mask for Halloween, so I could dress up as a fly.

We crossed the lift bridge, which was down, although I could see a freighter docked, waiting to pull in, probably full of limestone from northern Michigan. We had crossed just in time. Looking back, I could see the traffic lining up on the road as the bridge master prepared to make way for the freighter. Dad must not have noticed, since he would always pull over to watch the bridge whenever it was lifted.

We rounded a corner and climbed the steady incline of Lombardy Street. We were near my junior high. Past the school we topped another hill, which revealed the entire Slow Rapids skyline: the twin smokestacks of Lynxx, the coal chute arched above the harbor like a roller coaster, and the two halves of the lift bridge swung up like pinball paddles. Dad still didn't notice that the bridge was up and continued at the same speed. I could see all three of these landmarks posed together for just a moment, before they were all lost in trees.

Looking out the car window at all the shut blinds and curtains of the houses, all I could think about was my father, how concerned he was about Kyle, how he was always worried about my brother, Jared. How I was now the only one that didn't make those deep lines settle in around his eyes, didn't make him stare off at nothing as he sipped his endless cups of coffee. I knew I had that power, but I'd never want to do that to him. I would never want him to worry about my soul, my purity, about me reading Darwin or becoming godless. I watched him driving through town, his mind on everything but the road, but I was not afraid. My father was in control.

But now, I realized, I didn't have to worry about getting my father's approval to read Darwin. God had made it clear to me today with His message that it was okay for me to read it, and Dad couldn't argue with that. I had promised to give Beth to God in return, and I planned on doing just that. I was going to take Beth to the play, just like He wanted. Everything was set in motion for me to fulfill my Providential Destiny, and I wouldn't even have to worry my father by telling him.

I was in control and God knew. The problem with so many people buying in to Darwin's lies was that they were ignorant. I was not. I had the Bible strapped to my ankle like a dangerous weapon. I could slay Darwin with scripture, I knew. As I read, I could prove everything he said wrong. I would be a Warrior for Christ. It was clear that I was meant to do this. I was meant to spread the Good News to others. Beth was just the beginning. If I could save her soul, then I would prove to God that I was His servant, that I fit into His plan for the world. Just like Pastor Lyle's prophecy had promised. Right after I was born, my parents had taken me up to the altar, in front of the entire congregation. A simple dedication ceremony that was done for all babies. But Pastor Lyle felt God move in him the second he saw me. To everyone's surprise, he laid his hands on my forehead, listened to whatever it was God told him, and then informed my parents and the whole church that I was destined to do great works for God.

———

Mom had Caitlyn on her lap and was watching her favorite show, *The 700 Club,* when we got home from Werstyn's. I stood in the entry for a moment to watch. It was a special report from Thailand. "A land of idols," Pat Robertson called it. A golden Buddha came on the screen, with people kneeling all around it. "These people pray to golden statues," Pat Robertson said. "If only they could learn to ask for miracles from the true God, imagine the prayers that would be answered." The camera moved in on an old man, his dark, wrinkled face paused in an expression I had never seen before. He didn't look like he was praying. His face didn't seem to be asking for anything at all.

Pat Robertson came back on the screen, smiling, confident. "There is good news now coming from this primitive land of idolatry and despair. A group called Warriors for Christ has established over one hundred churches throughout the country. There has been an economic downfall in recent years, and since then they have freed over two thousand souls. We are reaping a large harvest for Christ!" His face grew serious again. "But there is more work to do. In this impoverished nation, where the starving worship golden statues, there is much more work to do." An address flashed across the screen telling us where to send donations. After scribbling the address on the back of an envelope, Mom flicked off the television and handed Caitlyn to my father.

"C'mon, Mel, we're going to the store."

I hadn't even taken off my shoes yet. I stared at her a moment, not knowing how to react. Her eyebrows were painted with more of an arch than usual today, making this statement seem more like a question. And I mistakenly interpreted it this way. "I just got back, Mom. And I'm supposed to go to Beth's."

She glared at me, raising a long fingernail in my direction but saying nothing as she brushed past me. She was already down the steps and on her way out the door when she said, "It won't take long. I need your help. We'll take you to Beth's later." Dad nodded after her, as if to tell me that all this had been planned long in advance and I had no choice in the matter.

Mom had never needed my help before. I lingered at the top of the stairs for a minute, hearing the car start in the driveway. I looked back to the television, the screen dead but I swear still humming on some frequency that just escaped me. Pat Robertson had confirmed my Providential Destiny, talking about Warriors for Christ. He was trying to prepare me for my mission.

I hated the Dollar Store. That was where my parents took me whenever I summoned the courage to tell them I needed anything. Usually I did without, just so I wouldn't have to go in there. If someone from school saw me going into the Dollar Store, I'd never live it down. In the sixth grade, when I showed up to school in a sweater my mother had bought at a garage sale, the sweater's previous owner, Rosemary Maddock, had informed me and everyone else that it used to be hers. My mother bought most of our clothes at garage sales, and it was not uncommon for some girl to approach me about her skirt or her shoes that I was wearing. Before the sixth grade, it had been more like a weird coincidence. But now it was something shameful. At Slow Rapids Junior High, the Dollar Store was no better than a garage sale. I found myself glancing around the parking lot as we parked, to make sure there was no one I knew around. JCPenney, with its golden doors, stood just across the street.

The Dollar Store always had a weird smell, sort of a combination between Tupperware and hamster shavings. A bell on the door announced our entrance, and my mom walked through as if she were going to meet the queen, her narrow hips nudging their way through cramped aisles. She plowed by stacks of pillows and legal pads, right to the back of the store. I followed her without paying much attention, until I found myself surrounded by racks full of white cotton panties, big as kites. My mother turned to me and smiled. "I thought we should come here and pick out some bras for you. It's about that time."

I didn't know whether to be happy or mortified. I glanced around the store to see if anyone else was around. The thought of owning a bra was definitely appealing, although I think I would have rather done this with my dad. But Mom seemed happy enough, sifting through bins of underwear that weren't even sorted by size or color. She picked through the lace straps with a delicacy I had never seen before. She used her long fingernails, not letting the fabric touch her fingers. Whenever she did anything, it was always so rushed: cleaning the windows, scrubbing the counters with bleach, even when she brushed my hair. She ripped through the knots fiercely, not even hearing my protests. But now, watching her untangle the complicated pieces of lingerie, I was reminded of the young, dainty woman in the red wool dress haunting our hallway.

I knew that anything I picked out would be vetoed, so I just stood by my mother while she contemplated different cuts and patterns. She even took her glasses out of her purse and put them on as she scrutinized. These glasses were supposed to be for driving, but she never wore them in the car. She only put them on when making an important decision, which I guess this was.

If I were to choose, I would get a black satin bra, one with lace trim and a little padding, no bow. I would wear it to school on Monday with a tank top, letting the black strap fall over my shoulder so P.J. could see. A black bra. Now thinking of it, I decided that there was nothing I wanted more than a black bra. But Mom seemed to be intent on the whites, as each colored bra she came across was immediately discarded.

"You know, Mel, I first met your father at the roller rink across the street. I was seventeen." She was holding up a plain white bra for me to see, not so much for approval, but to show me what was in good taste. It had a bow on the front.

I wasn't sure how to respond to this, so I just smiled. I never knew what to say to my mother. She continued. "I was with your aunt Ann. We were walking along the sidewalk when your father pulled up in his car. He started honking and whistling, but we just ignored him. You know what his first words to me were?" She did not pause for an answer. "He asked me whether I was smuggling melons out of the Food Lion." She looked up at me, her face stunned with laughter and fluorescence. "Don't tell him I told you that." I swear I saw her wink.

In the end Mom decided on three white bras, all made of the same boring cotton. They all had little bows on the front with thick straps. The cashier smiled as she scanned the tags. Three-fifty each. Mother sighed.

"Things always cost more than you think, Melanie," she said, as she rooted around in her purse. "Even at the Dollar Store."

I was still too overcome to be embarrassed.

On our way home, Mom pulled over without warning and parked at the Point, a small lot that overlooked Lake Michigan. Kyle had told me about this place. This was where high school kids went parking at night. This was where Kyle had lost her virginity to some guy named Hugh. She had told me all about it, about what "it" looked like, holding two fingers out for measurement. "About that big," she'd said with a straight face. She was fifteen.

Sitting at the Point with my mother, with traffic whizzing by, I had no idea what I was supposed to do. And on top of that, I couldn't stop thinking of my dad asking my mom if she had stuffed melons in her shirt. I tried to imagine him saying that to her, but it didn't seem right. My mother was pretty small breasted, especially in those days. It was my aunt Ann who had always had a huge chest.

Mom rolled down her window, letting in the sulfurous breeze of Lynxx. "Your sister's going to be staying with us awhile, sweetie," she said. A passing car honked; someone hooted. I sank farther into my seat.

"I hope you see now what can happen if you stray from the path. I hope you see how important it was for you to make that pledge."

I nodded, chewing on my thumbnail. I caught a hangnail between my teeth and pulled.

"Kyle's having a tough time right now, and she needs our guidance. I know she seems old to you, but she is really very young still. She has low self-esteem, Mel, and she needs us to help her make the right decisions."

And it was then, parked at the Sodom and Gomorrah of Slow Rapids, Indiana, where so many teenagers had been tempted and given in to sin, where kids had given up their bodies to youthful lusts, and where so many aborted babies had been conceived, that I decided what I needed to do. I realized then that there were countless kids who needed guidance, who needed to know the facts to be able to make the right decisions. I thought of Brenda Trickett, how she said she wished she could have known the facts. Our nation's youth *were* under attack, and I was going to fight back. I was destined to do great works for God, and it was then, sitting in the car at the Point with my mother, that I masterminded my first great work.

My mother and I pulled into the driveway, next to my brother Jared's car. He hadn't been home for a week, so I immediately went to talk to him. I was the only person in the family he was on any type of speaking terms with. He usually did most of the talking, though. The stairs to the basement led directly to his room, no door, so I knocked on the wall as I came to the bottom of the steps.

"Yeah?" I could barely hear him over the music.

"It's me. Can I come in?" I peered through the wooden hippie beads that draped from the ceiling, acting as his door.

"Sure."

I walked through to find him sitting on his bed, strumming his guitar, trying to imitate some song on the radio. I had heard it before. I remembered this song from one of my meetings with Pastor

Perle, how it was really singing about Satan's tool shed. When I asked Pastor Perle what Satan's tool shed was, he said he didn't know but assured me that it was clearly evil. Now listening to the song, I felt a chill up my spine. Was it a sin to listen to it?

"How's Pastor Lyle?" He leaned over to turn down the music.

I could feel my face turn hot. Somehow, Jared had found out that I had a crush on Pastor Lyle.

"Fine." I did not show him that this bothered me. Pastor Lyle was very handsome whenever he started pacing up and down the stage in his dark purple suit, throwing his hair back and calling on us all to repent. His breath would get all raspy, and I would feel my thighs burning. And then I would repent. Again. For the millionth time in my life.

To my relief, Jared didn't push it any further today. He just kept playing that song, struggling with a chord every now and then. He was missing the top part of his left pinkie, a good half-inch. When he went to live in Chicago a few years ago, he had left with a complete set of fingers. But when he came back, he had only a small sliver of white where his fingernail was supposed to be. He refused to tell anyone what had happened, and no amount of crying and begging from our mother changed his mind. My guess was it had something to do with that anarchy club he ran around with.

Jared's walls were covered in posters, scantily clad women and rock bands. Someone named Ozzy Osbourne stuck his tongue out at me from the far wall. There was a woman wearing a thong, posed, but more like bending over, in front of a yellow car. This was a sign, I thought. God telling me to get out of here, reminding me of my failure with Beth. In this room God's eyes were everywhere. He was testing me.

I turned away from the posters and decided to get this over with as soon as possible. I had come down for a reason. A reason that I thought transcended all this debauchery, the sound of my brother singing about Satan's tool shed.

"Mom said that Kyle has low self-esteem." I figured this was a good way to begin. My abstinence booklet said that having premarital sex would surely lead to low self-esteem, and I wanted to know if Jared thought this was true. I had to do my research, and I figured that if Jared and the abstinence booklet agreed, then there could be no doubt.

Jared did not look up from his guitar but exhaled a loud snort of laughter. "That's funny. I was just thinking the same thing about her."

"About Mom?" This was not going to be a productive conversation, I could tell already.

He nodded. "She has control issues."

My brother had never attended college. He had recently acquired a Psychology 101 textbook, though, and was sure he had everyone in the family pegged. To me, psychology was a shady area. Dad once told me that people shouldn't go fooling around with other people's heads. It was a dangerous business, he said. One that could open your mind to Satan without ever even knowing it. The subconscious was a scary place, I had decided. And Mom's subconscious was an even scarier place.

"Mom's what you'd call an obsessive-compulsive person with schizophrenic delusions." He paused to figure out the next chord, which fell flat against the music playing in the background.

"What does that mean?" I did not try to repeat the words.

"It's complicated, Monchi."

My brother always called me Monchi, but I didn't like it. It was the most horrifying nickname, especially for a girl my age. Not horrifying just because of the name itself, but also because of how it came about, and when I was too young to even defend myself. I was born during the popularity of the Monchhichi cartoon—the brother and sister monkeys who lived in trees and wore shirts. So when my father first saw me, the first word that came out of his mouth was "Monchhichi." I was hairy. I was so hairy that I had fur on my back. The hair on my head was so thick that, despite the nurses' attempts to put it in a bow for my first picture, it stuck out like I had put my finger in a light socket. In fact, the hair on my head was so thick and plentiful that it never fell out, as a newborn's hair is supposed to.

Mom and Dad had planned on naming me Hannah, but they said that when I was born I didn't look at all like a Hannah. I don't know what they expected a baby destined to be named Hannah to look like, but whatever it was, I wasn't it. I could imagine them bent over me, all hairy and dark, and shaking their heads, saying, "This is no Hannah; there's no way we can name her that."

So for the first few weeks of my life, I was a wrinkly primate-looking baby of which there are few pictures. I was Monchhichi. I was a monster. But after I smoothed out and started to look human, everyone called me Melanie. Everyone except for Jared.

Mother agreed to take me to Beth's after dinner. When someone's salvation was at stake, she was always willing to accommodate her schedule. The option of Beth coming over to our house was not discussed. She had never even been inside my house, and I was happy to keep things that way. Mother was very protective of our privacy. To her, a home was not a place to invite people. It was something much more private, even embarrassing. It was a notion that had rubbed off on me so well that I was shocked at the openness with which Beth's parents invited me into their home. When I was hungry, I would open their fridge; when I was looking for something, I would open closets and drawers, rifling through their everyday things. Hairbrushes, lotions, and credit card bills at their house held the significance of mere necessity, while at my house they were charged with something deeper, un-named. Going through their drawers, old pieces of paper were penned with innocent grocery lists, never the embarrassing scrawl of my mother's ramblings, hundreds of pages stuffed in books and cupboards all over the house—Bible verses, new uses for Vaseline, random toll-free numbers, things that God was telling her to do, words of wisdom from Pat Robertson, home remedies for hemorrhoids and mouth sores.

Mom dropped me off in the usual way, but this time she chose not to touch me when she said good-bye. With both hands gripping the wheel, she told me she'd be back to pick me up after play practice.

"Don't forget to tell Beth about the play," she said.

"I certainly won't," I told her.

Now that I didn't have to confront Beth directly about her religion, we were free to do whatever we wanted. I walked to her room, carrying my backpack, which held one of my new white bras and a permanent marker. It would carry out a black bra and Charles Darwin.

I wanted to tell Beth about my plan to battle premarital sex, but I had decided that this was something I was supposed to do on my own. I was working for God, and I didn't think it was appropriate to bring anyone else into it, especially someone who wasn't saved. Satan would try to thwart me in any way possible. If Beth was involved, he could use her to sabotage my plans. Beth was not educated in recognizing Satan's influence, and I did not want to risk anything. And soon enough she would be saved. After that she could help me with my other works. But this one I would have to do on my own.

As soon as I saw her, I invited her to the play and she said she'd go. I got an image right then of me and Beth spending eternity in Heaven together. Her family might be in Hell then, but she'd be so happy that she'd forget about them. Or maybe, I thought, they'd be in Heaven, too. Maybe after I saved Beth, we could both go to work on saving her parents. My influence could spread even further than that, to her grandparents and her aunts and uncles. Friends of the family, coworkers. And then they would go out and witness to their families. This was the beginning of my Providential Destiny. I could be responsible for the salvation of thousands of unhappy, confused, and lost people. The entire Methodist Church would crumble under my persistence. I was a fisherman for Christ, a fisherman of souls.

I was so relieved to not have to worry about her salvation anymore that I asked Beth to help me with a problem. I opened my bag and took out my bra, the one that hooked in the front. Beth didn't have a bra yet, even though most girls in our class had been wearing them since the fifth grade.

"Oh, it's horrendous." She sighed as she turned it over in her hands, stretching the straps, disgusted by their durability.

I nodded and handed her the permanent marker from my bag.

As I watched her color the cups, I again imagined the both of us in Heaven. We'd have eternity together. What would we do with all that time? I wondered if making sexy lingerie was an appropriate thing to do there. Probably not, I decided, since there was no sex in Heaven. Basically, as I understood it, Heaven was a place where you constantly praised God. So we'd probably sing and go to church forever, although I wasn't going to tell Beth that right away. I'd have to ease her into the idea.

We could hear Caitlyn screaming from outside. When me and my parents walked through the front door that night, the sheer volume was almost enough to knock me over. We found Kyle in her room trying to calm her, but she was on the verge of tears herself. She kept plugging up Caitlyn with a pacifier, which Caitlyn would only throw on the floor a few seconds later.

"That's not right," my mother scolded, rushing in with her angel costume flapping behind her. "You're going to spoil that baby and make things harder for yourself later. Let her cry." She stood between Kyle and the crib, her hands on her hips.

Confronted now with the obstacle of our mother, Kyle hesitated, wanting to say something, but whatever she was thinking didn't quite make it into words. Kyle had stopped trying to fight her long ago. She just shrugged, casting a forlorn look at Caitlyn before walking away. I hurried to my room to hide my backpack. Darwin was hiding in there, making me nervous. It was thicker than any book I had ever tried to read.

After an hour Caitlyn was crying loud as ever, choking and

coughing all through it as if her life depended on it. Mother, real-izing that Caitlyn wouldn't wind down by herself, switched strate-gies and whenever Caitlyn would start bawling, she'd walk briskly into the room and slap her on the hands.

I could hear the sound of it through my bedroom wall, the sharp staccato beats that started to work away at me. It sounded dif-ferent when someone else was being slapped. When I was the one being hit, there was no sound at all. When it happened to me, everything was muted and somehow far away. But now, hearing Mother slap Caitlyn, I realized that the sound was the worst part.

"Mother, don't you dare hit that baby," I said, crossing my arms in the doorway. "She's not yours to hit."

She spun around, stepping in close to me, making me flinch. I had no idea where my burst of confidence had come from, but now it was completely deflated by the dry, cracked finger she pointed in my face. Sometimes her hands bled, she washed them so much. "What did you say?"

I couldn't bring myself to repeat the words. I stepped back, right into my sister, who was suddenly standing behind me. Mom followed me with a step forward.

"This is my granddaughter, and I don't want her to grow up spoiled, like you." Her finger shook once for emphasis and then it dropped back to her side. "It worked on your brother and sister." Cait-lyn was crying even louder now. "When I first did this to you, you couldn't even talk yet." She was not looking at me anymore but giving the baby a stern face that she was supposed to take as a warning. "You know what you did? You slapped my hand right back. That's just what you did. And right there and then I knew you were a terrible child."

I didn't show it, but inside I was laughing. I had always wanted to hit my mother back and now felt a great sense of accomplishment, even though I didn't remember doing it. And standing there watching her slap poor Caitlyn's hands, I imagined little Caitlyn standing up in her crib and slapping my mother back, right across the face.

When Caitlyn finally settled down, I knew that I had no excuse not to begin Darwin, other than the fact that God might not want me to. I had liked the idea of keeping the book at Beth's and just skimming it. But that wouldn't work. I wouldn't be at Beth's nearly enough to pull that off, and I needed to start reading more closely. After writing my first entry, I realized that I needed the book, needed to really read it if I was going to prove Darwin wrong. I had to do this. My entire future depended on it. If I screwed up now, I would never get the scholarship for the high school camp next year. It all depended on now, this chain reaction that would determine what college I went to, what job I would have. There had to be some way to please everyone, God especially, my parents and my teachers, too. But I was pretty sure God was okay with it now. I had invited Beth to the play and kept my promise to Him. Besides, reading it didn't necessarily mean that I had to believe it.

><>

MONDAY, JUNE 3, 3:00 A.M.
CHAPTER II: *Variation Under Nature*

In this chapter Darwin uses the same rules from the first chapter (the rules of selecting and breeding farm animals) and applies it to animals in nature. But the main point of this chapter, I think, is how species classification isn't as accurate as we think it is. A lot of times scientists can't agree whether some animals should be grouped in the same categories, as variations, or as entirely new species. I thought science was more clear-cut than that. People always act like science has everything figured out, but clearly it doesn't. Even Darwin admits that. Putting all of your faith in science is like worshipping a false idol. "Although they claimed to be wise, they became fools and exchanged the glory of the immortal God for images made to look like mortal man and birds and animals and reptiles. . . . They exchanged the truth of God for a lie, and worshiped and served created things rather than the Creator" (Romans 1:22–23, 25). I think this is exactly what science and evolution do.

Darwin says there are a lot of animals that fit into a lot of categories. He thinks that using categories like species is useless because it implies "a separate act of creation." As if animals aren't different and that they are all a part of the same jumbled mess, without any order at all. I don't see why he is so against the idea of animals being created separately. He also says that the term "species" is a very loose one that just groups animals that look alike, as if looking alike is not very important. How else can you group animals? So I don't know about this in terms of evolution. The animals I see every day are very different from each other. A squirrel doesn't look like a dog or a cat, and there's no in-between. Where are all of these animals that seem so much alike that you can't tell them apart? Darwin doesn't give any real specific examples. He should be giving examples.

Definitions:

individual difference—the many slight differences that appear in the offspring from the same parents.

doubtful species—animals that possess in some considerable degree the character of a species, but that are similar to other forms or are so closely linked to them that naturalists don't like to consider them a distinct species. I can't give any examples since Darwin didn't give any.

On Monday during my lunch period, I went down to the principal's office to ask Mr. Vogel's secretary, Ms. Cook, if I could use the copy machine. I told her that Mr. Knutsen, the health teacher, had sent me down to make copies of the food pyramid.

"How many copies does he want?" she asked.

"A hundred."

She raised a single eyebrow and set down her pencil.

"He actually wants to give one to all his students," I said. "Have you seen what the kids here have been eating for lunch?"

"No," she said.

I ran my thumb and forefinger along the crease of the folded paper in my hand. "Yesterday, I had a pop and Chee-tos, and my best friend, Beth, ate a candy bar and chips and didn't have anything to drink at all."

"Well, that's not right," she said.

"Mr. Knutsen is calling it a crisis."

Ms. Cook got up from her chair and led me to the copy machine closet, which was right next to Mr. Vogel's office. As I followed her, I kept praying over and over in my head, asking God to forgive me for having to lie to Ms. Cook. She was a nice lady and I hated to take advantage of her, but there was a crisis in our school, and I was the only one who cared. I figured that for the Greater Good I had in mind, God would allow me a small lie every now and then. I was doing what He wanted me to do, so that had to count for something.

"You just put the paper there, punch in one hundred with those numbers there, and then press that big button," Ms. Cook said, and then walked away. She did not close the door behind her, and I considered for a moment easing it shut, but I knew that would be suspicious. So I scanned the flyer and then stood with my back to the machine, watching the hallway and Mr. Vogel's door, as it hummed and stuttered through all one hundred copies.

It wasn't until I had locked myself in one of the stalls of the girls' restroom that I could bring myself to look and see how the flyers had turned out. As I flipped through the pile, I decided that they were much more striking than I had originally thought:

SEX, SEX, SEX, SEX, SEX, SEX, SEX

Did you know that one out of every four teenagers will get an STD? That means that of the 316 students in Slow Rapids Junior High, **80 students in this building have an STD!!!**

Are there 80 students at this school that you don't know? **Then someone you know and trust has an STD!!!**

CHLAMYDIA, GENITAL HERPES, TRICHOMONIASIS, CERVICAL CANCER, GENITAL WARTS, SYPHILIS, HUMAN IMMUNODEFICIENCY VIRUS (AIDS!), GONORRHEA, PELVIC INFLAMMATORY DISEASE, SLOVODIMIA, URETHRITIS, HEPATITIS C, which may lead to STERILITY and DEATH!!!

Any sex that will land you in Hell is not safe sex! That includes any sex outside of marriage! Resist temptation, resist any activity that could possibly tempt you to contract a life-threatening illness! Know the boundaries:

FRIENDSHIP
God-Honoring Discussions
God-Honoring Activities
Encourage each other to grow in Christ

───────────**WARNING LINE**───────────

Petting   Lingering Hugs   Kissing
Suggestive Speech   Holding Hands
SEXUAL INVOLVEMENT

SAFE SEX IS A MYTH . . . JESUS IS NOT

I had been working on this flyer all during English class. For the past week, we had been in the computer room practicing our typing. Mrs. Richards had given us paragraphs and pages of gibberish that we were supposed to replicate and turn in at the end of the week for our Life Skills Portfolio. I had shown up to class early that day to be able to get the computer in the corner, where the screen faced the wall. No one could see what I was doing, and Mrs. Richards never checked on me since I was the best student in the class. But still, I had not typed the SEX, SEX, SEX headline until the very last moment, right before I printed the page out. It was obscene, I knew, but I also knew that I had to grab people's attention. I had to make this flyer impossible to ignore. ABSTINENCE, ABSTINENCE, ABSTINENCE would not cut it.

For the flyer, I had decided to stick with facts. I had wanted to include something about low self-esteem and suicide, but I decided that disease statistics would be more effective and to the point. I had gotten the numbers from my abstinence booklet, along with the names of the diseases.

I knew that not finishing the typing section would greatly affect my Life Skills Portfolio grade and maybe even my future, but I decided that it was a sacrifice I was willing to make. We were supposed to keep our portfolio all through high school and present it to our employers when we applied for our first job. But God would take care of it, I was sure. I had a higher calling right now, a calling that was more important than typing out a backwards alphabet. Both Mom and Dad had said that Kyle needed to start making the right decisions, and I knew that had to be a sign. There was nothing I could really do for Kyle now, but I knew I could try to help my peers make the right decisions. That was God's message to me; that was God's reason for Kyle coming home. It was a wake-up call. The lives of all my fellow students were at stake. There were already two pregnant girls in the eighth grade, one of them in my history class. While Mr. Knutsen incessantly lectured us on nutrition and exercise, my classmates were turning into fornicators.

That morning I told my parents that there was a Bible Study meeting after school. A few months ago, I had tried to start an after-school Bible Study Club that utterly failed. No one came but Beth, who sat with me while I waited a half hour for people to show up. She didn't even bring a Bible but let me read a few chapters from Revelations to her before we gave up and left. I had picked some pretty powerful chapters on prophecies and Armageddon, hoping that they'd move her to ask me more. But she just listened patiently, eating from the tin of cookies I had brought, and then suggested we go watch the baseball team practice out back.

I never had the heart to tell my parents that my Bible Study Club had failed. They had been so proud of me, and Pastor Lyle had even mentioned it in one of his sermons, calling me a Warrior for Christ. And so every once in a while, I told my father to pick me up an hour after school let out because we had a meeting. Usually, I would sit in the library and do my homework for that hour, but today I had different plans.

A half hour after the final bell rang, the halls were empty. I could hear the band playing in the auditorium, and there were a few teachers every now and then walking through the halls, but this was as good as it was going to get. I don't know where my courage came from, but I think it was from God. He had filled me with the Spirit so I could complete my first great work.

With the pile of flyers in my backpack, I wandered slowly down the hallways, pushing a folded flyer through the vents of every other locker. I didn't have enough for the whole school, but I knew word would spread. I kept the papers in my bag, taking one out at a time. If someone came down the hall, I just kept walking, skipping that group of lockers. By the time I was finished, my father was already waiting at the front of the school for me, honking the horn.

$$\propto \infty$$

That night Mother came into my room without knocking to warn me that Satan was sending demons to the house, to try to scare the family away from God.

"I saw one about an hour ago," she said with a stern face, her mouth drawn in a straight line. "He was about as big as you, green, with pointy teeth."

"Okay, Mom," I said, thankful that I had not been reading Darwin at that moment.

"If you see one, just say, 'Get out of here, Devil, in the name of Jesus,' and it'll go away. That's what I did." And with that she flicked off the light and closed the door.

My mother had been seeing demons in the house for as long as I could remember. At first the thought had terrified me. I would stay in my bed all night, not even getting up to go to the bathroom, praying over and over in my head, but now I just knew to stay out of her way for the rest of the night. Whenever she saw demons, she'd start cleaning the house with bleach, yelling at anyone who walked by or touched a doorknob. Sometimes we'd wake up in the morning to find furniture rearranged in bizarre ways—a couch facing the wall, kitchen chairs in the hallway. Reading in bed now, I could smell the familiar cleaning smells seeping in under the door.

Once when I was four years old, I actually got the courage to get up on one of the demon nights. Dad was out on storm duty that night, so we were alone in the house with Mom. I was having trouble sleeping, thinking of my father out in some storm around Gary. So when Mom opened the door to check on me and Kyle and found me awake, she decided to tell me about the demon, which she said she saw walking down the hall. Kyle and Jared were already asleep, so I was the only one to hear it that night. Mom had told me that as long as I was saved, he couldn't hurt me. This made sense. After she left, I lay in bed wondering what a demon looked like. I had never seen one before. It was a long time before I worked up the courage to get up and try to find one.

I found the living room empty, the television on, but Mother's rocking chair vacant. Pat Robertson was praying on the screen; the camera zoomed in on his face as he prayed. I scanned the room again, peeking into the kitchen and noting the darkness of the bathroom down the hall. Not willing to venture any farther into the darkened corners of the house, I sat on the carpet, listening for the demon. It didn't take long for me to finally hear it—a soft thumping beat from the dining room.

I rounded the corner of the dining room slowly. The noise was a bit louder, closer now. I quickly brought my hands together in prayer, the same prayer over and over, trying to imagine the demon, the effect of my words sizzling it away. I wasn't sure what a demon looked like, but Pastor Lyle once said that he saw one that was like a mist. *Thump thump thump.* It was knocking on something, maybe trying to make its way over to me. It had taken my mom, I knew, looking back to the empty rocking chair and suddenly becoming itchy all over. The demon had eaten my mom, and now it was going to eat me. I curled up, squeezing myself into the six inches of space behind the television. The back of the television was warm and still talking, alive. *Pat Robertson, pray for me.* I pressed my cheek to the heat of his voice. I didn't move, hearing that thumping, the demon going through our things. I closed my eyes and kept perfectly still, feeling the woolly itch spread around my body, crawling like the demon's hands. Demon's hands. The demon's hands touching me. I jumped up and ran into the dining room to get away from him, running for the light switch. He would disappear in the light, I knew he would, like the vampires on television. But when I turned it on, I found my mother. She was huddled up against the wall, eyes shut, arms thrust between her knees, looking like a crippled bird. I ran forward, bursting into tears at the sight of her, not eaten and in pieces, but whole. I stopped short when I heard the noise again. *Thump thump thump.* She was rocking back and forth, raising herself an inch off the ground, as if she were trying to get up but failing. As she fell back down, the side of her head thumped against the wall. Over and over.

"Mom?" This word coming out of my mouth like an echo. She did not hear.

"Mom!"

There was no response but that noise, like her wanting to knock my presence out of her head. I realized then that demon had possessed her—the way her eyes were half-closed but saw nothing, her body stiff and shaking. I noticed that the sock was missing from her left foot, which was clenched like a fist, and her skirt was hitched up to reveal a curve of black underwear. I remembered when a little girl in my preschool class had been possessed, had started kicking and crying for no good reason, and how Mr. Polinski and some other churchmen rushed in to cast out the demon. How she cried and kicked even harder as they held her down and prayed, making the demon even madder and madder. My tears by now had soaked the collar of my pajamas, making the fabric itch unbearable on my neck. Feeling the demon's hands trying to strangle me, trying to take me over, too. I ran away from him, away from my mother. Zigzagging so he couldn't catch me. In the hall I unzipped my pajama suit and ripped it off, leaving it headless and crippled against my parents' bedroom door.

I ran back to my room. The door, propped open with a shoe, flew open and then fell back noiseless behind me. The gap let in a thin sheet of light that cut through the center of the room.

"Kyle?" I could see the lump of her snuggled beneath her winter quilt.

I crawled up onto the bed, nudging her gently. She moved over to make room for me without saying anything. I peeled a corner of the quilt away from her bare chest and pulled it over me, moving close to her. The air underneath was warm and heavy against my cold nakedness. I tucked the edges beneath my legs and arms to keep it from escaping. I stayed in this position all night, watching the door, the hall light, for any shadow of intrusion. With Dad gone, I knew there was nothing to do. Even if I woke Jared and Kyle, there was no way we could cast that demon out ourselves. It had taken a group of men to help that little girl. So I just lay there, hoping that the demon would just go away by itself. I could not hear the thumping, but I could still hear the television. New voices now. Voices that could be my mother, returned to herself, talking on the phone.

I did not stay awake long enough to see the hall light turned off, and when I woke to the musky light of dawn, it was still on. I wasn't sure if it had been on all night. The only thing I could be sure of was the nakedness of my sister next to me. The humidity of her sweat sticking to me. And then I cried. I tried not to shake the bed and wake her, but my body would not listen. I wanted her to sleep all day, through her alarm, through any knocking on the door. She would have to get up in a few hours for school, and Jared would go to school. And Dad would still be at work. They all had responsibilities, but I did not. I wouldn't start kindergarten for another year. I would have to stay with Mother all day, alone and trying to act like I had seen nothing. Wondering if the demon was looking at me through her eyes.

$\infty \infty$

"Mel, is that the bus? You better get out there if you know what's good for you. I'm not driving you if you miss it." It was Tuesday morning. My mother was yelling from her bedroom. Still in bed, I imagined. She just packed my lunch the night before and called good-bye from the bedroom, shouting any last demands from her window as I walked down the driveway. My mother shouting at me through her window, making sure that I remembered to wear an undershirt, for all the neighborhood to hear. It was enough to make me think curse words.

As the bus honked a third time and drove away, I stared at myself in the bathroom mirror, at the blue shadows cast under my eyes by hours of late-night reading and contemplation. I certainly didn't feel like the Holy Spirit was with me this morning. I considered just going back to bed, to avoid the humiliation of going to school and facing what I had done. But I knew I couldn't do that. If I was absent today, then everyone would know it was me who made those flyers. And I also didn't want God to think that I was ashamed of what I had done. I was not ashamed and I had to prove it to Him. I was fit to do His work.

But there was no way I could let P.J. see me like this. I had to do something to make myself presentable. Kyle was in the kitchen by now, feeding Caitlyn, so I slipped into her room and stole a tube of her Passion Rose lipstick. With it tucked safely into the front pocket of my backpack, I went downstairs to ask Jared if he'd give me a ride to school. He was still in his white Lynxx jumpsuit, smelling like one of my mother's home perms.

"Sure," he said, "just give me a minute to change."

As we walked to his car, I heard my mother's window screech open, slow and painful. "Jared, pick up milk, peanut butter, laundry detergent, napkins, double-A batteries, and some bananas on your way back."

"Yeah, Mom."

"And some lunch meat. Ham."

Jared looked down at me and rolled his eyes.

I considered asking him what the words were he had used to describe Mom. Something about delusions and obsessions. I could look it up in my dictionary. But I couldn't bring myself to ask him.

He didn't seem to be in the talking mood; I was too tired to talk. I had stayed up late to read Darwin, only feeling safe enough to take the book from under my mattress after I heard Mom turn off the television and go to bed. That was at one in the morning. I thumbed a corner of it through the fabric of my backpack. I was going to try to finish the chapter in study hall, if I could stay awake.

My brother drove much faster than anyone I knew. Dad usually eased over our dirt road, trying to go slowly so the rocks wouldn't kick up and dent the car. Jared didn't seem to care. Huge rocks flew up from the tires, cracking against the doors and windows and disappearing into the tunnel of dust that expanded behind us. He turned on the radio and sang along with some secular song I had never heard. I clicked on my seat belt and watched the speedometer rise like a temperature gauge about to explode.

As we sliced through the distance that separated us from Slow Rapids Junior High, my palms started to get all slimy and my knee started bouncing. It was a nervous habit I had gotten from my mother. Inheritance, I thought, but then quickly pushed it out of my mind. Darwin had no idea what he was talking about, and I was well on my way to proving it. My reading was a holy mission, something to make my faith even stronger. Proving him wrong would be my second great work.

I watched the cornfields turn into farms and the farms into small clusters of houses, huddled against the highway. The courage I had possessed just a day ago was completely gone. What had I been thinking, making a flyer like that? I had included the SEX, SEX, SEX headline because I thought no one would suspect me of such vulgarity, but the God stuff could give me away. I really shouldn't have included the God stuff, I started thinking. But still, I told myself, I had done God's work. Even if I had to do some questionable things, I had still done what He wanted me to do.

But there was no way anyone could pin those flyers on me. Even if someone had seen me in the hallway, they just would have seen me with one piece of paper in my hand. I could have just been pushing a note into someone's locker. Lots of people did that. But still, I would have to lie low for a few days, which meant that I would have to postpone my plan to talk to P.J. Instead of talking to him, I would write him a note, or maybe even an anonymous note telling him that I loved him. Or I could just make eye contact, maybe a wink or a smile. I imagined how Emily Brontë would write the scene and suddenly felt depressed. Her characters wouldn't think about it; they'd just do it. Thinking about it would destroy its meaning. So I decided not to think about it. And doing my best not to, I chewed my left thumbnail until it bled.

The school was about twenty minutes away, but Jared made it there in twelve, running the red light that had just cleared the lift bridge for an incoming freighter boat. As he pulled up to the front door of the school, he turned off the radio and put his hand on my knee, stopping it with a firm grip. He smiled.

"You know, Monchi. It all seems like a big deal now, but in ten years you won't even remember it. Your life will be completely different."

"Yeah," I said, gathering my backpack from between my feet. "I know."

I could feel his eyes still fixed on me, but I did not look at him until he spoke again. "Do you want to see something really cool?" His hand remained on my leg, firm, as if he thought at that moment I might run away.

"I'm really late," I said. "I need to get to homeroom." I imagined my empty desk in the middle of the class, how everyone probably noticed I was gone. That would confirm their suspicions. And poor Beth there by herself, trying to defend me.

"Don't worry about it," Jared said, putting the car into reverse. "I'll write you a note."

———

The guard at the Lynxx chemical plant waved Jared's car through without even looking at us. We parked in the vast half-filled lot, apart from the other cars. The factory was on all sides of us now, the fence and the razor wire reminding me of a prison—which reminded me of prisoners, the type of people who probably skipped school when they were kids. We walked quickly to an unmarked side entrance as I considered the possibility of this moment, like peering over the edge of a slippery slope that would propel me into horrible things—drugs, sex, crime, prison. I will never skip school again, I told myself, but still I couldn't help the relief I felt, knowing that my morning humiliation would be postponed for just a little while.

"I'm not supposed to be here now," Jared said, opening the door for me and shoving me inside as he glanced around the parking lot. "But I think you'll really like this. I think it's something you'd appreciate."

Inside was dark and cool. As my eyes tried to adjust, I could see nothing, perceive nothing but a steady hum that seemed to be the floor itself beneath me. And no smell, astonishingly no smell. How a factory like this managed to stink up the entire town and have no smell inside was utterly baffling. I looked around some more, my eyes opening up finally to construct some large metal structures, pipes, my brother standing next to me—and then he was gone. I took a few steps and turned to focus on a shadow that could have been him.

"Jared, what did you mean when you said Mom had obsessions and delusions?"

No answer. I walked toward the shadow, with my hand outstretched, wanting to feel what it was.

"C'mon," Jared said from somewhere behind me. I turned and walked toward his voice instead, accidentally kicking something that let out a painful metallic screech as it scraped the floor. A hand grabbed my wrist and pulled me hard. "Fucking Christ," Jared said. "Do you want to see this or not?"

"Yes," I said, resisting the urge to correct his language.

I had no idea what we were going to see. I didn't even know what Lynxx made. They had huge metallic cylinders all over town and their smokestacks were almost always leaking something that smelled a tiny bit different from the last time.

My brother was pulling me through a series of more or less bare rooms, unlocking doors and checking to make sure there was no one inside before we entered. Walking this way, in seeming circles, I lost all concept of direction and just followed my brother, trying not to think of the absurd route we were taking, all of these rooms just strung together without any order. Trying not to think of mice in a maze. The way he was acting, I started to wonder whether Lynxx made things for the government, if my brother was under oath to keep these secrets. Whether he'd be sent to prison for this, maybe even kicked out of the country. It made sense that way, these rooms all clustered together to hide the one room that mattered. The room we were trying to find. I looked up at the ceiling, where a series of pipes led us around a corner and spilled us mercifully into a hallway.

"Jared, what do you do here?"

"I'm a janitor."

He stopped in front of a door that read "EMERGENCY EXIT" and opened it with another key on his huge key chain. He pushed me through the open door. I was expecting to be outside again but was completely surprised to find myself in another room. There was no real color to it, just the cool feeling of a blank room. The overhead lights didn't seem to be doing much other than sustaining this general feel—no light, no dark, just a room. I looked around disoriented, wondering if an emergency exit always had to lead outside.

Jared was fumbling in some cabinets when he called me over to him. I walked across the room, but he had found whatever it was he was looking for and met me in the middle, pulling me instead to a desk in the corner. He was holding a clear plastic bag full of something pale yellow—a distinct color showing through all the murkiness. Working at a corner of it with his teeth, he tore open the plastic and spit onto the floor.

"Hold out your hand."

I did as I was told and received a handful of cool powder that Jared smoothed out over my fingers and palm. Then he switched on the desk lamp.

"Hold your hand under there."

In the light the powder looked unremarkable. It could have been anything, really. A spice, some kind of explosive, a drug. I looked closer at the yellow grains and sniffed. No smell.

"What is it?"

Jared was standing over me, looking down with a smile that wanted to tell me right away, but he didn't.

"So what would an egghead like you do to find out what it was? What kind of tests would you do?"

I looked down again at my hand, which was beginning to shake as I considered the possibility that this was an illegal drug. It really wouldn't surprise me, my brother, listening to music that subconsciously told him to deal drugs.

"Jesus, Mel. C'mon. I thought you got some big scholarship to nerd camp. Think. What would MacGyver do?"

"Uh," I said, feeling the lamplight warming through the powder to my palm. "Maybe see if it dissolves in water?" And taste it, I told myself. The first thing MacGyver would do is lick his finger and pick up a few grains to put on his tongue. But I was not going to say that. There was no way I was going to put this stuff in my mouth.

Jared nodded, pleased with my answer. "What else?"

Smoke it, inject it, sell it to little kids on the street. This yellow powder was starting to feel heavy in my hand. I had sniffed it. Was it a bad idea to have done that? Had I just snorted drugs? I just wanted to throw it down and run back to school. This was exactly what reading Darwin and skipping school led to.

"How about this?" Jared switched off the desk lamp and then walked toward the door. He flicked the light switch off, and then he was gone. The whole room was lost in complete darkness. Except for my hand, which was glowing a stunning neon blue. Just my hand, amputated, floating in the darkness. I spread my fingers, letting some of it fall to the floor.

"That's alkaline earth aluminate," I heard Jared say, his voice still far away, near the door. "Pretty fucking cool, right?"

"Yeah." I wiggled my fingers. Dark creases had formed in the joints of my fingers, making it looked like they had been cut into pieces. "Is this what Lynxx makes?"

"No. We just mix it into paint. This stuff comes right from the earth. It's natural, Mel. Can you believe that? They just dig it right out of the ground, from caves or something like that."

"Here?" I asked. "Do they dig it out of Slow Rapids?"

"I don't know. Maybe."

I imagined the possibility of this, of the dirt in Slow Rapids containing something so incredible. The graves, the gardens glowing bright blue in the middle of the night, while everyone slept. I wondered if Darwin knew about this stuff, what it would do to his theory. This seemed to me to be something that could prove the existence of God. I looked down again at my hand, which was dimmer now. Much dimmer than before.

"It's going out," I said. "Why's it going out?"

Jared turned on the overhead light, returning my hand to me. Just a small pale hand, covered in yellow powder. "We didn't charge it enough under the light. It doesn't make light, it just gives back what light you give to it."

"So it doesn't glow underground?"

"No. Just when it's brought to the surface. Here." He kicked a wastebasket over to me, and I reluctantly brushed the powder off my hand. "Do you want a bag?" he asked. "You can take one if you want. You can make stuff out of it. Mix it with paint or water or whatever. You can paint your fishing lures. That's what some of the paint is used for, you know. To make your fancy fishing lures."

I wanted immediately to say yes but thought better of it. It would be a sin to steal from Lynxx, a sin against God, for sure, but maybe also a crime. I thought of the razor wire surrounding the factory, how far they went to protect this stuff. I couldn't live with that, with the fear of men in white jumpsuits knocking on our door in the middle of the night, searching my room, finding all of my secrets.

"No," I said. "That's okay. I think I just need to get back to school."

In front of the junior high, I sat in the passenger seat of my brother's car, watching him write something on the back of a brown paper bag. He then ripped it off and folded the note into what I could only call a trapezoid. He handed it to me.

"They won't give you any trouble."

"Thanks," I said, putting the note in my pocket and getting out of the car.

He leaned over before I could shut the door. "And wash your hands really good. Don't get that shit in your eyes or anything. You're supposed to wash your hands for, like, ten minutes or something."

I froze, staring at him, looking for a hint of a smile on his face. But there was none.

"I thought you said it's natural. You said it comes right from the earth." My heart was beating in my throat, as I tried to remember if I had touched my eyes or chewed on my nails in the past fifteen minutes.

"Yeah, it's natural," he said. "But that doesn't mean it can't fucking kill you."

As I walked the empty scrubbed halls of Slow Rapids Junior High, I kept my hands in front of me, about a foot from my body. I remembered putting my hands through my hair, scratching my nose as I waited for Jared to relock one of the Lynxx doors. I had chewed my fingernails, I was almost sure. I moved my tongue around in my mouth. My mouth didn't taste weird, but I knew that didn't really mean anything.

I made my way to the girls' restroom and saw a few of my flyers lying on the floor, but I no longer cared. Now I might die, and the thought of enduring the ridicule of other students, of having to sit through a year's worth of detention, didn't bother me. Even blind and deaf, I'd do it again, I told myself. Like Job, I would never blame God for my misfortunes but would continue to do His work without complaining.

I filled my palms with pink soap, emptying one of the dispensers. I washed my hands for about fifteen minutes and then moved on to my arms and face, my neck. I thought of my mother, at our house, doing the same thing. Standing at the sink with the scalding water steaming up the mirror. Obsession and delusions, I thought. Inheritance. But I didn't care. This was nothing like that. I was using cold water because the hot-water faucet was broken. Painfully cold water that made my skin ache.

I washed until I couldn't stand to do it anymore. And when I was done, I turned off the light in the restroom and stared at the darkness in the mirror. Looking for any hint of powder left on me. I couldn't see a thing.

When I finally made it to the office, my hair and shirt were soaking wet, my eyes raw and red from holding them open under the tap. I must have smelled like a janitor's closet with that pink soap clinging to my skin, refusing to wash off completely in the cold

water. Ms. Cook was standing at the front desk and saw me immediately, giving me a look like I had no clothes on. Her look made
me forget for a moment exactly what was expected of me. And then
I remembered the note. I had forgotten to read what Jared wrote. I
pulled it out of my pocket and considered reading it over before
handing it to her, but I knew that would just make her suspicious,
make her call my parents and find out that I had skipped school. I
handed her the note, telling myself that this was Jared's sin. Forgery
and lying. I had remained ignorant and therefore innocent. For all I
knew, he wrote down the truth.

Ms. Cook turned the note over in her hands a moment before
opening it. As she read, her face fell into distress. When she was
done, she set the note on the counter and looked down at me with
pity and painful understanding, as if everything about my appear-
ance now made sense. I hated my brother right then. I imagined
him in his car, laughing to himself about whatever it was he wrote,
thinking he was so funny. And thinking I was so dumb.

As Ms. Cook filled out a pass for me, I managed a weak smile,
although my insides were burning with anger and the knowledge
that all of the teachers, by the end of the day, would know this thing
about me. This one terrible thing that I would never know. I had
so much already, but now I had taken on another humiliation. I
would have to bear it for the rest of the year and it wasn't even mine.

∝ ⋊

"Who gave you herpes, Mel?" someone shouted across the hall, as
I was walking to my third-period science class.

"Hey, Melanoma," someone else sang. "I love it when you talk
dirty!" There was laughing, but I didn't care. These people would
sink their own life raft. And like my dad said, people who don't
even realize they need to be saved are the most important people to
reach, even if they mock you as you try to help them.

Trevor Hughes, a boy on the baseball team, a boy I knew was

not a virgin, walked over to my desk at the beginning of science class, before Mrs. Lucci arrived. "Don't take it out on all of us, just because *you* can't get laid," he said. There was more laughing. And right then I felt the Holy Spirit move in me, telling me exactly what to say.

"My body is a temple of the Holy Ghost," I said, looking him right in the eyes. "And no one but my husband is authorized to enter."

He stared blankly at me for a moment, as if I had changed his entire view of the world with that one statement. I saw a glimmer of hope right then in his confusion, in his half-open mouth that revealed rubber bands stretched between his teeth. But then he just burst out laughing, spraying spit on my face.

Mrs. Lucci had us dissecting bluegills. This was not the first time I had cut open a fish. I remembered my father teaching me when I was seven, the two of us kneeling over a sheet of plywood to fillet one for dinner. He had held the knife carefully, like a pen, the tip poised over the bass. As he dragged the knife along the top fin, tracing along the spine, I watched the cut lengthen into a line of blood that feathered out onto the wood. The inside of the fish shone a translucent white, parting easily, opening to the light. But then the fish opened and closed its mouth, as if it were trying to say something. I had screamed.

I was having a hard time focusing on my fish, with all the giggling and funny looks people were giving me. Dissecting was not like filleting, although I found myself cutting it that way. I didn't see the logic in doing it how the manual said and so decided to do it how I knew. I separated the flesh from bone, making two perfectly extracted fillets, which I set on my tray.

I had been dissecting my fish for about fifteen minutes, trying not to make eye contact with anyone, before someone came into the room and handed a note to Mrs. Lucci. I immediately knew

what was coming next, but still I tried to look surprised when she
called my name and told me to go down to the office.

Mr. Vogel wanted to talk to me, and I knew it was about one of
three things. The note Jared wrote immediately came to mind. He
could have written anything. It could have been something so awful
that the office called my house to ask my mother about it. And then
they would know it was a forgery, that I had been skipping school
to break into Lynxx. But also, it could be about the flyers. As I made
my way down the main stairway and to the first floor, I saw another
one lying on the ground near the bottom. SEX, SEX, SEX. It really was
eye-catching. I was glad I could read it clearly; the glow powder
hadn't affected my sight so far. Just to make sure, I walked back up
to the top of the steps and tried to read it from there.

There was no doubt the flyers had been a success, despite the
sarcastic comments and looks I got from some of the kids. As I
washed the fish scales off my hands, I heard girls talking about the
flyers in the bathroom. They were making some kind of joke about
not wanting to sit on the toilet seats because of herpes. They
laughed, but that didn't matter. The message was out. In my classes
I thought I noticed people looking at each other suspiciously. Yes,
I wanted to yell, it could be anyone. You don't know where people
have been.

Everyone was talking about the flyers. In between second and
third period, when Wendy Platt and Bill Geensley were walking
through the hallway holding hands, Dustin Wessler started heckling
them about giving each other genital warts. People laughed and that
was fine. All that mattered was that they were thinking about it.
People now had the information to help them make the right
choices. I really didn't see how I could get in trouble for what I had
done. The flyers were an issue of free speech. And anyway, there
was no proof, no proof at all, that I had made them.

But there was still another possibility. Mr. Vogel could have found out that I had forged the permission slip for the academic camp, the one that listed the required readings. The signature wasn't perfect, and I knew they had other letters from my parents to compare it to. This was probably the worst offense. Forgery was a real crime. That was something people went to jail for. Jared forged the one note, but this one I had done myself.

Mr. Vogel was sitting in his office, one leg crossed over the other, doing nothing but waiting for me. He was a middle-aged man, like all principals, with a shiny, bald head. And I had never seen him in anything but the same brown suit he wore to school every day. He was thick around the middle and thin everywhere else, making him look very solid even though he wasn't really. Many kids found him frightening, but he didn't intimidate me.

"Sit down, Melanie," he said, when I knocked on his open door. He did not change position as I put my backpack down and perched myself on the edge of the wooden chair that faced his desk. Just a few weeks ago, I had been in this same office, sitting in this same chair, when he told me that I had been chosen to receive the full scholarship to the academic summer camp.

Mr. Vogel's expression revealed nothing, and for a moment I thought he wasn't going to accuse me of anything. Maybe he just wanted to congratulate me again on the scholarship.

"Have you seen this before, Melanie?" He leaned across his desk without uncrossing his legs and handed me one of my flyers. I tried to look down at it like I had never seen it before in my life, with my eyebrows wrinkled, my mouth slightly open in surprise.

"No," I said, in a scandalized whisper.

I suddenly felt very embarrassed being in the same room with Mr. Vogel and this flyer. The fact that Mr. Vogel had read it and immediately thought of me made me want to melt with shame. There it was, "SEX, SEX, SEX," like an obscene note passed from him to me. I held a corner of it with my fingers, as if it disgusted me.

"You didn't get one of these in your locker this morning?" he asked, obviously not convinced by my performance.

I shook my head.

Mr. Vogel uncrossed his legs and leaned forward, putting his elbows on his desk. "Well," he said, "sometime between yesterday and this morning someone put these in a whole lot of lockers."

"Oh," I said.

Mr. Vogel pressed his hands together in front of him, as if he were praying. "Melanie, do *you* believe that a quarter of the students here have an STD?"

"No," I said, biting the inside of my cheek.

"Neither do I," he said. He paused, looked hard at me. "But somebody does."

Whatever Mr. Vogel had in store for me, I was willing to endure it. People had done greater things for God and been punished for them, punished in terrible ways that went beyond anything Mr. Vogel was capable of. I would suffer for Christ, too. And I would suffer for the good of my fellow students. It seemed to be my destiny.

"So you don't know anything about these flyers?"

"No," I said, feeling the pressure of tears behind my eyes. I hated this lying. I wanted to be able to confess, to show that I was proud of what I had done, that he was wrong in ignoring the facts. But I couldn't bring myself to do it.

"I know you've been very concerned by the moral decisions of your peers since you've been here, Melanie—"

I opened my mouth to defend myself, to say there were worse things to be preoccupied with, but he held a hand up and continued.

"Now I'm not persecuting you for your faith, Melanie. I admire your faith and your discipline and the work you've done here at school. I just want to find out who was behind these flyers. I want to make sure nothing like this happens again." He leaned forward even more, looking me right in the eyes, as if he were leveling with me. "I don't think that this person had bad intentions; I just think they need to leave this"—he pointed to the flyer still in my hand—"to the teachers."

I nodded my head, resisting the urge to tell him what I thought about the health program here. Yes, abstinence, they say, but if that's not for you, use a condom. That's probably what Kyle had heard for years from her teachers.

"We have professionals," he said, "who are trained in this stuff, and who can do a lot better job of teaching our students."

I nodded again.

"The point of education," he said, his eyes now set on the ceiling, "is to inform, not to distort facts—"

I couldn't keep quiet anymore. "Facts?" I said, my voice cracking. "The fact is that condoms are only fifty percent effective against the transmission of herpes, chlamydia, and gonorrhea. And there is no proof at all that they help to prevent syphilis, trichomoniasis, HPV, and chancroid. And pregnancy," I said, taking a deep breath before I dropped the bombshell. "If a fifteen-year-old girl uses condoms on a regular basis, she has a fifty percent chance of getting pregnant by the time she turns twenty." My sister, I wanted to yell at him. It happened to my own sister!

Mr. Vogel sighed and raised a hand to his temple. "I'm not saying that this isn't a problem—"

"It isn't a problem," I said, almost shouting now. "It's an epidemic. And no one seems to care. No one's doing anything about it."

"The point of education," he said again, his voice maintaining a patient tone, "is not to scare people into doing what's best for them. People have to learn to make their own decisions, and they have to learn to live with them."

"But people need the right facts to make those decisions. No one's giving kids the facts."

"Melanie, slovodimia isn't even a word." He pointed to the flyer still in my hand. "If you want to talk about facts, I think you have a lot more research to do."

I looked down at the flyer, at the list of diseases I had copied from my abstinence booklet.

Mr. Vogel continued, "The fact is, there will always be terrible facts about the world, Melanie. And I hope you'll learn soon that you cannot change them. The fact is that there will always be people who make mistakes and who don't make the right decisions for themselves. But think of it this way: If everyone were as disciplined and hardworking as you, you wouldn't be at the top of your class anymore."

I just stared at him, not knowing what to say.

"And please don't use office equipment for this sort of thing," he added, standing up and taking the flyer from my hand. "It really isn't proper use of the copy machine."

><>

TUESDAY, JUNE 4, 2:45 P.M.
CHAPTER III: *Struggle for Existence*

Darwin has finally started talking about "natural selection." Animals have many enemies in the struggle for existence: competition between themselves for food and space, climate, predators, and parasites. All this struggle and death, Darwin says, is not a scary thing. He writes that "we may console ourselves with the full belief that the war of nature is not incessant, that no fear is felt, that death is generally prompt, and that the vigorous, the healthy, and the happy survive and multiply." I don't know why he thinks everyone's worried. I know I am going to Heaven. I think Darwin was a pretty depressed person. I don't think he believed in Heaven.

Evolution is supposed to depend on lots of species going extinct. This is how animals evolve, according to Darwin. If you aren't well suited to your environment, then you die and then better-suited ones live. But what about Noah's ark? None of those animals were suited to survive that flood, but Noah saved them anyway. They didn't survive because they grew fins and gills; they survived because God intervened.

Darwin mentions people only once in this chapter. No mention of us coming from monkeys yet, but he does say that the human population has doubled in the past twenty-five years, and if we continued at this rate, in just a thousand years there would be no standing room left. Well, he wrote that in the 1800s, and we don't seem to be having a problem yet. So maybe he isn't so smart.

Definitions:

slovodimia—?

Darwin's definition of natural selection (evolution)—In the struggle for existence, "variations, however slight and from whatever cause proceeding, if they be in any degree profitable to the individuals of a species, in their infinitely complex relations to other organic beings and to their physical conditions of life, will tend to the preservation of such individuals, and will generally be inherited by the offspring. The offspring, also, will thus have a better chance of surviving" . . . and so on. This clearly goes against the second law of thermodynamics. Things can't be getting more complex and deteriorating at the same time. Why does no one else see this? Why are we even learning this if a law has proven it wrong? And also, if Darwin says that babies get their traits from their parents, where do these "variations" come from? On the one hand, he argues that babies are like their parents, and, on the other, he says that these fluke traits just appear from nowhere to help a species survive. So I guess his whole theory is based on anomalies, which he even said were very rare and usually die anyway. How can he base this theory on something that hardly ever happens?

～

When I got home from school on Thursday, Kyle was combing her hair in the bathroom mirror, trying to conceal her bruises with a dramatic over-the-eye look. She was going to the grocery store for Mom to get the stuff that Jared hadn't gotten on Tuesday. I asked if I could ride along to keep her company.

"Whatever, do what you want." She sighed and threw down her comb.

The ride there was completely silent, my sister staring daggers at the road and not saying anything to me. I didn't try to talk but sat back to pick dirt from beneath my fingernails.

It had been almost three days since my trip to Lynxx. I had not gone blind, deaf, or crazy. My hair hadn't fallen out, and I didn't glow in the dark. But I had been banned from the nurse's office at school. Whenever my eye twitched or my stomach grumbled, I'd go to Ms. Hern. She would look in my ears, down my throat, give me Tums, and send me back to class. Today she had refused to examine me. She said there was nothing wrong with me and then asked if I was having problems at home.

I considered asking Kyle's advice about the glow powder but quickly thought better of it. With all of the bad decisions she had made in her life, I did not want her giving me advice. She was my sister, but she was also a backslider and an unrepentant sinner. It had occurred to me right then that, being such a sinner, she may know something about slovodimia. I had looked it up in my dictionary, in three dictionaries at school, but couldn't find it. I had checked the spelling and everything from my abstinence booklet, but this sexually transmitted disease was nowhere to be found. I wondered what that could mean, if it was a sign from God, Him leading me on some kind of search that would make everything make sense: the glow powder, my mission, Darwin. If that was the case, then I didn't need my sister's advice on anything. And anyway, things had been working out for me lately. I had God on my side. This glow powder stuff would work itself out, just like the flyer incident. Mr. Vogel hadn't punished me at all. He knew better than to persecute me for my faith. The Church wouldn't let that happen, and Mr. Vogel knew what church I went to. After talking to me about the role of the teacher and my role as a student, he had released me. And I hadn't heard anything about it since.

As we drove, I watched Kyle tapping her elegant fingernails on the steering wheel. They were long and purple, with white roses airbrushed on them. Looking at her always made me self-conscious because she seemed like a glamorous, more cleaned-up version of me. When we were younger, we looked so much alike that our aunts often mixed us up, but now looking at her, I couldn't see any resemblance. She looked so grown up—her hair dyed with a reddish tint that made her entire head flare up when the sun shone on her, as it was at this moment. Guys always turned to look twice, but she'd slice through their stares without paying any mind.

The sun that made my sister glow was pounding on me through the window, making me hot and ashamed. My thighs were all wet and sticking to the seats, my armpits and my hair turning sour in the still heat of the car. I could smell myself now, like the musty odor of dirty laundry. How, I wondered, could anyone mistake me for her?

———

The Food Lion had an entire aisle dedicated to "feminine needs." Whenever I passed through this aisle with my mother, I usually kept my head down, spying things out of the corner of my eye: feminine sprays, panty liners. I could not bring myself to look straight on at anything, since my mother might notice and feel the need to tell me what these devices did in those vague, sometimes nonsensical explanations of hers. Sometimes she would outright lie, for lack of a decent explanation.

Without really knowing how I'd gotten here, I found myself now standing at the entrance to the feminine needs aisle with Kyle. I thought we were just picking up the things that Mom put on the list, but Kyle had stopped here and I had stopped with her.

"I need to get something," she said. "Wait here."

I knew from my trips here with Mother that the Kotex pads were at the end of the aisle, which I never understood. I thought that the normal feminine things should be placed at the beginning, so most women wouldn't have to walk through the more embarrassing sprays and squirters to get to the Kotex. If it were up to me, I thought, the weirder or more embarrassing a product was, the farther down the aisle it should be, making these awkward encounters necessary for only those loose and strange women who actually needed these devices. In my mind, the Kotex would be first, douches and crotch sprays a little before the Today Sponges, which would be near the end, where the aisle dead-ended into a wall. And tampons somewhere in the middle. I had not really made up my mind about tampons yet. I knew that my mother had refused to buy them for my sister because, as I overheard her telling my grandma on the phone, she didn't want to be giving her "any ideas." Kyle once told me that the Ladies of Vision group at church, who were responsible, among other things, for meeting feminine needs in all the church restrooms, had debated a full three hours on whether to mix a few tampons in with the maxi pads in the baskets that adorned all the vanities. My mother was in the majority who decided against it.

In my store pregnancy tests would definitely be the farthest down the aisle, right next to the wall. Pregnancy tests were for nervous women who did not want babies, who had premarital sex, and who were willing to get abortions. Decent, married women went to a doctor.

But despite the clear logic of my aisle plan, the Food Lion saw things differently. The pregnancy tests were smack-dab in the middle of the aisle, next to the home bikini wax kits. And this is where I watched Kyle stop and grab a box.

When she made her way back to me, I could see that Kyle was not holding a bikini wax kit. Without meeting my eyes, she took the box and shoved it beneath all the other groceries.

"Let's go," she said, trying to pull the cart forward, but I grabbed on to the handle and jerked it back.

"No," I said, in a stern voice that surprised me as much as her. "Not until you tell me what you're going to do with that." I pointed to where the box was buried, not allowing myself to say its name.

Kyle squinted, put her hand on her hip. "I'm going to make Popsicles with it," she snapped. "What the hell do you think I'm going to do with it?"

"Is it for you?"

She nodded. Her eyes, which had grown watery, were set on my chest.

I couldn't believe this was happening. I wanted to slap her right then. Crying in the middle of the Food Lion, as if she had no control over any of this. As if she were some type of victim. Didn't she realize by now that she had done all this to herself? Hadn't she learned her lesson?

"Well, are you surprised?" I asked in a voice that tried to be harsh again, but ending up sounding childish.

She glared at me, but I kept on. "I'm not surprised at all. I saw you pick up that box and I said to myself, yeah, that seems about right." Of course, it was a lie. Watching her take that box was more shocking to me than her coming home with a black eye. But I figured this was the way to go, to make her see that something like this was a result of her actions, not an accident at all.

"Shut up, Mel," she said, loud enough that a few people stopped their carts and looked. "You don't know fucking shit about anything."

We stood there for a moment, just staring at each other across the cart. And then she started crying. Not like before, but really crying. She folded her arms on the edge of the cart and put her head down. I thought then about what Dad said, about showing Kyle she has our support. Giving her grief right now wouldn't do anything. Kyle needed her self-esteem back, and I had to let her know I thought she was worth helping.

"Hey," I said, stepping over to her. "Hey, Kyle, I'm sorry. Just forget it, okay? I don't know, I don't know anything. All right? Let's just get this and get out of here."

Standing in front of the checkout, with our cart full of groceries, Kyle turned to face me. "Mel, I can't go up and buy this. She'll know it's for me." The "she" was the middle-aged cashier woman we had scoped out just minutes before. She was in checkout number 4 and was the least talkative, most pissed-off employee there. She barely looked at the items she scanned.

"What else are you going to do?"

She sucked in her lower lip and bit down on it, the way she liked to do when she asked Dad for something. "Can't you go up and buy it? I'll give you the money—"

"No way!" I squeaked, horrified.

Kyle put a hand on my shoulder. "If I go up, she'll know it's for me. It obviously couldn't be for you. She'll know you're buying it for someone else. C'mon, Mel."

I shook my head. "Why won't they think it's for me? It could be for me, why not?"

"Seriously, Mel, you're eleven."

"I'm fourteen."

"It doesn't matter. You look about ten. You couldn't even *get* pregnant yet." Her voice was half laughing, half crying. Her lower lip chewed up and dry like an old piece of gum. "I will just *die*, Mel. I'd just die right there, just faint in the middle of the checkout. I can't do this. Do you realize that in a few minutes I have to go pee on a stick? I have to go pee on a stick and wait, like, an hour to see if my life is over." She paused to consider this, the possibility of her life being over at the age of nineteen. I thought her life was already over, but I didn't say so.

"All you have to do is hand the cashier money."

Checkout 4 was occupied when I rolled up with the cart. There was a woman going through with a whole load. I used all of my weight to turn the cart into the lane. I situated myself right behind her, watching the cashier lady scan the items fiercely, as if she were being timed. As I waited, I decided that I would put the pregnancy test on the conveyor belt not first, but somewhere near the beginning as all the other items afterward would make her forget about it. Maybe third or fourth.

"Excuse me, miss," a male voice called. "I can take you in number three."

I was not expecting this. My hands gripped the cart defensively. "That's okay," I replied. "I'll just wait here."

Hearing this, the number 4 cashier lady paused, midscan, and scowled up at me as if I were every reason her day would never end.

"Okay," I said to the man cashier, who had already shrugged

and turned around. I backed the cart up and used my whole body to direct it into the next lane, where another woman had moved in on the vacancy. Not wanting to turn back to number 4, I waited here, in number 3, as the cheerful cashier man made small talk with the lady in front of me. He was an older man, with a patchy gray beard and smile-wrinkled eyes. His blue Food Lion smock had a button on it that said "NIETZSCHE IS DEAD"—GOD. Who was Nietzsche? A Bible character? It looked like a name from back then, although I couldn't remember reading anything like that in the Bible.

When my turn finally came, I set the batteries on the conveyor belt first, followed by the ham. I decided to put the pregnancy test third, immediately followed by the milk, which was large and would definitely make him forget about its predecessor. I piled the other items randomly afterward, trying not to make eye contact, but he spoke anyway.

"How are you doing today, miss?"

I glanced at my own reflection in his spectacles. "Fine."

The batteries were making their way toward him as the conveyor belt hummed. His hand was open, reaching out toward them as they came nearer. "Find everything you were looking for?" He grabbed the package as I nodded. The cash register bleeped. Six forty-five.

Putting the pregnancy test third was a mistake, I thought, as he reached for the ham. I should have put it near the end, so he'd be in a groove by the time he got to it, just grabbing and scanning. Bleep! Three thirty-seven.

His right hand was already on the box as he shoved the ham aside with his left. As he ran the bottom along the scanner, he paused and squinted at the lettering and then looked up at me, his eyes wrinkled but not in a smile. Bleep! Thirteen thirty-eight.

"It's for a science experiment," I heard myself say. "I'm going to see if it works on frog pee." Frog pee. Where this came from, I have no idea. I almost ran out of the store right then, ready to tell my sister that she was going to have to do it herself. That she might just have to faint in front of all these people because I screwed up. But right then, he smiled, setting the box to the side with his left hand and now reaching for the milk.

"Sounds real interesting," he said. "Don't know a thing about that, but sounds interesting. My grandson likes to figure out stuff like that. He's a real brain." Bleep! A dollar twenty-nine.

My sister was not pregnant. She came to the booth thirty minutes after she disappeared inside the McDonald's bathroom. I was just finishing my strawberry milk shake when she sat next to me, squeezing my knee so tightly I had a bruise the next day. "Everything's fine," she whispered, her lips touching my ear. "It's negative. Everything's fine."

On the ride home, Kyle leaned back, slipping her feet out of her sandals, and tapped her purple toes on the gas pedal. The windows were still up, even though it was hot as hell in the car.

"You must think I'm pretty stupid." She said this to the road.

These were not the words I was expecting. For a minute I just stared out onto a slice of Lake Michigan that showed itself through the trees. Surprisingly blue.

"I don't."

She laughed into her car's droopy fabric ceiling. "Don't think too hard about it, Mel." Her laugh dwindled into silence. A long silence. And then, "You're a good aunt. I mean, thanks for sticking up for Caitlyn. Mom shouldn't have been slapping her."

"No problem."

"It's not that I don't care. I just can't find a way around her." She sped up to meet an approaching hill. "You were always better at standing up to her."

———

As soon as we got home, I heard my mother's window screech open. "Mel, bring in the mail."

The sun was still high, the days getting longer, the air warmer. Across the street the pond sparkled as if glass had been shattered across its surface. God had given my sister another chance, I thought to myself. That scare was a sign, a sign from Him telling her that her lifestyle had to change. It was a sign she couldn't ignore. Maybe now she will start making wise decisions. God works in mysterious ways, I thought to myself as I trotted down the driveway toward the mailbox.

I looked across the street at all the homes clustered around the pond. The Arthurs' place stood three houses down, an exact replica of ours. There was a total of four houses on this street that looked like ours—split-levels with yellow aluminum siding and a matching one-car garage set off to the side. When I was younger, seeing the Arthurs' house used to give me a strange feeling, but after we became friends with Brody and his family, it didn't seem so weird. But Brody no longer lived there. He had moved to Alaska right out of high school—after he had asked Kyle to marry him and she had laughed—leaving his family extremely worried about him. He had wanted to become a king crab fisherman, but ended up working at a cannery instead. Now he lived in California, doing God-knows-what. Without Brody around, we rarely saw the Arthurs, but now I thought I might go and visit them tonight. Mom and Dad would be going to play practice soon, leaving me all evening to do whatever I wanted. I needed to do something with myself. I was afraid that I'd read Darwin.

Today, sitting in English class, I had decided that it was actually a sin to read Darwin, even if I didn't believe one word of it. Having the knowledge of it was a sin itself. Adam and Eve's first sin was knowledge, although I never understood how knowing the difference between good and evil was a terrible thing. My mother once told me that merely knowing was temptation and that temptation almost always led to a fall.

Opening the mailbox, I found a small bundle of letters, none for me. One big red envelope was addressed to the Wright family. I figured that as a member of the Wright family, I could open it. It was an anniversary card. Making my way up the front walk, I read the inside:

Dear Jake and Sarah,
  Wishing you a happy twenty-second wedding anniversary.

        Love,
        Mom and Dad Leary

It was June sixth. My brother would not be twenty-two until December. For the first time in my life, I did the math.

II.

GOD HELPS THOSE
WHO HELP THEMSELVES

I went fishing for the rest of the evening. To think, to figure out what exactly I had discovered. To try to wrap my head around the simple math that kept running through my head, the same equation over and over. What the answer was supposed to mean.

It was still light out, although I knew that my family was eating dinner. Kyle, my parents, all around the table. Jared—who knew where he was. Probably at work, sweeping, mopping, whatever it was he did, while that awful powder seeped into his body. Breathing it in, rubbing fugitive grains into his eyes. I wondered then if my brother would one day glow in the dark. Years from now he'd ingest that last grain that would put him over the limit. That one grain would join all of the others and make his entire body light up like a blue Christmas bulb every night.

Standing on the white dock next to my tackle box, I watched the surface of the pond, wondering where the fish would be hiding this time of day. The sun was low, the air cooling. No longer huddled under the shadows of the trees, the fish were coming out to feed just about now. I could see little wrinkles of concern forming on the surface and disappearing, where the basses' lips skimmed the water for bugs.

I searched my tackle box for the appropriate lure. I was too distracted to use the hula popper, to have to work its intricate dance on the water's surface, although it was the best thing to use this time of day. I needed something simple, something that would allow me to think. I chose a white rubber worm.

The lure was already pretty chewed up, but I managed to get the hook through its midsection without tearing it. The fish would be able to see this one in the dark water.

Just then something terrifying occurred to me. I placed the lure in my palm and closed the other over it. I peeked through my thumbs and saw a faint blue glow, as if the soul of this ancient rubber worm was hanging on with the last of its strength. It was painted with that stuff. How many years ago, I wasn't sure. But it was still clinging. I thought of Jared again, an old man, glowing weakly, just like this, like an old fishing lure. He was a bastard. A blue bastard. It sounded like the name of a fishing lure.

I cast the line out toward the exact middle of the pond, but my timing was a bit off, so the lure plunked short of my mark. I counted five seconds, imagining the light of the lure sinking deeper into the water, probably looking like a firecracker to those unsuspecting fish. And then I began to reel, slowly.

My parents were fornicators. This was clear to me. My brother was a bastard, which seemed to explain a lot of things. And now other things I had heard about my father were becoming much easier to believe. At family gatherings, my mom's cousin Harley would try to convince me of Dad's rebellious past, grabbing my arm and pulling me in close to breathe that yeasty breath of his. He'd tell me about my dad being arrested for marijuana possession. Dad had always admitted that he used to drink, and even that was unthinkable for me, but I would never have believed he did drugs. I chose to view anything Harley told me with skepticism, since he was a drunk. But now, with this new information, I guessed anything was possible.

The Bible said it was possible for kids to inherit their parents' sins. According to Psalm 37:28, "The Lord loves the just and will not forsake his faithful ones. They will be protected forever, but the offspring of the wicked will be cut off." And so maybe Jared was a sinner because our parents were sinners, and Kyle was a sinner because of them, so where would that leave me? Was I just a sinner by inheritance? Did it even matter that I had pledged my body to God? It made sense, this inheritance thing; it explained a lot of what had been going on. How these things kept happening to me. I wasn't trying to sin. Maybe it was just in my bones.

Darwin also said that you inherit things from your parents, but inheriting their sins didn't seem to be something very scientific. Darwin was scientific, but there were also a lot of other things that he missed. For him, everything had an explanation. But he only knew about science, which can't account for supernatural stuff. There were things, I knew, that couldn't be explained by science. Like the miracles at church. How Pastor Lyle had laid hands on a girl with a speech impediment and then demanded that she recite one of those tongue twisters right there onstage in front of everyone. "Peter Piper picked a peck of pickled peppers," she had said into Pastor Lyle's microphone, flawlessly.

I had reeled too fast. I found myself staring again at the chewed-up white worm. It dangled in front of me, dripping water, looking so unappetizing that I considered for a moment changing to a better lure. But I recast, aiming for the middle again and hitting it perfectly, with almost no splash.

But inheritance seemed to be something Darwin knew a lot about. With him, kids weren't always like their parents. What about monstrosities? Was it possible that none of this affected me at all? I didn't really think that Darwin had to be wrong about everything.

I felt a tug at the line. I stopped reeling and held the rod very still, hoping I hadn't noticed too late. I watched the point where the line disappeared in the water. It twitched a few times and then it starting running back toward the shore. Yanking the rod back quick and hard, I set the hook and pulled up to feel the weight of it. It was big. It was so big that the rod tip almost bent over and touched itself as I tried to pull the fish to the surface. I wanted it to jump out of the water, to splash around and make a huge fuss. But it wouldn't surface. It fought me to stay down deep, so I kept the rod low and kept trying to reel. The crank went around, but the line wouldn't catch. I knew I would have to tire the fish out before I could get anywhere.

With big, slow movements, I pulled the rod up and eased it down, feeling the fish resist me. I reeled in as much slack as it would allow me, which wasn't much. But as I continued to do this, I could feel the fish weakening, giving up more and more of the line.

By the time I had worked the fish to about ten feet in front of the dock, I began lifting straight up, trying to catch a silver glimpse of it under the water. The line was still, the fish lying on the bottom like a stone. I wondered for a moment if it was dead. It might have swallowed the hook, and I might have ripped up its insides trying to bring it in. I pulled again, using my whole body, and could feel it rising. I stretched up onto my tiptoes to get those last few inches, and when I finally saw it, I almost dropped my fishing rod into the water.

I had caught a monster. There floating on the surface of the water was a brown hairy animal, looking right at me with human-like blinking eyes. I screamed and shook the rod, hoping to jerk the hook free. But that just agitated it. It began to swim toward me.

I screamed again and tried to run away, but if I moved, I just pulled the thing closer. And I wasn't going to lose my fishing rod over this. I tried to cut the line by chewing on it, but I just sliced open my gums. The thing was now about three feet in front of me. It looked like a giant rabid squirrel from a horror movie. And the fact that it could swim made it even more terrifying. I imagined running from it on land, jumping into the water for safety, only to realize too late that it could swim. It would pursue me for miles, taking its time, just waiting for me to get tired.

Dad must have heard my screams because he came from the house right then, slamming the screen door and running across the lawn, across the street to me. By now I was frozen there, just staring at this thing that stared right back at me with brown eyes that looked very much like my own.

"Mel, what's wrong?" My father, the fornicator, ran onto the dock, lowering the whole thing farther into the water, even closer to the monster. He was out of breath. I imagined him right then all out of breath on top of my mother.

My father was staring at me, not sure what was wrong. I pointed at the thing attached to my line, realizing only now that I was crying.

"What is it?" I asked.

My father nodded, smiling down at the creature. "That's a muskrat, Mel. Haven't you ever seen a muskrat before?"

I shook my head.

"Wait here," he said. "I'll be right back."

Dad jogged off, leaving me and the muskrat alone. Now that it had a name, it didn't seem so frightening. Careful not to pull the line, I stretched out to get a better look. It was very still, just waiting for me to make the next move. The hook was set in its hairy cheek. I tasted the blood in my own mouth and wanted to vomit.

Dad came back with his hunting rifle.

"Reel it in a bit, sweetie," he said.

I looked at him blankly.

"We need to put it out of its misery. It's in terrible pain." He nodded at the muskrat. "It's the best thing to do."

I looked down at the muskrat, which was still looking at me.

"I'll do it in one shot. I promise. It won't feel a thing."

Reluctantly, I did as I was told, reeling the animal in as it held the line with its fingers. It had fingers. I closed my eyes while Dad put a bullet in its head. He took the rod from my hands, brought the hairy corpse to shore, and extracted the hook from its cheek. The white worm was gone, swallowed at some point during the struggle.

"I've been trying to kill that muskrat for months," Dad said, rolling the thing onto its back with his foot. "It's a nuisance. Digging holes and weakening the banks. You could be walking along the shore and the next thing you know there's a landslide and you're up to your neck in water."

><

CHAPTER IV: *Natural Selection; or, The Survival of the Fittest*

Darwin says that the changes brought on by natural selection are so slow that we do not even notice them. I guess he's just saying that people can't see everything and that just because we can't see it doesn't mean it's not true, which is fine with me. It sounds like Pastor Lyle's explanation of God and why, even though we can't see Him, He is always around and doing His work. Things happen before you are born, and just because you weren't around when it happened, or even if you can't imagine it happening, doesn't mean it can't happen, or that it didn't happen. Darwin's idea of time is very large, so large that it goes beyond people. So God's rules are for people, where Darwin's rules are for time and nature and things like that.

Darwin says that he can't help but personify natural selection, talking about it like a deity. But the acts of natural selection are laws, he says, just like gravity. It is just metaphorical, he insists, something that's hard to avoid. I don't think it's this at all. I think Darwin just can't help but acknowledge God's influence. "For since the creation of the world God's invisible qualities—his eternal power and divine nature—have been clearly seen, being understood from what is made, so that men are without excuse" (Romans 1:20). When the Bible says God is clearly seen through what has been made, it's talking about His creations. So Darwin doesn't want to imply God, but he insists that everything happens because of natural laws. Who, then, makes these laws? And also, some laws like gravity can be broken. Like birds. And glow powder is a natural thing even though it seems to go against laws of nature. If anyone can break the rules, it's God. Nature can't break its own rules. I think I may be on to something. Maybe these things prove that God does exist, and that Darwin has no idea what he's talking about.

Definition:

metaphorical—"A word or phrase applied to an object or concept it does not literally denote, suggesting comparison, as in 'A mighty fortress is our God.'"

∝

Kyle, Caitlyn, and I spent Saturday morning at the local zoo, which was basically a farm that had been opened up to the public for a fee of three dollars per person. The farmer had lost a whole crop of corn the previous year to the locusts, according to my dad, and was trying to get out of debt. He sold hay and oats to feed the animals for fifty cents a handful.

We toured the fields first. The stroller would not roll on the gravel pathway, so Kyle took Caitlyn on her hip as we walked by the cattle. There were a few calves that stuck close to their mothers. Kyle pointed for Caitlyn. "Baby," she said. "See the baby cows?"

Caitlyn did not seem to care about the baby cows. She was more interested in Kyle's hair, which she would gather into her small fists and pull.

There wasn't any semblance of weather. The temperature was more like a lack of temperature, making me perfectly comfortable in my skin. No wind or direct sunlight. The sky was hazed over with a thin veil of clouds, the position of the sun determined only by a vague sense of light just above the eastern tree line. Everything, even the grass and the trees, was drained of color. Without the sun, Kyle's hair was no longer edged in fire, but hung limp and dull at her shoulders, almost her natural color, if I remembered correctly. Caitlyn was now pulling at it and stuffing it in her mouth.

The farm was just down the road from us, a couple of miles. We were on a slight hill, which allowed a view of my neighborhood. The houses looked strange from this distance, the way they all loitered near the shore of the pond, like large awkward animals contemplating a drink. And even the pond itself seemed strange, dark and shapeless, like a puddle of spilled coffee.

I turned to watch the cows lying in the field. The corn, I knew, had all been eaten by the locusts, but what about the cows? There were some swarming insects that could pick the bones off of an animal, I was almost sure. I wondered if any cows had been eaten by that frenzy of wings and mandibles. They had been so close, but somehow my neighborhood was safe. Dad said that they came and went just like that, like a tornado.

Kyle was already wandering off to show Caitlyn some wildflowers, leaving me alone, leaning against the splintered fence that limped along the path. The cows were clustered in the middle of the field, not getting up or doing anything very interesting. The mothers and babies, I could see, had a lot of the same coloring, the patterns slightly different sometimes but clearly related. Like puzzle pieces sorted by color and texture, I could tell that even though they didn't line up perfectly, they all belonged in the same pile.

I was satisfied with myself for thinking of this. A puzzle, I thought, scanning the landscape to determine the difficulty of a puzzle like this. Lots of monotonous grass, the overlapping black and white of huddled cows, the huge bland sky. My tiny neighborhood in the background, almost looking like trees. All this would be very difficult. The fences and power lines would make it a bit easier, though, cutting right through the middle and giving some context to work with in the muddled expanse of grass and cows. I imagined myself in the foreground, leaning just as I was now against the fence. How even I would be a difficult part of the puzzle in my brown shirt and jean shorts. The pieces of me mingling with bits of sky, grass, and cow, completely disassembled.

I found Kyle and Caitlyn inside one of the barns, petting the horses. Kyle was holding Caitlyn up to touch a horse's snout, which she did with a shriek that sent all the animals shifting in their stalls. This horse seemed used to it, though, and didn't even flinch as Caitlyn tried to stick a finger in its nostril.

The pigs were on the other side of the barn. We made our way through a dark narrow corridor, stepping through thin blades of light that cut in through gaps in the walls. Caitlyn reached out to grab them, screaming when they touched her. "Light," Kyle said. "Dark." Stepping in and out of shadow, we made our way toward the faint grunting sounds of the piglets.

The mother was huge, lying in a corner of her pen in a stupor as a litter of piglets squirmed at her tender pink belly. One, I could see, was black. All the others were pink and sturdy looking. I pointed it out to Kyle.

"That's an anomaly," I said. "Or maybe a monstrosity." I squinted through the hay dust and darkness for a better look. It had a huge tail that didn't curlicue like the others'. "It's a monstrosity," I decided. "See that?"

Kyle did not look at the pig but was staring at me, one tweezed eyebrow raised. "What the hell is a monstrosity?"

"Something that deviates greatly from the structure," I said.

"Structure?" She rolled her eyes. "I think *you're* a fucking monstrosity, Mel." This is the way she treated me, my sister, for whom I had risked my reputation to help just a few days before. There was no recognition, no change in her attitude toward me. It was like that day at the store never happened. But I guess that was fine. I didn't want things to be awkward with us. I just hoped she hadn't so easily forgotten the lesson in it.

Hoisting Caitlyn higher on her hip, Kyle sauntered out of the barn and toward the baby goat feeding area. I stayed a moment to watch the piglets as they struggled to feed. The black one had been pushed to the edge of the pile and was now trying to nose its way back in. It was smaller than the others. Raising myself up onto the pen wall with my arms, I hooked a foot into a crevice and swung my right leg over to the other side, straddling the wall. The mother pig raised her head and snorted, keeping her head in profile so one red eye pulsed in my direction. Completely still. The piglets didn't seem to notice. The black one was still on the outside of the horde, looking tired and small. This one would die, I knew, and the mother didn't even seem to care. I shifted my weight and lowered a foot down into the pen. Another snort, and then the mother jerked herself to attention, making me pull myself right back up onto the fence, leg still dangling. The mother was staring at me full-on now, intent on protecting the death of this helpless piglet. I could just run in and scoop it up, tucking it under my shirt and leaping the fence before the mother could even collect her fat self from the ground. I thought maybe she would lie back down and forget me for a moment, giving me just enough time to do it. But after a couple of minutes, we were still locked in a staring contest, and the black pig had given up fighting the others. It loitered on the outskirts now, willing to wait out the frenzy. And the mother's red eye was boring holes in me, as if the lives of her children depended on the death of this little black one. It made no sense, I decided, and she would not give up. So I swung back over onto my side of the fence, my feet finding the ground in a single solid motion.

I knew it would die, and there was absolutely nothing I could do about it. I glanced back to see the little black pig teeter on its young legs, still waiting for its turn. From outside I could hear Caitlyn squealing and Kyle laughing. I followed their voices, digging into my pocket for some change. Fifty cents to feed the baby goats, a dollar for a bottle of milk. I counted the change in my hand, a dollar fifteen. I found them crouched along a fence petting a spotted baby goat.

"Do you want to feed one a bottle?" I asked.

Kyle swiveled around to face me, a sarcastic smile on her face. "No, Mel. I don't need to play house." She sighed. "I have to do that enough."

Mom and Dad were fussing with dinner when we came home from the farm. As we walked up the stairs, I tried to think of how I could avoid Dad hugging me. I hadn't told anyone about the anniversary card yet and was reluctant to give it to my parents since the envelope was gutted beyond repair. I knew that if they read it, they would probably deduce from my math skills (I was already in my second year of algebra) that I had figured out the dates. And I knew that they would probably try to explain it to me, in that awkward and embarrassed way of theirs, about making mistakes and how God always forgives. I wasn't interested in any of that. They'd been lying to me for fourteen years. And I wasn't going to be as forgiving as God.

As Kyle and I walked up the stairs, my body was operating on pure memory: Take off my shoes, twelve steps up. I felt as if I were watching myself do these things, a spectator floating over my own family, unaware of my involvement as my parents bustled around the kitchen, acting as if everything were perfectly normal. I could not feel my legs beneath me, but somehow they carried me into the kitchen, where I placed the day's mail on the counter. I hadn't even checked if there were any more anniversary cards.

Dad was already walking toward me, a hug or even a kiss hovering in the air between us. And then his arms parted slightly, moving in closer for a hug. "There's my Born-Again Child!" I winced. Mom gasped.

"No, you don't, Jake. I don't want any of those barn germs in my kitchen." I loved my mother right then, her pointing a rubber glove in my face. "You and you"—she swiveled over to point at Kyle—"go take a shower in the basement. I don't want you upstairs dirtying up my clean shower."

Dad had stopped about a foot in front of me, hands now useless at his sides. He offered a smile instead. "I'm making meat loaf!" He winked at me. I felt my throat tighten. "It's Kyle May's favorite." That what he likes to call her, Kyle May, because people used to mistake her for a boy when she was a toddler. She was named after one of our uncles, which didn't help things. Kyle used to cry when someone mistook her for a boy, so Dad started tacking on the middle name to avoid any confusion. He never fell out of the habit.

Dad returned to preparing supper. Mom stood behind him, supervising his work. She had to make sure that he didn't touch anything with his raw-meat hands. She followed him across the kitchen, with her rubber gloves on, putting all of the utensils he touched into the sink with one hand, while she opened cupboards and drawers for him with the other. He whistled, trying to ignore her.

Without saying anything, I backed out of the kitchen. I couldn't be near either of them. After having a few days to contemplate their sinfulness, I did not know whether my face could reflect any kind of innocence. With the mere sound of his voice, my father would send my stomach lurching into my throat. The sound of my mother's footsteps made me chew my fingernails. The second I turned to walk down the hall and toward my room, I heard my father giggle and a cupboard creaking open. It was obscene. I imagined them in bed together, the sheets pulled up to their armpits, laughing at themselves and their sin. I ran into my room and slammed the door on the sound of them, repeating my abstinence pledge three times in my head.

The big red envelope was still in my backpack, along with Darwin. The safest place, I had decided, because I took it with me wherever I went. But I hadn't taken it to the farm with me. Stepping out into the hallway that morning, my sister had yanked it off my back. The weight of it caught in the crux of my elbow, making my body almost follow it to the ground. "Mel," she said, "we're not going to school. We are going to a *farm*. No studying, just relax and have a good time. Can't you ever just relax?" My father had been standing there, too, and heard it all. If I had insisted on taking it with me, he would have become suspicious. So I had left it at home.

My parents often went through my room just to make sure that I didn't have any secular music, hypodermic needles, or anything like that. These searches often took place while I was at school, so I took all of my contraband with me, carrying these sinful indulgences around with me all day. I had a large backpack, my parents thought, because I had a lot of books. This wasn't true. I had a large backpack because I had a lot of secrets.

I knew that I needed to find another place to hide the anniversary card. I couldn't keep it in my backpack anymore. The thought of carrying it around with me all day was horrifying. Just taking it to school with me on Friday was unbearable. Every time I opened my bag to take out a book, there it was, reminding me of my stupidity. The color was accusation enough of my ignorance. I had opened this envelope and found my own naïveté inside, folded carefully and presented in my grandmother's handwriting.

Between classes I was paranoid that it would fall out in the hallway, for someone else to discover. And I would never know who had it, who knew this awful thing about my family. I had considered throwing it away at school, but just thinking of not having control of it, having no idea where it would end up, was enough to make me lug it around on my back all day.

After careful consideration, I decided to use psychology. Instead of stashing the card under my bed or hiding it in a shoe box in my closet, I placed it on my desk and covered it with a copy of my school newspaper. I knew that Mother would turn my closet upside down and crawl under my bed, but she would never look on top of my desk. I had seen this once on *MacGyver*.

Darwin was also getting to be too much to carry around. Having it with me all day was just tempting me to read it. I decided to hide the book under my mattress for the time being, not wanting to invest too much in my new strategy. If my parents found the anniversary card, I might be able to act ignorant and talk my way out of it. But for Darwin there was no explanation, no excuse.

When the red envelope and Darwin were safely concealed, I went to the living room, so as not to arouse any suspicion. Mom and Dad were still in the kitchen. I avoided looking at them and focused on the television instead. Caitlyn was buckled into her car seat, watching *The 700 Club*. Pat Robertson was praying with eyes shut so tight that it looked like God had shot pepper juice in them. He prefaced every sentence with some kind of name for God, as if giving himself time to think of what he was going to say next. "*Gee*-zus!" Caitlyn's eyes would widen into dark blue pools every time he said it.

Kyle unbuckled Caitlyn and handed her to me. I took her, careful not to touch the bruises that still shadowed her fat little arms. A long line of drool stretched from her mouth and landed on the carpet. She turned to watch Pat Robertson again just as the phone rang. Dad picked it up in the kitchen and poked his head in the living room to tell Kyle in a low voice that she had a phone call. She hesitated, our eyes meeting for a second, before she walked into the kitchen to pick it up. I could see her behind the partition as she took the receiver from my father and immediately replaced it on the hook.

She and Dad stood there, his hand on her shoulder. She was turned in profile, the puffy side of her face distorting any sign of emotion into apathy. As Dad asked her a question, which I could not hear, she turned again, revealing her entire face to me. Its duality no longer surprised me but reminded me of a perfectly good piece of fruit that had been dropped on the floor.

Caitlyn was trying to squirm loose from my arms, reaching out toward Pat Robertson, who was praying for someone with headaches. "God is telling me right now that there is someone out there who has been suffering from headaches. And He wants you to know right now that you are being healed." Mother screamed and ran in from the kitchen.

"I claim that in the name of Jesus! I *claim* that!" She was looking at me with a big smile on her face.

Dinner was a quick affair. Kyle set Caitlyn on the table in her car seat and gave her a bottle. After Dad said grace, changing his usual prayer to thank God for healing Mom's headaches, Jared shoveled his food down as quickly as possible and returned to the basement. Mom picked a little at the food, but in the end decided to have a Twinkie instead. She drifted to the living room to watch television. Kyle and I stayed at the table with Dad, trying to ignore the phone, which was now ringing about twenty times every fifteen minutes. Mom wanted to leave it off the hook, but Dad said that would be rude. We had a party line that we shared with some farmer in Beaufort.

"Kyle May, did you hear your sister got a scholarship for some reading camp this summer?"

Kyle set her fork down. "Really?"

Dad kicked me under the table. I tensed, bringing my legs up to sit Indian style in my chair. "This one's going far. To college, I think."

My eyes remained fixed on my plate. I could hear him chewing his potatoes. Out of the corner of my eye, I watched Kyle pick up her milk and drink noiselessly. Replacing the glass, she swallowed and said, "Well, good for her."

I suddenly wanted to talk but couldn't think of anything to say to either of them. I concentrated on my food, trying to think of what to do with all this meat loaf. All I could think of was those cows lying in the field, how their tails swatted at the flies. This silence was making me feel ill. To my relief, the phone started ringing again. Dad cleared his throat and spoke over it.

"Haven't you girls been down to Clearwater Park yet?" We shook our heads. "You should go. They've done it up real nice, and they even have a duck pond now. Better than the pond here. You girls should go."

Without looking at each other, we both nodded. The ringing stopped.

He seemed satisfied. "I've been trying to get Mom to go, but you know how she is."

Right then a strange smell filled the room. Caitlyn had puked something brown all down the front of herself and was looking at Dad with an expression of shock. Kyle laughed.

"Dad, did you give her meat loaf?"

He got up and wet some paper towels under the faucet. "I ground it up real little. I thought she'd like it."

After my parents left for play practice, I spent the rest of the night in my room, preparing for my encounter with P.J., which just had to take place on Monday. Friday was the last day of school, and if I waited until then to talk to him, it would be obvious that I was a chicken and that I was only talking to him because I knew that I would have the entire summer to recover from any embarrassment. So I had to do it Monday with a whole week of school ahead of me, just to show that I wasn't afraid.

The only makeup I had was the lipstick I had stolen from my sister. But I knew I would need something a bit more, so I perched in front of my dresser mirror all evening, making the most of what I had. From just that one tube of lipstick, I was able to produce a near-complete cosmetics kit. Smearing a little on my fingertip, I rubbed the Passion Rose onto my eyelids and cheeks to create a dramatic effect. Just that little bit of color gave me high cheekbones and enhanced the depth of my eyes. I then practiced what I would say, fluttering my eyes and turning in profile so P.J. could see my new cheekbones and mysterious eyes. I taught myself to suck in my cheeks and cast my eyes downward, glancing up coyly and puckering my lips. When I did them all at once, I looked like a starved fish, but one at a time, each placed at the right moment, I was like Audrey Hepburn. I had dark eyes and thick eyebrows, like her. I just didn't have any eyeliner.

I was so pleased with my rehearsal that I decided to get some reading in before bed. I needed to get deeper into Darwin, but I found that I was too excited to give it my full attention, and with the phone ringing and my sister screaming at Lance to stop calling every five minutes and to please stop calling her a whore, I knew I wouldn't be able to concentrate until things got quiet. So for the time being, I took my little blue booklet out of my backpack and started reading about the prostate.

I awoke that night to the sound of car tires popping gravel on our driveway. My alarm clock said it was 3:14 A.M. Through my open window, I heard a car door half close in a way that would probably leave the interior light on to drain the battery. This person was not planning to stay long. I could hear the footsteps on the front walk, gravelly, grinding against the brick as if small stones were lodged in the treads of the shoes. No one in the house made any noise of movement. No one else had heard the car.

The steps were large. I counted only seven to get from the driveway to the walk right beneath my window. Then I counted five to the front door, where they stopped. I was too afraid to look out my window, so I just listened to the short shuffling at the front door, hoping they would just walk away. And then I heard the moan of hinges. He was coming for Kyle.

I leaped out of bed, possessed by a bravery that transcended the fact that I was only wearing my underwear. Lance was coming to hurt Kyle or maybe even take her away. Calling all night, saying those things to her. What he wanted, I wasn't sure, but he wasn't going to get it. Through the darkness and through the terrible thoughts that were taking control of my head, I tried to think of the best weapon. I scanned the blackness of my room until it revealed itself to me with a faint glow. My silver baton with rubber stoppers on the ends. Dad had put pink glow tape on it for me a few years ago, so I could twirl in the dark. That was a sign. God wanted me to use the baton. I grabbed it from the floor. The rubber end fit perfectly into the palm of my hand.

I crept to my bedroom door; no envelope of light slipped beneath, so I knew the house must be perfectly dark. For a moment I considered waking my parents, but I knew that they wouldn't do anything to keep him from coming again. Mother would scream and my father would come out in his blue bathrobe and ask Lance to leave. Maybe he would and maybe he wouldn't. Maybe he would punch Dad right in the face.

Emerging into the hallway, I twirled the baton in my hand, somehow exhilarated by the fact that I was going to clock this bastard good. The adrenaline pumping through me made it feel like I was walking in a dream. A good dream. I would make him look just like Kyle, maybe even worse. There was no fear now, just anger and pride. The pink glow of God's wrath stood cocked and ready in my hand.

I could hear him dragging up the stairs, slowly, trying not to make any noise. One, two, three. There were twelve steps, which meant that I only had a few more seconds to get to him. I sprinted to the end of the hallway and pressed my back to the wall. Six, seven, eight. I closed my eyes and concentrated on the sounds, trying to locate his body. One swing, just one swing to disable him. Eleven, twelve. I jumped around the corner.

"Fucking bastard!" I yelled, swinging too low and catching something soft that seemed to absorb any pain that I was trying to inflict. My victim screamed a high cowardly scream. I reeled back to deal another blow, higher this time, but was disarmed midswing by a big pillowy knock to the head.

"What the fuck are you doing?" The voice was familiar, too familiar. A light snapped on at the end of the hall. Mom and Dad came running from their room, followed by Kyle. Caitlyn, I could hear, was sucking back sobs as they all ran down the hallway. A light above flicked on to reveal my brother, standing over me. Somehow,

I had become sprawled on the floor, clutching a zebra-striped bed-sheet in my fist. Jared was holding a full laundry bag.

Dad reached down to help me up. "What happened?"

Jared gave me a look up and down, which made me realize that I was wearing only a bra and panties. "That's one hell of a vocabulary, She-Ra."

I raised the sheet to cover myself. I would have run back to my room, but Dad was holding me firmly behind the neck, like a poisonous snake. My baton lay at my feet. Right then I desperately wished that someone would use it to put me out of my misery, like that poor muskrat. My ears were pounding with blood and anger. I was out of breath.

Kyle, wearing a T-shirt and a pair of boxers, was peeking over Mom's shoulder with a mocking grin. Not grateful, not even understanding that it was her I was protecting. Right then I wished that Lance would come and abduct her, take her kicking and screaming from the house so I could stand there, like she was now, smiling and cruel. She would never even admit that she was completely vulnerable in sleep and that I could have saved her life. She opened her mouth, I thought to laugh, but instead she spoke in a serious voice.

"Mel, if you wear a bra to bed, they'll never grow."

Kyle hadn't always been so cruel to me. Although she was never one to really say thank you, I could always tell that she was grateful when I tried to help her. For just a few minutes, she'd lose that disinterested look, would make me feel like I was the only person in the world for her. But that was before Lance, before she started wearing lipstick and perfume. Before I was old enough to even understand her problems. She seemed to like me better that way, ignorant of what exactly was going on but still willing to help her in ways that didn't really help at all.

When Kyle outgrew Superchurch, things started to change

between us. She was thirteen. She had been baptized by Pastor Lyle, and she had taken the necessary classes to finally move into adult church.

After her first Sunday in adult church, I asked Kyle how she liked it. She just shrugged and said, "It's okay." The next Sunday, when Dad came to wake her up for church, she said that she was sick.

I didn't really question it at the time, seeing how she had always been excited about church before. And adult church, I knew, was much better than Superchurch. She had been so excited about making the transition, sauntering through the house the entire week before and even taking her Bible to school. But when we got home from church that second Sunday to find her up and about, not sick at all but doing her new beauty routine to go to the mall with friends, I knew that something was wrong. And so did Mom and Dad. The next Sunday, when she again claimed illness, they made her go.

I couldn't ask her what was wrong. Whenever I so much as mentioned church, she'd just ignore me. Eventually, Kyle gave up on avoiding church. She would get up and get ready without protest, although she didn't show any enthusiasm, either.

Kyle had been going peacefully to church for about a month when I decided that she needed to be rescued. From what, I wasn't sure, but it was definitely ruining our friendship. On that Sunday morning, Kyle went to the adult sermon, while I obediently went my way to Superchurch. About a half hour into Pastor Perle's message, I excused myself to go to the restroom, leaving the gymnasium and starting the long trek to the main complex.

Originally, the church complex was built to look like a cross. But when they later decided to add a gymnasium, the members didn't want to compromise the design, which could be clearly seen from airplanes flying between Cleveland and Chicago. This gentle reminder from thirty thousand feet was considered part of the Outreach Ministry. So they finally decided to build the gym as a separate building, far enough away from the foot of the cross to prevent any confusion. And so I walked all that distance, through an open field, the empty school, and finally by the bustling church offices, to rescue my sister.

When I reached the sanctuary, I could hear the painful dragging beat of drums. I circled to the doors that bordered the back. From the small windows on the doors I scanned the crowd, looking for my sister's long chestnut hair, the awkward shape of her sitting among adults.

The speakers above were blaring some kind of slow prayer song that dragged along with the drums as people screamed, moaned, and waved their hands in the air. This back hallway was virtually soundproof, only letting in the noise of the sanctuary through these speakers in the ceiling that were now transmitting my father's voice. I could hear him above everyone else, the static faraway sound, even though I could see him onstage. His beautiful liquid voice made the speakers crackle, overtaking the general noise of the congregation. He was singing a song I recognized, "We Will Live Forever," but his lips did not match up with the words that were transmitted to me.

Finally, I spotted her in the ninth section. Slipping through the back exit, I was hit with the sudden reality of all this chaos. The noise was deafening and thick, no longer far away; the air almost unbreathable, my father's voice assaulting me from every angle. But through all of this, I did not lose sight of Kyle. I rushed over to her and pulled on her sleeve, dragging her out into the aisle. Then stepping behind her, I pushed her toward the exit. Under my coaxing, she moved mechanically, her legs resisting at first but eventually acting under my momentum. And then we were back in the hallway.

As we crouched below the glass and out of view, Kyle gathered her surprised smile into an annoyed grimace. She straightened her glasses and put a hand on her hip. "What are you doing here? You know what'll happen if Dad sees us?"

I shrugged, glancing toward the stage, where Dad was still leading the song. "I thought you might want to go to the playground."

She rolled her eyes. "Well, let's get out before anyone sees us." She ran to a fire exit and flung the door open. I considered for a moment whether this was a sin, ditching church to go out and play, but I figured that seven years of loyal service had to count for something. And so I stepped through into the sunlight, letting the heavy door fall behind me in a single definitive slam that would not even let our father's voice follow us out.

"How did you get out of Superchurch?" Kyle was swinging in time with me, her hair flying back as we rushed forward and obscuring her face as we fell back. She pumped her legs trying to get higher than me, but I kept up.

"I just went to the bathroom. No one will notice." I squinted through the noon sun back toward the Church, about two hundred yards away. There was no noise now, no drums, only the low groans of the chains as we pumped, swinging higher and higher.

Kyle smiled through her tangled mess of hair as we fell back together. Her hair was much more beautiful than mine. Although we both had naturally wavy chestnut hair, hers was smooth and shiny. Mine was coarse and frizzy, like Mom's. Watching her rise beside me, her hair flying back and her mouth partly open in an unguarded smile, I felt like I had rescued something helplessly beautiful, like a butterfly. Like the endangered butterfly with a really complicated name in my Wildlife Treasury card collection.

I glanced back toward the Church. Against the sun, the blond brick looked almost gold from this far, like gold bricks stacked into a fortress. I imagined the scene inside, trying to recollect the smudged details of my haste. The music jamming my ears, the sweaty bodies squirming against each other, the thousands of hands lifted, fingers sprawled or cupped gently toward Heaven. And there were tambourines shaking from somewhere, the noise leaping out of aisles, harassing me as I tried to reach Kyle, whose mouth I now remembered moved vaguely to the lyrics. I had glimpsed some dancing in the aisles, more toward the front. Through the loose wall of torsos I had to nudge my way through, I thought I saw a body lying on the floor, but that could have been something else.

"Is church always like that?" I addressed this question to the sky, leaning back to take the sun full on my face, my body straight as a rocket shooting through the air.

Kyle didn't answer but flung her feet out in a violent kick, sending her sandals sailing out in front of her. With this, she fell out of sync with me, lagging a split second behind. I slowed down to let her catch up, but I couldn't get the timing right.

Kyle was pumping wildly now, her nylons snagging sunlight, making her legs sparkle as her skirt flew back. I watched as she shed weight, her feet grasping at the air, climbing the slightest wind. Before long she had exceeded the capacity of the chain, which was trying to shake her loose by bunching up, lifting her body a few inches above the seat, and then snapping down. Her knuckles gripped the chain so hard that they were turning white. I watched her body being jolted up and down, envious of her courage but still maintaining a safe distance from the ground.

After about an hour outside, Kyle said that she needed to get back for the end of the service. "I can't miss altar call. Mom and Dad will be looking for me." She bent down and snapped her sandals into place.

"What's *altar call*?" It sounded strange, even a bit scary. I thought of Abraham setting his only son on the altar and raising the knife to sacrifice him. That split second before God told him to drop the knife always bothered me. What if the wind was blowing in his ears at that moment, causing Abraham to miss God's message?

Kyle looked off toward the Church, her face serious, her mouth set against any type of explanation. "It's nothing, just the end of the service."

⋉ ⋊

I didn't realize until the next morning that I had called Jared a bastard. I didn't even think of the current situation; it just popped out of my mouth. I found that a lot of surprising things had been popping out of my mouth lately. Did Jared know that he was a bastard? Probably not. Did he care? I didn't think he would. But my parents were another story. If they had heard me say it, would they then assume that I knew? I had learned the word from Jared, who had used it to refer to, of all people, Lance. Months ago Jared told me that our sister was stuck on bastards and that Lance was just more proof of his theory. I looked it up immediately after I heard it. The word had a nice ring to it, I thought, and so I began using it in my head whenever I encountered people I didn't like, usually people at church like Tessa Goodman. I never said swear words out loud, but thinking them was different. I felt guilty thinking them in church, but that seemed to be the place where they just popped into my head without any source, as if being in God's presence made me think them even more. And so I would torture myself, sometimes screaming curse words in my head during prayer, and then immediately asking forgiveness, just to start cursing again. Before I had thought that "fuck" was the worst of them. But now "bastard" had taken on new significance.

I was so mortified by Saturday night's events that I avoided my family for the rest of the weekend, other than going to church, which I couldn't get out of. I considered asking whether I could go to church with Beth's family, but I knew what my parents thought of Methodists, and that would make them ask if Beth wanted to come to church with us instead. And I knew I wasn't prepared to deal with that. I was supposed to be an example to Beth, but ever since I opened that anniversary card, I had been doubting. I now distrusted everything my parents had ever told me. I still couldn't figure out exactly how this would affect my mission to convert her. Maybe it wouldn't affect anything. All I knew was that I was no example for anyone right now. I had to figure out things for myself before I even began to worry about Beth.

That Sunday, from my room, I listened to my family's daily routines with complete contempt: Mother doing the dishes, Kyle drying her hair, Jared's car pulling in and out of the driveway. My stupid brother, I kept thinking. What kind of person does laundry at three in the morning? My parents wondered the same thing. Through my door I had listened as they questioned him about the strange wildlife-themed sheet that fell out of that laundry bag when it hit me. I felt intense satisfaction as I listened to his stumbling replies, his eventual admission that he had been bringing his friends' laundry over to the house, using our detergent, and charging a dollar a load.

I was relieved to go to youth group on Sunday night, where I could be away from my family for a while, forget their sins and hypocrisy, and focus again on God's plan for me. Pastor Lovely, the youth pastor, liked to make our meetings like this, a refuge from the pressures and difficulties we experienced daily. Usually, we would listen to a short sermon and then play kickball or have a bonfire. This time there were about thirty of us. We met in the gymnasium and sat on blue aerobics mats underneath one of the basketball hoops. The stage and lights, the hundreds of chairs from the abstinence rally were gone, folded away and stored beneath the complex. I was surprised how different the gym looked now, so empty and bright. Sitting with the other teens underneath the harsh fluorescent lighting and distant ceiling, I imagined saying my pledge here now. Without the close feel of darkness and the audience, it seemed like a much smaller gesture. When Pastor Lovely began to speak to us, his voice was blurred by echo. His words swallowed each other, fighting for dominance, as if this huge space weren't enough to contain his message.

"I want to talk to you guys a little bit today about trust, and learning to trust God's role in your lives. I know it can be easy to doubt His involvement, but I think that after tonight we will all have a renewed trust in His presence."

Pastor Lovely was rather fat with the perpetual gloss of sweat on his face and neck, which under the right light made him look as if he were shining with supernatural joy. But tonight he just looked sweaty and nervous, unaccustomed to talking to a bunch of teenagers.

He had been the youth pastor for only four months, replacing Pastor Wells, who moved to Tennessee.

A few kids were lying down on the mats as they listened to him; others were leaning against each other for support. I sat up, my legs crossed in front of me, my back slightly hunched forward. Deanna Whegler, who was sitting directly in front of me, was braiding Joy French's hair. They, like all the other girls in youth group, had become pretty easy friends. We were all polite to each other, but I found it awkward trying to talk with any of them. They were devout, but in a more passive way, since they were more concerned with volleyball practices and clothes than spreading God's Word. Deanna went to my school and had not shown up to the Prayer Around the Pole, even though I had personally handed her a flyer.

"God is with you at all times," Pastor Lovely continued. "A lot of kids come to me saying that they feel alone, they feel as if God has abandoned them, but I want you guys to know that this isn't true. Many of you may believe that you are giving all you can to God, that you are following His Word and doing good works, and that He doesn't notice. But He does. Too many of you believe that God is silent, and I want you guys to know that He's not. God speaks to us every day. He is always giving us signs, revealing truths to us. He is constantly guiding us through our lives. We just have to learn *how* to listen and how to see what God is showing to us. Second Corinthians 4:18 tells us that we are to 'look not at the things that are seen but at the things that are unseen. For the things which are seen are temporal, but the things which are unseen are eternal.'"

I knew this verse, although I thought it was meant to explain Heaven, not everyday signs from God. But either way, it was a good verse, and I thought that this was a good message. Pastor Lyle had given a variation of this one a few months ago.

"Seeing and hearing traffic, or a storm, are not the same as hearing God. Your eyes and ears are made to perceive things of this world, but if you train them, if you learn to pay attention to small things, then they can also perceive God's messages to you. And when you learn to recognize the signs, you will realize that God is always there. He is always speaking to you and guiding you."

I shifted on the mat, trying to ease the ache in my back from sitting without support. My mother always said that she had heightened perceptions and was constantly getting messages from God. I wasn't sure about any of that, but I knew that her hearing was excellent. Other than God speaking to her, she could hear any secular music playing in the house, even if you had it turned all the way down and had to press your ear to the speaker to hear it.

Pastor Lovely was sitting in front of us now, trying to get into a comfortable position on the mat. "I know some of you are already attuned to God's everyday messages. So let's have some testimonies. Does anyone have testimonies of revelation to share from this week?"

Someone moved behind me. I twisted around to see Hannah Klug gathering herself from the mat. Hannah was in the ninth grade. I had heard that she had been persecuted for her faith at the high school, where she had lobbied for schoolwide daily prayer after the morning announcements.

"Last week my cousin was staying over at my house for a few days while his mom was out of state on business. They are not religious people, and I had been trying to get them to come to church for a while, but they never came. Anyway, his mom was supposed to get back on Saturday night, but she got a flat tire in Pittsburgh and had to stay in a hotel. So Ray, my cousin, had to stay with us an extra night and then come to church with us in the morning. Well, once he was here, God spoke to him, and he got saved. And now he's going to get his mom to come and get her saved, too."

Pastor Lovely nodded and smiled to this testimony, and Hannah sat back down. That wasn't a sign. That was God taking matters into His own hands because Hannah couldn't do the job. There was no heightened perception involved at all, I thought, as Ron Powers stood up and started in on his testimony.

"A couple days ago I was really sad because my grandma died. I was walking home from school, thinking how could God allow people to die? Then I looked up and saw this billboard that said 'SHE'S WITH ME.' It was right there, God speaking to me, telling me that she was in Heaven."

"That's a good one," Pastor Lovely said, and I agreed. "If you keep your eyes open to small details, God's messages are everywhere."

I knew that billboard. It was on Route 33, across from the Clark gas station. There were a bunch of people on that sign, all crowded together, with one man and woman in the middle—his arm around her waist while all the other guys were ogling her. It was a beer ad. Everyone was drinking and laughing. But this beautiful woman wasn't looking at anyone but the guy who was holding her with one hand and a bottle of beer with the other. I thought maybe I should mention the fact that this was a beer ad, that God could even use the most corrupt mediums for His message, but I decided not to. Ron might take it the wrong way.

"Anyone else have a testimony?"

I wanted to share one, but I thought that mine might sound stupid out of context. What would I say, that I discovered something called glow powder and that through the powder, God was giving me signs? There had been definite messages with it, like the rubber worm and my glowing baton, but I hadn't yet figured out how to decipher them. The muskrat was baffling, and I had thought that God was telling me to use the baton as a weapon, but then I didn't think He really wanted me to attack Jared. It seemed as if I were taking these messages the wrong way. They were so confusing and bizarre. Why couldn't my messages be on billboards?

There were no more testimonies, so Pastor Lovely had us all stand up and break off into groups of three. I ended up with Deanna and Joy.

"Now we are going to do an exercise that teaches us to put our trust in something that we cannot see. I want everyone to spread out over the gym and give yourselves plenty of room."

We did as we were told, choosing the far end of the mats, under the basketball hoop. Pastor Lovely told us that in order to be able to listen to God, we had to abandon our eyes.

"Two of you hold hands and spread out like this, and the other person stand with your back to them and fall backwards." He had a group demonstrate for us. "The people behind you will catch you. They won't let you fall."

Deanna and I held hands while Joy stood a few feet in front, with her back to us. Closing her eyes, she tipped back slowly, waving her arms in panic as she lost control and fell back into our arms. She was much lighter than I expected.

"That was fun," she yelled, jumping back up to her feet. She situated herself to do it again. We did this for Joy about five times. Each time she gained more confidence, and by her last turn, she threw herself back in our arms and Deanna and I had to hold each other's wrists tightly to keep from dropping her.

I went last. With Joy and Deanna standing behind me, holding hands and breathing heavy from adrenaline, I rocked on my heels, eyes closed, contemplating. I could hear the other kids talking and laughing as they fell into each other's arms, getting much more comfortable with the idea.

"Hold on," Pastor Lovely yelled. I opened my eyes to see him jogging over to us. "Move off the mat," he said, pulling Deanna and Joy back. "You don't need that mat, Mel. Put your trust in God. He won't let you fall."

When Deanna and Joy had become God, I had no idea. But everyone else seemed to make the transition, so I figured I'd let it slide. Now the three of us were standing on the wooden gym floor, Pastor Lovely watching, telling me to go for it. I closed my eyes again, hearing the giggles of Deanna and Joy behind me. They wouldn't drop me, I decided, especially not with Pastor Lovely right there. I swayed back a few times, testing the limits of my control. I found the boundary after a few tries, got myself there and hovered, for only a second, before I pushed myself just a fraction beyond. I fell back, not letting myself flap my arms and look ridiculous. A spike of adrenaline lifted my arms just slightly, as if in rapture. All my senses were heightened for just a moment, just in time for me to hear the awful sound of my head hitting the floor.

I didn't get knocked out, as far as I could tell. I opened my eyes and saw Pastor Lovely, Deanna, and Joy kneeling beside me, asking me if I was okay. The back of my head throbbed without pain at first, but quickly my ordinary worldly senses returned to me like a screw embedded in my skull.

"Oh my God, oh my God," Deanna kept saying. "I'm so sorry—are you okay? It's just you're so short. We didn't realize you were so short."

><

SUNDAY, JUNE 9, 11:45 P.M.
CHAPTER IV: *Natural Selection; or, The Survival of the Fittest* (*continued*)

In sexual competition, the struggle is between individuals of a species. Between female and female, male and male. In male competition, females will settle with the mate that is either the most attractive or the one that defeats all the other males fighting. Yesterday I saw some squirrels fighting in the front yard. Maybe they were fighting over a female. They actually growled, something I didn't think squirrels did.

Darwin says that when nature works in natural selection, it works on much more than appearances, because the survival of the animal depends on many unseeable things. He says that appearances aren't the only things that are important in improving animals, which I can agree with. Just because animals or people look alike doesn't mean that they are the same. I agree that the inside is much more important than the outside of a person, or an animal, I guess. The Bible says that you can't judge a book by its cover, and I think that's right. "Stop judging by mere appearances, and make a right judgment" (John 7:24). So I guess that Jesus and Darwin are in agreement about one thing.

Darwin hasn't stopped referring to natural selection as if it is a single person, even though he insists that it is just laws. He writes that "natural selection is daily and hourly scrutinizing, throughout the world, the slightest variations, rejecting those that are bad, preserving and adding up all that are good." This reminds me of God keeping records of everyone on earth, marking down their sins, their good deeds, who has premarital sex and who doesn't, who lies to their children. In the end, deciding who goes to Heaven and who doesn't.

✼

I waited until my father had left for work to get up and get ready for school on Monday. I had about seven minutes, but it was difficult to hurry. My head felt precisely like it had been bounced off a gymnasium floor.

Everyone else was still asleep, so I tiptoed around the house, trying to hurry, but it was useless. By the time the bus pulled in front of the house, I hadn't even brushed my teeth. Waking my brother up to take me again was out of the question. Stuck in the car with him for all that time, he'd just make fun of me. So I grabbed my backpack, jerking it on as I ran down the front steps, with my hair uncombed and my mouth all slimy. It wasn't until I had gotten on the bus that I realized I was braless. Kyle was probably so proud of herself for making that terrible remark about my chest not growing, for making me feel humiliated. I knew that she was just being cruel, but the logic had struck me when I returned to bed. Breast growth could be stunted by constriction, just like a princess's feet remained infant-sized by being wrapped up all her life. The possibility was so disturbing that I now took my bra off before bed every night. Kyle would never know. But now, sitting on the bus in a T-shirt and no bra, I hated my sister. Everyone at school would be able to tell. I wasn't even wearing an undershirt. I sank low into the seat, crossing my arms across my chest and holding tears down in my belly like vomit. It wasn't until then that I remembered P.J.

✂

Nothing, absolutely nothing. I cast the line out again, watching the plastic line silver as it hooked the last of Wednesday's sunlight. I had caught nothing all evening, hadn't spoken to anyone all week, except for Beth, who was sympathetic, as always, to my situation. As soon as the bus dropped me off, I went straight for the garage to get my pole. Mom's window had screeched open, but I ran across the street before I could hear the message, saying, *Leave me alone, you fucking whore* over and over in my head. From the white dock, I watched Jared's car pull into the driveway (*bastard!*) and then Dad's company truck (*lying asshole*), both trapping Kyle's car, which hadn't moved all day. *That vain, self-satisfied bitch.* No one came to get me for dinner.

The sun was getting low, so I reeled in my line and switched my rooster tail for a hula popper, which was more appropriate at dusk. Instead of flashing its sexy tail as it spun underwater, a hula popper rested on the surface, moving slowly in an epileptic attempt at swimming as I reeled and popped the line like the lure was a puppet. It looked like a fish, having little indents for gills, its mouth open in a big red painted O, but it also had legs and swam across the surface. I thought it might be an amphibian. This confused me at first, but the fish didn't notice, so I didn't worry.

As I snapped the lure across the water's surface, it cut the lake into ever-expanding V's that eventually made it far enough to nudge the shore. I was pleased at this and concentrated on making the lure's dance as regular as possible, so the moving lines were all exactly the same distance apart. Soon my half of the lake looked like an endless line of parabolas, a new word I had learned in my study guide for camp. Such a beautiful word. It could almost be a swear word. I said it over and over in my head, trying to come up with profane meanings for it.

I was so engrossed in the rhythm of my hands that I became annoyed when I finally did get a nibble, which screwed up the pattern and threw ugly squiggly lines across my beautiful pond. At that moment I thought of the muskrat, of all the possible things that could be nibbling at my lure. Monstrosities. Freaks of nature living at the bottom of the pond, never having seen light. I did not set the hook, but let the fish taste the lure and spit it out. I waited for the disturbance to erase itself before I started the pattern again.

The water was dark and stagnant, too gross to swim in. Mother never allowed us to swim in the pond, and we never had any desire to. There were leeches and snakes, not to mention the muck that stunk to high heaven. But I knew Mother had been in it before. Years ago, before I was born, she went jumping into this water to save Jared. He was four or five, and had snuck out in the early morning to catch frogs. She said she heard the splash all the way across the street, inside the house, while she was sleeping. She shot right out of bed and went running outside, not even bothering to wake up Dad. Without any hesitation whatsoever, she jumped into the water—pajamas still on—and hauled Jared out. By the time my father woke up, she was pulling leeches off herself and Jared in the bathtub. Thinking of this story now, I just couldn't believe her doing something like that. I imagined myself drowning in this same water, screaming for help—my mother staring down at me and, only after great hesitation, putting on her yellow rubber gloves to hold a half-hearted arm out to me.

Across the street I heard the screen door sigh and slap shut. Dad was making his way across the front lawn. He waved and jumped the ditch, headed right for me. I stared down at the water, at my own wobbly reflection.

"Are the fish biting?" Dad called from the road, now jogging toward me.

I didn't answer, but let the tip of my rod drop into the water as I continued to reel, trying to become as small as possible, so maybe Dad would forget I was standing a hundred feet away. It didn't work. He came jogging up behind me, a little out of breath but smiling nevertheless. He placed a hand on my shoulder and presented a sandwich with the other.

"I thought you might be hungry."

His hands felt like claws. I took the sandwich and the opportunity to slide out of his grip, putting the sandwich on my tackle box. "Thanks," I said through clenched teeth. I don't know if he even heard me. I didn't care. I stared at the trees now, to avoid his reflection standing next to mine. I still could not look at him after reading that anniversary card, and him seeing me in my underwear made it even worse. Apart from that humiliation, I knew I had been lied to my entire life. Them always acting like they were some kind of example, telling me that God wanted me to do this and that. How this and that were evil. How my own sister was a backslider. Like they had the right to condemn her for doing exactly what they had done. I now knew that all this stuff about walking in Christ's path was something they just told us kids to make us do what they wanted us to do. They just wanted to control me. If they couldn't follow God's rules, how the hell was I supposed to do it? They tried to make it seem so simple. The Ten Commandments. Don't watch soap operas. Don't listen to secular music. Do what we say. It meant nothing. What was the real path? Did it even exist? How was I supposed to save Beth if I didn't even know what was true?

I wanted nothing more than to scream obscenities at him. My father, standing next to me, putting that hand on my shoulder again, like I was the one who needed guidance. *Fishers of men,* he used to tell me. *As Christians we need to go fishing for souls.* He was not a Christian. He was an animal. I wanted to throw my fishing rod in his face, but

I just kept reeling. I knew what Pastor Lyle would say. *What would Jesus do?* My parents would think that in this situation, Jesus would beg forgiveness of His parents and tell them everything, about Darwin and the anniversary card and about the little blue booklet and the Janet Jackson tape, the thong, and the terrible swear words that were whirling around in His head. Who knew what Jesus would do? Who were they to say what He would do? I had as much right to decide what Jesus would do as they did, even more. I wasn't the sinner here. I decided that in this situation, Jesus would just run across the water, away from all this. But I was not Jesus, and my parents weren't Jesus. Jesus had never worn a thong or thought these awful things. I could never know what He really wanted from me. I felt like the world was falling away right from beneath me. *Shit fuck bastard. Shit fuck bastard!*

"How's your hula popper working?"

"Fine."

A bat swooped overhead, making an elegant arc through a finger of light that had wiggled its way through the tree line. A sign. Of something. That I was on the right track.

"I got some special feed for your worms today. Good dirt. They'll like it."

I nodded, trying to find the bat again without looking up. Bats could be messengers from God, I decided. Why not?

Dad began shifting his weight from one foot to the other, rocking the dock slightly. Why wouldn't he just leave? I was reaching the limits of my self-control, I could feel it, the awfulness wrenching in my skull. At any moment it would all spill out.

He patted me again on my shoulder. "It's a good feeling having you around." He cleared his throat. "I mean, if Jared were a burglar, you'd be a hero. That was very brave of you the other night."

"Yeah." But Jared wasn't a burglar; he was something else. The word was working its way up my throat. I pressed my lips together as if to make the *b* sound and kept them there, the word filling my mouth.

I hadn't been paying attention to my reeling but was watching the bats. The hula popper clinked against the rod tip, jerking my hands to a stop. I slackened the line and cast again. A bat scooped down in pursuit but, to my relief, turned away at the last second. Would it have been another sign if I had hooked the bat, or was it a sign that I hadn't?

"I think you get it from Babka, being so brave. Your great-great-grandmother. You remember her?" His hand slid off my shoulder and traveled down my back. Like a line of insects migrating down my spine. And then it was gone. Scratching his head.

I didn't say anything. He knew I knew who Babka was.

"She was only nineteen when she came to America. All by herself. Left her whole family, everyone she knew."

"Why'd she do that?" I asked, already knowing his answer, but thinking that maybe he'd tell me more. Why would a girl nineteen years old just leave her whole family like that, hop on a boat, and move halfway across the world? No one ever told me why, but Jared said he had a good guess. He didn't tell me, either.

"To work," Dad said, shifting his weight from one foot to the other. "Like most people those days."

"Why couldn't she just work in Poland? Why did she have to leave everyone she knew?"

"I don't know, sweetie," he said. "That's just the way things happen sometimes." He started picking at his beard as I reeled in my line and recast, over to the left this time, under a willow tree. The lure landed perfectly, without snagging any branches, right into the shade of the tree, where the fish liked to hide in cooler water. "Nice cast," my father said, nodding.

I resisted saying thanks.

I worked the hula popper through a patch of algae, thinking that maybe I did want to catch a fish now, just to have something to do, to keep my father from saying whatever it was he was about to say. I reeled slowly, making the hula popper's dance more natural, more appetizing.

My father cleared his throat. "There are worse things a person can do than try to show God's love." He said this to his shoes, not requiring an answer from me. "People aren't generally happy, Melanie. I think you're smart enough to know that by now."

I wanted to say that he seemed to find a way to have a good time but didn't. I bit the inside of my cheek, thinking of his sin.

"People feel like you just want their money or their"—he paused—"other things." Other things? I stopped reeling for a moment, but he just kept on. "But God's love doesn't want anything from you, you know that. I know you know that. But other people don't. They see us trying to spread the Good News, and they persecute us, just for trying to show these people love. I know you've put up with that at school."

I pulled in my line. What did he know about that? I didn't think I ever mentioned being called a Jesus Freak to my parents. I wondered then if he had heard about the flyers, if Mr. Vogel had called my house, or if one of the church kids who went to my school had told their parents and it had gotten back to him. What would he think of something like that? I imagined the headline—SEX, SEX, SEX—spread over the top, in bold. Would he believe it was necessary, or would he be shocked that I was capable of such vulgarity?

"Just remember, Melanie. There are worse things you could do than share God's love."

I nodded, recast in the same spot.

"Our friends are a gift from God, put in our lives for a reason. So we can share love. So they can find happiness and truth and meaning in their lives. So we can show them the way to Heaven." He looked up at the sky—at Heaven—the dark bruise of night spreading from the east. I looked down at the water, thinking of Beth. I certainly couldn't show her truth or happiness.

"We are responsible for our friends, Melanie. God has given them to us so we can save them from Hell. It's our responsibility to God and our friends. If we fail, their blood is on our hands."

Blood from what? I imagined my hands covered in blood, like Pilate in the Church's Easter play—him washing it off in a big glass punch bowl, the water turning pink. What kind of gift was that, these friends, whose blood covered us? I imagined myself in Heaven, walking around with Beth's blood on my hands, not being able to wash it off. Everyone I passed seeing my bloody hands and shaking their heads at me. Selfish me, who kept Heaven all to myself.

"I am not proud of the person I used to be," he said, clearing some debris off the dock with his foot. "I was a very unhappy person, Melanie. And because I was unhappy, I couldn't love anyone. But that changed. People don't realize that things can change." He stepped into me and put an arm on my shoulder. "That's why I call you my Born-Again Child. Because it all happened when you were born. God spoke to me and I was changed. And then you came along right after. When you were born, I was reborn."

I felt a tug at my line and immediately jerked the rod, making the lure fly up out of the water and hit the dock. Dad shook his head.

"You have to wait to set the hook," he said. "Give them a few seconds. Let them take it in their mouths and run with it. Then you set the hook."

I reeled in the slack, recast.

He patted me once on top of my head, just missing the sore spot that lingered from Pastor Lovely's exercise in trust. "God changes lives, sweetheart. He changed my life, made me a better person, and now He helps me help other people." I looked up at him, and he gave me a tired smile. "There are worse things we could do."

He was watching the bats now, five of them, flying over the pond. He reached into his pocket and then tossed something into the air, making a pair of bats swoop cleanly just a few yards in front of us. Watching those bats, I decided right then that I wasn't going to let my father's sins ruin Beth's salvation. I was not going to have her blood on my hands. She was my best friend—how could I live with myself if I let her go to Hell? I imagined Beth stuck on earth after I had been raptured away, her living under the rule of the Antichrist. My booklet told me if you knew someone who wasn't going to be raptured, you should warn them about the Mark of the Beast. I would be floating away through the trees, screaming down to her, telling her not to let them put a bar code on her forehead.

Across the street the screen door slapped shut; I could hear Mom's heels clicking down the walk. Dad stepped off the dock, making the whole thing rise about six inches off the water. "Mom and I are off to play practice. We'll be back at around ten or so. Kyle May and Jared are inside. I got tickets for you and Beth for the night of the thirtieth—that's a Sunday. Opening night."

∝ ✕⟩

When I finally packed up my reel and tackle and made it inside, it was nearly eight o'clock. I had been waiting for all the lights in the house to turn off, so I wouldn't have to face anyone, but I knew that wouldn't happen anytime soon. All the lights in the house were still on, even my bedroom light, which meant that I had either forgotten to turn it off in my morning haste or Mom had been in there. I sprinted through the front door and up the stairs. I wanted to make it to my room without running into anyone, but the weight of my backpack made me almost fall backwards at the top of the stairs. Stopping to balance myself, I noticed Kyle and Brody Arthur, the neighbor boy, sitting in the living room. He was home, maybe for a few days, but probably longer since he lived in California. I wondered then if Kyle would have moved away with him if she had known he would end up in California.

Brody looked older, dressed in a collared shirt and khakis. I was struck by how respectable he looked, but then I saw his face. He was laughing. Kyle had told him about me in my underwear and attacking Jared with my baton. I was just about to scream and stomp off when Brody spoke.

"Hey there, kid." He sniffed. He was not laughing.

"Hey, Brody."

Kyle's head was turned to the front window. I could see her face in the glass, the bruises obscured in the simplified reflection. She was studying the darkness for something specific when a tree limb tapped on the glass. She ignored it.

Suddenly embarrassed for Brody and not knowing what he needed me to do, I turned down the hallway and ran to my room. I didn't have time to really think about him crying. I had to make sure Mom hadn't been nosing around.

As I surveyed my bedroom, I relaxed my arms and let my back-pack fall to the floor like a stone. Nothing seemed disturbed, although I had to check my traps to make sure. But first I looked under my mattress. Darwin was still there. And the red envelope was still on my desk, under the newspaper.

My first trap was under my bed, where I had balanced a small bead on the edge of the shoe box that contained all of my pictures. If Mom had looked through it, the bead would have fallen off. I reached under my bed and brought it out carefully. The bead was gone. I moved over to my closet, where I had placed a silver crayon in front of the door. Whenever I opened the closet, I would replace the crayon, which would be pushed out onto the carpet. The crayon was sitting about a foot in front of the door. I knew Mom had been here some-time today, probably while I was at school. She hadn't found a thing.

Unwilling to venture out again into the rest of the house, I thought of Kyle and Brody and what they were saying to each other. Confident that there would be no mention of me in my un-derwear, I pressed my ear to the wall of my room, anxious to catch a stray syllable, but there was nothing. I was sorry for Brody, for the fact that he couldn't think of anything to say to her. Actually, I knew exactly what he wanted to say to her, but they were both silent, Kyle not willing to ever say anything that mattered. I knew her. I knew that she was cruel. I wondered if either of them had ever read *Wuthering Heights,* if they had any idea that all this had been played out before and that it wouldn't lead anywhere. Probably not. Like Heathcliff and Catherine, they thought they were the only ones.

✝

Wednesday, June 12, 8:40 p.m.
Chapter IV: *Natural Selection; or, The Survival of the Fittest* (*continued*)

In natural selection, monstrosities rarely survive. Even though nature depends on monstrosities to develop new and better traits, rarity almost always leads to extinction. Darwin says that it is essential that in a flock of white sheep, a lamb with the faintest trace of black must be killed. I guess that means that the flock has to kill the baby themselves? How do they know they need to kill it? Do they know what they are doing? How can the mother allow this to happen? Does she help to kill it?

All this talk about black sheep actually reminds me of a Bible story, where Jacob tricked Laban into giving him almost all of his sheep (Genesis 30). Basically, Jacob convinced Laban to give him all of his goats and sheep that had dark markings as payment for watching Laban's flock. All the white ones Laban got to keep. But what Laban didn't know was that Jacob made all of the marked sheep and goats mate with Laban's white ones, so that all of the livestock born were marked. So they all got turned over to Jacob. So I guess Jacob knew all about inheritance and could predict what the offspring would look like, just like Darwin says farmers pick traits out of their animals and can control what kind of babies are born. Jacob also let all the strong females mate, while the weak ones he kept from reproducing.

In a state of nature, Darwin says that natural selection can act on animals at any age. Different traits develop at different ages, and offspring accumulate all these inherited traits over their lifetime until they are just like their parents. It's like these traits are just sleeping inside them, waiting for their time to wake up and take over. Is this really possible? I don't think so, since this goes against the second law of thermodynamics. As these traits accumulate, an animal would be getting more complex when, in fact, they are supposed to be deteriorating.

There is a diagram on page 117 that shows the "divergence" of a species. This is what Darwin thinks the long-term effects of natural selection would be like. It maps the "original" species and shows how it has changed over millions of generations. Some varieties have arisen, then died, arisen and thrived, sometimes overtaking other varieties, sometimes living next to other varieties peacefully. It looks like the family tree hanging in our living room that Dad made, dating all the way back to Poland. Darwin actually calls his diagram "the great Tree of Life." He writes: "The affinities of all the beings of the same class have sometimes been represented by a great tree. I believe this simile largely speaks the truth. The green and budding twigs may represent existing species; and those produced during former years may represent the long succession of extinct species. At each period of growth all the growing twigs have tried to branch out on all sides and to overtop and kill the surrounding twigs and branches, in the same manner as species and groups of species have at all times overmastered other species in the great battle for life." This sounds pretty awful, but I guess I understand what he is saying.

Definition:

simile—"A figure of speech in which two things are compared by using 'like' or 'as': 'She is like a rose.'"

Later that evening Kyle knocked on my door to ask me if I would watch Caitlyn. She was going down the street to Brody's, she said, to watch a movie. I said yes, because I wanted them to be together. And because saying yes to my sister was always easier than saying no.

No one had ever asked me to be in charge of Caitlyn before. I sat in the living room, watching her for that first half hour, not really sure what I was supposed to do. Kyle said I could put her to bed, but she seemed happy enough watching the static of the television. I had decided to watch MTV, even though my parents had blocked it out. Pastor Lyle was always talking about secular music, how it spoke backwards to people and made them do crazy things. I wanted to know if this was true. And how was I to know if I never listened to it? I figured that if I did anything crazy in the next few days, I could remember the songs I had listened to and go back to them. Beth said she could figure out how to play tapes backwards on her stepdad's stereo.

The picture was distorted, but the sound came through pretty clear. I watched ghostly images on the screen, while some woman sang about having brass in her pocket. Whatever that meant. It sounded like something to do with sex, although I couldn't be entirely sure. I wrote it down on a piece of paper and tried to read it backwards. No swear words as far as I could tell.

I tired of this pretty quickly, feeling like I was neglecting Caitlyn. She really was a good baby, just watching the television and chewing on her fist. Too good. I figured that as her aunt, I should do something with her. I remembered my mother complaining that I fought back as a baby, and suddenly it occurred to me to teach Caitlyn the same thing. I thought of her crying as my mother slapped her on the hands. And then I thought of those bruises on her arms, the ones Lance had to have given her. And I decided then that I would teach her to fight back. Slap someone right back if they tried to mess with her. That would be something to see. And so, sitting her on my lap, I tapped Caitlyn on her hand. And then I took her hand in my own and hit myself across the face with it. Caitlyn squealed, seeing this as a game—which was fine with me. It was better that way anyhow.

We played like this for a while, me tapping her hand and her hitting my face. With me, it had been instinct to fight back. I was going to give her that same instinct. She caught on pretty quickly, although once I had hit her hand a bit too hard, which made her face wrinkle up in distress. After that I couldn't do it anymore. So we watched more MTV until I heard my parents pull into the driveway.

"Where's Kyle?" my mother asked, trailing her long white robe behind her as she looked through the house. Her wings, still tacked to her back, bobbed up and down uselessly as she walked. "Did she leave Caitlyn with you?" The concern on her face made it clear she thought I was the last person on earth to be left with a baby.

"She's at Brody's."

"Well, go get her," she said, taking Caitlyn from my lap. "Go tell her she has to take responsibility for her child." She turned Caitlyn to face her. Just tap her hand, I thought to myself. Touch her hand and see what happens. But Mother had her face buried in Caitlyn's belly, rubbing her nose into the little sleeper suit. Caitlyn's mouth opened in silent laughter. I wondered how long it took for something to become instinct, if Darwin was going to get into stuff like that.

I knocked on the Arthurs' door, but no one answered. The family car was gone, although there were some lights on in the house and the front door was open. I stared at the front staircase, identical to our own. The light in Brody's room on the second floor was off.

I placed my fingers around the handle of the screen door and opened it.

"Kyle?"

I didn't really expect there to be an answer, but I called anyway. Called a few times as I made my way up the stairs and into the yellow light of the kitchen. I knew exactly where they were but was hoping they'd hear me and come down. I waited. Not a sound.

Being in the Arthurs' house was always weird for me. No matter how much their house looked like ours, with even the same green carpet in the living room, it was so incredibly different inside. I could never understand what it was. Their furniture and walls were pretty bland and forgettable, like ours, and there was nothing else that really stood out. But now, standing in their kitchen and looking around, I knew. The Arthurs' house seemed lived in. It wasn't dirty or messy, but there were still traces of the people that lived there: fingerprints on the microwave, a licked spoon in the sink. These small clues of family life did not exist in our house, where Mother would wipe your breath marks from the windows every time you looked outside.

After drinking a glass of water and eating a cookie from a package left on the counter, I worked up the courage to walk down the hall. I hadn't been in the Arthurs' in a couple of years, but I knew that Brody's room was right where mine would be. The door was closed, the cracks showing no light, but I could hear faint noises inside, something rustling. I knocked, timidly at first, but there was no answer. I knocked again, louder, which caused some commotion inside.

"Kyle? Are you guys in there?" I tried the doorknob, but it was locked into place.

My sister's voice answered. "Mel?"

I pressed my ear to the door. "Can I come in?"

"No. Just go away, would you?"

"Are you coming home?"

"No."

I certainly wasn't going to break in and catch them at whatever they were doing. I imagined them naked in bed together, rolling around, just like my parents, just like her and Lance, just like everyone else in the world. Leaving teeth marks on each other's shoulders. I absolutely couldn't believe it, after all that had happened. After we had sat in that McDonald's, like prostitutes or something, waiting for a stick to turn blue. I was the only person left with any sense of decency. I pressed my back against the coolness of the wall and slid down to sit on the floor, deciding to wait there and confront my sister with her sin the second she came out. Haven't you learned your lesson, I would ask her. God will only give you so many chances. Do you want to get pelvic inflammatory disease?

I hoped they would be done soon. Sitting there, the wall was getting colder on my back. Shadows from outside were moving on the ceiling, projected from a window I couldn't see. The silence was getting louder, made of a million slight noises that couldn't be heard alone, but now were rising and disappearing just as quickly: the electrical buzz of the ceiling, the furnace, confused by a draft, kicking on and then falling dead in the walls. I repeated my abstinence pledge over and over in my head, trying to remember exactly how the last sentence went. And then I thought I heard someone moan. I held my breath, waiting to hear it again.

A few minutes later, there was a thump and then the door swung open and coughed up my sister, who was all red and out of breath. Her barrette was half pulled out of her hair and her bra was twisted to the side, exposing the hardened bumps of her nipples beneath her tank top. She didn't seem surprised to find me curled up near the door. Grabbing my wrist, she hoisted me up, not stopping to let me find my feet or my voice. She pulled me down the staircase and stormed out the front door, letting the screen slap rudely behind her.

Walking down the street and back to our house, I couldn't remember anything I had decided to say to her. I just stared at her, wondering how far they had gone. Her face looked different than it had in the Arthurs' house. When she came flying out of the room, she looked furious, but now in the streetlamps she was almost glowing, her chest heaving and her tongue sampling the sweat beaded on her upper lip. She was smiling.

>◯

Thursday, June 13, 12:04 a.m.
Chapter V: *Laws of Variation*

The strangest thing I have ever heard of is a type of bird that cannot fly. Useless wings. Darwin tries to explain this weird occurrence. Darwin believes that natural selection can affect the variation of a species by what body parts are used more and which are used less. Like the logger-headed duck of South America can fly along the water, but they can't do much else. Their wings are like the wings of farm ducks, pretty weak. But what is so weird is that the young logger-headed ducks can fly. They lose the ability when they reach adulthood. Darwin thinks this may be because they do not need their wings to escape predators on the water. I guess this makes sense. Ostriches also have wings that are pretty much useless. Even God recognizes that. Job 39:13 reads, "The wings of the ostrich flap joyfully, but they cannot compare with the pinions and feathers of the stork." This verse is a little weird, because in it God admits that ostrich wings aren't as good as stork wings, making one of His creations imperfect. But God made up for it. Instead of wings, He gave ostriches large powerful legs that they use to kick. So legs were more effective than wings in self-defense. Instead of flying away, they fight. Most of their enemies are on land anyway, so this makes sense. So because their wings were used less and less and their legs were used more and more, their legs and bodies got larger. When their bodies got large, their wings couldn't carry them anymore. So they lost the ability to fly.

In nature sometimes it's better to not use a helpful body part if it's not very strong. Darwin gives the example of beetles on an island, and how some evolve to have large wings and others have none at all. There are none with middle-sized wings. This is because the ones with very large wings survived the strong winds that would normally blow them out to sea. The ones with not-so-large wings, when they tried to fly, were blown out to sea and killed. So it was better for these beetles with medium or small wings not to fly at all. The ones that stayed on the ground survived. Because they don't fly, their wings disappear from not being used, and so they become ground beetles. This is getting very complicated, but I think I understand what he is saying. It explains how two very different animals could be related without having any animals that link them in the middle. Like the flying and the ground beetles. It is not good to be in the middle and try to raise yourself up. Just be content with what you are and work with it. Like Paul says in Philippians 4:11, "I have learned to be content whatever the circumstances." And Hebrews 13:5 says to be content with what you have. And Proverbs 14:30 says, "A heart at peace gives life to the body." For these beetles with small wings, being content with staying on the ground literally gives them life, while those who try to fly are killed. Darwin says sort of the same thing about swimming: "As with mariners shipwrecked near a coast, it would have been better for the good swimmers if they had been able to swim still further, whereas it would have been better for the bad swimmers if they had not been able to swim at all."

"Why don't you come over here and do something about it, *Jesus Freak*!" Tanya Thayer's head snapped back around and disappeared behind the high bus seat in front of me. I could hear her and Jason Starner continuing to grope at each other, despite my disapproving remark. They had been going at it ever since I got on the bus, making sloppy kissing noises and breathing all heavy. I gripped my backpack and tried not to think of what Jesus would do.

The bus was chugging along Day Street, groaning up hills, the engine out of shape, but continuing on some innate sense of survival, as if it were being pursued. I cringed in my seat, trying to ignore the sin that was being committed just a few feet in front of me. Trying to ignore that awful name Tanya had called me. I looked at my watch. Only ten more minutes until we pick up Beth, then everything would be okay. This is the last day of school; just get through this last day. I hunkered down in an attempt to ride out the fury that swirled in my gut, the embarrassment of the snickers around me, and the fact that I was sitting alone. No normal fourteen-year-old would have said anything like that, about kissing being only for married people. Why had I said it? Was that actually in the Bible? I didn't think so. No, actually, it wasn't. I knew it wasn't. It was just one of those rules my parents had made up that I always thought was from the Bible, like the one against swearing. What would Jesus do? He wouldn't give a flying shit, I decided. *Shit fuck bastard*. It didn't matter to God. Just as long as I didn't take His name in vain and just as long as I didn't have premarital *sex*. Who did my parents think they were kidding, saying all these things were in the Bible? I wish I had thought of all this just five minutes ago, then none of this would have happened. My ears burned with shame. Everyone on the bus now knew that I had never been kissed by a boy. A wad of crumpled notebook paper came flying out of somewhere and landed on my lap. A message? A sign from God? I opened it only to find that it was blank. I slumped down farther into my seat, feeling so heavy, unable to move. I stared out the window, up into a flock of birds, their perfect V in the sky. Just wait until Beth gets on, then everything will be fine.

Staring out onto the houses on Day Street, I watched my own reflection wandering over the cornfields, the cows lying down in Mr. Palmer's field, the pumpkin patch, which was now nothing but a huge square of dirt studded by posts. The Pumpkin Festival wouldn't be until the fall. I thought of the stands lined up along Main Street, pumpkin ice cream, pumpkin cider, pumpkin magnets, orange balloons, pumpkin butter, the pumpkin beer and wine—not that I had ever tasted wine, not that my parents would ever allow even cooking wine in the house. The bottles were so beautiful, though, silvery labels with scripted writing. Last year I wanted to buy a candleholder made from one of the wine bottles, but my parents wouldn't allow me to support the business. I then asked if I could buy one made out of a nonalcoholic bottle. Mom hesitated, lifted the bottle to her nose, sniffed it, and shook her head. "It's the idea of it, Mel. It doesn't matter if it doesn't actually have alcohol in it."

This was a lie, too. Jesus never said that drinking alcohol was bad; He just said that being drunk all the time was bad. Beth's dad drank beer at dinner, but he didn't get drunk. Jesus turned water into wine. Where were my parents getting all of these rules? From now on, I decided, I would only listen to what came directly from the Bible. Right now I knew from Galatians 5:19–21 that "adultery, fornication, uncleanness, lasciviousness, idolatry, witchcraft, hatred, variance, emulations, wrath, strife, seditions, heresies, envyings, murders, drunkenness, and revellings" would keep me from Heaven. Of these, I knew what idolatry, fornication, uncleanness, witchcraft, murder, hatred, drunkenness, and envyings were. The rest I would have to look up when I got home. These would be my new rules, I decided. And variance. What about variance? That was a Darwin term. Was God making some comment about Darwin in this verse? He must have known that Darwin was going to come along before he did—thousands of years before he did. Natural selection was based on variance, so would natural selection be a sin? Variance was being different from your parents. Was it then a sin to be different from your parents? I was going to figure all of this out on my own. God helps those who help themselves, I thought. But then I paused to think of where in the Bible even that was. I didn't recall ever reading it. So where was it from? And slovodimia, that STD no one had ever heard of, that I couldn't find in any dictionary or encyclopedia. Was it just made up to scare people? Was absolutely everything a lie?

It was all getting to be too much to think about. I checked my watch. Five minutes until Beth got on. My best friend, I thought, her blood on my hands. Did the Bible really say that? Did Methodists really go to Hell? To distract myself, I opened my backpack and took out my tube of Passion Rose lipstick and my portable mirror. Actually, it wasn't my mirror—just like it wasn't my lipstick. I had stolen Caitlyn's clown rattle, which had a small mirror in the center, where the clown's face was supposed to be, where she'd look at her reflection and smile at herself in a colorful hat and orange hair. As I held the mirror through the bumps of the road, I tried to keep it still so it wouldn't rattle, but it did. I quickly traced my lips and then smudged a bit of lipstick onto my fingertip and rubbed it into my eyelids. I could still hear Tanya and Jason slurping each other up in the seat in front of me, but I didn't care. I stuffed the rattle back into my bag and turned my thoughts back to the Pumpkin Festival, the pumpkin candy, pumpkin Popsicles, Miss Pumpkin Pie. Every year the Rotary Club chose a Miss Pumpkin Pie, a high school girl who would ride through the parade in a white convertible and wave to everyone in the crowd. I don't know how they chose a Miss Pumpkin Pie every year, but sometimes riding in the car when I was little I would imagine that I was her. I'd wave to the mailboxes, their little red flags raised in return. But now, staring out onto the fields, thinking of all these festivities—the contests, the orange banners and brewery floats that rolled through the streets, leaving the reek of alcohol in their wake—I was struck by the absurdity of it all. Thinking of the billions of years I hadn't even existed in the world, I completely understood that it didn't matter. Darwin might be wrong about a lot of things, but he definitely knew about time. He knew that we all existed in a huge ocean of time, like little pieces of bacteria. Plankton, even, too tiny to make any difference. Even the Bible said that the world was very old, although I doubted that a single book could account for the billions of years the earth existed. Was the earth that old? Was it a sin to listen to Darwin at all? My parents had told me what this book was all about in the first place. They told me that it merely stated in a few hundred pages that man came from monkeys and God doesn't exist. So I didn't really need to read it. I hadn't gotten to that part yet. All Darwin talked about so far was pigeons, dogs, ostriches, beetles, and sheep. No mention of God or monkeys. But would all of this add up to some awful "truth" that was in fact a lie but was impossible to disprove? My parents said that Darwin tricked people with a lot of fancy talk. By the end of the book, I could be an atheist without even knowing how I got there. But I was getting carried away with myself. I couldn't let a few chapters of reading begin to contradict a lifetime of study. The beautiful thing about God was that He made it clear that I did matter, although in what way I wasn't sure. But yes, I mattered, the Pumpkin Festival mattered, the parade mattered, the men in Kiwanis hats driving those Krazy Kars in circles, avoiding collisions by mere inches, they mattered. I was positive that it all mattered. If it didn't, what was the point? Darwin and all his talk about death and not mattering, it was making me doubt God; it was making me "variant." And that was my new rule, not to be variant, not to read Darwin and learn about variance. I shouldn't even think about it. God would be reading my thoughts, marking down all my doubts. I didn't doubt anymore. I still believed in Him. I didn't believe my parents, but I believed Him. A hundred pages of fancy talk couldn't make God disappear. But when I thought of my parents, I doubted it all, and when I thought of the Bible, I believed. Forget my parents. Forget their sin; don't even think about them. Don't even think of them unmarried and sweaty and naked and fornicating all over each other, while God watched. Ignore the wet kissing noises in front of me. How could I prove myself to God? It was all a rush, thoughts buzzing through my limbs, lifting my body from the seat, directing my hand over the back of the seat in front of me. My mother's and father's faces staring up at me, saliva on their chins. I watched in horror as my fingers twisted in her hair, closing hard and pulling her out of his loose grip and into the aisle of the bus, still roaring and coughing and jerking into higher gears, all in slow motion until the final moment when I wound back my other arm, taut at the shoulder, and released it like a rubber band to smack her in the face.

Mr. Vogel's office was a cramped room stacked with file cabinets and papers, no plants, alive only with the hum of fluorescent light. He was flipping through some of those papers when Mr. Klein knocked on his door frame, pushing me out in front of him like a human shield. I had not heard Mr. Klein's voice much before, as it was usually drowned out by the noises of the bus, but now he spoke clearly.

"Had a little incident this morning on number seventeen."

Mr. Vogel glanced up from his desk, but he caught himself as he cast his gaze downward again. "Melanie?" His eyebrows wrinkled, pulling his entire face into concern, the look he often used with Mrs. Hoyle's LD class. That look reminded me of Jared's note, making me wonder if this pity came from whatever was on that note. "What happened?"

Mr. Klein cleared his throat, waiting for me to say something, but my mouth was set shut. He sighed. "A fight. Pulled a girl twice her size out into the aisle and walloped her good. A little bit of a bloody nose. She's with the nurse now." I could hear him shuffling his feet against the grit of the linoleum, anxious to get back to whatever it was he was supposed to be doing. Mr. Vogel did not take the hint.

"Who?" He rose from his desk, pushing back his chair, which let out a shrill protest.

"Tanya Thayer."

Mr. Vogel walked over toward us, but stopped midstep, searching the middle distance for the name. After a moment his head snapped back in recognition and then looked down on me, questioning. Mr. Klein tapped his fingers on the door frame. Mr. Vogel cleared the distance between us with a single step. He placed his hand on the door in a gesture to close it.

"All right, Ed. Thank you."

After closing the door, Mr. Vogel motioned for me to sit down, and I did, with my bag still strapped to my back. It made me sit very straight. He sat on top of his desk, peered down at me through his bifocals, and said, "This has been a bad month for you, Melanie."

I looked down at my hands.

"This is the second time in two weeks, and Ms. Hern is also concerned about you. You've been in to see her a lot. Something about your eyes burning?"

I knew he was waiting for me to clarify, but I could not open my mouth. I just stared at his right shoe. There was a rumor going around school that Mr. Vogel had webbed feet. I had just decided that this rumor wasn't true.

Shifting uncomfortably against the clutter on his desk, Mr. Vogel finally gave in and asked me the question. "Do you want to tell me what happened?"

For a moment I considered telling him everything, how I had read Darwin and how God was mad at me for doing that and how Tanya had called me a Jesus Freak because I merely pointed out that it was not appropriate for unmarried people to be necking on the bus, let alone necking at all at such an age. I could tell him all about variance and how my parents were fornicators, about the blank note from God falling in my lap, telling me to do something.

"I just got carried away. Tanya called me a name, and I got carried away. I'm sorry."

Mr. Vogel stared straight at me, unconsciously fingering through a cup of pens and pencils. He looked doubtful. "That's all?"

I hesitated. I could tell him about Darwin, but then it might get back to my parents that I was reading it, not that I cared at this point whether they took the book away. Frankly, I would be happy to never see that book again. It was the forgery I was afraid of. If my parents found out that I was reading Darwin, they'd ask how anyone came off assigning something like that without parental permission. Mr. Vogel would say: "But we did ask for your permission." And he'd pull the yellow slip out of one of these metal file cabinet drawers and say, "I have your signature right here giving permission for her to read Darwin, in addition to that trashy romance novelist Emily Brontë, who writes about sexy men digging up the corpses of women and violating them in unspeakable ways." And my parents would take the slip of paper from his hands, and my mother would say, "This certainly is not my signature. See how the *S* in *Sarah* has been traced too carefully, too slowly. Here." And she'd grab a stray piece of paper and a pen from Mr. Vogel's desk and sign her name with that dramatic flourish with which she signed checks. That quick, careless scribbling that I had tried over and over to emulate, but it was impossible to copy without actually tracing with a slow, careful pen tip. Mr. Vogel and my father would look from my mother's signature to the forgery and back again, shaking their heads and finally turning to me, sitting in this same chair with the bare backs of my knees sweaty and stuck to the pockmarked wood. What could I say?

"That's all."

After I sat alone in the secretary's lobby for a half hour, Mr. Vogel called me back into his office and told me that Tanya was fine and that he wouldn't put this incident on my permanent record and that he wouldn't tell the scholarship committee as long as I promised to go to an adult the next time I had a problem. "I certainly will," I told him. And then he said that he thought I should go home for the day. Just take the summer to cool down. I wouldn't be missing anything on the last day anyway. I'd had a tough few weeks and should use the summer to consider how to act like a lady in trying situations. Maybe spend more time thinking about my own actions instead of worrying about other people all the time. He had already called my mother, he said, and told her about what happened. And she would be here any minute to pick me up.

Mother. At first, the word meant nothing, just a pair of syllables that failed to trigger any response. Something had been stunted in the transaction, and it took me a full five seconds for the word to register. *Mother.* My body was unable to respond to this, but my mind kicked into gear. And then a bunch of other words fell into place in my head. *Shit fuck bastard! SHIT FUCK BASTARD!* I could think of nothing but *shit fuck bastard.*

I stood completely still, thinking these awful words, when a sudden thud made both me and Mr. Vogel jump. He turned to look at his office window, where a bird had just flown straight into the glass. He shrugged and turned back to me. My body sagged under the sudden weight of my backpack, unbearable and cramping my shoulders.

"Have a great time at camp," Mr. Vogel said as he led me back to the lobby to wait for my mother.

Those words still fighting for dominance in my head. *Shit fuck bastard;* and now a new one, *bitch!* I had to use my last bit of energy to summon a decent response, not to scream these words and spit in his face. It took every ounce of self-control to mutter, "Thanks."

∝ ✕⊃

I waited in the office for my mother for over an hour, convinced that she was purposefully trying to prolong my agony. I tried to imagine the punishments she had in store, but I really had no idea what to expect. She was so unpredictable that she might just usher me into the car and not say anything, or she might stomp into the office screaming and shake me right there in front of Ms. Cook. I knew it was useless to try and guess what was going to happen, but still I couldn't clear my mind of it.

I sat there, my left leg shaking like crazy, making the small table next to me jiggle nervously, too. Ms. Cook sat typing at her desk, raising her eyes every once in a while to check if I was still there. I wondered if she remembered me from the other morning, as the pitiful, soaking-wet girl who had dragged herself through Hell to get to school. Probably showing my note to all of the teachers. But she didn't seem to remember me. Her typewriter never paused, even when she glanced around the room. It clanked on that entire hour, some keys producing an off-note that snagged my ear every time I managed to tune it all out. The frequency with which she kept looking at me, I wondered whether she was typing out a report on my misconduct.

Clank, clank, clank, clank. Clank, cling, clank, clank. Ms. Cook was pumping out words like artillery fire. This and the clock hanging right in front of me in the skinny room were enough to make me start chewing my thumbnails, running the jagged tips over my bottom teeth until I tasted blood. It was the longest hour of my life, staring at the clock, and then the doorway, then Ms. Cook looking at me. *Clank, cling!* I braced myself against the moment when I would see my mother framed in the doorway, and then her walking toward me with what kind of look on her face? It did not come that way, though. Despite my frantic, shifting eyes, I did not see her come in. I saw her sandals. I was staring at the floor when they shuffled into view. The red strappy sandals that Mother wore all the time. They were a size too small; the imitation leather straps looked like they cut off her circulation, making her skin overflow from every possible space. She thought they made her feet look dainty. I thought they made her look like she'd tip over at any moment.

I watched her feet waddling in my direction, the red, irritated skin stepping carefully around the pain. An injured version of my sister's walk. I did not look up until I felt her fingers grasping my arm, yanking me up from the seat. The backs of my thighs ripped from the plastic with a slight sting and a horrendous noise that made me look directly in her face. She was crying. Her eyelashes were wet, separated into clumps, and her eyebrows were drawn into pity, not anger. She knelt down in front of me and started rubbing at my face with her thumbs. Hard. When her thumbs came back tinged red, I knew she was wiping Tanya's blood off my face. Her nose gushing blood as she held her hands to her face. I shuddered thinking of her. Mother leaned into me now, wiping harder and harder, her thumbs digging into me like she couldn't get the blood off. But now her thumbs came back pink, Passion Rose pink. I must have looked like some kind of demented clown. Now aware of my own disarray, I could feel my hair matted around my head. The tear tracks that had dried on my cheeks now cracked as I tried to smile at my mother.

Ms. Cook was still hacking away at the typewriter as my mother began smoothing my hair down, her palms caressing my scalp. I closed my eyes to stop myself from crying again. *Clank, clank, clank, clank, cling!* The next thing I felt was Mother's left hand driving hard against my right cheek. The typewriter had stopped just a second beforehand, registering the sound through the hallways and, I imagined, to my own classroom upstairs. *Smack!* Ms. Cook's mouth had dropped open. I had never heard her say much, but now she looked like she had too much to say to get anything out. As Mother dragged me into the hallway, I looked back at Ms. Cook, still frozen in that dumb expression, which, I now realized, I was giving right back to her.

The ride home was completely silent. I rode in the back of the minivan, looking out the window onto all the homes. I could still feel the imprint of my mother's hand weighing on my cheek, burning. She turned the radio on, probably to drown out the sound of my breathing, to forget that I was in the backseat. The preacher's voice on WJCR was majestic and soothing, like how Dracula sounds on television. "It's good to be with you again, here in the presence of God. Today we will discuss the omnipresence of God, and we will begin with Proverbs, chapter fifteen, verse three, which reads: 'The eyes of the Lord are in every place, beholding the evil and the good.'" I sank into the seat. This, I knew, was the Word of God. This was truth. I could imagine God pulling out my file, taking notes, counting every bruise on Tanya's body, every drop of blood released. But would He know the good that I intended? "'Whither shall I go from thy spirit? Or whither shall I flee from thy presence? If I ascend up into Heaven, Thou are there; if I make my bed in Hell, behold, Thou art there. If I take the wings of the morning, and dwell in the uttermost parts of the sea . . .'"

I stopped listening to his words and let only the rhythm of his voice enter my ears. Outside, all of nature seemed to dance to the cadence of his words, from God's hand. Squirrels twitched to the short syllables and wind-blown branches swayed with the long, drawn-out vowels. The world and all of its creatures were in perfect harmony. There was no conflict, no battle for survival that was comparable to my own. Mine was the only struggle, everything else so tranquil in contrast, so permanent. The trees sipped water from the soil, perfectly content with the wind that tousled their branches. And the dogs ran jubilant circles in backyards, returning to their food bowls whenever they felt hunger. Everything was so peaceful, so perfect, like pieces of a jigsaw puzzle snapping in place to make this roadside scenery. These thoughts were so calming on that ride home, making me forget the horror to come from the driver's seat. This was the view of the world I had grown up with, that I had tried to reject—the simplicity of a rabbit sprinting into the underbrush of Day Street was utterly remarkable, even though I knew this wasn't how Darwin saw things at all.

Nietzsche Is Dead

Friday night's storm was in no hurry. It lingered for a while in trees and shadow, rustling leaves and casting a pink tinge on everything while preparing for a dramatic entrance. There were low grumblings on the horizon and an exceptionally warm breeze that inflated my bedroom curtains, snapping them occasionally like an unaligned sail. I had nothing to do but sit and listen as the air whipped itself into a frenzy outside, trying the seams of the house, which cracked and groaned as it relinquished itself. Like a ship about to sink.

By eight o'clock it was clear that there wasn't going to be a compromise. That was when the phone rang. A ringing phone at our house in the middle of a storm only meant one thing: that Dad was being called to work to repair downed telephone lines. I hadn't seen him since he'd gotten home a few hours before. Mom had sealed me off in my bedroom ever since the morning, when she brought me home from Mr. Vogel's office.

Right when I stepped into my bedroom, I knew what had taken Mother so long to pick me up. She had completely ransacked my room, probably looking for something to blame for the inci- dent. First I checked my desk, and to my relief the red envelope was still there. But only a few seconds later, I realized that she had found something. She had found Darwin. I flipped the mattress over, looked under the bed, even under the box spring. But in the wake of a gutted closet and open drawers, it was gone. When I discov- ered it was missing, there was nothing to do but remain in stunned silence, too petrified to even clean up the mess Mother had left behind, afraid to make any noise to remind her that I was still in the house.

I had no more fingernails left to chew. In bed I had to sit on my hands to keep myself from chewing the live raw crescents that were left. I imagined my mother calling up Pastor Lyle, my grand-parents, telling my father about the morning's events. I had no idea what she knew, what Mr. Vogel had told her, but I knew that didn't really matter. She had found Darwin.

I had made notes in the margins. I had put Bible verses in some places, where God agreed with Darwin and where He disagreed. They would see those, and they would see that I was trying to prove him wrong. But some of the notes, I knew, would disgust them. I had underlined some words, words I had to look up, like procre-ation. And there were passages with stars next to them, some with three or five stars. Really important points, like monstrosities and deviation. Stars didn't mean that I believed what it said; it just meant that it was important for understanding what Darwin was saying. I thought I put a star next to the section titled "Sexual Selection," but I couldn't be sure. I could see them shaking their heads, reading about procreation and sexual partners, seeing my stars.

A few minutes after I heard the phone ring, I heard my father descend the front steps, tell my mother to unplug the television and all other appliances, and then close the door behind him. I knew he must be furious at me. He didn't even come to say good-bye.

By the time he left, the rain was pelting the house with heavy sporadic drops. I closed my window, fighting the breeze as I turned the crank with both hands. When it clicked into place, the house took on the thick silence I had been dreading. There was no tele-vision, no music, not even the sound of the dryer to comfort me. Kyle and Caitlyn were hiding out somewhere, silent and probably forbidden to see me. There was nothing but the knowledge of my mother in the house, and her knowledge of me. With no television or music to distract her, she had begun pacing.

I simply lay in bed, thinking of my father tackling electrical wires that thrashed and sparked violently in my imagination. Dad had always told me that downed wires did not do this, that they just hung limp from the poles, looking as harmless as pieces of ribbon. *Never,* he always said, *never touch any wire, even if it looks dead. It will kill you.* Even though he worked for the phone company, he found himself dealing with electric wires during storms like this. There'd be a whole mess of fallen trees and poles, telephone and electric wires all tangled up and indistinguishable in the dark. And my father was the one who decided which was which. I had no idea how he could tell them apart, but he did. All I knew was that it was extremely dangerous. So dangerous that him being out in the middle of the storm got Mother pacing all around the house and praying for God to keep him safe. And now, I thought, Dad could die. Something could go wrong, a loose wire could swing down and hit him, and his last thoughts would be of me, his Born-Again Child, fighting and cursing and ungrateful to God. And so I started to pray, to make more deals with God. I told Him that if He let Dad come home safely, I would never read anything but the Bible ever again.

At around ten o'clock, I began mapping out my rules, the rules in Galatians I had decided on. The rules that God Himself had given me. I knew that something was about to happen very soon, and I knew that I would need these rules to help me through, to deal with it the way God wanted me to. I needed to know how He wanted me to deal with Darwin, although I knew that my parents had already dealt with him for me. I began by looking up *variance.* The definition said that it was a disagreement between two documents or people. Something that was against known facts. This was now a sin. I wrote it on a piece of paper, copying the definition out exactly. I paused at the end of the definition on something I thought was just my imagination. Under *variance* it said, "at loggerheads." Loggerheads. Like the logger-headed ducks that Darwin talked about. The ones who lost the ability to fly when they became adults. I ripped a few pages as I flipped back to the L section. My fingers were shaking. Under *loggerheads* it said that being "at logger-heads" involved an argument in which both sides stubbornly refused to give way. I wrote this down under *variance* and considered it. It had to be a sign. Of what, I wasn't sure. God was trying to tell me something, and I was completely unable to figure it out.

I decided to go on with the rules, hoping that I'd get another clue. *Strife* is a prolonged struggle for power; *sedition* is inciting hostility against the government; *revelings* are taking intense pleasure, in what it didn't say. In anything, I guess. I wrote, "taking intense pleasure in anything." And then scratched it out. I moved on to *heresies,* which are any beliefs opposed to orthodoxy. I looked up *orthodoxy* and put the definition under *heresies. Emulations* are when someone tries to do as well as someone else at something or to be a rival. And *lasciviousness* is the expression of sexual lust, which didn't surprise me at all.

I copied all of these down with a careful hand, adding the others I already knew to the list. I sat there staring at all of them, re-arranging their order, trying to find some links. They all were so similar, pointing to something. I thought of the blank piece of paper that fell on my lap, and how it looked just like the piece of paper I was staring at now. Variance leads to loggerheads, which leads to strife, which leads to wrath. What came after wrath? I was considering this when the entire house went black with a dead click.

I sat up in bed, frantic at first, waiting for my eyes to adjust. I thought of Tanya's nose leaking blood, me standing in the aisle of the bus with a clump of her hair in my hand. Beth stepping on the bus a few seconds later and finding Tanya crumpled at my feet, holding her face. Beth seeing the blood on my hands, giving me this look like I had murdered someone. Mr. Klein stopping the bus in the middle of the road to come back and see what was going on. But it wasn't so bad, I told myself. It wasn't so bad as that. I waited for the familiar outlines of my room to emerge—the desk, the chair, the closet. Just as I began to recognize the room again, my door flung open, spilling a thick orange light into the room.

Mother walked in with a plateful of candles. She held them out in front of her with both hands, as if presenting me with a birthday cake. The individual flames sent contradicting shadows all over the room, making the bureau lurch, the walls shiver as she moved. Shuffling around the mess on the floor, she made her way to the desk, where she switched the plate to one hand while she cleared a space with the other. I did not move but watched in horror as she shoved my papers aside and set the plate down.

"What's this?" She turned to me with a slight smile, holding up something that I could not make out at first. I shrugged. She turned the thing over in her hands, flinging a corner of it into the light for an instant. There was no form to it, only color. Red, just a flash, and then black again. My stomach twitched with nausea.

"It's nothing, Mother. Just something from Beth." I tried to get out of bed, but the action was somehow too complicated to pull off. All I could do was try to distract her. "I think my window might be cracked. Could you look at it?"

She did not hear me but was now opening the envelope. Her fingers slipped inside and pulled out the card. She read the front and looked at me. Her face was bland and questioning at first, but something, a draft maybe, sent the candles shaking. The question was immediately transformed, the shadows twisting her face into accusation. I could feel my stomach now working its way up my throat as she opened the card and read.

"What *is* this, Mel?" The card dangled from the tips of her fingers as she held it out to me again. She stepped forward into half shadow. The orange light and shadow smoothed over her face, making her look much younger. Like Kyle.

I shook my head as she stepped even closer. "Are you stealing from me now?" Her lips didn't seem to go with the words. "Are you *stealing*?"

She didn't wait for an answer, but started half crying, half screaming words that I could not understand. As she screamed at me, her face began to look like my own. I could not even hear her. I just watched her face contort in the candlelight, a puffy, wrinkled version of my own sneering back at me one second and looking stunningly beautiful the next. I looked at my hands.

"There is no reason to be hiding this," she sobbed. "Why are you hiding this?" The words meant nothing to me. *"Why are you hiding this?"* She lunged forward. She grabbed my hair and twisted my head, making me look directly into her face. "Are you listening to me?" She no longer looked like me. She was herself again. "First fighting, now stealing?" And Darwin, was all I could think, you forgot to mention Darwin. "Do you know that you are going to *Hell*?"

She hoisted me from the bed by my hair and started toward the door, yelling words that missed profanity by only a few letters. Not giving me time to find my feet, she dragged me behind her through the doorway and into the hall, my legs thrashing behind me like a panicked swimmer. I could feel individual hairs ripping from my scalp each time I fell back on my knees, but she did not stop. With my hands clasped to my head, I tried to loosen her grip, but she kept pulling. I ripped my nightgown trying to pull myself from the carpet.

The carpet burned my bare legs as she hauled me down the hallway. *"You are a disgrace to this family."* When she reached the stairs, she grabbed my shoulder with her other arm. Looking back down the hall for help, I glimpsed my sister rooted at the end of the hallway, candle in hand, unmoving as Mother pushed me down the steps. I could not feel the pain, but only heard the terrible sounds of my bones striking each wooden step as I toppled down in slow motion. Calmly, I watched my legs rotate over and over each other until I hit the front door.

"Get out of my house!"

There was no blood to speak of, only the tenderness of bruises on my back and shoulders, rug burn on my knees. Huddled on the front step under the overhang of the roof, I tested my bruises. I knew it was too early for them to take on any color. I imagined the yellow and green, the shades of blue that were working their way to the surface of my skin. Now, under the faint battery-powered light of our doorbell button, my skin had taken on a pink glow.

Beyond the small circle of comfort this light afforded me, the world was translated into sound, my knowledge of it defined only by the forces of wind and rain: the wind bringing branches, bushes into existence; the overhead gush of the gutters outlining the house, the heavy sound of rain on the front walk, the muffled patter of it on the lawn. By listening, I could locate certain objects that I had only known before in the light, the hollow drumming of garden pails, the crackling of weather tarps. Turning my attention across the road and toward the pond, I was sure I could hear the wind skimming along its surface.

The overhang of our roof was not much, only two feet or so, which made it difficult for me to stay dry in the hard rain. After only a few minutes outside, the random drops that infiltrated this shelter had soaked my pajamas and left a cold, musky film on my skin. My back was starting to cramp as I hunched forward to keep my bare legs warm.

Unsure of what my mother expected me to do, I was content to stay outside, on the edge of this storm, drawing some comfort from the predictable movements of the dark.

After ten minutes or so, a new sound came. I jumped at the jarred, metallic banging. And then the pained screech of a window opening in the darkness to my left, low to the ground. A basement window.

"Monchi," a voice half whispered, half yelled.

I leaned out into the rain, looking around some bushes to see my brother extending a hand the wrong way.

"I'm over here." I stepped carefully down the walkway and toward the window, which was edged in candlelight from the inside. When I came near enough, he placed his hand on my shoulder and brought his other arm out into the rain and under my armpit. I curled my legs into my chest as he lifted me through the window and back into the house. After he set me down, he replaced the screen and closed the window.

"Rough night, huh?" He grabbed a crumpled towel from under his bed and handed it to me.

I nodded and brought the towel to my face, but the thick smell of mildew made me pull it away and start wiping off my legs.

"Aren't you supposed to be at work?"

He shrugged. "Probably."

He handed me a dry T-shirt, also from the floor, and turned away. I pulled off my nightgown. Despite the awful moldy taste, I put the towel in my mouth and held it in front of me with my teeth as I changed, to shield my body from any funny ideas he might come up with. In my haste I fumbled the T-shirt and gagged on the fuzzy taste that spread down my throat.

The black T-shirt hung only to my knees, making me consider leaving my damp, cold underwear on. A moment's consideration prompted me to choose warmth over decency.

Jared was moving around the room now, lighting more candles. There must have been at least thirty, all at different levels, making the walls look as if they were on fire. I moved over to the bed and plopped down.

"Did you plan on staying out there all night?" His back was still to me. I shrugged in reply. With the lighting of more candles, the room returned to familiarity, dark corners relinquishing stacks of cassette tapes, posters, and piles of dirty laundry to the light. As the heat returned to my body, I ached even more. My shoulder joints felt hot and swollen. I tried to distract myself from the pain by counting the candles. Thirty-two.

When he was finished, he sat down next to me on the bed and took a cigarette from his front pocket. He held it out to me, no trace of a smile on his face. I shook my head, and he shrugged as he stuck it in his mouth. But why not? Why had I automatically refused it? Smoking wasn't in variance with the Bible, by my new rules. Fornication, wrath, adultery, revelings, that *L* word—I considered asking him for a cigarette after all, but saying it seemed somehow worse.

"Want to play poker?" The unlit cigarette wagged from his mouth like a scolding finger.

"Yes."

He leaned over, sticking the end of the cigarette into a nearby candle flame. As he sucked in, smoke billowed from his lips, which held the filter end loosely in a relaxed smile. I breathed in the curls of smoke that unfolded across my face. And then, just for a moment, I forgot myself.

"Jared, what did you write about me in that note?"

He looked at me, not sure what I was talking about at first. But then he remembered and a smile spread across his face. "You didn't read it?" He shook his head. "Nothing that wasn't true." He got up to find his deck of cards.

I sucked my cheeks in and bit down on them, not letting myself ask any more questions.

I had never played cards before. In our family, cards were a tool of the Devil. According to Pastor Lyle, money spent gambling went straight to Satan, via casinos, which, and I am not sure how, would buy misery and suffering to dole out onto the masses. But if instead of gambling you gave your money to the Church, the money went directly to God. Exactly what God and Satan did with this money was never really explained, but the forces of good and evil seemed to operate on the same capitalistic playing field as Burger King and McDonald's.

I watched Jared shuffle the deck. The cards were red and shiny, a new stiff deck that flashed in his fingers like jewels as he threw cards from one palm to the other, flipping and cutting the deck in elaborate ways. His defective pinkie didn't seem to slow him down at all. When the show was over, five cards lay in front of me. Jared scooped his up and considered them. He didn't notice that I hadn't picked up mine.

"I don't know how to play," I said, after he already had decided whatever he had to decide about his hand. He threw two cards on the floor and frowned down at them.

"You want cards that are the same or in numerical order. Throw down ones you don't want."

"Okay." I picked up my hand. The cards were slick and cool in my fingers. I was surprised by the innocence of the pictures on them, how harmless they were. Just numbers and faces. There couldn't be anything bad about this. It was just like playing go fish.

"You'll catch on," my brother said.

The thing about gambling, according to my dad, was that it left things to chance. When I had asked him why it was bad for Catholics to play bingo, he told me that with God, there was no chance. Everything happens for a reason because God is in control, he had explained. And when you go into a game of cards, you are putting yourself out of God's hands. There is chaos, he had said, and there is order. "God's world is ordered. We know that He looks out for us and that we are not left on our own. But when you put yourself into a card game, you are choosing chaos, and that, Melanie, is a scary place."

I tried to think of how gambling could possibly be a sin. The only way I figured was if I intensely enjoyed it, then it would be reveling. I was a bit afraid of this at first, but as the night went on, I realized that with gambling there was no pure enjoyment. I won and I lost. All night we bet everything we could think of. We haggled fiercely over the value of bandannas and fool's gold, bantering and laughing, trying to ignore the sound of Mother pacing overhead as the ceiling cracked and groaned under her weight. And when I thought I might be having too much fun, I lost on purpose, just to keep myself in check. Since I didn't have much money, we had to get creative in order to keep the bets equal. After I squandered five dollars, I started betting my favorite fishing lures and even my pet turtle, Moses. I wasn't sure if I had lost more than I had won, but by early morning I had lost, among other things, Moses (after betting him back and forth about five times), my hula popper lure, my Rubik's Cube, my stamp collection, my rooster-tail lure, my walkie-talkies, and I had to take out the trash for a month. Weighing this with some of the stuff I had won, I decided that I had broken about even: his inflatable raft, four cigarettes, three dollars, a candle shaped like a frog, a Madonna tape, an expensive-looking pen. I even won a vial of Lynxx glow powder that Jared kept in his sock drawer. I hadn't won it on purpose—I actually had tried to lose that hand. But God had given me three kings. I had no idea what I was going to do with a vial of that lethal stuff, but I wasn't going to show Jared that I was afraid of it. So I kept playing and resisted the urge to put it back in the betting circle to lose it. And then at around five in the morning, Jared called the last bet.

The ante was the usual, one cigarette, but things quickly escalated. I had a pair of jacks and a pair of nines, nothing to be too confident about, but Jared kept pushing. I raised him; he raised me, sauntering over to his dresser. He opened the top drawer and brought something out, hiding it behind his back. Returning to the game, he slapped the thing down between us.

"You've gotta match this, Monchi."

I recognized Darwin right away, the worn paperback cover, corners peeled back, the *Beagle* slanted on rough water. I went to grab it from the betting circle, but Jared caught my hand.

"That's mine," I yelled, trying to wrench my wrist loose.

"No. It's mine. I found it; you lost it." He threw my hand back.

So Mother didn't find it. Dad didn't know; Grandma and Pastor Lyle had no idea. Something that had been wound up in my chest all night was released, although that didn't stop tears from filling the corners of my eyes. It was all in my hands again. I was back to where I started.

"You know, Mel, you can't hide things worth shit."

"Give it back," I whined, moving again to snatch the book.

Jared slapped a hand on top of it. "You should be thanking me for saving your ass. Do you know what Mom would have done if she found this? I got in there, like, two minutes before she did. She was all screaming on the phone, telling Dad what you did, saying she thought you were on drugs." He leaned back with a satisfied smirk. "But now it's mine and you're going to have to win it back. So what do you have?"

"My marker set."

"Not valuable enough."

"How about my fishing pole?"

He shook his head.

"My bike?"

Jared snorted. "What the hell would I want with your little pink girl bike?"

"What, then?" I was about willing to bet anything, even my painting easel.

"I figure a book for a book. That's fair."

I nodded, trying to remember all of my books. "How about *Wuthering Heights*?"

"How about your Bible?"

My Bible had been given to me by my parents when I was in the fourth grade. It replaced my children's Bible, which summarized all of the important Bible stories in pictures: Jesus walking on water; Noah and all the animals peeking from windows in the ark, a hole cut in the roof to accommodate the giraffe's neck. Although I had moved on to the adult Bible years ago, these pictures still exemplified the stories in my mind. Reading pages and pages of small print did nothing for me. I memorized them and could recite them on command, but the Bible in my mind was still these series of pictures: the woman of many sins washing Jesus' feet with her chestnut hair; Lot's wife turned to a pillar of salt, the grains of her nose blowing away in the wind. And there were other pictures, ones I would turn to in half-horror, half-pleasure, like David holding the severed head of Goliath, a generous layer of blood rimmed around the giant's jaggedly cut neck. And the picture of Abraham, knife in hand, reared back and ready to plunge the blade into his own son's throat. I often wondered if God would ever tell my parents to do that to me, to sacrifice me without question. They'd tie me up in the back-yard, holding the butcher knife over me, the one they used to hack the legs off the Thanksgiving turkey, and saying that they were sorry but they had no choice in the matter.

And then there was the picture of Adam and Eve tasting the fruit of knowledge, elbows and knees bent awkwardly in order to cover their parts. I always wondered why knowledge was the worst thing for people to have. Why not violence or hate? Why not killing your own kid? Adam and Eve running from the Garden of Eden, covered in ivy and thorns.

I often wondered whether it was a sin to read at all, whether the Bible itself, which was meant to teach us the will of God, counted as knowledge of good and evil. I knew that variance and heresies were bad, but writing them had to be different from read-ing them. I wasn't being variant by reading them. Darwin was the one who was sinning, not me. I could read it, as long as I knew these things weren't corrupting me. Not all knowledge was corrupt, I knew, but how were people supposed to figure out what was good and what was bad knowledge? If I couldn't read something like Darwin, how was I supposed to know that it was bad? My parents had never read it, but they knew that it was evil somehow. Who told them? Probably my grandparents, but I knew that they had never read anything like that. It seemed to me that the rules of knowledge and ignorance were governed by authorities that were present in our minds, but absent in form. Who decided that Darwin was about man coming from monkeys and God not existing? It seemed to me that he was all about which pigeons were eaten and which survived to reproduce. There were no monkeys, only sex. But not fornication. Animal sex was different from people sex. And variance, who was to say? Was Darwin variant to the Bible, or was the Bible variant to Darwin? I could feel all context slipping away, all context but my own nakedness, my skin burning with shame under my brother's T-shirt. Jared was watching me, waiting for an answer, making me twist uncomfortably through the feel of my own skin breathing under the thin cotton shroud. Nakedness, the worst sin, I thought. I wished I had left my damp, cold panties on. I thought of the picture of Salome, the curvy outline of her body just perceptible under her thin robes, her tiny hand holding the silver platter, John the Baptist's head placed on one side, his eyes half-open, glazed. This Bible, in pictures, in my brain. I knew it already, the pictures, the words. Did it really matter if I owned it or not?

"C'mon, Mel. I haven't got all day." I glanced out the window to spy a slice of pink sky on the horizon. It was almost morning, the storm having passed by probably hours ago. The candles on the shelves had burned down into abstract forms, like hardened lumps of clay.

"All right."

Jared gave me a startled look. "Really?"

Ignoring his surprise, I mustered my best poker face. "What do you have?"

Jared paused, gave me a look up and down, as if checking whether it was really me he was playing poker with. I refused to acknowledge this, keeping as straight a face as I could as he slapped down three sevens. I hesitated, unable to remember which was the better hand. I laid down my two pairs and watched Jared's face, which remained blank, staring right back at me.

"Well, who won?" He looked amused, but his expression gave no hints.

"I can't remember which is better," I mumbled, staring down at the betting circle, imagining my Bible with cigarettes on top of it, placed right next to Darwin. The soft leather cover, golden script, the words of Christ in tiny red letters, like fire ants on the page. Crossing my arms over my indecent chest, I could feel my tears return, burning the back of my throat. I could not squeeze them back as they filled in underneath my eyelids. I tried not to blink, but the instinct was too powerful.

A tear landed on my open palm. Others I could feel tracing the crevices along my eyes and cheeks, which I had wrinkled up to keep from crying. Seeing me, Jared's face fell from blankness to pity. He leaned forward and swept the cards up in a neat pile. "Christ, Mel, don't cry." He sighed. "Two pairs beat three of a kind. You won, ya little shit."

I woke up at seven curled up at the foot of my brother's bed. He was gone, to where I had no idea, but he had taken his pillow with him. Crumpled underneath my cheek was Darwin, open halfway with some of the pages wrinkled. When I lifted my head, the cover stuck to my skin and then released itself from the deep groove it had pressed into my cheek. Running my fingers along the indentation, I discovered that my right shoulder was tight and sore. I then rolled over onto my back, feeling the mattress nudge the bruises that had sprouted overnight along my spine. Not wanting to settle into this pain, I continued rolling back up and into a sitting position to look out the window. The light outside was fierce, skidding off slicked surfaces and saturating everything in brilliant color.

All of my winnings were still on a pile on the floor, along with my ripped nightgown and my underwear, which was rolled up inside. I stretched the damp nightgown out on the rug and piled all of my new possessions on it, careful to put the cigarettes and the vial of glow powder on top so they wouldn't break. I tied the arms and the bottom together and slung the whole package over my shoulder as I made my way up the steps. Twelve steps up and into the light of the foyer, where the windows that edged the front door threw rectangles of light on my feet. I turned and made my way up the next twelve steps, slowly, stepping carefully around the tenderness of my legs and back. I could feel the temperature rising with each step, taking me out of the cold basement and into the hot and humid upstairs. When I reached the top of the stairs, I turned right into the hallway but stopped short at the sight of my mother.

She was asleep, sitting on the floor with her back against the wall. Her legs stretched across the width of the hallway, her knees bent slightly to allow her feet to rest against the other wall. Her breath was shallow and measured. I crept forward, small steps toward her and one large step over her. My left foot went first, making a slow, exaggerated arc over her body and finding the carpet on the other side. I leaned forward, my body following my left leg and my right trailing behind. Lifting it up and over, until it snagged something, fleshy and warm. My heart leaped into my head, suddenly pounding behind my eyes as I looked back. My mother's hand placed on my bare calf. She was staring up at me, the sleep still clouding her eyes, her mouth hung open in a lost question.

I remained perfectly balanced there, my nakedness under the T-shirt exposed, ready to move in either direction. My bundle of sins hanging from my shoulder like an overripe piece of fruit—heavy, near bursting. The smooth surface of Mother's expression did not shift as she gathered herself up from the carpet and knelt beside me.

"Melanie, sweetheart. Where did you go?" Her black eyes were large and liquid in the morning light. She was trying to convey concern, but something was terribly wrong. She looked hideous, and then I realized why. Her eyebrows were gone, completely rubbed off, leaving her forehead blank, her eyes unprotected and desperate. She raised a hand, and I instinctively flinched as she cleared stray hairs from my face. "Baby, why did you run away? I was so worried. I waited all night." Her fingers groped lightly at my shoulders and back, as if she were trying to gather me into permanence, give me a definite shape, as if I were a melting ice-cream cone. The exact pressure of her fingers against my bruises held a precise medical tenderness.

I leaned into her hands. I don't know if I was taking comfort in her touch or in the completely unpredictability of the situation. I expected this offering, this small movement, to snap the safety cord, to plunge us into some kind of violence. She would lunge, but I would meet her in the middle, ready to claw and bite my way past to make it to the safety of my bedroom. And so I leaned into her, but it did not come to that. She accepted my muscles relaxing against the teetering wall of her body. She didn't even look at my bundle as I let it pull my arm down to my side. She didn't take it from me or ask me to open it. But still, my eyes remained wide open, not trusting her in the dark. I shuddered under the kiss she could only bring herself to breathe on my forehead. I was unclean. I was a sinner, a monster, a deviation. And at that moment, she accepted it. And so did I.

✠

SATURDAY, JUNE 15, 5:14 A.M.
CHAPTER V: *Laws of Variation (continued)*

I have been thinking about my last entry and I am confused about one thing. Darwin was explaining how not using certain body parts makes them shrink in size, which makes them lose their functions. Like wings. Darwin says that there is no greater anomaly in nature than a bird that cannot fly. And I agree. He gives the example of ostriches, which I understand. Over time the ostriches with bigger legs and bodies survived and reproduced because their powerful kicking was better for defense than just flying away. So over a long time, their wings got small and useless. This I understand. And it doesn't seem to go against the Bible, which admits that ostriches weren't made perfect. What I don't understand is the example of the logger-headed duck of South America. It seems like natural selection, which we are not supposed to see and which takes millions of years to make any change in a species, is doing something here that doesn't make sense. The logger-headed duck can fly at a young age, but when it reaches adulthood, it loses that ability. Now I can understand how the entire species would lose the ability to fly altogether (like the ostrich). But how can the individual birds evolve in this way over just the period of a few months? Why do the adults lose the use of their wings so suddenly like that? It doesn't seem to agree with Darwin's theory, and I think that there is something in this whole logger-headed duck business that is very important. Maybe this disproves his theory. Maybe the logger-headed ducks are just one of the many animals that don't fit into this plan. I don't think anyone has ever noticed this before, but I have a very big suspicion that there is something here that Darwin was just trying to skip over. I will think more about it.

Clearwater Park was very different from what I remembered as a little girl. Kyle and I finally took Dad's advice and went down there on Saturday evening, after Dad got home from storm repair. When he walked in the door at around six in the evening, he had been working nonstop for almost twenty-four hours. He was so tired that he went straight to bed, ignoring the dinner Mother had set out for him and refusing to take off his shoes at the door, despite her pleadings. After he closed the bedroom door behind him, Mother came into the living room, where Kyle and I were watching television. The deep, exhausted lines under her eyes and the look she gave Kyle when she walked in to find the TV playing too loudly were enough to make us get up and get our shoes on. As we walked out the front door, Mother told us not to hurry back. "I'll take care of Caitlyn; don't worry about us." I could see my sister's shoulders stiffen on hearing this.

The park's playground that was once a brilliant green was now sharp with rust. There was a newer playground on the other side of the road, but we climbed this one instead. From here we had a clear view of the Lynxx smokestacks, which stood breathless at the moment behind a line of tall trees. As children, we came here with Mom and Dad to feed the seagulls and play in Lake Michigan. That was before Mom stopped going outside, and now Lake Michigan was so polluted in this area that it was illegal to swim in it most of the time. The color of the water seemed off to me, but I could not be entirely sure. Maybe Lynxx was dumping glow paint into the lake at night. Maybe if someone dove down to the bottom, they'd see fish that glowed neon blue. But no one would do that. There were warnings posted all over the beach that read "SWIMMING PROHIBITED: TOXIN LEVELS DANGEROUSLY HIGH."

The new duck pond our father had mentioned was still under construction. A bright orange construction fence surrounded the area, but there were still ducks inside puttering around to pick at the sparse grass. They didn't look like they could fly over. The adult ones were large and awkward, their wings tucked into their sides as they waddled on two legs. I couldn't imagine this awkward walk being more advantageous than flying. I wondered if they had really flown here or if someone had just put them behind the fence. Maybe they could fly at one point but couldn't now, but that idea was absurd. Watching the chicks, I decided that they couldn't fly, either. They were fragile and fuzzy looking, milling around the fence near my feet. I stomped the grass, making them jump and run away, but they did not fly.

Kyle and I bought stale bread from some girls who had set up a stand nearby. The little girls paused to check my sister's face before handing over the bread, cautiously.

"Don't think he's such a bad guy." Kyle was trying to throw bread at the ducklings, huddled over to the side.

At first I thought she was talking about Dad, but then I realized she was talking about Lance. This didn't surprise me one bit. "Well, you know what I think."

She nodded. The ducklings were running away from the pieces she threw at them. Not even trying to fly. "He's got a bad temper, that's all."

"I noticed."

"He had reason, you know."

The mother duck was now squawking as she ushered her chicks into the water.

All this time I had wanted more information, had studied the bruises on her face, looking for some kind of clue, but now I didn't want to hear any more. I tossed the last of my bread into the pond and walked toward the beach. She followed, a few feet behind.

Clearing the line of trees that edged the park, we could now see the barbed-wire fence of Lynxx. The buildings on the other side looked deserted, but the parking lot was nearly full. I wondered if my brother was at work now, lost in that maze of rooms. Cameras mounted on the ceilings watching him to see what happened to a person if they were exposed to that glow powder. And none of us would ever notice or be able to save him. He slipped in and out of the house and even my own consciousness so easily now. I hadn't seen him since our poker game, I suddenly realized. The only trace he'd left of himself actually being there last night was the missing pillow, which had for some reason begun to bother me. Where he went for days at a time I couldn't even begin to guess, but I hoped it wasn't to Lynxx.

The sand on the beach was soft and cool. I kicked off my sandals and walked down toward the water, cutting through a flock of

seagulls that were standing in my way. They got restless as I neared, taking uneasy steps in all directions until they decided to fly. I did not stop as they parted for me like an ugly gray curtain. Flying low, they moved down toward the break wall and settled again on the beach. Kyle was still behind me. I turned around to see her carrying her shoes and dragging her toes in the sand. She was looking toward Lynxx, where the smokestacks were discreetly coughing something up. Soon there was a steady flow that collected in large tufts, like thought bubbles. Then they rose up to mingle with and eventually become indistinguishable from the clouds.

"There goes the Twinkie factory," she said, and then inhaled deeply.

"Twinkie factory? They make Twinkies in there?"

Kyle laughed. "No, just the stuff that makes them live forever. You know, food preservatives." She stopped to consider something. "When we die, Mel, they aren't going to have to embalm us, since we've been breathing this shit in all our lives."

I just nodded, not wanting to mention the glow paint. Maybe it really was a secret, what Lynxx made.

We walked up and down the beach all evening, not saying much. I watched the flock of seagulls rise up and settle down repeatedly along the shore, when kids threw rocks at them or a sudden traffic noise startled them. They never went far, just far enough away not to be bothered.

As the sun sank down behind the trees and the park was emptied of visitors, Kyle and I moved closer to the water. With each pass we made, we came closer until we were watching the rust-tinted water move over our toes. As we got bolder, we began touching the waves with our hands and splashing each other.

"I bet we get cancer from this." Kyle laughed, kicking water into my face.

———

The sun was setting and the park was supposed to be closing. Kyle and I were now sitting on the beach, digging our hands into the cool layers of sand. Everyone else had left, even the kids who were throwing rocks at the birds. The sun was just about to touch the parking lot, sending the longest shadows of the day across the sand. With our legs straight in front of us, we both leaned back on our arms, my right and her left crossing behind us. Our shadows, stretched side by side, looked like paper dolls holding hands.

"Mel, why did Mom throw you out last night?" Kyle lay back on the sand, stretching her arms over her head, burying her toes in the sand. Her shadow disappeared, leaving mine alone.

I had considered telling her the minute I found out—all about the red envelope, the anniversary card, about Jared being a bastard. I knew that Kyle would never suspect our own parents of such a thing. She thought she was alone in this. And if I did tell her, I knew that she would be able to hold her head up again. Not in that deliberate way she always did, but really hold her head up, not even having to think about it.

And now I had the power to do this for her, to give her something that she could either throw back in their faces or keep to herself for encouragement. I could do this for her, but something was holding me back, had been holding me back all week. My mouth opened to answer, "I don't know."

She just nodded and said, "Do you want some advice, Mel?"

"What kind of advice?" There was a pinch of hopefulness in my voice that immediately made me ashamed.

"You know. Boys. Don't you want them to notice you?" She hooked a finger through a belt loop on my jeans and pulled me into her, down into the sand. "I know there's one you like. Don't you want him to stick his tongue in your mouth?" She slipped her tongue between her lips and sucked it back in, like a lizard.

I couldn't help but laugh. "No! Ugh, no!"

Kyle smiled devilishly and stuck her whole hand down the front of my pants. I rolled back, screaming. "What are you doing?"

Shaking her head mournfully, she said, "Those jeans are way too loose. If you want to get the good guys, you have to wear tight jeans."

"But I don't have any tight jeans."

"Wear your jeans from last year."

"But they don't fit."

She smiled. "Yeah, they do."

Our noses were so close they almost touched. I breathed in her breath, staring at her perfectly preened face. Like me, Kyle had inherited Mom's dark bushy eyebrows, but since the age of fourteen she had diligently tweezed them into thin, tapering arcs. And then there was the makeup: her lips red, bloody looking; sweeps of blush on her cheeks, making her look just slightly flustered; the blue tint of her eyelids. I usually envied her for this mastery, standing in front of the mirror, brushes and pencils flying violently across her face. Doing three things at once, throwing combs aside as if she didn't even care. But now this makeup reminded me of when she first came home, the blood, the bruising. I couldn't tell where her black eye ended and the eye shadow began.

Out in the parking lot, a patrol car passed by. Without saying anything, we both jumped up and ran behind a Dumpster.

We remained hidden as the officer locked the gates behind him. By the time he was gone, Kyle seemed to have forgotten about her questions. She pulled her shirt over her head and yanked her shorts down to the ground. "Are you coming?" She gave me that lopsided smile, standing there buck naked on the beach, her frail arms stretched out to test the wind.

I hadn't seen her naked since she was a little girl, and somehow I was shocked to see breasts. I remembered exactly how her body looked when she was young. When Mother wasn't watching, we used to sneak outside and dance naked in front of the garden hose, taking turns spraying each other. Her legs were so sleek, and her entire body as straight as a board, slipping easily through the summer air. Turning cartwheels and somersaults in the spray, her spine braided down her back, the hard nub of her tailbone. Now she looked so heavy, so slow, standing there with her hips edged in a golden light. I could see the stretch marks laid across her abdomen like a bandage and the dark hair that hid the crux of her body in a vague, shapeless shadow.

Before I could reply, she dashed off toward the water, making some kind of yelping sound that startled the birds. She ran awkwardly through them, her buttocks bouncing in time with her ponytail, and her breasts making her run much more slowly than she used to. The one thing I recognized was her tailbone, the stubborn knob having refused to change with the rest of her body. I glimpsed it briefly, and then she was gone in a white splash.

I was throwing my clothes off as fast as I could. The rushed motions reminded me of the bruises along my shoulders and back. I immediately crossed my arms. I was not embarrassed by my nakedness, but by the bruises. I sprinted after my sister despite the pain, silent and quick. My body was much sleeker than hers; I could not even feel it resisting my stride. Everything was still held tight to my body, which allowed me to leap unburdened as I ran, dashing like an arrow into the low waves to hide myself.

The water was much colder than it was on my feet, but it made me conscious of my skin in a new way, so I didn't care. My sister stayed underwater for a long time, but finally she emerged with her hair slicked back and her eyes blinking away water like an otter as she adjusted her contacts. Her face was washed clean. Her shoulders rested just above the surface, smooth and shiny. Tipping her head, she leaned forward to touch the water with her lips. She sucked a mouthful and spit it back at me. I winced and ducked under, opening my eyes to the opaque murkiness. I could not see her legs. I tried a handstand but lost my balance somewhere along the way. When I surfaced, Kyle was floating on her back with her breasts flattened into her body. Her nipples, barely submerged, were gathered into tiny hard knots.

"My eyes burn." I rubbed my eyelids and then placed a hand under the small of her back, feeling her bob easily in my palm as if she weighed nothing at all.

Her eyes were closed. "My throat burns."

I laughed. "You *drank* it?"

"I was thirsty." Her body began to shake as she giggled. With her weight returned to her, she slipped under and out of sight.

That night Beth called to ask if I could spend the night. I said I didn't think so. I didn't know how I'd face her after she saw me like that on the bus, out of control, like an animal. She had pulled me aside to sit with her, helped Tanya to her feet, and when Mr. Klein came to the back of the bus, she spoke for me. I just remembered sitting there, looking at the blood on my hands, hearing Beth tell Mr. Klein that I was all right now. That I would sit and be good for the rest of the ride. Me, the animal. Me, who was supposed to be an example of God's love. It was me who was supposed to save Beth, not the other way around.

I tried to apologize to Beth over the phone for what happened, but she just blew it off. "I'd give anything for a tape of that," she said. "Tanya's a bitch. She had it coming to her. I'm just glad you finally stood up for yourself."

The events of Friday still weighed on my mother's memory, I could tell, and she would never let me go to Beth's anyway. Her dealings with me were more clouded than usual, even though we never had been comfortable with each other. But now the few words she said to me were drained of all meaning, her eyes skimming the top of my head. "Mel, go get the mail," she'd say with such disinterest, as if challenging me to find another anniversary card, to go through the math in my head again and try to find something to accuse her of. We would unexpectedly find ourselves alone in a room together, and she would stay there for no good reason, even follow me to the next room and pretend to have something to do there. She wanted me to know that she wasn't afraid of me, of what I knew. She treated me with such indifference, as if I weren't even there, like she was trying to convince herself and me that I was just a child and had no idea what these things meant.

I did not tell Beth any of this. She accepted my excuse that I had church in the morning. But also I wanted to read that night. With Mom and Dad gone to play practice, I could finally read at a decent hour. Darwin had been waiting for me all day, stuffed between the mattress and the box spring, despite my brother's warning that it was a bad hiding place. That poker game, I decided, was a sign. It wasn't beyond the hand of God. Actually, when it came to cards and chaos, I thought it would be easier for God to intervene in that than in the whole free-will thing. I had been passive, waiting for my cards to be dealt and waiting for my answer in those, the codes of faces and numbers that would make my choice for me. God making my choice for me. And in that final hand, He'd told me that I could have both. I could have Darwin but not without the Bible. And so I accepted this, telling myself I could read Darwin as long as I held the Bible as reference. And with that, I could either confirm or deny the validity of Darwin's points. It was a job I was going to take very seriously.

Before Beth and I hung up, I reminded her of the play at the end of the month, that my Dad had already bought her ticket. I didn't really want her to go at that particular moment, but I didn't say this. I had to keep my promise to God; I had to atone for my sins. I was a fisherman, a fisherman for souls. And although the thought of hooking Beth in the mouth and dragging her to shore fighting and ripping her skin in the process was horrifying, I was looking forward to having someone to sit with during the play.

While Mom and Dad were away at play practice, Kyle seemed

to want company. I went to my room to read, but she knocked on my door just a few minutes later, asking if I was busy. She had our old Curious George puppet on her hand. "No," I said, closing the book, "I'm not busy."

Kyle and I sat on the living room floor with Caitlyn, trying to make her laugh. Kyle had found the puppet in the garage in a box marked CANDLES in my mother's handwriting. Caitlyn liked to stick her fingers into Curious George's mouth, which would chomp down to her screaming delight. We played like this for a while, Caitlyn never seeming to tire of the game. She would look back and forth between us, as if she couldn't get enough, her blue eyes watering from laughter. When she laughed, I would bury my face in the delicate bluish skin of her scalp and kiss the dark fuzz on her head. She smelled like sour milk and bananas, and she looked just like Lance.

When she was first born, she didn't look much like anyone. I remember being led by my father into the recovery room where my sister looked ugly and exhausted under the unforgiving fluorescent light. She was covered in a stiff white sheet, so starched that it spiked up and stayed where she had, probably only a few minutes before, had her knees propped up so some doctor could inspect her. Those ghost knees up and spread made me stare at the floor until they brought in Caitlyn for my mother to hold. She was the first in the family to hold her, other than Kyle. Maybe even before Lance, who was frozen in a far corner of the room with a stunned smile on his face, rocking from foot to foot and fiddling with something in his pockets. And when I leaned over and first saw Caitlyn, I understood what he was so nervous about. She was ugly. Her purple skull had been squeezed into a cone, and she had fur on her cheeks. And her eyes—what creeped me out the most were her eyes. So deep blue and attentive that she seemed to be registering everything. A prune with eyes, a California Raisin. I almost laughed out loud thinking this, but seeing Lance's stunned face, I knew to keep my mouth shut.

After just a week, Caitlyn looked normal, although she still didn't look like either Kyle or Lance. I don't know when she started having his face, but now, watching her grab at the puppet, I could see only him. Not even a trace of my sister. Maybe Kyle's genes wouldn't kick in until a little later, I thought. Darwin said that a lot of traits from your parents would lie dormant until a later age. I hoped for Kyle's sake he was right.

When the phone rang, both Kyle and I got up to get it. I thought maybe it was Beth calling again. Leaving Caitlyn lying on her blanket, we both raced to the kitchen like we used to when we were small. I let Kyle win because at the last second I got a bad feeling. Raising the phone to her ear, she said hello, listened for just a second, and hung up the phone. In the next room, Caitlyn began crying. With no trace of anything on her face, Kyle walked over to the fridge and opened it. She stood in the cold breath of it, considering something, as I returned to the living room. The second Caitlyn saw me, she stopped crying and burst into a smile, just as impassioned. She reached out with her hands as I walked back to her, but as I got closer, her face fell again into distress. By the time I sat down next to her, she had figured out that I was not her mother. Maybe I didn't have the right smell. Her lips quivered and her eyes shut as she let out a wail, which persisted until her entire body shook with the effort of it. And then she'd suck in more air and start over, even louder. When Kyle walked in with a bottle and a cloth thrown over her shoulder, she again stopped crying and held out her hands.

By the time our parents got home from play practice, Kyle and I had abandoned the puppet. We were both watching a muted television, hoping Caitlyn would fall asleep. Dad was the first one up the stairs, with Mom following a few steps behind. When she saw us, she immediately turned down the hall and disappeared in their bedroom. Dad lingered at the top of the steps awhile before walking into the kitchen to get himself a drink of water.

I could hear him opening cupboards and drawers, closing them too softly, and then letting the water run for a long time. And then there was no sound at all. Kyle noticed, giving me a weird look but choosing to ignore his glaring caution.

"When's your first day of camp, Mel?" She reclined back on her elbow, vaguely jiggling Curious George for Caitlyn, who would not fall asleep.

"Saturday, the twenty-ninth."

"How about that Sunday? Do you have classes then?"

I nodded.

"Are Mom and Dad going to let you miss church?"

"Dad said it was okay as long as I went to their play that night."

Kyle made a face. "Dad's trying to get me to go, but it always makes me cry."

"Yeah."

Caitlyn, still wanting to play the puppet game, stuck her fingers in my mouth. I curled my lips over my teeth and chomped down on her fat-ringed fingers, making her squeal.

Giving up on the whole sleep idea, Kyle turned up the volume on the television, which immediately grabbed Caitlyn's attention. I was turning myself on the carpet to get a better view when I noticed Dad standing in the entryway. He lingered again, looking over Kyle's shoulder at me. His face was the color of ashes, at first I thought from the stubborn shadow of his stage makeup, but the slack weight of his entire face, the way the pad prints from his glasses had settled deep into his skin, I knew it was not stage makeup. He did not rub them now as he usually did, pressing his thumb and forefinger to massage away the deep grooves. He stood there, hands useless at his sides, looking very old. I immediately knew. Mom had told him about the anniversary card.

∝ ✕⟩

On the weekend of my thirteenth birthday, Kyle had called off a date with Lance to celebrate with us. My birthday was on a Saturday. Kyle was eighteen, just about to graduate from high school.

Lance had been kicked out of school months before for threatening the principal.

Mother had baked an angel food cake, and Dad had dug the old ice-cream maker out of the garage. Since Mother wouldn't allow anyone to help her with the baking, Kyle and I churned the ice cream while Dad added ice and chocolate syrup. After about forty minutes, the ice cream was the consistency of eggnog, so Kyle and I wandered onto the back deck, leaving Dad to salvage the mess. We both settled into the porch swing, her long elegant legs tipping us back and forth, while I drew mine up to my chest to ward off the steady Lake Michigan breeze. It was a lukewarm April evening, rare in northern Indiana.

Our backyard was flanked by another backyard, the Crajacks'. From our back deck, we could watch the Crajacks on their back deck, and the McCormicks on theirs, to the left. Although it was a breezy evening, everyone seemed to be out enjoying the air. Mrs. McCormick, an older woman, was hosing off her house in what looked like a nightgown. I was squinting through the half-light, trying to determine the nature of her outfit, when Kyle came out with it.

"I'm pregnant, Mel." Her voice wasn't weak or frightened, but detached, as if she were just trying the phrase on for size, turning in front of a mirror to decide whether it was really "her." *I'm pregnant, Mel.*

I focused more on Mrs. McCormick, who must have felt my stare. She turned and waved, letting the garden hose spew off onto her car. Kyle and I both raised a hand in unison, the rhythm of our swinging unbroken.

"No one knows yet. Not even Lance. I'm afraid of what he might say."

Too stunned to actually speak, I could only parrot back her own words. "Well, what might he say?"

She shrugged and looked off onto the grass, pretending that something had caught her attention. "Anyway," she said to the lawn,

"I think I can do it. I took care of you and you're still alive." She turned to look directly at me. "You knew that, didn't you?"

"Knew what?" I barely heard her, still trying to wrap my head around the idea of her being pregnant.

She stared at me a moment before she continued. "When you were a baby and Dad was off at work, Mom wouldn't feed you. She locked herself in her bedroom all day and wouldn't come out. So I started feeding you baby food, and then, when we ran out of that, I taught myself to make instant oatmeal. I was five." Her eyes drifted away, back over the lawn. Through the window, I could see Mom and Dad in the kitchen. Dad had evidently given up on the ice cream and was standing behind Mom, his arms wrapped around her waist, lifting her backwards and slightly off the ground. Her mouth opened in what looked like a laugh as she batted at his head with an oven mitt. I couldn't believe she was laughing.

"I have to tell Mom and Dad tonight."

Kyle was looking over my shoulder at Mom and Dad, her face perfectly symmetrical, expressionless. "If I tell them before Lance, he can't make me get rid of it."

A chill was coming up in the air. Soon, dogs would be calling up and down the street, their barks ranging from anger to desperation. The chain on the porch swing had settled into a deep, methodical groan as Kyle's heels tapped lightly on the wood. "No. I'll tell them tomorrow." She sighed.

The light bakery smell of angel food cake had found its way through the seams of the house and wafted into the turning night air. Kyle inhaled deeply through her nose and stretched her legs out in front of her to stare thoughtfully at her feet. She had big feet.

"I don't want to ruin your birthday."

I still hadn't seen Jared since our game of poker. I usually worried about him when he disappeared, but that Sunday I was glad he didn't come home for church. I could take my brother and sister separately, but sitting through church with both of them was unbearable. With Jared's smart-ass remarks filling one ear and Kyle's devout sniffling in the other, I felt like an impressionable cartoon character with an angel on my right shoulder and a devil on my left. Sitting between them, I would find myself simultaneously teary-eyed and laughing at Pastor Lyle's sermons. Kyle would nod, thinking of the perverse world her child was being raised in, while Jared whispered obscenities in my ear. Kyle would lean over, give him a look. She liked to call Jared out on his sins, although her devoutness had become very specific. Christian principles, for her, were either readily embraced or rejected, depending on her opinions. Her version of God was not as all-knowing as everyone else's.

Kyle and I sat in the middle of the sanctuary, waiting for the service to begin. Mom and Dad had somehow convinced her to come to church, or maybe she had come to repent for her sins. Caitlyn was at the Arthurs' house. Brody came over in the morning to get her so Kyle could go to church. She had stood at the front window a long time to watch him carry her child down the street.

Whatever the reason she chose to come, I was happy to have my sister at church with me. I wasn't embarrassed by her anymore, not after learning about my parents. When I looked around the sanctuary now, I would pick out people and try to imagine their worst sins, the ways in which they had disappointed God. I knew that no one here was in any position to judge. Except maybe Pastor Lyle, but he was up onstage and could be easily avoided.

There were about five hundred people present for the day's sermon. Everyone milled around under a general buzz, looking puny under the fifty-foot domed ceiling and the massive wooden rafters. The sanctuary was located right at the intersection of the cross design, allowing for its huge size. I watched Mom and Dad file onto the stage with the rest of the choir, taking their place front and center and kicking off with my favorite song, "The Walls of Jericho," which was about how Joshua marched around Jericho with his army playing trumpets. They played so loudly that the walls of the city crumpled. This Jericho song was exhilarating. I could feel the trumpets in my head, the drums in my chest. It was like I was in Joshua's army, marching around the walls of a great city, armed with nothing but a trumpet and the fire of God's wrath. I liked to think of music in this way, powerful and destructive. I raised my hands and clapped along with the choir.

By the end of the song service, almost everyone was out of breath and sweating. It was so hot that the slow drool of the air-conditioning vents couldn't keep up. The choir members had all unzipped their purple robes, which now flapped behind them like useless wings. Above and to our left, I could see the big aluminum cross swaying just slightly from its cables. The ceiling fans were spinning real slow, as if stirring a thick batter. Everyone was waving their arms and shouting hot, breathy lyrics, making the air so thick it felt unsanitary to breathe. There were people laid out on the ground mumbling and shaking, including my mother, who during "God Is in Control" had snapped straight like a struck lightning rod and tipped back slowly onto her heels while the choir members behind eased her down to the floor.

I didn't look at Kyle through all of this but was still aware of her reactions in my periphery: the jubilant bounce, the hushed sway, the reverent stillness broken only by a single hand raised toward Heaven. She always did that, placing one hand on the pew in front of her as she swayed, and then, as the last few songs dwindled to a whisper, she'd become completely still. With one hand raised in worship, she would leave the other still gripping the pew, as if bracing herself for the lightning bolt. But Kyle never spoke in tongues; I had never seen her filled with the Holy Spirit or even become weak-kneed. But she was always prepared, watching my mother first in envy and then in shame, thinking herself too impure to be blessed with such an event. If I wasn't so afraid of saying it out loud in God's presence, I would have told her right then about Mom being a fornicator. I wanted to tell her that if the Spirit could fill Mom, it could fill her. If she wanted it to. I watched my sister now, her body relaxed with the music and begging for the Holy Spirit to enter her. I stiffened, like I always did during the end of the song service, when the Holy Spirit seemed to just buzz around the room, taking people over. I slowed my breathing way down. I clenched my jaw and took short quick breaths through my nose every thirty seconds, hoping I wouldn't breathe Him in. I had gotten good at this over the past few months, holding my breath longer and longer. I did not want to be taken over. I did not want to lose control of myself and go flopping on the carpet like a caught fish. And so I'd stand there for a good fifteen minutes every Sunday, trying to close off every orifice of my body as the people around me swooned and dropped to the floor.

Pastor Lyle's sermon was from the book of Deuteronomy and, according to the program in my hand, was entitled "The Test of False Prophets." He came up to the stage in his burnt-sienna suit, a color from my old Crayola box I had never really used.

Deuteronomy, I knew, was written by Moses between the dates 1450 and 1410 B.C. It is one of those summary books of the Bible and was titled "The Law Restated" in my Bible. The only verse I could recall from Deuteronomy at the moment was chapter thirteen, verse four: "Ye shall walk after the Lord your God, and fear Him, and keep His commandments, and obey His voice, and ye shall serve Him, and cleave unto Him." Opening my Bible, I wondered if Pastor Lyle would be reading that one today.

After taking a sip of his water, Pastor Lyle ran his fingers through his hair, letting it fall back over his eyes. He then looked down, reading through this unruly mess. "If there arise among you a prophet, or a dreamer of dreams, and giveth thee a sign or a wonder. And the sign or the wonder come to pass, whereof he spoke to thee, saying, Let us go after other gods, which thou hast not known, and let us serve them; thou shalt not hearken unto the words of that prophet, or that dreamer of dreams; for the Lord your God proveth you, to know whether ye love the Lord your God with all your heart and with all your soul."

He looked up, brushing the hair from his eyes in that way that made my throat ache. He leaned out to survey all of us with those fierce little eyes of his, small, striking, blue. I loved the way they half closed when he spoke, as if trying to search each one of us out of the darkness. "Brothers and sisters, there are many people out there who will try to tell you how the world works. They will present you with other religions, other gods, alternative ways of thinking. A false prophet is not only a person who tries to predict the future, but is anyone whose message opposes the *objective* Word of God. Oh yes, my brothers and sisters." His perfect sliver of a moon smile now shone as he drew his lips back like a curtain. He paused there a minute, just to torture me, I was sure. "No one can make that decision but you. You, I say, have to stay strong in the face of temptation. I know, I *know* the temptation. I know the world doesn't make sense all the time. I know that the desire to know, to *know,* can make you seek answers. But I can tell you that the right answers are right here." He held up his Bible, the worn black leather so limp, the whole thing drooped in his hand like a string of black licorice. Head nods crested over the congregation, weakly culminating to a few *amen*s and affirmative grunts.

Pastor Lyle kept the Bible up. "Well, *am I right?*" He rode a bit over the altar, on tiptoe, leaning out toward us. The congregation now roared in agreement. "Who wants to give you answers? Do you know who?" A few head nods. He leaned out again and whispered, half laughing, "I can tell you Buddha does." I straightened at this. The congregation laughed freely now, Pastor Lyle joining in with that light, controlled chuckle of his. What would the Buddhists try to tell me? Whenever I saw them on *The 700 Club,* they never said anything. They were always sitting around with their eyes closed, their faces completely relaxed and blank. Looking like they were praying but at the same time not. What were they doing?

What would they try to tell me about how the world works? My palms were sweating, leaving a wet spot on my lap. I pressed them into the pew, trying to concentrate on the message. I closed my eyes to shut out the sight of Pastor Lyle, trying to erase all thoughts of him, his surprisingly muscle-roped arms grabbing me and dunking me under the baptismal waters.

"Those philosophers, those scientists, those Jehovah's Witnesses. They will try to tell you how the world works." My breath caught in something in my chest, the lump of guilt working its way up like the urge to vomit. "Nietzsche said that God is dead. But I say that Nietzsche is dead." I had heard that before. Where? I could imagine his eyebrows raising in amusement, causing a few people to laugh again. "But what those people don't understand is that only God can know all of the answers; only He can show us those answers. And they are right here." I knew he must be pointing at the Bible again. I kept my eyes shut. "Ye shall walk after the Lord your God, and fear Him." A slight smile spread across my lips as I recited the rest with him, my lips, I imagined, moving with his. "And keep his commandments, and obey his voice, and ye shall serve Him, and cleave unto Him." I stopped, but he went on to the next verse. "And that prophet, or that dreamer of dreams, shall be put to death." To this, I opened my eyes. "Because he hath spoken to turn *you* away from the Lord your God, who brought you out of the land of Egypt, and redeemed you out of the house of bondage, to *thrust* thee out of the way . . ." I spied a short hip motion here, as Pastor Lyle moved out from behind the altar and to the front of the stage, leaving his Bible behind. I lost a good thirty seconds of the sermon there, trying to clear my mind of that image. And when I could focus again, he was in a completely different book. I flipped through my Bible, unable to keep up. My fingers were sweaty, shaking and sticking to the pages.

"Zechariah thirteen:three: 'When any shall yet prophesy, then his father and his mother that begat him shall say unto him, Thou shalt not live; for thou speakest lies in the name of the Lord: and his father and his mother that begat him shall *thrust* him through when he prophesieth.'" I stopped turning the pages. Thrust him through? Pastor Lyle laughed, tilting his head to the side to look at the emergency exit to his right. My throat was suddenly so dry I could barely swallow. "But this is before the New Covenant, folks, and we can't just go around killing people in this day and age. But there is something you can do. You can kill *the ideas*. You can meet those ideas head-on and slay them with scripture." He turned abruptly and scurried to the other side of the stage. "And even better, you can slay them where they came from. You can reach out to that misguided person who has tried to *thrust* thee away from the Lord thy God and slay that beast within them." He was out of breath now, pacing as if pacing itself were breath.

"But sometimes that beast is very big. Sometimes it is far too big for us to confront, and we need a little help. Chapter seventeen, verse eight, tells us to seek counsel in the Church." He whizzed past the altar, snatching the Bible and flipping to another section, all in one motion. I looked down at my Bible. In the confusion, it had been opened to Ecclesiastes. Was he in Deuteronomy again? "'If there arise a matter too hard for thee in judgment, between blood and blood, between plea and plea, and between stroke and stroke, *being* matters of controversy within thy gates'; verse nine, 'And thou shalt come unto the priests, the Levites, and unto the judge that shall be in those days, and inquire, and they shall show thee the sentence of judgment'; verse thirteen, 'And all the people shall hear, and fear, and do no more presumptuously.'" He sucked in another mouthful of air and wiped his forehead with his sleeve. Then, as if his clothing had become too much to bear, he jerked at the buttons of his suit. With his coat now open, I could see sweat stains working through the front of his shirt. "There are books, there are television shows, there are people who can trick you—they will try to take advantage of you. There are enemies that are too much for the common man to conquer. Too eloquent, too deceptive, there are enemies that do not seem like enemies at all. But the Church will always help you with this; the Church will guide you, will tell you what books, what television shows, what music is harmful. Harmful in ways that you can't even understand, and when you are tempted by these beasts, you must trust the judgment of the Church, the judgment of the Lord our God."

I had sunk low in my seat by now, my thighs burning, my stomach churning with disgust and desire. Pastor Lyle's body was thrusting and heaving onstage, speaking with as much ferocity as his breathy, exhausted voice. I swear he was looking at me each time he punctuated his sentences with a pelvic thrust or a head toss. I glanced over at Kyle, who was leaning back, perfectly calm in the turbulence of his hips. It was me; it was just me. My dirty mind had put all those things there. Poor Pastor Lyle, up there spending himself, trying to just give the Word of God to his congregation, and here I was imagining all these dirty things, thinking he was putting a show on just for me. It was all for me. He was looking at me, now I knew. His eyes would graze the audience, but they always seemed to fall on me. He knew about Darwin. God had told him, just the way He told him about sick people in the audience. Just like Pat Robertson, he'd say, "God's telling me that there is someone out there who is struggling with drugs and alcohol." And he'd give a special message to that person from God, something like "God wants you to know that He is stronger than those addictions, and that He will help you to overcome if you will just give yourself to Him." And now, as if Pastor Lyle or God had read my mind, the sermon took a drastic turn.

"I know that there is someone here today who is struggling against these false prophets. Someone who isn't sure what the truth is. That someone is being led astray from the teachings of our Lord." He paused to scan the audience, squinting. No one moved or looked around, lest they put themselves under suspicion. The pressure rising in my body, to my head, made me feel like my eyeballs were going to pop out. I closed my eyes. "These lies always seem more complicated than the truth." Another pause. "There's a lot of fancy talkers out there, and there are things that we can never hope to understand. The workings of the Lord are beyond us, are beyond our understanding, and it is *a sin* to try to find answers to things we are not meant to know. Those dreamers of dreams, those false prophets, want you to want those answers, and worst of all, they want you to accept *their* answers. You need to kill those false prophecies, those dreams in your mind. There is no truth greater then the truth of the Lord, and no ally greater than Him."

I would repent, I decided. I would go up for altar call, ask the Lord to forgive me, and maybe even try to open myself up to the Spirit. *Take these evil thoughts out of me,* I'd pray over and over. Yes, I would go down deep within and hollow myself out so I could be filled with the Spirit. I would shake and start babbling in tongues, letting God completely take me over. And then Pastor Lyle would see. He would see me, all weak-kneed and shaking, and he'd come over and place his hand on my forehead, gently at first, whispering a prayer for me, and then his arm would stiffen and he would push my head back, sending me back onto my heels, just enough force for a brief pause of weightlessness before I fell all the way back into the hands of so many strangers waiting behind me, their soft, fleshy fingers touching me and easing me down to the floor. And Pastor Lyle standing over me, having the power to take me if he wanted, would rush to get his burnt-sienna suit jacket and smooth it down over my exposed thighs.

∞ ⧓

When Kyle and I got home from church, Lance was sitting on the front stoop getting ready to light a cigarette. Mom and Dad were still at church, helping to redecorate the sanctuary with new banners the Ladies of Vision had sewn. We pulled up and saw him at exactly the same moment he saw us. He stood up, flinging the unlit cigarette aside and putting the lighter in his pocket. Kyle braked in the middle of the driveway, not even pulling up to her usual parking spot. Lance's car was nowhere in sight. He must have parked farther up the road. Kyle put the car in park, but we did not unclick our seat belts.

"Kyle, do you want me to go talk to him?" The words came out with as much surprise to me as to her. She swiveled to look at me, her face melting from amusement, to anger, to fear, until it decided on nonchalance. She whipped her hair back and checked her lipstick in the rearview mirror.

"Mel, I can handle this. It's no big deal. Just go inside while I talk to him."

"Are you sure?" I knew she wasn't, by the way she gathered her face into determination. She smacked her lips together in the mirror to even out her lipstick.

Without looking at me, she nodded. "Yeah. Go in through the back. I won't be long."

She undid her seat belt, and I did the same. Placing a hand on the door handle, she stared hard out the window at Lance, who was making his way toward the car. I just wanted to shake her right then. She must have known that she wasn't fooling me. Why did she keep this up? I swallowed these emotions down and kept swallowing as my mouth overwatered in protest. I was not going to puke, and there was no way I was going to leave her alone with this creep, I decided, even if she yelled and kicked at me to go in the house. I would follow behind her. I wished I had my baton with me. Kyle jerked the door handle, and I went for mine. But just as I was going to open my door, she reached over and grabbed my hand, yanking me over the gearshift and through the driver's side door. She held on to me as she walked over to meet him. I struggled to keep up but finally found her pace, sashaying in time with her as she marched to meet him in front of the house.

He stopped to make us walk to him, an amused grin on his face. "You don't need your bodyguard, Kyle. Mel, get in the house."

"Don't you dare talk to my sister." She squeezed my hand fiercely, making my fingers cramp in her palm. It felt like she had crumpled all the tiny bones of my hand into one huge knot, one that might not come loose when she let go. But I did not pull away. She squeezed again, and I leaned into it. I knew she was terrified, but when I looked up at her, her face was perfectly calm. "She's staying."

Lance shrugged. "Fine, then. I don't care." He smiled down at me, showing a small gap between his front teeth. His face dirty with stubble, his nose wrinkled as he looked me up and down. His wavy black hair was a bit rumpled, and his pupils just kept opening up to absorb me. He was so sexy, the way his eyes traced my body. He was Heathcliff, dark and violent and sexy. I stared right back at him, still swallowing and swallowing, as fast as I could, trying to keep the spit from collecting in my mouth. But it didn't seem fast enough. "You're growing up. A little taller than I saw last." Heathcliff. I wanted to spit on him, to get rid of the flood in my mouth, and to defile him in the process. But Kyle pulled me in behind her before the thought could become any more than a thought.

"Stop it, Lance, just stop." She was holding me against her back now, half shielding me with her body. "I told you not to talk to her."

He ignored her, keeping his big blue eyes on me. Caitlyn's eyes. But then they narrowed at me and weren't Caitlyn's eyes anymore. "I hope you don't grow up to be a fucking whore like your big sister."

"Shut up! Don't be making up lies about me. I can call the police. You aren't supposed to be here."

"Calm down. I just think your little sister should know what you've been up to." He stared down at me again with no hint of a smile in his eyes. "Don't go through life lying on your back, Mel."

Kyle screamed, "You're disgusting, you're a filthy bastard! Filthy fucking bastard!" She let go of me, reached down, grabbed a handful of stones, and flung them at him. He ducked, moving in to grab her. She leaped back, stumbling over me and losing her balance. She was tipped back on her heels, flapping her arms forward, but it did no good. She fell back, almost on top of me, but Lance grabbed her wrist and yanked her up. I had fallen to the ground and was now scrambling to get up.

Lance was holding her right to his face, hissing something I couldn't hear. I finally found my feet and ran for the back of the house. As I ran, I turned around, running backwards the way I did in dreams, to see if he was chasing me. There was no one. When I reached the back deck, I sprinted up the wooden steps, taking two at a time, but I missed and my shin scraped down through the gap in between. I crawled up the rest of the way, clambering on my hands and feet all the way to the back door, which flung open and slammed behind me as I reached for the kitchen phone, a rotary, mint green with a long coiled cord. I picked it up and began dialing, keeping my finger in the holes and pushing the dial back after each number, fighting its determination to take its time, like it always did. I swore in my head, wondering why our family couldn't have a push-button phone like normal people. Reeling and pushing, reeling and pushing. Just these seven numbers took an eternity, my finger reeling the dial all the way around and forcing it back: the nine, the seven, another nine. For some reason, Brody's number had nothing under five in it.

After I hung up, I ran to the front window to see Brody already making his way across the street. He was running so fast, taking the ditch in a single jump and not breaking his pace as he cleared it and ran up to the house. When he was close, I ran down the front steps and opened the door, stepping out to see Lance and Kyle, his hand not locked around her wrist, but holding it loosely with his fingers. They were silent, just looking at each other.

"Kyle." Brody was not even out of breath but spoke evenly as he ran up to them. Lance turned around, letting go of Kyle's wrist and putting his hands in the air.

"I'm not doing anything; we're just talking," Lance said. "Just talking." Kyle kept her wrist up for a second before letting it fall to her side.

Brody slowed and walked the last few steps toward them, walking straight up to him and finding that Lance was a good three inches taller. Lance smiled down at him, that same gap-toothed smile he'd given me, too amused to even expect Brody's right fist to split that smile wide open. Even I was shocked, though I was expecting it all along. It was so fast, I still wasn't sure it had happened until I saw the blood brightening the inside of Lance's half-open mouth. I thought there would be some words exchanged, maybe a shove, but Brody had come right out with it, and Lance, after a brief pause, straightened himself and stepped right around Brody's next punch, catching him off guard and lining him up for something. I don't know. I instinctively looked away, only hearing Lance punch Brody three times, and when I looked back a second later, Brody was doubled over on the ground.

Kyle did not scream. She did not cry or break up the fight, but ran straight to her car, fumbling the keys from her purse and not looking back as she closed the door and started the engine. The car jerked into reverse, a single spasm propelling her backwards and out of the driveway. I watched her hands cutting the wheel back around, and then she was squealing down the street. Brody was bent over, holding his stomach. I could see the pained blush of his scalp underneath his buzzed brown hair. He stayed on his knees, gasping at the grass, leaving me and Lance to watch Kyle's car turn left, without stopping, onto Colfax Street and disappear behind a row of houses.

Lance turned to me, his face serious with blood and concern. He shrugged apologetically, looking down at my left shin, which was also streaked with blood. "She's gonna kill herself driving like that. I've tried to tell her, but she don't care. She's a fucking maniac."

⋈

When Kyle came home about an hour later, she peeked into my room, saying nothing but looking me up and down and nodding, just to make sure I was still alive, I guess, or maybe to thank me for not saying anything to Mom and Dad about the whole thing. Caitlyn was asleep in her crib. I picked her up after walking Brody back to his house, finding nothing to say to him but "Thanks for taking care of Caitlyn."

He nodded and said, "Anytime," still bent slightly around the pain in his stomach. And then he disappeared into the house as his little sister brought the baby to the front door.

Kyle did not call Brody when she got home, and he didn't call the house, although I'm sure he heard her pulling into the driveway in that fantastic way she always did, tires squealing, gravel flying. Whatever romantic notions I had for them were now gone. At first I didn't know why I had called Brody instead of the police, but once my sister just ran away, not even looking back at Brody, I knew why. I had expected her to scream, maybe even to jump in front of Brody, trying to hold Lance off. I would have been happy if she had just cried. I had imagined her whimpering in her Sunday dress, biting her knuckles, tears streaming down her cheeks as she pleaded with them to stop. But the way she just shrugged at me (I remembered this now), she shrugged and ran to her car, not even caring who won, not even flattered that these guys were fighting over her.

When Mom and Dad got home a little while later, I told them that Kyle went to get gas for her car. And when she got home, she just settled into the couch to watch television with Mom. I could hear them from my room chatting away, Mom being more talkative than usual. I walked in to find Mom talking about the Ladies of Vision and the new banners they had sewn.

"We hung four today, right behind the baptismal pool. They have gray trim to match the new carpet. Right above the pool, it says 'WASHED IN THE BLOOD OF THE LAMB.' Isn't that clever?"

I shuddered visibly at this, the thought of a whole baptismal pool filled with blood and Pastor Lyle wading in it in his Hawaiian shorts, reaching out for me to come and get baptized in it. "What does that mean?" I asked. "People always say that, and I don't understand what it means."

Mother smiled and looked directly at me, for the first time in days. "Before Jesus, people had to sacrifice animals to God in order to be forgiven for their sins. But when Christ was crucified, He was the last sacrifice. He sacrificed Himself like a lamb so we could be clean. We can be forgiven without sacrificing animals now. We just have to *ask*. So they say we are washed in His blood."

So we had turned from sacrificing animals to sacrificing people? How was that good? What about fishers of men, reeling people in instead of fish? Them flopping on the ground in front of the altar to ask forgiveness. And all of us supposedly covered in blood. Parents stabbing their own children just for being a little misguided. I glanced over at Kyle. She was nodding, smiling, which infuriated me. She of all people, pretending to care about these things, with Brody just down the road, probably waiting for her to come and see him.

I found it impossible to sit there and watch Kyle act so aloof about poor Brody. As she started regluing her nails, laughing with my mother at the television, pretending to care about *Wheel of Fortune* reruns, I got so angry at her. And Mom just ignored me the entire time, making a big effort to talk to Kyle and to forget that I was in the room. Dad had gone back to church to help take down the aluminum cross for the play. I volunteered to go with him to help out, hoping to get away from the house, but he'd said, "That's okay." He had smiled when he said this, an offering that my mother would never give me. The way he put a hand on my shoulder and said that he might need my help later this week, I knew he was asking me to forgive him. For being a fornicator, and maybe even for leaving me alone with Mother during the storm. But I doubted that he even knew about me being thrown out of the house. He just wanted me to forgive him, and for the moment I did, because it was easier than forgiving Mom or Kyle, and I had to have some ally in the household. Jared wasn't home nearly enough.

I went to my room to escape my mother and sister, their new solidarity. And I locked the door behind me. There was something that

I needed to do today, something that I had been thinking about for a while. I had finally decided what I was going to do with my glow powder. I was no longer afraid of it.

For a while I had considered taking it to Beth's house to make glow-in-the-dark underwear, but that was before I understood its importance. This powder was holy, I now understood. God had given it to me in that hand of poker, and I knew that I needed to do something with it to prove my loyalty to Him, something that would remind me on a daily basis, something between me and God and no one else.

Glow powder was beyond evolution. Its existence was constantly reminding me of the things I could never understand, of the things Darwin never knew about. And that was why God wanted me to have it, I decided. It was not alive, it did not evolve, it was as it had always been, and because of this I knew that the world was ordered.

I took the vial of glow powder from an inside pocket of my backpack and dug through my closet for my art box. I had half a bottle of clear glue left, just enough to do what I wanted. With a new courage that I knew must be inspired by God, I opened the vial for the first time and emptied it into the bottle of glue. Stirring it all together with a pencil, I watched the pale yellow grains disappear.

With a paintbrush and the bottle of glue, I stood on my bed and stretched to reach the ceiling. The paintbrush just reached. I dipped it into the glue and began to write out my rules, the ones from Galatians. Slowly, I painted out the word *wrath*. It was hard to see where I had painted the letters, but I tried to keep the word as straight as possible. When I was done, I tried to make out the letters and could just see the shimmer of wet glue where the word was supposed to be. I blew on it, watching all traces of it disappear.

Next was *lasciviousness,* which ended up being much longer than the space I had allotted for it. With my notebook open at my feet, I carefully spelled it out and smooshed the last four letters together, right against the wall.

I went on this way for about a half hour, spacing all of the words out over my bed, so they would completely cover me at night. *Adultery, fornication, uncleanness, idolatry, witchcraft, hatred, variance, emulations, strife, seditions, heresies, envyings, murders, drunkenness, revelings.* After reading Darwin, I would turn off my bedside lamp and stare up at these rules and know that I was doing God's work. These words would remind me of my duties; they would keep me from getting lost in doubt. And I would be the only one who knew they were there.

I knew I would have to wait until nighttime to see if it had worked. So I left my bedroom light on to charge the powder and decided to read.

SUNDAY, JUNE 16, 4:30 P.M.
CHAPTER V: *Laws of Variation (continued)*

The most interesting trait that Darwin claims can disappear is sight. Many ground-dwelling animals, like moles, are blind and have their eyes covered in skin and fur. I have seen a mole before, so I can say that this is true. The cause of blindness, he says, is often inflammation of the eye that is caused by constant irritation from dirt. And since eye infections are not advantageous and sight really isn't needed underground, natural selection would make the eyes go away from disuse. Some animals lose their eyes altogether, while others just have eyes that don't see. I haven't seen any kind of animal with no eyes at all, so I can't say if this is true. Darwin says that he has seen blind animals called cave-rats that have eyes, but they are blind. Some guy or scientist took these blind cave-rats and exposed them to gradual light over the course of a month. After a month of this, Darwin says that these cave-rats gained "a dim perception of objects." I don't know if this is true, and after I figure out what is going on with the logger-headed ducks, maybe it will turn out to be a lie. But for now I think that it is the most interesting thing in this book I have read so far.

∝

I was going to go fishing that evening, but when I started down the stairs, I noticed Jared's work boots standing at attention in the foyer, still tied.

He must have heard me descending the stairs, because when I got to the bottom, he was standing in the middle of his room, ready for company, rubbing his eyes. He had been sleeping. He always slept during the day. From the way I ran down the steps, he must have known it was me.

"Don't you knock?" He didn't look mad. This was only a formality, I knew, something he always said. There wasn't actually a door to knock on when you went downstairs to his room. We used to knock on the walls as we descended the stairs, until Mom complained about all the smudges on her white walls.

"Sorry."

"Did Mom throw you out again?"

I shook my head, but he didn't see. He walked back into the shadows of his room. "I guess you can wait it out here, until Dad gets home. You'll be okay then, right?" His voice was sarcastic. "Born-Again Child."

I stepped in. Rubbing my feet against the scratchy blue carpet, I walked across the room and sat down Indian style, tucking my feet under my thighs for warmth. There was a single bare lightbulb hanging in the room that struggled against the darkness, a weak yellow. The pull chain was just swinging to a stop.

"You know, Mel, it's not her fault." He located his glasses on the nightstand and put them on. "She's crazy, but it's not her fault."

I didn't say anything. My feet were freezing. I tried to wiggle them farther under my thighs. I was hoping he was looking for

201

socks for me, but he turned back around, empty-handed. He closed the drawer with his hip and walked over to sit on his bed—that slow, gangly walk of someone who's all legs.

"You get the worst of it, though. I don't know why, but you do."

"The worst of what?"

"Mom's bullshit."

I stiffened.

"Don't be such a fucking infant." He rolled his eyes. "You think God cares about swearing? You think He takes time out of His busy schedule to mark shit like that down? God doesn't even speak English, Mel. You should know that." He smiled. Above, the floorboards creaked.

I was just about to tell him that Mom hadn't thrown me out and that I had just come down to talk. I wanted to tell him about Lance coming to the house, about the anniversary card, and maybe even get him to tell me what he wrote about me in that note, but instead I heard myself say, "I hate her." I didn't know where this came from, but I said it. This didn't surprise Jared at all.

"I know you do." We both glanced up at the ceiling, which creaked as someone walked overhead. Probably Mother. "But, Mel, like I said. It's not her fault."

"Then whose fault is it?"

He took a breath. "You wouldn't believe me if I told you."

I could hear the phone ringing above, my mother's footsteps racing after it, down the hall and into her bedroom. We were alone.

My voice cracked. "I know what you think." That shut him up. He leaned back, as if that was his cue to stop talking. But I didn't want him to stop. I said, "Why's it Dad's fault?" Although that was the last thing I wanted to hear, I had a feeling it was true. And it was better than telling him what I came down to tell him. That he was a bastard.

He considered for a moment. "He used to be really bad, Mel. Before you were born. I remember stuff."

In as light a voice as I could gather, I sighed, saying, "I know," as if I were bored with the topic. I had always tried to imagine my father drinking, smoking cigarettes, and, recently, fornicating with my mother.

"I know, Jared. Cousin Harley told me all about it."

"No, Monchi. I'm not talking about what Harley told you. There's a lot more. Stuff no one talks about."

I didn't move. Jared was about to tell me something, and I felt that if I moved, he would change his mind. He liked me here, on the floor, palms flat behind me, legs crossed, freezing. And although the carpet was getting unbearable against my hands, itchy and burning, I remained still.

"He left us a lot. He'd be gone for days, maybe a week. He'd go off with other women."

He paused, waiting for a response. I could feel my face trying to work itself into an expression, many expressions. But I fought it. I felt more and more weight pressing back on my hands, rubbing the delicate skin of my palms into the carpet. There were a few loose pieces of gravel digging into the meaty part of my thumbs. I leaned into them. The pain kept me focused.

Jared continued. "Anyway. He would tell her about it. About all the other women. He'd come home and scream at her if there was a spot of dust anywhere, and he'd tell her he was going to go screw some other woman. He'd be gone for days." He paused again to look at me, but I just kept on, stone-faced. "He'd bring his friends home, and they'd all talk about it, too. Insulting her and stuff. And then when she was pregnant with you, it got really bad. I remember."

Upstairs a door slammed, and the footsteps started up again, faster and harder than before. She was calling my name. "What happened, Jared?"

He shrugged. And then he told me. He told me how Dad had once left, how he had screamed that he was never coming back. Jared was playing in the living room and the phone started ringing, kept on for a good ten rings, so Jared went to find Mom. He looked everywhere and finally found her under the kitchen table, pregnant with me and completely naked. She was soaking wet, having just walked straight from the shower to the kitchen. Sitting there in a puddle of soapy water, ripping at her fingernails with her teeth. They were beyond bleeding, but she just kept gnawing at them, trying to rip them out of her fingers, not responding as Jared tried to get her attention.

I heard the back door slam shut. More footsteps. "I tried to help her, but she was too heavy. She was about eight months with you. So I ran to get Mrs. Arthur."

The footsteps were now coming down the stairs, heavy and slow. "Mel?" Jared stood up and ran over to his dresser, opening the drawer again and shoving something inside. He turned back to me. "They were going to put her away, but they didn't because of you."

The front door opened. Mom called for me outside, and then the door slammed shut. And she called down the stairs, her voice softer now.

"He hasn't done it since then, Mel. I swear he hasn't, so don't worry." Jared crossed the room and opened the basement door that led outside. "I wasn't here, okay?"

I blinked, still trying to understand what he'd said before, about her being *put away*. "Why?"

He didn't answer but closed the door, leaving me alone with the sound of my mother's footsteps descending the last of the stairs. As I rose to meet her, I glanced out the window. Outside the air was dark pink, about time for my father to come home. Soon the sound of his tires on the gravel, the slam of his car door, his careful steps up the front walk. For the first time in my life, I did not look forward to his return.

∝ ✕⃝

My dad said that he found Jesus on a little dirt road in South Bend, Indiana. It was right before I was born, he said, but from that moment on, he never had a drink again. Dad had always admitted to the drinking. For a few years, he was a traveling speaker in churches all over Indiana. He'd bring all of us with him to sit in the front pew and listen to his life story, at least once a month for three years.

When my father was up onstage in front of a congregation of people, he always started by singing a few songs. He had a beautiful singing voice, one of those voices that would even make the babies in the audience be still. As he sang, my mother would give him hand signals from the audience, telling him to adjust the bass or the treble on his ancient mixer. She loved sitting there, making those signs while Dad would fiddle with the knobs as he sang. She had a good ear for those things, my mother, and she'd always be making those signs, always trying to adjust something. "Your mother has a superior sense of hearing," Dad would joke after the service. "Be careful what you think around her."

After a few songs, Dad would launch into his sermon, his sermon of salvation, as he liked to call it. He didn't preach like Pastor Lyle; he didn't pace up and down, flipping his hair out of his eyes, yelling and getting all out of breath. My father didn't stir the audience up with yelps and hip thrusts. He would stand in the middle of the stage, with both hands gripping the microphone, his voice low, just asking for everyone to hear him out. He was a big man, but looked very small onstage. Sometimes he shook, staring down at the floor as he spoke.

He would always begin with his childhood in Slow Rapids, with his father. Finding him passed out on the kitchen floor in a pool of vomit and urine, finding his mother hiding in her bedroom with clumps of hair missing from her head. How he'd go through the house sweeping up the balls of hair before his brothers and sisters woke up. As the oldest boy, he had to do things like that.

I never really connected the woman sitting on the bed with bald spots with my grandmother. And the eleven children, all crowded around a kitchen table for a dinner of spaghetti and ketchup, they didn't seem like my aunts and uncles. They were all characters in this story that my father told. I would listen, half-aware of its truth. Whenever I saw my aunts and uncles at Christmas, they were happy, even beautiful people. They had kids; they bought me dolls and puzzles; they wore bright sweaters with matching turtlenecks underneath. The only story my father told that connected him to these traumatic events in my mind was the story of Bella. That story always made me cry, and sometimes it made him cry, too, onstage in front of all those strangers.

Bella was a mutt that my father adopted when he was about ten years old. Just when he said this, I would feel tears filling the corners of my eyes. He had her for about a year, but during that year, she learned to hate my grandfather. Dad would have to tie her up when he was around. But one time when his father had come home drunk and started to beat up on my grandmother, Bella came pushing through the screen door, dragging her broken rope behind her and locking her teeth around my grandfather's ankle. He grabbed Bella by the neck and ordered my father to hold her in his arms, to hold her tight. And he did. He said he never held anything so tightly in his life, pressing her to his chest while his father took a hammer from underneath the kitchen sink and started beating her. Dad talked about how he was afraid to let go, even when he felt her bones cracking and she yelped so hard trying to wriggle loose. He had the power to let her go at any moment, he said, but he just couldn't disobey his father. And so he held her tighter and tighter to his chest until she stopped fighting him altogether and just whimpered as his father beat the last breaths out of her with that hammer.

My mother, sitting next to me in the audience, would nod all through this story, as if she understood it perfectly. She never even sniffled or wiped at her eyes. The story of Bella made perfect sense to her. But it did not make sense to me. The way he told it even now, he didn't seem to regret it. He told it like he didn't have a choice, like his father was the one to blame. And so every time I heard the story of Bella, I couldn't help but think of Abraham sacrificing his own son, how God had ordered him to slit his son's throat, and he had prepared to do it without question. I'd think of the picture in my Bible, Abraham standing over his son with the knife in the air, his muscles tense as if he had every intention of doing it. Was it so awful to question God? If He demanded that my parents tie me up in the backyard and slaughter me, would they do the same? And I would look up at my father onstage, him shaking and talking about what he had to do; and then I'd glance over to my mother, right next to me, nodding her head, unmoved, completely understanding such a terrible situation. If this was the way they treated the authority of a drunken maniac, then I knew what would happen if God told them to sacrifice me. I knew right away that they'd do it without question.

Dad's story would continue through his teens and meeting my mother, although he never mentioned asking her whether she was smuggling melons out of the Food Lion or making her naked and hysterical, hiding under a table. He didn't go into much detail after his childhood; he mostly said vague things about how he was becoming just like his father. And it would all lead up to that little dirt road in South Bend, Indiana, where he said that God spoke to him, just days before I was born. His Born-Again Child, he would say, pointing at me. The entire congregation would turn their heads to look as I smiled weakly, taking credit.

I never questioned that God spoke to my father. When Mom talked about God speaking to her, I was always skeptical, but with my father, it just seemed right. Dad never said exactly what God said to him—He just spoke and my father understood. He pulled over to the side of the road and cried for hours, he said. He sat there and cried, and from that point on, he was a changed man.

IV.

FAMILIES WHO PRAY TOGETHER
STAY TOGETHER

Somewhere along Route 71 in Kentucky, Mom unfastened her seat belt, jerked around from the passenger seat, and yelled, "That's just fine, Jake. You should just drop her off right here, if she's going to complain. Just leave her here for the bears to eat her."

"Sweetie, put your seat belt back on." Dad did not take his eyes from the road. We had been driving for about seven hours now, nonstop, if you didn't count the gas stations and the McDonald's on the Indiana border. I watched his eyes in the rearview mirror, intent on the highway. "Mel, I promise we'll be back in time for your camp. Don't worry. We have to be back for the hearing next week anyway."

I didn't say anything but slumped down in the rear seat of the minivan, propping my knees up on the middle of the seat, where Kyle's head, which was lolling back and forth in sleep, suddenly shot up, ripping her hair from under my shins. She spun around. "Jesus, Mel! Watch my hair!"

As she said this, Dad pressed the brakes, just enough to send Kyle rolling onto the floor and making my seat belt lock. It must have been only an instinct, for he stepped on the gas again without saying anything.

Again, Mom unfastened her seat belt and spun around, this time pointing a finger at Kyle. "What did you say? What did you say?"

"Geez, Mom. I said 'geez.'"

Dad glanced back in the rearview mirror at my sister. "Kyle May, put your seat belt on."

————

We had left on Thursday morning, two days after Mrs. Arthur called to ask if Lance had been to the house again. My mother was the one who answered the phone.

"Lance was here?"

I was at the kitchen table, trying not to attract attention to myself as I listened.

"He hit Brody? Oh my, Carol, I'm so sorry. No one told me."

After she hung up the phone, she ran past me (to my relief) and woke up my father, who had gone to bed early that night. A few seconds later, he came storming out in his blue bathrobe, tying it as he came into the kitchen. I wondered if he slept naked, my father, the fornicator. A few weeks ago, this would have surprised me.

Mother followed Dad into the kitchen, a few steps behind. "Where's your sister?" she asked.

I shrugged. "She went out."

"Out with who? When did she leave?"

"I don't know, Dad."

"Did you know about Lance coming to the house?"

"No." God forgive me, I had to lie.

We could hear tires spinning through the gravel in the driveway when Kyle got home a few hours later. Mom and Dad were waiting at the top of the stairs, firing questions at her as she walked in the door and kicked off her shoes. She did not come up the steps but remained below in her bare feet. She was surprisingly cooperative.

"Was Lance here on Sunday?"

"Yeah."

"What did he do?"

"Nothing. Well, he hit Brody. But other than that, nothing."

"Why was he here?"

"I don't know."

"Why didn't you tell us?"

"I just didn't want to worry you."

"What? You didn't want to *worry* us?"

"Sorry."

"Honey, he could have hurt you again. You should have told us."

"Sorry."

"I'm calling a lawyer tomorrow, Mr. Anderson from church. Will you talk to him?"

"Okay."

"I think we should file a restraining order."

"Okay."

Mom and Dad seemed pleased at this, not in a happy way, but in an official, serious way. They marched down the hallway and disappeared behind their bedroom door for the rest of the night. I waited at the top of the stairs as Kyle came up, looking beaten, even though she hadn't put up any fight at all.

"Kyle, please don't tell Mom and Dad I knew about it. I told them I didn't know."

She hoisted herself up the last step. "All right."

"Are you really going to do that restraining order?"

As she stepped into the light of the hallway, I could see her face. The makeup she had left the house in was now melted away, revealing the shadow of bruising around her eye. I had grown accustomed to the makeup. I winced. "Are you going to?"

"Mel, I'm so fucking drunk right now. I really don't care. I just want to go to bed."

The court date was set for Friday of the next week. When Mom and Dad found out that Mr. Anderson was out of town and wouldn't be back until then, they decided to pack up the minivan and head down to Kentucky for a week. They didn't trust any other lawyer with our personal problems, and they decided that they could miss play practice since neither of them had a major role. "Your mom just has to stand there and look pretty. I just have to look mean. I think we have it down by now," Dad said. I made a conscious effort not to bite my nails, thinking about Mom almost being "put away" because of him. But the worst thought of all was my mother ripping her nails off like that. I always thought I was the only one in the family who bit my nails. Kyle and Mom, for as long as I could remember, kept their fingernails long. But now my habit had become a terrifying inheritance, something that could take me over in just the same way, leaving me speechless and ripping at my own skin. I looked down at my hands. All my nails had been strictly disciplined for the past few weeks, chewed back whenever they tried to emerge from the raw stubs of my fingers.

We left Caitlyn with the Arthurs, who were more than happy to take her. Brody was going back to California in a few days. Jared stayed at home. He told Mom and Dad that he'd watch out for Lance, although I doubted he was even going to be at home most of the time. Laundry and food were all he was ever home for anyway.

My family had been to the Mammoth Caves many times over the years. Whenever Dad got an extended vacation, we went down to Kentucky to tour the caves. Overall, I had been there about six times, although I was too young to remember two of those times. The last trip down, I had just finished the sixth grade and was tired of the Mammoth Caves. Both Kyle and I complained, asking why we always had to go there for vacation. Kyle wanted to go to Florida. I wanted to go to Australia to see the Great Barrier Reef, but my family had never flown before. I knew they never would.

"There's over three hundred miles of underground caves in Mammoth, and that's just what they have mapped," Dad had said. "It's the largest cave system in the world, and I figure we've only seen about twenty miles of it. That won't do at all."

And so we kept going, each time taking different tours. We had taken the Historic Tour, the Frozen Niagara Tour, the Travertine Tour, the Grand Avenue Tour, the Making of Mammoth Tour, and lots of other tours not offered by the National Park Service but by small businesses in the surrounding towns. Businesses run by people whose families owned sections of the cave system way back when it was first discovered. This year I hoped we would finally take one of the lantern tours.

By the time we were three hours from the park, Kyle was still asleep and Mom, thankfully, had relaxed enough for a small nap. Having only two days to physically and mentally prepare for this trip, she had been tense the entire ride. Normally, she'd need at least six months' notice for an outing like this, but, she said, for the safety of her family, she was willing to change her schedule. It was not easy. But I knew that as soon as we were at the caves, she would calm down. Mother loved the caves and knew them well, having visited there more times than she could count.

With the car finally quiet, I slipped off my seat belt and slid to the front, careful not to wake my mother or sister. I leaned in close to my father's ear. His big, hairy ear that looked disgusting to me. But I had to ask him. It had to be done. I closed my eyes so I wouldn't have to look at him, to think of him with some other woman nibbling on that ear.

"Dad, can we please take the Violet City Lantern Tour this year? You promised last time we would do it next time, and it's next time now." I didn't like nagging and, worse, begging him to do me a favor, but I needed to establish a plan early, before Mom and Kyle voiced their preferences. Two weeks ago I would have put my hands on his neck to massage at his sunburned skin, watching the white marks from my fingers disappear as the blood returned, as he said yes to whatever I asked. But not now.

"Sure, Mel. We'll do that one this year. Now put your seat belt back on."

I had taken Darwin with me. Why, I don't know, but at the last minute of packing, I had stuffed it into my pillow, bringing it to sit next to me on the long car ride, like an old companion—like I used to bring my teddy bear along and strap him into a seat belt. I didn't plan on reading it necessarily, not after Pastor Lyle's message, but I figured, like any enemy, keeping it in sight was the best plan. The only problem was that I forgot to bring my Bible. I wondered what that meant, that in the haste of packing I had thought of Darwin and not God. What kind of person did that make me? But in the end, I decided not to worry about it. I didn't need my Bible because I wasn't going to read Darwin anyway. So he stayed zipped up in all those feathers, the corners working their way through to the surface and scratching at my head as I tried to sleep through most of Kentucky.

We arrived at the Cave Inn at around midnight. A busty teenaged girl at the front desk registered us. She had a clean and pretty face, her hair pulled smartly in a low ponytail as if daring me to find a single blemish on her. She wore a pressed blue suit with an orange scarf tied around her neck. The end of the scarf rested flat on the shelf of her chest, and I could not help but think of melons at the Food Lion. My dad saying that to my aunt Ann and my mom thinking he said it to her. I watched my father fiercely as he spoke with this girl, filling out the forms and making small talk about the caves. I watched his eyes for any sign of desire, that long, sexy *L* word from the Bible I couldn't remember. When she handed Dad back his credit card, he overreached and touched her fingers with his own. I shot a glance at Mom, who didn't seem to notice anything. She thanked the girl and smiled at her, the way she smiled at all young women who seemed to have it together. Dad had already stepped away from the desk and was picking up our luggage, his tired eyes showing no hint of betrayal.

As we walked down the hall to our room, Mom, calmed from her long nap, lingered behind me, scooping my hair up into her fingers and twisting it back, too tightly, behind my neck. I could feel my eyes pulling back and narrowing as she twisted.

"Mel, you should wear your hair back more. The kind of hair we have looks best when it's up. It would look so beautiful if you would just let me do it." Her fingernails scratched lightly down my neck as she situated a bun. I walked carefully so I wouldn't discourage her. "Will you let me do your hair tomorrow? I'll even use hair spray and one of my clips. The turquoise one."

"Okay." I couldn't remember the last time she'd done my hair.

She patted my shoulders, directing me to room 156. Dad was already fussing with the key in the lock, which gave in with a loud click. "After you, ladies." With a swooping hand gesture, he stepped aside, letting Kyle pass through first.

Our room was just big enough to hold two double beds, with a nightstand in between. Dad left us three inside while he went to pull the car around and get the rest of the luggage.

"Well, isn't this nice?" Mother was admiring the mini coffee maker in the bathroom, which was big enough to make a cup at a time. When she came out of the bathroom, she found me and Kyle plopped down on our bed, sprawled out and staring at the ceiling.

"Oh no," Mom gasped, rushing over. "Get up, get up. Please!" She grabbed our arms and pulled us up. "Don't lie on that comforter. They don't hardly ever wash those. Don't you know?" She lifted a corner of the paisley-printed comforter between her long nails and pulled the whole thing onto the floor. "You could catch scabies or something. Ugh!" She shuddered and moved over to the other bed to do away with the second one.

We slept under the coolness of stiff white sheets, the fabric light and teasing my skin as it shifted over my body in peaks and valleys every time my sister moved. She had always been a restless sleeper. We shared a bed often when we were young, whenever I wet my bed in the middle of the night. I would curl up to her, changing my position to fit with hers as she thrashed around all night, not even noticing me until the morning. "Eew, you smell like piss, Mel," she'd say. But she would never kick me out.

It was always difficult for me to sleep in hotel rooms, with my sister's restlessness and my parents a few feet over. Even more disturbing than seeing my parents in bed together was the thought of having them hear me moan or say something awful in my sleep. Maybe swearing or saying one of those words I looked up in the dictionary. And even if I wanted to sleep, I wouldn't be able to. My mother had this awful habit of bouncing her foot while she slept, making the bed and, it seemed, the entire room shake with it. And Jared, usually sleeping on the floor in between the beds, would whisper under his breath. "Christ, Mom, just cut it out."

But there was no Jared this time. Lying there with everyone asleep around me, I missed him. I missed his being unable to sleep, too, through the instinctual movements of our family. Dad's uneasy half-snore like a steady background to my mother's and sister's thrashing movements, their erratic breathing, the kicking.

I lay on my back for a long time, just looking at where I knew the ceiling should be. I thought of my glow-powder experiment and how it had utterly failed. I didn't know what went wrong, but that night after I had painted my rules on the ceiling, when I turned off the light, I was greeted by gibberish. Only a few smudges glowing so faintly that I had to squint to see them. They seemed green to me, not blue like they were supposed to be. I was still trying to decide what this meant, if it meant anything at all. I had stared at these smudges for hours, trying to find a word, a picture, anything that God might be trying to tell me.

I woke in the very early morning with my sister curled up to my back, her shallow breath in my ear, making the air around me sour. Her hand had somehow worked its way up my shirt, just far enough that her fingers rested in the hollow right below my sternum. She was calm now, her breath even, her body perfectly still. I didn't want to disturb her, so I stayed there in her embrace. I could feel her heart beat steadily against my back for a good half hour until the air turned from dark blue to dusky brown, until she kicked away and settled back on her side of the bed.

———

Mom and Dad wanted to do the Travertine Tour first. It was the easiest of the tours, no incline, all walkways, and led to the Snowball Room, which I had seen about a hundred times. The Travertine Tour was my mom's favorite, but I was sick of it, seeing the same rooms, the same old gypsum flowers. It was the tour all the old people and little kids took.

Mom, Dad, and Kyle left me in the hotel room, promising to be back by suppertime. We had just got out of bed at noon. "Don't worry, Mel," Dad said. "We'll take the Violet City Lantern Tour. We have all week to take all the tours we want." Mom and Kyle were lingering in the doorway, impatient to leave. "Are you sure you don't want to come? You can see the Snowball Room."

"No, Dad. I really need to do some reading." This was true, although I hadn't brought any other books but Darwin. There were a lot of other books on the reading list, but I hadn't gotten them yet. There was *Slaughterhouse-Five* and *Othello*. I wondered if this town had a library.

Dad gave me a kiss on the forehead. I did my best not to pull away, did my best not to think of him kissing all those women Jared told me about.

After they left I went down to the front desk to ask directions to the town library. The big-chested girl from the previous night was gone, replaced now by a small molelike man who was wearing the same blue suit, but with an orange tie instead of a scarf. "Can I help you, little lady?" he chimed, as if I were five years old. I did my best to ignore his tone.

"Can you tell me if there's a library around here?"

He squinted through his thick glasses, searching my face as he leafed through his own thoughts. "Well," he said, "I'm not really sure. Never had anyone ask about a library before. Donna!" He spun around to speak to a woman who was drinking coffee behind him. "You know anything about a library around here?"

Peering over her mug, she shook her head. "Maybe try the phone book?"

"Good thinking." He took the phone book from under the phone and flipped it open. "I think it would be in the yellow pages, right?" He was asking me now.

"Sure," I said.

After a moment he shook his head. "Nope. None close to here. There's one about a half hour away, in Brownsville."

><

FRIDAY, JUNE 21, 5:30 P.M.
CHAPTER V: *Laws of Variation (continued)*

Darwin has been to the Mammoth Caves in Kentucky! My family goes there for vacation every few years to tour the caves, and we are here right now. I think that this is a sign, being here while I'm reading about Darwin being here. Now I can really see what he saw, maybe check out his research methods and maybe even conduct some experiments of my own. He's not the only person who can come up with theories, and I'm positive that I can poke some holes through his argument with my own observations down here.

In this part of the chapter, Darwin talks more about the disuse of parts, about eyesight and the "effects of disuse" in the eyes. Darwin thinks that ordinary seeing animals in America slowly migrated by generations deeper into the Mammoth Caves because of fierce competition in the outside environment. This theory is supported by the very close similarities between the aboveground animals and the cave animals. When we go into the caves tomorrow, I will have to see if this is true. Maybe they have cave squirrels or something like that.

After many generations, the animals that went to the caves for protection lose their sight because their eyes aren't used in the caves. What is more helpful to them down there are superior senses of hearing or touch, so the animals evolve to have really good ears or very long antennae. These super-senses make up for the blindness and make it easy for the animals to live in the dark. So a lot of species that would have been extinct aboveground are able to survive because they moved down and adapted to the caves, where there is less competition and not many predators. This makes sense. There are a lot of biblical characters who went into caves for protection. Lot hid in caves with his family, and the five Amorite kings in Joshua hid in a cave. In 1 Samuel the Israeli army hid from the Philistines in caves when they saw they were outnumbered.

Not all blind animals are cave dwellers, but all cave dwellers are pretty much blind. Some animals, like bats, are blind because they are nocturnal. They live in the outside world, but because they only move at night, they are blind. Only going around at night and living in a cave are pretty much the same thing, as far as eyesight goes.

Darwin says that there are some cave species that have no members outside of the caves. This probably means that they were extinct on the outside and only survived in their protected cave homes.

Darwin explains that there are many types of blindness for these animals in the Mammoth Caves. They all seem to have had sight at one point, but over the generations it was lost. There are crabs in the Mammoth Caves that still have a foot stalk where the eye would be, but the actual eye is gone. The blindfish has absolutely no eyes. Their faces are blank, not even an indent where their eyes are supposed to be. The cave rat still has eyes, but they are blind. As Darwin said before, these rats still have the ability to see. If exposed to graduated light for about a month, they will regain "a dim perception of objects." I guess it all just depends on—

✦

When I heard Dad jiggling at the doorknob at six in the evening, I jumped out of bed, threw my notebook under the sheets, and stuffed Darwin back into my pillow, accidentally sending a flurry of feathers into the air. I zipped it back up and threw on the pillowcase just in time. When my family finally filed in, they stopped in the doorway to stare at the feathers drifting down around my head.

Kyle snorted, posed in the doorway in her cutoff shorts and tank top, her legs long and muscular. "You get in a fight with a bird?"

"What's going on, Mel?" My mother walked over to the bed, trying to pick feathers out of the air. I started to make a pile of them in my hands, scooping them up and taking them to the trash.

"Sorry. I was looking at the different kinds of feathers in my pillow. Look. There's black ones and brown and white. Are they all from the same kind of bird?"

"Ducks, I think," Dad said, still regarding me from the doorway.

"Oh. That's interesting," I said. "That's real interesting."

We didn't go on the Violet City Lantern Tour until Sunday. Saturday we all went on the Mammoth Caves Discovery Tour and the Self-Guided Tour. I hadn't seen any cave animals yet, not even as much as a cave spider. But I knew they were there somewhere, the blindfish and the crickets and the rats. I had seen pictures of them in the gift shops. The blindfish, I decided, looked just like the little minnows I sometimes used as bass bait, except for the no-eyes thing. It was incredible to see the pictures of it, the utter blankness of its face. But I needed to see one up close, to see the hard, scaly skin where the eyes were supposed to be, to really believe it.

I bought a postcard with a picture of a blindfish on it and sent it to Beth. On the back I wrote:

Dear Beth,

The blindfish (*Amblyopsis*): American animals, having in most cases ordinary powers of vision, slowly migrated by successive generations from the outer world into deeper and deeper recesses of the Kentucky caves. By the time that an animal has reached, after numberless generations, the deepest recesses, disuse will have more or less perfectly obliterated its eyes.

—Mel

On Sunday morning Dad pushed back our hotel window curtain to show me the bad weather. The clouds were all congealed, thick and dark. A few heavy drops splattered on the window. But Dad patted me on the back in a happy way. "That's the beauty of caves," he said. "It doesn't matter what's going on above, because below-ground it's always the same. If there was a tornado, we'd pack up and go on an extended tour, because there would be no safer place."

Before we got dressed, Dad offered to read a chapter of the Bible, it being Sunday and all. "We can have our own little church service here," he said, as he unzipped his Bible from his suitcase. There had been a Bible here all along. I had felt so guilty for reading Darwin all by itself, with nothing to counter it. Next time I read, I would have that Bible with me, I promised myself, just to be safe. Dad was thumbing through the pages now. One of the things I loved so much about the Bible was how thin the pages were, like onionskin. The care involved in just turning a page constantly reminded me of the importance of these words. God's words were almost too delicate for mortal hands. Pastor Lyle and the congregation treated them more like Silly Putty, I thought, throwing them around to let them bounce off the walls, stomped under dancing feet, chewed up, and spit out.

"What do you want to hear?"

Galatians immediately came to mind, but Mom came out of the bathroom smiling, her face gleaming with age-defying lotion. "I know what I want to hear," she chimed. "Mel, do the chapter on love. I just want to hear that, and I want Mel to recite it. Will you, please?"

Dad snapped his Bible shut. "That's a good one. Do that, Mel."

I sagged back into bed, saying nothing. I wanted to hear Galatians. I wanted to hear my father say "fornication" without the blood rushing to his face and him fumbling at the pages. And "wrath," I wanted him to say "wrath" and to think of my poor mother crouched under the kitchen table. I wanted him to choke up and not be able to go any further. I wanted him to fall on his knees in front of all of us and beg our forgiveness.

"Don't you remember it?" Mom asked.

"Of course I remember it," I snapped. I fixed my eyes on the ceiling to locate the words. "Do you want King James or NIV?"

Mom clapped her hands together softly and sat down on the bed next to Dad. "Oh, King James is so pretty. I want King James. Kyle, come in here, Mel's gonna preach to us."

I could hear Kyle rifling through her makeup bag in the bathroom. "I can hear her from in here, Mom. Go ahead, Mel."

King James was always much easier to recite than NIV. With NIV I would have to think of the words and try to remember the actual message of the verse. But with King James, all I needed was the first word, and the rest would just come out so easily, like a song. But for some reason, people were always more impressed with the King James, to hear a girl my age saying "doth" and "thee."

"Though I speak with the tongues of men and of angels, and have not charity—"

"Oh no, Mel," Mom piped. "Do 'love,' not 'charity.' It sounds better."

"But that's the NIV, Mom. Do you want the NIV, then?"

"No, no. I want the King James. But could you say 'love' instead of 'charity'?"

I sighed impatiently. "It's the same thing. Charity means love."

There was silence, except for Kyle combing her hair in the bathroom. I thought of Pastor Lyle standing up onstage while the golden collection plates circulated through the congregation, talking about giving to charity. I guess it wasn't the same thing at all anymore. "All right," I said. "I'll start over."

Mom and Dad both smiled and snuggled in closer to each other. Mom put her hand on Dad's lap, and he took it in his own. I didn't know the last time I had seen them holding hands.

"Though I speak with the tongues of men and of angels, and have not love, I am become as sounding brass, or a tinkling cymbal. And though I have the gift of prophecy, and understand all mysteries, and all knowledge; and though I have all faith, so that I could remove mountains, and have not love, I am nothing. And though I bestow all my goods to feed the poor, and though I give my body to be burned, and have not love, it profiteth me nothing. Love suffereth long, and is kind; love envieth not; love vaunteth not itself, is not puffed up. Doth not behave itself unseemly, seeketh not her own, is not easily provoked, thinketh no evil; Rejoiceth not in iniquity, but rejoiceth in truth; Beareth all things, believeth all things, hopeth all things, endureth all things. Love never faileth: but whether there be prophecies, they shall fail; whether there be tongues, they shall cease; whether there be knowledge, it shall vanish away. For we know in part, and we prophesy in part. But when that which is perfect is come, then that which is in part shall be done away. When I was a child, I spake as a child, I understood as a child, I thought as a child; but when I became a man, I put away childish things. For now we see through a glass, darkly; but then face to face: now I know in part; but then shall I know even as also I am known. And now abideth faith, hope, love, these three; but the greatest of these is love."

Mom and Dad both clapped as I rolled over and looked out the window, pretending to be checking on the weather. I could see our minivan in the parking lot, the bumper sticker in the back window that read "FAMILIES WHO PRAY TOGETHER STAY TOGETHER." But after a while, I could only see my own self in the window, the simplified reflection that did not show the tears welled up in the corners of my eyes. With a quick finger, I swept those corners dry.

"Mel, let me do your hair now," Mom said when I came out of the bathroom from brushing my teeth. She had a comb in one hand and a can of hair spray in the other. Her eyebrows were freshly drawn, replacing the old faded ones from the day before. She was wearing a dress, even though we were on vacation. "You'll look beautiful for your special tour. Here." She grabbed my arm and yanked me over to sit on her side of the bed as Kyle squeezed past to reclaim the bathroom. "You never do anything with your hair."

I braced myself as Mom situated herself behind me on the twisted sheets. Her fingers picked delicately at my scalp, the way she did when I had lice in the first grade. "I'm going to make a side part, starting right here." She placed the sharp, thin handle of the comb a little to the right of center. Starting at my hairline, she traced back with a surgeon's care and precision. I could feel the sections of hair falling against their will to the wrong sides, a slight ache in my scalp as Mom pushed them down. With this new part established, she just began ripping through my hair with the comb. "Don't you ever brush your hair?" She pulled the plastic teeth through, her hand hitting the mattress as she wrestled with the knots at the bottom. She pulled through the entire length of it with a sudden sense of urgency. I could feel hair ripping from my head but did not say anything. I stiffened my neck and leaned into my mother's force, just wanting it to be over. After a few minutes, I could feel Mother relax again behind me as she dipped the comb deep into my thick hair, running it all down my back, satisfied to find no resistance.

Mom gave me her hand mirror to see the back of my hair in the bathroom mirror. She had snaked various sections all around in braids and twists, all collected into a high bun. The front was clean and smooth, a perfectly straight side part, all stray hairs plastered down and gleaming like a newly waxed wood floor. I raised a hand to touch it. As I pressed down, it crinkled, making a noise like tissue paper. Kyle and Mom stood back to admire my new hair.

"Good job, Mom. She actually looks like a girl now. How does it feel, Mel?"

I walked over to sit on the bed again, afraid to move my head and mess it up. "Okay."

Kyle laughed. "You're walking like a pigeon. Try to look more natural."

I shrugged and lowered my new self onto the bed.

Mom's smile was almost bursting into teeth as she admired me. "You know, I think we could give her a little lipstick. Don't you think?"

As they worked on my face, Kyle licked her thumb and started smoothing out my eyebrows. She and Mother exchanged meaningful glances, but I shook my head and covered my eyebrows with my palms.

"No way," I said. "No."

The tour started at eleven. We waited at the visitors' center for the ranger with about forty other people crammed under the eaves. The sky was still thick with clouds, overcast in every direction. The rain was in no hurry, falling straight down in unimpressive drops. Ranger Rick came and saved us at exactly eleven o'clock, right when the drops started to take on weight. "All right, folks," he shouted. "Let's get this tour underground before this storm lets loose."

We entered at the Natural Entrance, the only known entrance to the cave for a long time. It wasn't as majestic as I remembered it from only a few years ago, much smaller actually, just big enough for a person to walk inside. It seemed almost accidental, the way it was overgrown, vines trying to mend the abrupt edges of rock. Ranger Rick said that it was discovered by a hunter in 1799 when a bear he was chasing sought shelter there.

Once we were inside, the rain was translated into sound, heavy resounding drops from dark crevices, the light trickle of water running off the entrance. Mom and Dad made their way to the back of the group to join me and Kyle as Ranger Rick proceeded through the Narrows.

According to Ranger Rick, the caves took two hundred fifty million years to develop. During that time Kentucky was farther south on the globe, about where the Bahamas are now. "Three hundred fifty million years ago, this was all covered in sea, a sea filled with shell animals." I glanced back at my parents, to see how they'd react to this information. They certainly didn't think the earth was that old. According to the Bible, it was only a few thousand years old. But Mom and Dad were lagging behind, looking down a dark corridor we had passed, not even hearing Ranger Rick's commentary. Did they think these caves could be made in a few thousand years? Did I?

I tried to imagine the span of two hundred fifty, even three hundred fifty million years. What the animals could have looked like, what they would look like now. I didn't know how much adaptation could take place over a period like that, although it was obvious that land animals couldn't have lived here during that time. And if this place had moved from a much warmer climate, wouldn't it just make sense that the types of animals who lived here would change? So sea animals and tropical animals lived here at one point, but they couldn't survive here now. That made sense. But the animals that were here now—did they evolve from the shells or did land animals migrate from other places?

"When the shell animals died, they collected on the bottom, layers and layers building up, with so much weight that the water was squeezed out to form limestone. Between five hundred and a thousand feet of limestone was deposited over the next seventy million years."

Seventy million years for all this. I decided that if seventy million years was enough time for the caves to develop, then in three hundred fifty million years anything could happen. But then again, it could have been that nothing happened at all.

Without a word, my family regrouped and proceeded down a dimly lit limestone corridor, high but narrow, cold but looking like warmed red clay under the weak wattage of the overhead lights. We followed Ranger Rick's voice, which echoed violently from unseen surfaces. Father in front, Mother, Kyle, and then me in single file. With a hand placed on either side of the chilled layers of rock, I ran my fingers along behind me, tracing the Narrows as if they could be read in Braille, the jagged painful ends of my nails catching on each syllable of a million years.

By the time all this limestone formed, there were tectonic shifts. This I could grasp. Their change disrupted the surface, causing the limestone to crack and allowing water inside. Over the years groundwater, which collected carbonic acid from decomposed life-forms, ran through these cracks, eating through the stone and making more cracks, according to Ranger Rick. Everyone in our tour was inspecting the ceiling as he explained this, searching out weaknesses in the structure, as if the water were a malicious predator—the concept of a million years failing them. As everyone looked up, I looked down to inspect the cracks in the floor where the water seeped into deeper layers. "These cracks eventually became passages. The water keeps working its way through, dropping down to levels as it works deeper into the rock. Currently, the fifth level is being carved out by the Echo River, three hundred sixty feet below the surface."

Again, the death of things. All of this cave, it seemed, was a product of death, even though weaker animals came here to avoid extinction. The dead shells packing down, the carbonic acid from dead animals carving it all out. And with Darwin, the death of animals is necessary for the survival of others. The cave animals, the blindfish, the beetles Darwin talked about are all a product of death. I wondered how death had suddenly become so useful a thing.

Underground the scenery changes dramatically, even violently. A narrow passage loses itself suddenly in high, rounded rooms. Smooth, caramel walls collide with jag-toothed formations. And all along it, a string of weak orange bulbs rounding corners, struggling against the predictability of a tour route. I watched my family in front of me, their heads almost bowed, reverent as they proceeded.

The limestone had been cut in many different ways by the water. Ranger Rick pointed out different alleys and routes as we moved along. Fast-moving water left steep inclines, winding curves and canyons, and even gravel-covered floors. Slow water made level floors, round passages. These places were preserved because of a layer of sandstone that now acts as a roof to the caves. Again, everyone looked up, including Mother, who nodded, her hands pressed together in appreciation. This sandstone prevented more rainwater from cutting through and eventually weakening the caves. If it weren't for this protective roof, the caves would have collapsed a long time ago. "That's why it's the largest cave system in the world," said Ranger Rick. "Time has virtually stopped here, preventing further erosion."

It all seemed contradictory to me: The formation of these caves depended on vast amounts of time, the accumulation of death, and now being protected from the very things that formed it. No carbonic acid was able to make it through. It seemed unnatural, the way it was now exempted from death, from the passage of time, even though that's the reason it existed at all.

The Rotunda Room we had all seen before, a large, rounded room, carved out by slow water and used in the 1880s to make gunpowder. The old vats were still in place, huge and wooden, where cave soil was soaked and dried. About four thousand years ago, the Adena Indians found shelter in these caves. They did not explore far, maybe three miles, but they did mine the precious gypsum, which they thought had magical powers. When Ranger Rick said this, I thought of glow powder, how Jared said it came from caves, too. Maybe gypsum glows in the dark when you bring it to the surface, just like glow powder. I couldn't imagine anything else it could have done to make them think it was magical.

Unbuckling a flashlight from his belt, Ranger Rick shot a powerful small beam right above his head to illuminate small white blisters along the ceiling. He told us that in dry parts of the cave, water seeps through and deposits gypsum, which builds up around its center to form a snowball. As more gypsum builds up, forcing its way through, the snowball bursts into a flower. "Please don't touch the gypsum," he said with a serious face. "The oil and acid from skin stops gypsum from growing. And at a growth rate of a millimeter per century, these formations have been preserved for a long time."

As Ranger Rick led the group across the Rotunda Room, I stayed to look at the gypsum snowballs, flowers, and blisters, to see if they glowed from the flashlight shining on them. But it wasn't dark enough to be able to tell. They almost looked like marble decorations, out of place against the jagged limestone. There were a few lower flowers I could inspect up close, on tiptoe, studying their texture. It was strange to think that they didn't even belong here, their presence a fluke that has lasted thousands of years. But if you looked at it from my parents' idea of time, these gypsum formations may have been here since the beginning of the universe. A hundred years wasn't that long—it was like a second down here where formations took millions of years to take shape. Stepping into the path of a nearby lightbulb, I shaded myself and one of the flowers while

I raised a hand to touch it. It was rougher than I expected, like my mother's pumice stone. I quickly smeared my hand across its face, turned around, and trotted back toward the group, which was just leaving the Adena Indian display. Father spotted me and grabbed me by the hand to lead me to the front. I stiffened at first, thinking he might somehow feel the gypsum on my hand. But he didn't. The guilt on both our hands mingled warm and dry, his hand completely swallowing mine. I let him lead me. "Can you see, Mel? These are the people who used to live in here, look."

The mannequin's face was the color of the rock, a warm clay expression, staring off with wide eyes as he hoisted himself from a tight crevice. In his hand was clasped a chunk of fake gypsum, more yellow than the original. Only able to see his upper half, I wondered if they even bothered to make a lower half; if he was finally able to make it out of that wedge of rock, would he even have legs to walk away?

"We are unsure whether the Adenas actually lived inside the caves. We know they occasionally used them for shelter, even hiding from enemies."

Father was crouched down to my level, regarding the Adena man's face. "I think they lived here. Who wouldn't? It's so beautiful, isn't it? And they were protected from everything, from bad weather, from bears and other tribes. Especially other tribes. What do you think?"

I hesitated as the group shuffled off into another narrow passage. I stared into the mannequin's face, his eyes large and seeking light. I didn't think the Adenas lived in here. By the looks of the mannequin, their eyes were way too big for that. But Darwin never talked about people's eyes going away when they moved to caves, only animals. That seemed to be the problem with all this Darwin stuff, knowing whether changes that happened to animals could happen to people. "I don't know, Dad. It's so dark. How would they see?"

But he hadn't waited for an answer. He had already dropped my hand and was walking after the group. Mom and Kyle lingered behind to wait for us, their faces bland, expectant, like the Indian's. They were holding hands.

When we caught up with the group, Ranger Rick was clapping to get everyone's attention. "All right, folks. This is where the lantern tour begins. Everyone please stay put so I can distribute the lanterns. No one under thirteen can have a lantern, please, so don't ask. This is for your own safety. No one under thirteen, please."

As he zigzagged though the group, distributing lanterns, I moved over toward a dark gap low on the limestone wall. It was just big enough for me to crawl through. I placed a hand inside, watching the darkness nibble up my arm, until my entire forearm was completely gone. I regarded the stub of my elbow and imagined that my arm was amputated there. Focusing on the line of skin that divided me from the nothingness of the gap, I actually believed for a moment that my forearm was completely gone. What happened, I thought, when you couldn't see your own body? I wanted to crawl inside the opening and experience losing my entire self. Would I just be a soul, then? Disconnected from my body and merely existing without it? Or would I become sound, my body transformed into a sound wave that the animals in the cave could recognize? The faint intestinal grumblings, my breathing, my voice would become my face, the way I was perceived.

I jumped when Ranger Rick tapped me on the shoulder. I turned around to face him, my arm still extended into the hole. He smiled. "I wouldn't go sticking my arm in random holes like that," he said. "Something may just chomp it off." He winked and handed me a lantern, which I took dumbly. No one had ever mistaken me for being my own age before. I looked so young, people usually thought I was ten, sometimes younger. At some point Kyle had moved over beside me, or maybe she was there all along. She said, "I think Ranger Rick likes you, Mel." I turned to see her smiling dev-ilishly in the light of her lantern, holding it up to her face for effect.

I shrugged, only then remembering my morning makeover. I lifted my hand to my hair, feeling it stick to my fingers, damp from the rain but still plastered into shape. I felt silly all of a sudden, tour-ing a cave in gobs of makeup and hair spray, but thrilled at the same time. I actually looked like a teenager. And I had a lantern.

I followed my family into a dark passageway, where the long line of lanterns snaked downhill like a procession of fireflies. The mounted lightbulbs now gone, I lingered in the back, turning back-wards to watch my own lantern light move steadily along the walls, the last light in the procession. The darkness crept just a few feet be-hind me. The faster I walked, the faster it came, threatening to take over the small tail of light that I inhabited.

From the front of the line, Ranger Rick yelled for all of us to stop and inspect the corridor walls. "I bet you guys had no idea you were walking right through a hallway of fossils. Get in close to take a look." Everyone stopped where they were and stepped up to a section of the wall. I moved next to my family, who were running their fingers along the stone. Their mouths were open, paused in wonder. Mom was pointing out different shapes. Ranger Rick started to yell again, "There is a wealth of fossils in these caves, mostly crinoids, blastoids, gastropods, and sharks' teeth." Mother gasped, her lantern light faltering. I wondered how many people knew what a crinoid, or even a blastoid, was. No one asked, and I wasn't about to. Even Mom and Dad, who I knew had no idea what any of these fossils were, were rapt with the idea of them. The unpronounceable species, happy with the mystery of them, the mere fact that they would never know.

We proceeded, following the sound of Ranger Rick's narrative echoing back to us. "As you probably have figured out, animals who live in these caves do not need their sight. They have learned to rely on other senses to guide them through this underground world. They compensate with a superior sense of hearing, or even touch. A lot of animals down here have very large ears or long whiskers. There are over one hundred thirty species of regular inhabitants in these caves . . ." I lost his voice just then. He must have rounded a corner. Mom, Kyle, and Dad were taking their time, not caring if they heard Ranger Rick or not. I wanted to sprint ahead and catch all of it, but I couldn't. Mom would yell at me the second I tried, telling me to stop acting like a child and walk like everyone else. I stepped a few paces ahead of them, trying to hurry them along, but they were stubborn. Mom was wearing dress shoes, not to mention her dress. I strained an ear to hear something about otters and some kind of program to reintroduce them to the caves. We finally rounded the corner and were met with Ranger Rick's booming voice.

"Troglobites are by far the most interesting animals here, since they live their whole lives inside of the caves. They depend on the cave for shelter and food. They are extremely fragile animals who will die if ever forced to the surface, by a flood or some other source. There are about twenty-seven types of troglobites in these caves. Millipedes, flatworms, six kinds of beetles, and two types of water life, the blindfish and the white crayfish—"

"Do we get to see the blindfish?" I heard myself say. Everyone turned to look at me. Even my family seemed surprised.

Ranger Rick gave me a weird look, as if no one had ever asked him a question before. He paused to make out my face in the darkness before he answered, "No. They're in the Echo River, the lowest level of the cave system. It's all filled with water." Kyle snorted and Ranger Rick turned back to the rest of the group. "The interesting thing about the blindfish is that it has no eyes at all. It navigates its way through the water, finding food using small sensors on its head. The fish is only about the size of a human finger."

The people seemed unimpressed by this, more interested in the smoke names on the walls he had pointed out. Early explorers had written their names in smoke all over the caves. The smudged black letters were eerie looking, as if written by a ghost. I wanted to ask whether there was a type of seeing fish that lived on the surface that resembled the blindfish but didn't. I would have to find out myself. I scanned the floor, kicked at a few cracks, hoping to frighten a beetle or salamander into my lantern light. We were about two hours into the tour, the farthest down, the darkest, the coldest. The animals here would have smaller eyes, maybe, larger antennae, less color.

Elizabeth's Dome was a huge room, Ranger Rick assured us when we spilled out from a corridor into a wide space. He asked everyone to spread out over the chamber so we could see all of it. The crowd dispersed in every direction, Mom and Dad walking one way and Kyle in another. As the points of light moved out toward slowly materializing walls, I remained in the middle, as a sort of center. As the lanterns spread, I could make out the high-domed ceiling, the stalactites like rafters hanging down. It was huge, big enough to fit a thousand people, I thought. About as big as the sanctuary of the Church.

Lanterns swung around all over the room as people tried to extinguish the last bits of darkness left. After a few minutes of this, Ranger Rick spoke again. "Now, folks, I am going to ask you in a second to turn off all your lanterns. It is quite an experience being in total darkness, and you will experience no darkness greater in your life than this." I turned to locate my family but couldn't find them. "If you want to really experience the caves, you need to experience it with your ears, with touch. This is how the cave really looks. Everyone please switch off your lanterns."

One by one, clumps of darkness fell onto the room, some small, some whole sections going out at once. I was so busy watching the room disappear that I was the last one to turn off my lantern.

Complete silence. No one moved or spoke, as far as I could hear. I held my hand in front of my face and saw nothing. The room was no longer large; I could not feel the expanse of the ceiling above me, the walls. It wasn't small, either. There was absolutely nothing, no room, not even myself inside of it. I knelt down to touch the floor, gravel scraping against my fingertips, a faint noise. I closed my eyes and could not tell the difference. I could hear someone whispering from somewhere to my right and was relieved.

"All right, turn 'em back on," Ranger Rick's voice came, nearer than I thought. The room was filled with the clicking of starters before all the lights came on at once, including mine. As if someone had raised the houselights in a theater, the flames grew into an altogether insufficient light.

As the group moved on, I lingered in the dome, reassured by the warm lantern glow of the narrow exit as they left. Turning back to a wall, I held my lantern up to inspect some more fossils and wondered if they even looked like animals at all. They looked like a bunch of screws and coins embedded in rock—small spiraled cylinders and discs, looking almost rusted. I thought I could make out some vertebrae stacked and curved like a spine, like a question mark. Running my fingers along a series of them, left to right, I felt the bumps and indents of their bodies.

Finally turning away from the wall, I found myself alone, inhabiting only a small circle of light. The rest of Elizabeth's Dome had fallen away, existing only in my memory. I constructed the blackness into walls, a ceiling, a room made up from pure memory of sight. The far wall I figured to be about a hundred paces ahead, the exit about twenty to my left. I could feel the ground beneath me, the gravel grinding under my sneakers as I tested my feet. Stepping back to the wall, I lowered my lantern flame, watching the room shrink even more, closing into my circle, until the knob clicked off and I was left with only the wall pressing my back.

In this, nothing but black, I ventured, leaving my lantern on the ground against the wall. Counting ten steps out from the wall, holding my hands in front of me, or at least I thought I was. As far as I could tell, my hands weren't even there. Ten steps, feeling the gravel shift as I dragged my feet. I stopped to relocate myself, squinting to see any light from the exit, but there was none. Ten steps, I told myself, back to the lantern.

Standing there, I considered the possibilities in a room this size and decided to go on. A little tougher this time. Five steps to the right. I turned sharply on a heel and measured out the steps, casual, as if I were walking down the street. I stopped to relocate. Five steps back, ten steps to the left, and then the lantern. From there about twenty steps to the right to get to the exit. I repeated this again, feeling my lips mouth the words as I took twelve steps to the left. I stepped carefully this time, trying to make no noise at all, just feeling. The air was still and just too cold, as if I were in a huge refrigerator. I could feel the floor changing, less gravel now but deep cuts in the rock. I lifted my feet high over any possible obstacles, knowing that if I fell I could lose all orientation. On my twelfth step, thinking of the possibility of getting lost, I immediately swiveled and ran eight steps to the right. I was going to try to run all the way to the right wall, but my foot caught on something and made me stop short. I tried to calm myself. I tried not to think of what might happen next. I peered over my shoulder. Yes, that way. The lantern was definitely that way, and I wasn't even going to think of it being anywhere else.

I stopped breathing, just trying to hear something. Maybe the tour group, Ranger Rick's deep powerful voice. But there was nothing. This was the deepest silence I had ever experienced. I thought that not being able to see, I would be able to hear or even feel something, but the ground was now bald, refusing to exist under me. I couldn't even hear myself think in this silence. No more, I decided, trying to convince myself that I knew exactly where I was. No more.

I turned around and walked the eight steps back, turning and walking the twelve steps to the left, five to the right. The gravel returned, and I toed it as I considered my last steps back to the lantern. Ten steps to the left, casual steps. I retraced my retracing, making sure I hadn't lost myself somewhere along the way. If I had screwed up, if I took those ten steps and could not find the lantern, I would scream for help, I decided. I would scream complete nonsense until they found me. I didn't care.

I took nine steps and ran into a wall. Kicking a foot out to the right and left, there was no lantern. I swear I felt my heart fall down into my belly as I knelt down to the ground and swept my arms all around. I scooted over to my left and swept my hand again. Nothing. A bit more to the left and my fingertips brushed something warm, metallic. I grabbed the lantern, immediately dropping it and hearing it hit the ground. The metal roof was still burning hot. I brought my hand to my mouth and licked my palm as I reached out with my other hand to carefully find the handle. With the lantern now in my hand, I sat on the ground a moment to feel the fire burning through my palm and to consider my next move. I did not turn on the lantern. By now my eyes had adjusted to the darkness, not adjusting so I could see, but its complete impenetrability was no longer a lack of sight but an enhancement of my other senses. My right palm throbbed with pain, and I pressed it to the coolness of the limestone wall. I listened to the tiny sound of my hand touching the wall, the sound of my own heart in my ears. My ears felt like the ends of a stethoscope, my hand covered in raw newborn skin. The darkness was now like a cool bath, which I glided through with only a hint of resistance. Isaiah 42:16 came to mind just then, even though I hadn't thought of the verse in years: "I will lead the blind by ways they have not known, along unfamiliar paths I will guide them; I will turn the darkness into light before them and make the rough places smooth." I placed the lantern back on the ground and started from there, turning and stepping toward the exit.

I ran into a wall at twenty-four paces, feeling it with my hands, the cold, damp stone again a relief to my burning palm. Another verse from Isaiah came to me. I heard myself recite it out loud: "Like the blind we grope along the wall, feeling our way like men without eyes." The verse sounded so small and personal in the endless darkness. Hugging my body to the wall, I sidestepped twenty-three paces, groping for the exit. Not able to find it, I sidestepped back those twenty-three, stopped to relocate myself, and sidestepped to the left. At seven steps, my left hand fell into a gap. Easing myself into the hole, I traced it out with my arms, about five feet wide. I walked inside, bouncing side to side against the opposite walls with my outstretched arms, so not to lose track of the passage. I had no idea what I would do if it branched off.

There was a steady incline. I could feel the walls warming as I stumbled around curves and cleared debris with high steps. The passage narrowed, my arms shrinking in, still tracing the stone, smaller and smaller, until they were at my sides and I had to turn sideways to continue, the walls slimy wet now, warmer against my shirt.

I sensed the ceiling lowering, but I could not be sure. Reaching a hand upward, it caught nothing, and so I proceeded. This narrow passage, I decided, was too narrow for my parents to make it through, maybe even too narrow for my sister or for any of the adults in the tour group. I began to panic.

Reluctant to turn around, I quickened my steps, not caring if I stumbled, if the tight walls scraped me. Turning a sharp corner, still pressing uphill, my hair caught on something, a tree root maybe, and ripped out a section of my bun. I felt the hair release, falling in front of my eyes, but it didn't matter. My scalp eased under the reduced strain, a dull ache from the weight of my long hair spreading across my head. Raising a hand, I felt the damage and ripped the other half down.

Shouldering my way through, too frightened to care as the jagged ends of rock cut into my shoulders, I groped forward with my hands, feeling the tightness, the intricate details of the rock. Fossils lined the walls. Millions of them.

It seemed darker now, not dark like a lack of light, but dark like my own blindness. I widened my eyes, searching for anything that would convince me otherwise: a glimmer of light, a trace of glow powder in the walls that would outline the corridor, the fossils, and lead me in the right direction. But I knew down here it wouldn't glow. Not without ever being exposed to light. The stuff was naturally useless. I wished I had brought my charged powder with me, wished I hadn't wasted it on my ceiling like that. I would spread it on the rock with my hands, giving the cave form again, giving myself something to see.

It was useless to search the darkness ahead of me, so I turned my head and focused on the walls as I stumbled through my blindness. But without sight they weren't even walls, just obstacles my mind had put there to keep me on some sort of path. A path that I at first thought was leading me forward, but now it seemed to be going nowhere at all. But my legs just kept working, as if on a treadmill, frantic to gain distance. I kept my hands on the rock, hoping I could make the walls disappear. But then where would I be? How would I know where to go?

A hairpin turn now, to the left, and suddenly I glimpsed a sharp sword of light angling in from the left, about twenty yards straight ahead. I ran, the passage widening slightly to allow me to straighten, still feeling the walls scraping my shoulders. About halfway there, I tripped over a shift in the floor, falling to my knees and feeling the skin give way against the gravel. I crawled as I found my feet again, not stopping until my legs hit the light, my lower half returned to me, looking strange. The hole was about three feet wide, four feet or so from the ground, where I could see grass and twigs, glistening with water. It must have stopped raining. I lowered myself, feet first, dropping onto the ground and suddenly finding myself completely blinded with light. Nothing but light, not even sky or ground.

My eyelids immediately closed, injured from the sun's assault, or at least I believed it to be the sun. I felt as if my skin were sizzling. Raising a hand over my brow, I attempted to look around. Forms began to materialize, human forms, standing all around, still. Staring.

"Holy shit, Mel," a voice ventured, unsure of itself. A familiar voice.

Someone rushed over to help me up. It was Ranger Rick, I could see, his green uniform floating above me, lifting me to my feet.

I could see the tour group now, the familiar strangers all staring at me, and someone rushing forward. "What's the matter with you? What did you do?" It was my mother, flapping over in an awkward trot, running right past the sign that read "VIOLET CITY ENTRANCE." I had made it to the end of the tour.

She barreled right into me, my mother, screaming gibberish and smacking me hard, right across the face.

><>

MONDAY, JUNE 24, 11:30 A.M.
CHAPTER V: *Laws of Variation (continued)*

"Acclimitisation" is the term Darwin uses to describe how animals from one environment can still survive in a new environment completely different from the one they're used to. It's another type of adaptation that animals can go through to become better fitted for their environment. I believe this. I believe that animals can change and that they need to be fit to live where they live. But what about when the environment changes so much they can hardly keep up? How can we even know what "best fitted" means if things are always changing?

Darwin says that the ability to adjust to a different environment isn't rare. He says that there is a "common flexibility" in animals that only needs "peculiar circumstances" to be brought out. The conditions he's talking about, the "peculiar" and "extreme" ones, I wonder how often these occur. Once in a million years, or maybe every billion—the point is that with these huge shifts, only a tiny percentage of animals survive to even adapt.

Darwin mentions God for the first time on page 158. He argues that the evidence that species have developed out of other species is very strong, but that some people still argue that all animals were created independently. These people believe that the similarities between different remote species aren't inherited but merely chance. Darwin says that to believe this "makes the works of God a mere mockery and deception. I would almost as soon believe with the old and ignorant cosmogonists, that fossil shells had never lived, but had been created in stone so as to mock the shells living on the sea-shore." I remember when they found that Lucy skeleton, Mom told me that Satan would put fossils in the ground to trick us into thinking that things were different from how they actually were. She said this about carbon dating, too. According to the Bible, the earth is only five thousand years old, or something like that, but fossils in caves and carbon dating on dinosaurs and rocks tells us that it is much older. Mom said that carbon dating is wrong and that anyway our faith is stronger than the carbon in old rocks.

I wasn't allowed to go on any more tours. For the next three days, I stayed in the hotel room while Mom, Dad, and Kyle continued their exploration of the caves. I didn't really mind since this gave me time to read Darwin and try to find anything that contradicted what I had seen in the caves. My experience was limited, I knew, without actually seeing any of the animals. But I decided I would do my best. I also wrote more postcards to Beth, telling her about the cave rats and cave crabs and the blind cave insects. I didn't mention the play on Sunday, or Lance coming to the house, or getting lost in the caves. I let Darwin speak for me, copying down his descriptions of the animals on the front.

We would be back on Thursday night, the hearing against Lance being on Friday morning. No one told me what this hearing would entail, but I assumed that to obtain the restraining order there would have to be witnesses, and I would have to tell my parents that I saw all of it. I would have to swear on the Bible. I imagined myself on the witness stand, questions being asked about what Lance said to her, me having to repeat the words.

"'Fucking whore,'" I'd have to say. "He called her a 'fucking whore.'"

My parents in the audience, their faces, I have no idea what they would express.

"You heard him say 'fucking whore'?" The words coming out of Mr. Anderson's mouth, the judge's mouth, the opposing attorney. Repeated over and over.

I would nod.

"You heard him say 'fucking whore,' yes, I understand that. But what did you see?"

"What did I see?"

"Did you see Lance strike your sister, on that day or on the first of the month, when the initial assault supposedly took place?"

"No."

"Where were you when all this was going on?"

"Sleeping. Upstairs calling Brody."

"Which one?"

"The first time, probably sleeping. I don't know. She came home later. I wasn't there. The second time upstairs, calling Brody."

"So what, exactly, did you see?"

The numbers on the phone, the dial taking an eternity, my hand forcing the rotary around and back, around and back.

"Did you see Lance hit Brody?"

"No."

"But you were there?"

"Yes, but it was too fast to see. I was looking across the street."

"At what?"

Geese. I remembered now, I was watching geese landing on the pond across the street, their legs extended to meet the water, their wings open and finding wind in the still air.

"What exactly did you see? Did you see anything at all?"

The white pulse of my sister's Sunday pumps, running away. The blood on my shin. Geese landing. Yes, I clearly saw the geese landing.

×◯

TUESDAY, JUNE 25, 4:18 P.M.
CHAPTER VI: *Difficulties of the Theory*

Darwin thinks that people who argue that all animals were created separately by a superior Being who chooses which type of animal replaces another over time support his theory. It's all the same rules. I guess it just depends on whether you want to call the same process natural selection or God.

In a section called "Organs of Extreme Perfection and Complication," Darwin talks about the evolution of the eye, the most complex organ. There are many different kinds of eyes for different animals, so Darwin defines the simplest eye as a group of pigment cells that cannot really see. They can only tell light from dark. More complex eyes have optic nerves, lenses, and other stuff—I was just going to say that the human eye is the most complex, but I think that is just a habit, thinking like that. Actually, I think that some animals have much better sight than people do (like hawks). But whatever animal has the most complex eye, between that and the simplest eye, there are a ton that fall in the middle. Eyes seem to be linked by a bunch of stages of development, connecting the simplest eye to the most complex. There don't seem to be any "missing links" between them. A starfish has a transitional eye. It has the beginnings of a cornea that concentrates light but doesn't form a picture. In order to form a picture, all there needs to be is an optic nerve just the right distance from this concentrating apparatus. There are tons of animals with this nerve at varying distances from the "cornea," making some animals picture-seers and others somewhere just short of that. Once the perfect distance was achieved in certain animals, other things, like the pupils, can be added to make vision more perfect. In human embryos the eye seems to evolve from the very simple to the complex right in the womb. It begins as a group of epidermic cells that lie in a saclike fold of skin, and the "vitreous body" is formed from "embryonic subcutaneous tissue" (whatever that means). But the point is that the human eye is very simple in its beginnings. I can't help but think of the cave animals with perfectly good eyes that eventually lost their sight after moving into the caves. With them, the eye is evolving in the other way. But it is still evolving. I guess when you think of it this way, evolution and the second law of thermodynamics can go together. When things evolve, it doesn't necessarily mean things are getting more complex. But the second law of thermodynamics still seems go against a lot of things in nature: like reproduction and growth. When embryos grow, they get more complex as they turn into babies. This makes me think that maybe I've misunderstood the second law of thermodynamics. It's possible that this law isn't a biological law. It might have more to do with existing molecules and atoms and stuff and how they break down in individual animals as they get older, not the overall evolution of millions of generations of animals.

So these blind cave animals have evolved so they can live in the dark. I tried to see this for myself, but I didn't see any cave animals when I was down there. There are pictures of them, though. So I guess they do exist. But what about when they are brought into the light? Darwin said that after a month, they regain a dim perception of objects. But would that dim perception eventually become perfect sight? Do these animals have the ability for perfect sight? I wonder, either way, what would happen if they were thrown back into the cave. I bet they wouldn't want to go back.

⊂✕

On Tuesday night we went to eat at the Mammoth Buffet in Cave City. Mom, Dad, and Kyle had been out on the Great Onyx Lantern Tour and came back starving. Dad said the prayer over the food, battling with the pop music playing in the background, the bustle of customers in line for the buffet, the yelling that drifted in from the kitchen, demanding "more fucking baked beans." The buffet line snaked right by our table. I kept my eyes open during the prayer, trying to look natural. Everyone else, even Kyle, kept their eyes closed as Dad thanked God for His protection, for the wonderful food we were about to eat.

After the prayer Dad went over the details of the Great Onyx Lantern Tour, recapitulating with Kyle and Mom, but I knew it was only for my benefit.

"Those lantern tours are really the way to go, I think," he said through a mouth half-full of chicken wings. "You can experience the caves just like the olden times, how the explorers and Indians saw it."

Mom and Kyle didn't seem interested, but he continued. "You know what my favorite part was? Seeing those chirpless crickets." I stopped chewing. They had seen the crickets? "Those cave crickets look more like spiders than like crickets. Don't know why they call them crickets."

I was about to say something but didn't. Dad really didn't seem interested in knowing why, and I didn't feel like talking. So I just listened as he went on to describe the flowstone and gypsum deposits. Mom and Kyle ignored him, going back up to the buffet in the middle of his descriptions. He would look up after them and keep talking, as if talking to himself. I kept eating, pretending that I wasn't listening, but I was absorbing every word. I hoped he would talk more about the crickets or maybe some other cave animal he saw. His eyes looked tired, but his face was trying hard at enthusiasm. He was talking about the Tuberculosis Huts now, jabbing a chicken wing in the air for emphasis. "Wasn't that neat, the way all those TB patients lived down there?" He was asking Mom, who just nodded into her plate. I felt sorry for my father right then, the way he had to keep going, trying to get all the details in for me. I watched him fiddling with the food on his plate, not eating much as he spoke. He picked up a dinner roll and turned it over in his hands, only to discover that a bite had been taken out of it. He put it back on his plate.

"Could you imagine living down there?" he asked us.

A manager stopped by the table, asked if everything was okay.

"Great," my dad said. "Everything's great. Thank you. There are other towns. We don't have to do the National Park tours. We can see the Crystal Cave if we want. We haven't seen that one yet."

After a while Mom got impatient with Dad's summary and directed the conversation to more Biblical matters.

"These caves are beautiful," she said. "But I'm getting sick of all this scientific stuff. Slow change and millions of years." She waved a hand in the air, as if at a fly.

Dad nodded. "I know. It's a shame scientists are the only ones allowed to have an opinion on natural wonders. But I hear they've started Bible tours of the Grand Canyon. They need something like that down here."

Bible tours? Kentucky, I knew, certainly wasn't in the Bible.

What would a Bible tour of the caves be like? Probably a lot of talk about the Great Flood, although that seemed a little absurd. Thinking of the caves forming in just a few thousand years seemed too short a time, but forty days?

Dad sighed. "Well, what other tours are we going to take?"

"We could take the Travertine Tour again," Mom said. "I like that one."

Kyle sighed. "We've seen that one a million times."

"Well, we've been on all of them, sweetie. What else do you want?"

Kyle wrinkled her nose; Dad started eating again. I kept quiet, stirring my mashed potatoes, making gravy rivers with my fork. Overhead the toy train passed by again, the track set up just below the ceiling, all around the restaurant. Around and around. Mom smiled at it.

The only National Park tours they hadn't been on were the Wild Cave Tour and the Trog Tour. The Wild Cave was only for experienced cavers, and you had to be at least sixteen to go. The Trog Tour was only for kids twelve and under. I was excluded from both, even though I knew I could definitely pass for twelve. I had planned on going on the Trog Tour to see the cave animals. A ranger would lead the kids around with flashlights to find the chirpless crickets, cave beetles, salamanders, maybe even the blindfish. I wanted to see the blindfish more than anything. But it didn't matter now. I couldn't go on any more tours. Mom and Dad (although mostly Mom) decided that I had to stay in the hotel room for the rest of the vacation. And there was nothing I could say in my defense. Yes, I had been careless. Yes, I had cost them twenty dollars for the lost lantern. Yes, I could no longer be trusted to behave, and yes, I could have been lost forever in those caves. What would have happened to me if I had wandered into some unmapped section of the caves? Crawling around on the ground like an animal, eating cave crickets, and making up my own language to talk to myself. I imagined what I would look like without eyes, my face blank, eyebrows arched over nothing. The slow process of blindness as the skin grew over my eyeballs and thickened. Would I even be able to tell or would I have forgotten by then what sight was?

As I spread my mashed potatoes evenly over my plate, stretching my gravy into the longest and shallowest river possible, my family continued their dialogue, which I didn't even hear. Using my fork, I then scraped away layers of potato, eroding bit by bit until there was no river left, just a big pile of brown mush, a muddled sea too watery to be land and too solid to be water. I then began pressing down with the bottom of my cup, trying to squeeze the gravy from the potatoes to make them solid again, but it would not separate.

Mother reached across the table and grabbed my wrist midtask. My fingers gave up the cup, dropping it on the table like a murder weapon. "That's just disgusting, Mel. Why don't you act your age for once, and stop playing these baby games. Really." Her face was twisted in real concern as she looked down at my plate and then back up at me. "Unbelievable."

By the end of dinner, they decided to go on the Crystal Cave Tour the next morning. No one asked for my opinion. I knew I wouldn't be invited to come along, but that was fine. I wasn't interested in the Crystal Cave. I'd had enough caves to last me a lifetime.

><

WEDNESDAY, JUNE 26, 12:38 P.M.
CHAPTER VII: *Miscellaneous Objections to the Theory of Natural Selection*

I think it is possible that both God and natural selection exist. As long as there were a few single acts of creation, like Genesis says, I think it could have happened. Many people say that the seven days of creation weren't really days but more like "God days," which are much longer. To God, a day can be a million years. Pastor Lyle uses this argument to explain why Jesus hasn't come back yet. Jesus told His disciples He was coming back soon, but it has been thousands of years. So God days are different. This makes sense when you think of how long He has been around. The Bible says that on the third "day," plant life was created. On the fifth day, God made fish first and then birds. On the sixth day, He made land animals, and on the last day, He made people. This order seems to suggest progress in the complexity of the animals, although birds seem a little out of place. Darwin thinks that flying animals came from land animals (like the flying squirrel), which means they would have to be created after land animals, not before like the Bible says. But then again, he did give the example of flying fish. Flying fish could be the link that shows that birds came right after fish, and then the birds evolved into land animals. Darwin says that with birds like penguins and ostriches, their wings became useless and they started to hang out on land. So the progression from fish to bird to land animals could be correct according to Darwin. And so the evolution of animals follows the "seven-day plan" of Genesis. I guess those days were just a few million or a few billion years. As long as God supervised the whole thing, I don't see how it is bad to say that animals evolved from other animals. I guess you could say it is bad to think that God created imperfect animals that needed to adapt to the world, but Darwin says that life in the Middle East area hasn't evolved much for a long, long time. This is where life began, so maybe God did create perfect animals for this area. But when they started moving around the world to different climates, they needed to adapt. And this is how animals started to evolve. Animals created by God can change. Why not? And since man was created on the seventh day, is it that horrible to think that

maybe we were created from the animals God created before us? Ecclesiastes 3:18–20 says, "As for men, God tests
them so that they may see that they are like the animals.
Man's fate is like that of the animals; the same fate awaits
them both: As one dies, so dies the other. All have the same
breath; man has no advantage over the animal. Everything
is meaningless. All go to the same place; all come from dust,
and to dust all return." And if anything, doesn't evolution
show how elaborate and well thought-out God's plans are?
Instead of just making a man right away, He orchestrated
billions of years of change that led to the creation of man,
which I think is much harder to do.

∝

We headed back north on Thursday morning, rising with the sun
and packing up the minivan in a half-asleep stupor. I didn't even
change out of my pajamas but curled up in the back of the car with
my feather pillow.

I woke up around the Indiana border and could already sense a
change in my mother. She was uneasy, surveying the flattened landscape from the passenger seat, her head jerking around like a deer in
an open field. She read all the billboards aloud, until we passed the
one for the adult toys and videos store in Great Plains. Its place on the
side of the highway marked an uncomfortable silence in the car that
caused my mother to start pointing out interesting livestock instead.

"Ostriches!" she'd yell, snapping her head back to get a better
look as we passed. "That was an ostrich farm! Of all things!"

Turning to look out the back window, sure enough I saw a
bunch of ostriches, lined up along a fence, watching traffic. One of
them had its wings flapping, but they were useless, I knew. They
were kickers, not flyers, with extremely powerful legs and puny
wings. I wondered if they couldn't fly over the fence, why didn't
they just kick it down?

I nudged Kyle to wake her up. "See the ostriches?" I pointed, but they were already lost in the distance.

Without even raising her head, she rolled her eyes and said nothing, stretching her beautiful long legs out to rest her feet on the window.

As we passed through Indiana—the landscape becoming more familiar—I thought more about the verse from Ecclesiastes, the one that said man and animals are the same. Pastor Lyle and my Sunday school teachers always said that no one was sure who wrote Ecclesiastes. They said it was written by someone who had lost faith, who was questioning God and confused about his own purpose. But thinking of it now, the first verse of the book said that "the Son of David, king in Jerusalem" was the author. Then that had to be Solomon. That didn't make sense. Solomon was supposed to be one of the wisest men in the Bible. 1 Kings 4:29–30 proved that: "God gave Solomon wisdom and very great insight, and a breadth of understanding as measureless as the sand on the seashore. Solomon's wisdom was greater than the wisdom of all the men of the East, and greater than all the wisdom of Egypt." And anyway, how could something like that even make it into the Bible if it was written by a doubter? The entire Bible was supposed to be God-breathed, and so wasn't this passage just as valid as any other? Maybe even more so, since Solomon was obviously smarter than anyone else during that time. Maybe he was so smart that he thought of evolution thousands of years before Darwin did.

We arrived at my grandmother's house in time for dinner. My dad's mother, who smoked and drank beer. She lived in Franklin, about a half hour from Slow Rapids. Her house was almost two hundred years old, the oldest house I had ever been in. It was the house she was raised in by her mother.

She answered the door wearing all black, a leopard-print scarf tied around her neck. Her nails were painted red. "She's Catholic," my mother would say at times like these, like when I found Grandma's *National Enquirers* sitting on the toilet tank.

She posed in the doorway a moment, standing there like Kyle always did when she answered the front door to talk to Brody or the Jehovah's Witnesses. Her hand on her hip, Grandma took us all in at once and let out a raspy squeal. We stepped eagerly into the smell of pot roast, my stomach almost leaping up my throat from hunger. Grandma grabbed my face with both hands and kissed me on the mouth. She was a mouth kisser and always tasted like peppermint and charcoal. "You get prettier every time I see you. You got a boyfriend yet?"

I shook my head.

"Well, give them time, dear. Boys are a little slow." She winked at Kyle when she said this and bent down to straighten the entry rug. I could see her scalp through her hair, pink and tender through a delicate nest of dyed red curls. I winced, thinking of Grandpa ripping those curls out, my father sweeping them up off the floor.

"So how were the caves?" She walked toward the living room; we followed. "Did you see any bears?"

"Praise be to God, no," Dad said, sitting on the couch with a sigh. "Nothing like that."

The living-room walls were smoked nicotine yellow, with large squares of white. After Grandma's surgery a few years ago, Dad and I came to rearrange her furniture to make it easier for her to get around. After moving the couches and tables, we found we needed to move the clocks and pictures to correspond. Lifting them off their hooks, I remembered discovering the patches of clean white, which still lingered on the walls like ghosts. The octagonal shape of an antique clock that never worked loomed over my mother now, still present even though Grandma had thrown it away years ago.

Grandma lit a cigarette and continued talking to my father. The second she reached over toward the pack sitting on the coffee table, his smile fell into tired, loose pouches of skin around his mouth and eyes. She had learned to ignore his concern and kept talking, raising her voice to a slightly higher pitch just to show that he didn't move her. "I'd rather live five more years and be happy than live twenty more in misery," she told me once, soon after she got out of the hospital. "Some people get it in their heads that living as long as possible is what we all want. Hell, not me." She spoke to my father now, laughing loud and occasionally turning to me and Kyle to ask about our impression of the caves. She moved her head a lot as she spoke, turning it dramatically to suck on her cigarette. As she moved more, the pink surgery scar wriggled its way from underneath the leopard-print scarf tied loosely around her neck. Like a small finger placed at the hollow of her throat, extending each time she lifted her head to laugh out loud into the ceiling. I thought of the cigarettes I had won from Jared in poker, hidden in my crayon box. I would flush them down the toilet as soon as I got home, I told myself.

My mother didn't say anything all evening. She ate quietly, seated next to Dad at the dinner table. When the meal was over, she sat on the couch, still saying nothing, just staring at those white patches on the walls, watching them as if they were filling in with each cigarette Grandma tapped out of her pack. She was afraid of Grandma, I knew. The lightness with which Grandma treated everything, especially death, was a personal insult to her.

"I tell you," Grandma said at the dinner table, "if I ever see that Lance in the street, he better run for his life. He can't punch an old lady, but I can sure kick the shit out of him." She laughed.

Kyle caught my eye from across the table, both of us stifling laughter. Mom's and Dad's heads remained bowed, focused on their food.

I liked to go into Grandma's bedroom alone and look at things. Whenever we came, I would go in there and sift through her old dresses and jewelry boxes, things that belonged to her mother and a hand mirror that was once Babka's, who was her grandmother. She had old tins of face powder that smelled like dust and tubes of lipstick in the most scandalous colors: fire-engine red and even gold. Her perfumes leaked the faint smell of cleaning products, and the books she had were so old I was afraid to touch most of them. They were stuffed with flowers she had pressed so long ago that they had disintegrated into the pages.

I came in here after dinner, relieved to have a few moments to myself among these things, old things I could touch and smell that people long dead had touched and smelled. I liked to think of these things as existing longer than me, imagined them being used even before my parents were born. I wondered if anyone would ever look at my things in that way, maybe Caitlyn's grandchildren handling my hairbrush or one of my books as if it were something that had had a life of its own. And my life being something they could never comprehend, filled with these astonishingly everyday objects that I had used and thrown aside.

Grandma never minded me being in here alone and told me that if I saw anything I wanted, I could take it. But I was always afraid to take something out of this room and was even uneasy moving anything. Without picking up Babka's hand mirror, I would stretch myself up on tiptoe and peer into it laid flat on the high dresser. I would stare down at myself like this until my toes cramped and I couldn't hold myself up anymore. Moving anything, especially on this dresser, seemed wrong. Everything had its place, and none of those places had changed in the fourteen years of my life. The perfume bottles were lined up in perfect order, like an army of chess pieces that had never been played.

Grandma also had Babka's Polish Bible, the one she brought on the boat with her when she came to America. She traveled by train, then by boat, the whole trip taking about a month. She was nineteen and had in her possession two suitcases. What was in those suitcases I have no idea, except for the Polish Bible. I don't know if she ever read it on her trip, but I liked to think that she did. Taking the

Polish Bible off a shelf and fingering its delicate pages, I thought of the time I met Babka, when I was about five years old. She was one hundred two years old at the time and looked like she was made of papier-mâché. I sat across from her in the nursing home, wanting to say something, looking into that dry cobweb mouth of hers, but she had forgotten English long ago. Dad tried to explain to her who we were by using his hands, saying names and moving his fist down an imaginary line on his lap. I don't think she understood, but she nodded and then her eyes rolled back to somewhere else.

I sat on Grandma's bed awhile and looked through the Polish Bible. I recognized the letters and started sounding them out. Slowly, at first, then I picked up speed, not caring if I was right. When I read the letters quickly, it sounded like an actual language, like I knew what I was talking about. I started reading even faster, pleased at the result. It almost sounded like I was speaking in tongues at church. When I tired of this, I flipped through pages of gibberish, looking at the chapter headings and translating them into English, according to their order. I knew the word above the first chapter must have been the Polish word for "Genesis." The first word under that heading would be the Polish for "in"; the fourth word would be their word for "God." I wished I had been older when I met Babka. I could have used this Bible against my own to learn a few words to say to her. Maybe "I love you" or "Hello." I tried to find the Corinthians chapter on love, to find out how to say "love" or "charity" or whatever they called it, but I lost track of the order of books.

On her nightstand Grandma had a framed copy of the family tree that my father had compiled. He had given a copy to all of his brothers and sisters, too. Somehow he had found a picture of an oak tree that perfectly fit our family. The exact number of branches, each with a name next to it, none wasted. It was made before Caitlyn was born, so she wasn't on it. I was just a little twig on top, but that twig had a bud on it. What that meant, I wasn't sure, but I figured it was just a mistake.

I located Babka on the oak tree and counted four branches from me to her. She was so old, a hundred seven when she died. It seemed like there should be more than four branches' difference. With Darwin's Tree of Life, all the branches were different species that had taken over other species—all those branches competing for food. Some of them had to die so others could live. This oak tree sort of looked like that, like a bunch of branches competing for dominance, fighting each other for space. Jared, Kyle, and I were all crowded together on a little extension of my father's branch. Grandma's branch was thick, thick enough to support the eleven branches of her children and the thirty-seven grandchildren on top of that. On her half, the tree looked a little lopsided, even unnatural. I had never noticed that before. Dad probably went to a store where they would create a tree that looked just like your family, I decided. There could be no tree like this in nature. It was all deliberate. I looked again at the bud on my little twig and wondered what it could mean.

There was also a picture of Babka on Grandma's nightstand. I picked it up and lay back on the bed to stare at it awhile, just to make sure that I hadn't forgotten anything about her. She was nothing like the half-deflated old woman I had met in the nursing home. Here she was puffed up and proud, looking like she had just taken a deep breath and was holding it in forever. She was standing in a rickety doorway, wearing a dress down to her ankles. She had a boxy jaw, almost manlike. So heavy, it seemed to weigh down her entire face. Her hair was wound tightly back to reveal a wide forehead, a mole on her left temple. Her feet were set apart, one forward as if she were walking. Her hands were behind her back. She didn't look like the type of person who owned a hand mirror. She was far from beautiful and she knew it. I could tell by the way she glared down at me.

Now looking at her, I tried to picture her large, alert eyes crying as she said good-bye to her family, but it didn't seem right. She didn't leave her home to get a job. She left because she was angry at them, I suddenly decided. That's what Dad and Jared wouldn't tell me. She had hated her family. She hadn't cried at all. I wondered what she had said to them before she hopped on the boat to America, if anything. She was only nineteen, my sister's age. I imagined her telling them to take one last look, because that was it. They would never see her again.

"Mel, it's time to go. Say good-bye to Grandma."

I walked out of Grandma's bedroom to find my family waiting at the front door, the screen ajar against my sister's hip. Gram was in the kitchen washing dishes. Her hands, covered in thousands of tiny bubbles, reached down to give me a hug. "Nice to see you, dear."

Talking over her shoulder, I asked, "Grandma, what was Babka like?"

She pulled back to look at me, the water from her hands soaking through my clothes, warm. She searched my face a moment, as if looking for the answer. "She was a woman who should not, under any circumstance, have been fucked with."

V.

SAVING BETH

FRIDAY, JUNE 28, 12:00 A.M.
CHAPTER VIII: *Instinct*

There is a big difference between habit and instinct. Darwin says that an instinct is "an action . . . performed by an animal . . . without experience, and when performed by many individuals in the same way, without their knowing for what purpose it is performed." Habits are not like this. They are learned in some way, even though the learning and even the actual action may be unconscious. This makes sense. Instincts you are born with, and habits are formed by your environment. Habits are often associated with certain times and emotional states, like washing your hands after going to the bathroom or something like that. Sometimes habits are associated with other habits, too, so you get a whole string of habits that all go together, Darwin says. Like after you go to the bathroom, you crack the bathroom door open just a little, wash your hands three times, shake them dry, open the door the rest of the way with your hip, take a clean towel to dry your hands from the alcove, and then maybe put rubber gloves on your hands to keep them clean for the next hour or so, until you have to go to the bathroom again.

Things start to get a little fuzzy between habits and instincts. Darwin says that habitual actions can be inherited. When this happens, you can't tell the difference between habit and instinct. Like when a mother bites her nails and then her offspring gets the same habit. It gets a little confusing here, but I think I understand. He says that in changing environments, the change of instinct is profitable for a species, so instincts are improved upon by natural selection just like other physical things are. I don't understand how nail-biting could ever be advantageous, but the evolution of physical things, like wings and sight, are a lot of times brought on by different habits, like the use and disuse of parts in caves. So the evolution of instincts can also be affected by habit, but Darwin says that this doesn't happen very often.

✧

There was no trial. Mr. Anderson told my father over the phone that there was enough evidence to grant the restraining order. The judge had signed it earlier that morning, and the papers were in the process of being served to Lance. Fifty yards, I think it was. Lance was not allowed to come within fifty yards of my sister.

Mother was back to her usual self on Friday morning, flitting about the house, all afluster at the state in which we left. "Who left the curling iron plugged in?" she demanded, storming down the hallway to confront my sister, who was the only person in the family who even used a curling iron.

"It was off, Mom. It doesn't matter."

Already marching back from where she came, she yelled to the ceiling, "It could still burn the house down. We could have come home to smoldering ash, and I'm the only one who cares."

Kyle rolled her eyes.

"I can hear you!" Mom shouted from one of the bedrooms. "I can hear you thinking those curse words!"

When she ripped open a new pack of yellow rubber gloves, Dad announced he was taking Caitlyn to the park. By the time he left, she was scrutinizing every room, flipping light switches and opening doors with her elbow, touching clean things with her right elbow, touching the dirty with her left. She had already color-coded the hangers in the coat closet and was looking for anything else that was out of place. From the living room, I saw the bathroom light turn on and off three times before it decided to remain on. "Who left the toothpaste tube open?"

It was then that Kyle and I decided to leave. Without even saying good-bye to Mom, we slipped out the front door and almost ran right into Jared, who was on his way inside.

"Hey. How was Kentucky?" he asked, taking the door from Kyle and holding it open for us. He was wearing his white Lynxx jumper suit, zipped down in front to reveal a solid black T-shirt underneath. I wasn't used to seeing him in daylight like this and was struck by how exhausted he looked.

"Fine," Kyle said, not even looking at him.

"Where you guys going now?"

"Away from here," she said, rolling her eyes in the direction of the house.

"Aw, Christ."

All three of us were in Jared's Corolla, Jared driving, Kyle in the passenger seat, and me hunched in the back, battling for space with a mildew-smelling blanket and a pair of speakers. I was the only one who put on my seat belt. Dad had told me that I wasn't allowed to ride in Jared's car. Ever. "That car should be illegal to drive," he told my brother one day. "The bottom's completely rusted out; the exhaust flows in through the heating vents. It's a death trap."

My brother didn't seem to mind this. In fact, I think he enjoyed riding in a dangerous car. "It's better than riding in the minichurch," he said.

We drove on the highway. The entire car shook as we neared fifty, so loud that I couldn't hear what Kyle and Jared were talking about up front. I held on to the door, thinking of the bottom rusted out beneath me, the possibility of falling through onto the highway, run over by my own brother.

Right before we hit the county line, Jared exited. They must have been discussing where to go, since Kyle asked no questions. With the car settled into a more comfortable speed, the cab had become quiet again. My brother and sister were done talking. Jared flipped on the radio. We were in Beaufort, a sign announced. I leaned my head against the glass, wishing I had brought my pillow.

The Acawan River was the home of one of the few surviving covered bridges in the United States. Jared braked, easing the car on the single-lane bridge. I watched through the windshield, hoping another car wouldn't come through the other end. The car became dark under the wood roof. The tires rumbled along the planks as we coasted through the strobe light of passing windows. Light, dark, light, dark. I closed my eyes to keep from getting dizzy.

We came out the other end into full sunlight. Jared pulled over immediately and got out; Kyle and I followed him through some underbrush and toward the shore of the river. A few families were settled on beach chairs on the other side of the river, but we were alone on our side. Jared selected a rock and threw it across, watching it skip three times before sinking in the middle. Kyle did the same, hers only skipping twice. I sat down to watch them, my hand in my pocket, turning a Kentucky souvenir over and over in my palm. It cost me the whole three dollars I had won in poker.

The river was higher than usual; it had rained here during our vacation. The water spilled over large concrete slabs in a few places, showing us the real color of the water—a rusted orange. There were a few children who had waded out about knee-deep, holding on to each other in the current. Their parents kept yelling out to them, telling them not to go any deeper. The children waved, pretending not to hear and taking a few more steps out into the rush of cold water. There were a few fishermen perched on the side of the bridge, letting their lines run all the way down into the water. I had fished from there before. From that high you could see the silhouettes of the fish in that water and cast out near them. There was no guesswork, like in pond fishing. You could choose which fish you wanted to go for and get it most of the time. Kyle, Jared, and I watched as one of the men reeled a good-sized catfish up to the top of the bridge. The fish flopped on the hook, its mouth probably ripping from the weight of its body. I wondered what Beth was doing right then, if she'd received my postcards. Kyle and Jared were still throwing stones, trying to skip them all the way across.

Kyle was the first to speak. "Did Lance stop by during the week?"

Jared stiffened. His answer was uneasy, as if he were trying to turn back but couldn't. He threw the last stone in his handful and reached down for more. "Why do you even care?"

"I don't," she said, giving up on the stones and lowering herself onto the pebbled ground to take in the sun.

"Then don't fucking ask."

I moved over to sit near Kyle. We watched Jared hurl stones, not caring if they even skipped anymore.

Kyle sighed. "Don't swear in front of Mel."

"I don't care," I said. But no one paid attention.

Jared snorted. "Fine." He swiveled around to face us. "Let's not swear in front of Mel, but let's parade our fuck-ups in front of her. Introduce her to your sleaze-bag boyfriends, but for fuck's sake, don't fucking swear in front of her."

"I'm fine," I said. "I don't care."

"You're just like Mom, the way you let men suck all the self-esteem out of you."

"No, I'm not."

He raised his voice, his Adam's apple bobbing furiously as he spoke. "You're going to end up just like her, controlling your own pathetic little house, too afraid to walk out into the real world. Caught up in some reality some asshole has set up for you."

"No, she's not."

The family across the river was picking up their chairs, calling their kids in from the water. We all watched them move farther down the river, out of earshot.

"I love how I'm the fuck-up in the family," Jared snapped. "I'm the fuck-up because I don't believe in their petty little God, who makes sure that Mom's rice turns out for dinner, but who somehow missed Lance kicking the shit out of you—"

"God can't control everything," Kyle interjected. "I don't blame Him."

"I can't believe you've bought in to their shit, Kyle. It's pathetic you believe all that."

"I believe in God," I said.

"No, you don't. You just think you do."

Jared turned back to Kyle. "And it's not enough that you're fucking up your own life, but now you're fucking up Caitlyn's. You have to think of more than yourself, you know."

I thought of Caitlyn staying with the Arthurs all week, what she must have thought in that house that looked just like ours. Did she think we abandoned her?

"Oh, like you're one to talk, making Mom and Dad pull their hair out over you, making them bail you out of jail when you know they don't have the money. They should have let you rot there a few days. Maybe then you wouldn't feel so fucking privileged, so enlightened."

"You went to jail?"

Kyle jumped up from the ground, hoisting me up with her. "Why don't you fix your own life before preaching to me about mine."

She pulled me back toward the car, getting in the driver's seat and leaving me staring at her through the windshield. "Get in the fucking car," she yelled through the open window.

I climbed in, watching Jared's back, turned to us. He was probably wishing about now that he hadn't left his keys in the ignition, but he didn't come after us.

Fumbling for my seat belt, I clicked it on just in time for Kyle to drop the transmission. She didn't know how to drive stick.

The tow truck dropped us off at home. Me, Kyle, and Jared, and the man in the blue jumper with CARL stitched on his left breast pocket, all of us squeezed in the front, touching shoulders. He agreed to give us a lift when we said we didn't have any money for a cab. Since I was the smallest, I had to sit next to Carl, whose sweat-slicked forearms brushed mine each time he went to change gears. He looked down apologetically when it was decided I was to crawl in next to him, as if I were some sort of lady or something.

Kyle sat next to me, her head cocked slightly in my direction, whether that was to ignore Jared or to keep an eye on how Carl shifted gears for future reference, I wasn't sure. As soon as we had slid into the truck, she grabbed my hand and held it on her lap for Jared to see our solidarity. I let her hold it there, even though I wasn't on her side. I wasn't on her side, and I wasn't on Jared's side, either. There were no sides anymore.

To my relief, Carl didn't try to make small talk. I was grateful. I knew that Kyle would jump all over the opportunity to get in a few jabs at Jared, some subtle remarks that only family members would recognize. I didn't want her to use Carl like that. He seemed embarrassed enough by his grimy hands, his huge thighs rubbing against mine. I imagined the grease mark he would leave on my white jean shorts and felt my spine tingling.

When we walked in the front door, Jared immediately went downstairs, Kyle upstairs. I stayed in the foyer to take off my shoes and watch Carl pull out of the driveway before following my sister. I didn't know what I would say to Jared. I guess I would have to ask

Kyle what he went to jail for and then decide. If it was for fighting, I guess I could forgive him. But anything else, I didn't know.

I went immediately to my room, hoping that Kyle would be there sitting on my bed, ready to tell me all about it. But when I closed the door behind me, I found my mother there. Her head buried in my pillow, not moving. Darwin was still zipped up in there. She must have felt it.

"Mom?"

She turned to reveal a shiny wet cheek, her eyes swollen and red. She sat up and wiped her eyes with her thumbs. Seeing me clearly now, she put a stunned hand over her mouth and shook her head.

"Mom, what's wrong?" She had found Darwin.

Sniffling, she sat on the edge of the bed and spoke. "I was just cleaning in here. I was doing laundry." She paused as her throat spasmed around her next words. "I found something. I don't know. I—"

Darwin. She had found him, taking the pillowcase off; she had felt him hiding in all those feathers. She knew I was a heathen. It was all wrong, and it was bound to happen. All these false alarms, all the signs, God had been trying to show her, and now she knew. What had I been thinking? That it was all okay with Him? I had to stop doing this, putting words in His mouth and convincing myself it was all okay. Take it away, please. I almost smiled, thinking of her burning it in the fireplace, like she had burned my sister's Elton John posters.

Mother stood up and stretched a fist toward me, opening it. I watched something colorful bloom in her palm. A ragged flower, magenta. "Mel, what happened to you? Please tell me." She bit her lower lip, hard. "Did someone touch you?"

I stepped into her and took the thing from her hands. Dangling from my finger, it took shape. My underwear. It was the underwear

Beth and I had cut into a thong. It was frayed now, just a pile of loose threads held together by elastic.

"Baby. Who did this?" She knelt down, her face close to mine. A bead of blood quivered on her lip where she had bitten. "You need to tell me, sweetheart. Don't be afraid."

My mouth hung open, unable to come up with anything. My Lord, what could I say?

Mother's fingers pressed into my shoulders, kneading, squeezing tears up and behind my eyes. "Who did this to you?" Her eyes were now painfully empty of tears but still trying to cry. The violent blush of her cheeks had spread down her neck. I watched the blood collecting on her lip reach capacity and spill into her open mouth.

I held my head up and tried to balance my tears in my eyes, but they fell anyway. "Mom, it's nothing. I'm okay."

She didn't even hear me. Her eyes flicked vaguely around my face, taking nothing in. "You're ruined. My God, you're ruined." She bared her teeth, clenching down and shaking her head as if she were ripping apart flesh. I had never heard my mother take the Lord's name in vain before. I became afraid.

Her nails were now biting my arms as she shook me hard. "You have to tell me. Who ruined you? Who was it?"

My teeth clamped down on my unsuspecting tongue, which curled back into my mouth like a frightened animal. I stiffened, fighting her. "It's nothing, Mom. Beth and I cut them to make a thong. We were just fooling around. It was in Frederick's of Hollywood."

Her hands dropped to her side, setting me free so suddenly that I stumbled forward. Her eyes settled for a moment on my chest, heaving as I tried to fuel some more tears. But it was too late.

"You're a monster," she said, her mouth set in a straight line. Not even looking me in the eye, she got up and walked out of the room, closing the door behind her.

FRIDAY, JUNE 28, 9:00 P.M.
CHAPTER IX: *Hybridism*

I know what circular logic is, and Darwin talks about it when he tries to explain why different species can't reproduce with each other. He says that a lot of people say that different species couldn't be related because they can't reproduce together. Darwin says that this is stupid to say because most species are classified as separate based on the fact that they can't reproduce with each other. He doesn't say that it's circular logic, but it is. It makes me mad when people don't think about their arguments and just care about saying something cute or witty, or to say something just to be able to argue, but it ends up making no sense. A lot of people who opposed Darwin back then did this. Even I can see through their arguments. Like the guy who said that since giraffes evolved to have long necks because it was advantageous, why haven't all animals grown long necks? This is so stupid. And I guess this guy was a scientist. Isn't it obvious that if all animals had long necks, long necks wouldn't be advantageous anymore? All the food at the tops of trees would be eaten and the little shrubs would go uneaten. Short necks would then be advantageous. It's all really stupid and I don't think Darwin should have wasted his time even addressing this argument. It's like this guy didn't even read what Darwin wrote. How come people do this? They decide what something is about without even reading it, and then they come up with ridiculous reasons for why it's wrong. It's like all they care about is arguing with it, and they don't even bother to find out what it's really about. Even the Bible condemns doing that. In Jude, it says that false teachers "speak abusively against whatever they do not understand; and what things they do understand by instinct, like unreasoning animals—these are the very things that destroy them." So they condemn things they know nothing about and then participate in animalistic pleasures. That sounds familiar.

Darwin gives his principle of life at the end of this chapter, which begins to explain these "peculiar" and "extreme" circumstances that are so important to his theory and that he keeps mentioning. He says that "life depends on the incessant action and reaction of various forces, which, as throughout nature, are always tending towards an equilibrium; and when this tendency is slightly disturbed by any change, the vital forces gain in power."

I awoke to "The Lord Is on My Side" playing on my alarm clock. It was 7:30 and the first day of camp. As I rolled over to shut it off, I felt something crunch under me. It was Darwin. I had fallen asleep with six chapters to go. I picked up the book to inspect the damage. Over the course of the night, I had managed to rip a few pages and crease the rest of them. Smoothing the paper down over my lap, I sat up in bed and started reading chapter 10. I needed to be in Beaufort at nine o'clock for orientation, so I figured I had an hour to read as much as I could. I didn't think I had to have the whole thing read for today, but I wanted to be prepared just in case. No one else in the house was up, so I felt safe enough to read in the daylight.

At around eight I heard my sister's bed squeaking on the other side of the wall. I tried to ignore the sound of water in the bathroom as she brushed her teeth and took a shower. Self-exiled in my room all the day before, I hadn't spoken to or seen her since we had been dropped off by Carl. I was hoping she would come in to visit me, to tell me about Jared going to jail, but she didn't.

A few minutes after the water shut off, there was a knock on my door. Kyle was wrapped in a towel, her hair dripping off her shoulders. From across the room, I could smell the clean chemical scent of her skin mingling with my own musty night-sweat smell. Thick, like mildew. I didn't have time to shower.

Kyle smiled at me with a familiarity that caught me off guard. I glanced at the clock. It was 8:22.

"I need your help today." She was looking at the floor, wiggling her purple toes against the carpet. "I'm going back to Fort Wayne to get some of my stuff, some stuff for Caitlyn, too."

I looked down to reread a sentence. "Can't Jared go with you?"

"Fuck Jared."

"What about Mom?"

She rolled her eyes. "C'mon."

I closed Darwin and set him on my lap. "I can't. Today's the first day of camp. Orientation's in a half hour."

She paused a moment to adjust her towel. Her elbows tucked in at her sides, like wings. "It'll only take a couple hours. I just need to get some toys for Cait and my checkbook. That's all." She smiled again.

I knew I could spare those few hours, but I heard myself saying, "I have to go to this. I'm sorry."

She flapped her elbows once in protest as she stepped forward. "Mel, I can't go by myself."

"Then don't go today. Wait until someone can go with you."

"I have to go today. He has Sundays and Mondays off. He won't be home now."

"Then why are you so scared?" It came out too harshly. I felt tears welling in my eyes but kept my head down. I almost said yes right then, just to counteract those words, but my mouth was cemented shut.

"Forget it," she said.

I watched her feet shuffle out the door.

I sat there a moment holding Darwin tightly. The thick paper cover buckled and cracked in my hands. On the other side of the wall, I could hear Kyle rousing Caitlyn with soft cooing. A car horn blasted outside. My ride was waiting. Caitlyn began crying. I jumped out of bed, throwing my book to the ground. I was not yet dressed and had more than five chapters left.

Camp that day was as I expected. Orientation was useless and the eleven o'clock lunch was terrible. Hot dogs and French fries. Classes went until about five, and I sat in the back of each one, keeping my mouth shut and my books opened thoughtfully in front of me. If God really didn't want me to be here, I thought, this could work in my favor. I could still maintain some kind of innocence if I didn't participate. We wouldn't be covering Darwin for a while, which was a relief. It would give me time to think.

When I got home, Kyle wasn't there. When I mustered the courage to ask Mom where Kyle was, she said, without meeting my eyes, she hadn't come back from Fort Wayne yet. Hearing this, I felt my stomach drop. I was a monster, I knew. I deserved to have my mother ignore me. I deserved to be punished for all this. All these things I had done that I couldn't even keep track of anymore. Things were going to catch up to me very soon. Kyle hadn't come home, and I knew that it was God's punishment for me. He was going to make me think about my choices, my choice to go to camp and not go with her.

After dinner Mom and Dad left for their last dress rehearsal before opening night on Sunday. I went to my room to read. I would speak up in class tomorrow. I promised myself. If I was a monster, then there wasn't anything I could do about it now. Everything was already in place, I knew, and there was no changing it.

It wasn't difficult reading those last few chapters since I wouldn't have been able to sleep anyway. Maybe Lance had been home and something terrible happened. As I read, I envisioned every possible scenario, the film running in front of my mind as I plowed through the chapters. Lance beating her up again, Lance locking her in a room and holding her captive, Lance holding a gun to her head and telling her to get in his car, Lance tying her up and stripping her naked. Four chapters. I read each word furiously, failing to grasp the larger picture outside of single sentences. Everything was blurred in a nervous urgency that pushed me to the next page, the next. If God was going to punish me for reading, then I may as well get as much reading out of it as possible. I read until my eyes couldn't read anymore. Only then did I close the book and turn off my light. I lay there for hours, begging God to leave her alone, to keep this between me and Him, and listening for the sound of her tires on the gravel driveway. That loud grinding and popping that would finally allow me to sleep. It came at 4:30 A.M.

SUNDAY, JUNE 30, 7:00 A.M.
CHAPTERS X, XI, XII, XIII

Time is really incomprehensible to us humans. Darwin says that the geological records we humans keep are so incomplete that we can't figure anything out from them. He says that what we know is like reading a history of the world that is written in a changing dialogue, and of that history we have only the last volume, which only covers a few hundred years, and in that volume only a short chapter here and there remains, only a few lines to each page, and each word evolving through the chapters. And so when we read what we have, it is impossible to come up with a view of the world. It is impossible to come out with any answers. When we try to imagine the huge numbers that are the basis of geological time, "the consideration of these various facts impresses the mind almost in the same manner as does the vain endeavour to grapple with the idea of eternity." I can see this. I can see myself in bed trying to understand what it means to be in Heaven forever or what it means to be dead forever—depending on my mood. Darwin says that we look at time in years, but that it is a completely inadequate measure. He says to imagine a roll of paper eighty-three feet and four inches in length. When you mark off a tenth of an inch, that's one hundred years. The entire strip represents a million years. Babka's life would be that tenth of an inch. My life would only be a tenth of that tenth of an inch.

∝

At breakfast the next morning, Kyle poured milk over her Cheerios, stirred them around for a few minutes, and announced that she was going back to Fort Wayne to live with Lance. When Mom asked why she would do such a thing, she said just this: "He asked me to marry him." She shrugged and looked down into her bowl, continuing to stir with her spoon. My father excused himself from the kitchen table and disappeared behind the soft click of his bedroom door. I sat there a moment, unable to swallow. Then I went on eating until Mother hurriedly began clearing the table, taking my toast right from under my elbows.

No one helped her pack. Mom and Dad left for church a few minutes after her announcement, and I had to go to camp. I didn't want to go, but if I went, I wouldn't have to go to church. Mom and Dad said they would let me miss the morning service for classes if I came to their play that night and brought Beth. And even though I knew it was a sin, I decided that I would rather go to camp than go to church. If I had to hear one more sermon that God and Pastor Lyle intended just for me, I had no idea what I would do. I would lose all control and do something terrible, something that I couldn't help but do. I would lose control and it would not be because of the Holy Spirit. I had tried that. There was no repenting for me anymore. I had gone up to the altar after Pastor Lyle's "Test of False Prophets" sermon and tried to clean myself out, but God wouldn't have anything to do with me. I had relaxed my whole body and asked for the Holy Spirit to enter me, with my mouth and eyes open, breathing deeply, just begging. But nothing happened. I was beyond hope and even God knew it. I *was* a monster. Darwin was a permanent stain on my soul. I couldn't go to church, put up with that disappointment again. But camp wasn't much better either, with all these facts and words I had to remember. It was like I couldn't even think anymore with all these voices in my head. I didn't want any more of them. I just wanted to lie in bed and think of nothing for once. I wanted to feel the mattress beneath me and nothing else.

When I got home from camp in time for an early dinner, Kyle was already gone. Mom and Dad ate their dinners without saying much, just the prayer. Dad turned to me after a ten-minute silence. "How was camp?"

Classes had actually gone better that day. I sat closer to the front and raised my hand furiously. I wanted God to see it. I wanted Him to see that His punishment didn't bother me, and while everyone in church was singing, raising their hands to Heaven, I wanted Him to see me raising my hand in class. Not to Him, but to questions about the fish we were dissecting. About where the stomach was and the heart. I had cut up my perch in a new way, not like I was filleting it, but like I was a scientist. I saw organs I had never known fish had, organs like human organs. I saw the swim bladder that Darwin said is used as lungs in some fish. I had cut it out carefully and laid it on the dissection table. If He thought it didn't bother me, maybe He would send Kyle home.

I needed distraction. I found that when I didn't occupy myself with the lectures and the labs, I just replayed the previous day in my mind. I reconstructed that morning, where I would agree to help Kyle and we would buzz in and out of the apartment, paying Lance no mind. She would have done that if I had gone with her. She would have plowed right by him, calling him a no-good bastard and ignoring every word he said. We would have held our heads high and slammed the door behind us. We would have gone out to lunch. She would have splurged and taken me out to a nice restaurant, and we would have sat in some corner booth, powerful, refusing to even talk about him. We would have talked about the most trivial things, with sly smiles and nods that held a conversation all their own. Maybe I would even have told her about Mom and Dad being fornicators, and she'd just smile and nod, as if it really meant nothing. These are the thoughts that drove me deeper into the lessons of the day, deeper into the body of that poor perch, making me slice its tail off and pop its eyes out, just because. When I was done, it didn't even look like a fish anymore, it looked like roadkill. Like it had just grown legs, wandered out in the street, and got smashed by a pickup truck.

"Fine," I said.

Both Mom and Dad nodded, lifting their forks. Opening their mouths, chewing as if they didn't want to taste any of it.

＞○

SUNDAY, JUNE 30, 4:15 P.M.
CHAPTERS X, XI, XII, XIII (continued)

Darwin's concept of time makes right now pretty meaningless. It makes it hard to care what happens today and what happened yesterday. It makes it hard to believe that I actually cause some things to happen, although I guess I do. It's just that the things I affect don't really matter, which is hard to accept. But no matter how small the thing I do is, it affects other things. There can be chain reactions that go out and become bigger and bigger until it does matter. So something so small, one tiny wrong thing, leads to countless others, and eventually they add up to something. What that something is, I have no idea, but I think that people can do a lot more damage than Darwin says here. They don't do damage on their own, so much as they cause God to do damage. The things we do, I think, determine what God does. And God does matter. He can see all those millions and billions of tenths of a tenth of inches and pick out what you do. He can see them all at once and decide what He's going to do about every one. Sometimes we make God happy, and other times we make Him mad. But the point is that because of Him we matter. He makes us matter, although sometimes, like right now, I wish I didn't matter at all.

✁

I went fishing to get out of the house for a while, away from the whispering of my parents and their efforts to talk to me about Beth, how important this night was for her. I stood on the dock, just casting, not really wanting to catch anything. I got a few nibbles, but I couldn't bring myself to let them take the hook. I just kept reeling, just to reel, to look like I was fishing for whoever might be watching. Whenever I felt a nibble, I'd suddenly think of the tenderness of their little bass mouths, the hook inside, how I had the power to yank it through if I wanted. The pain must be awful, I thought, testing the side of my cheek with my tongue, finding a patch of raised, tender skin.

I heard the front door close. My brother, in his white Lynxx jumpsuit, was leaving for work. He saw me and immediately detoured, cutting through our front lawn, across the street, his jumpsuit swishing as he walked purposefully toward me. I stopped reeling, letting the lure sink in my imagination, down to the bottom of the pond to collect all kinds of muck and leaves. I watched the slightly rippled surface, trying to determine where, exactly, I had let the lure sink.

"Hey!" Jared yelled, collecting himself into a casual jog. "Hey!"

I turned around.

"Don't you ignore me." He fell back into a hurried walk and pointed in my direction. "You owe me five hundred dollars. I'm not fucking paying for that shit." He was shielding his eyes against the sun as he walked. "I don't have a car now, you understand? You *broke* my fucking car, and I can't get it fixed—" He stopped at the edge of the dock, squinted at me. "Christ, Mel. I thought you were Kyle."

"No," I said. "It's me."

He looked out over the water as if seeing it for the first time, shaking his head, reaching into the front of his jumpsuit for a pack of cigarettes. "Kyle doesn't fish, does she?"

"No. Not anymore."

"I thought that was funny, her fishing." He looked at me again, puzzled, fumbling with the package. "Where is she?"

"Gone," I said. "Gone back with Lance."

He didn't say anything at first, just nodded as he stabbed the cigarette into his mouth and lit it. He stepped onto the dock, making it sink a few inches into the water with a bubbly gush. "Well, fuck." He sighed, blowing that curse word right past my face, making me breathe it in. We stood there, side by side, him smoking and me just watching him smoke for a long time. I thought about that note he wrote about me, wondered what he could have come up with to explain everything, to explain me. I was about to ask him again what he had written, but I realized right then that it didn't matter. Instead, I heard myself ask, "Why did you go to jail, Jared?"

He didn't answer for a while, not until he had sucked that cigarette down to a stub and dropped it in the water. I watched a couple of bluegills rise to the surface to nibble at it a few times before they descended back into darkness. I wanted to reach in the water and scoop it out but found that I didn't care enough.

"You know, Monchi, I could tell you a lot of terrible shit about Kyle. She's not so sweet as you think she is." He paused to let me imagine this terrible shit, but I just wondered where he got the idea I thought she was sweet. "But I don't," he said. "I don't tell you these things. Do you know why?" He was staring down at me, his eyes perfectly clear of sarcasm.

"No."

"Because it's none of your fucking business."

I looked away.

"We all have our vices. I have mine, Mom and Dad have theirs, and you have your Darwin and that blue penis book of yours—"

I stiffened.

"And that's fine," he said. "That's fine."

At that moment my fishing pole went jumping from my hands, and I caught it just before it would have fallen into the water. I could see the line running out, so I jerked my hands instinctively to set the hook.

"I don't know how you do that," Jared said. "I thought you loved animals."

"I don't know, either." And I didn't. But I kept reeling anyway, the rod tip bent, the line taut and going in crazy circles. This was a young bass, I could tell. It fought the entire way, and all I could think of was that hook ripping through its mouth, how young fish never let that keep them from fighting. I could see its body flashing silver in the mucky water, about five feet in front of us now. I reeled a bit more and lifted it out and onto the dock, where it began flopping at our feet with its mouth opening and closing.

"It's a little one," Jared said.

"Yeah." I knelt down and placed a firm hand on its body, pinning it to the dock. I couldn't see the hook. I put a thumb in its mouth and held it up, like a fisherman on TV, which made its mouth open and its tail curl. I looked inside and could see the tender pink machinery of its insides. The gills and throat, looking almost like gears. The line, I could see, disappeared into the pink cushiony hole way in the back. Blood lined the opening. It had swallowed the hook.

"Get the pliers out of the tackle box," I told Jared.

The fish was utterly still, paralyzed by its own weight hanging off my thumb. Jared handed me the pliers, leaned over to peer into the bass's mouth. "Are you really going to get that thing out?" There was blood now dripping from the gills.

I opened the pliers slightly and moved them into the fish's mouth. Its eyes were perfectly round and unblinking, staring me down. I suddenly got the feeling that the fish could see me. Not just light and dark or outlines, but really see me. I didn't remember Darwin talking about fish eyes, but now looking at the veins and the pupils and the golden iris, I knew that this was a complex eye.

"Hand me the knife."

"Are you just going to kill it?" Jared gave me the knife. "Put it out of its misery."

I set the fish back down on the dock, which was dotted with blood. Returned to itself, it flopped and gasped again. I put my hand on top of it and pressed down, which caused a new rush of blood to flood from its gills. I pressed harder to keep the bass still while I repositioned the knife in my other hand and sliced the fishing line as close to the mouth as I could get. I stood up and let the fish flop across the dock and back into the water.

"I don't know how you do that," Jared said.

"I don't know, either."

"Can it live like that? With a hook in its stomach?"

"I don't know," I said, throwing the knife and the pliers back in the tackle box. I should have killed it, I decided. I imagined the hook traveling slowly through the fish's digestive system. Kneeling over the edge of the dock, I rinsed the blood and slime off my hands. The cigarette butt was out of reach now, riding the ripples I had caused out toward the center of the pond.

"I didn't kill anybody, or anything like that," Jared said to my back. "I drove my car down a sidewalk."

I lingered with my hands in the water. "Why did you do that?"

"Because I was drunk."

I got up and wiped my hands on the back of my jeans. Jared just stood there watching me, expecting me to say something, I guess, but I just picked up my pole to inspect the cut line and to consider whether I was going to tie another lure on and fish some more.

"I know you worry about me, Mel. I know you think I'm going to Hell. And I know you think you're going to Hell sometimes, too."

I selected a red rooster tail lure and began tying it on the line.

"Are you really going to fish again after that?"

I shrugged. He said, "Why do you want to go to Heaven so badly?"

I tightened the knot with my teeth, careful not to snag my lip on the hook. "Why wouldn't I want to go?" I asked.

"Because I don't think you'd like it."

I looked at him. His face was completely serious.

"Do you really want to go to Heaven and hang out with Pastor Lyle and Pat Robertson and all those pricks at church? Hell would be much more interesting, I think." He was smiling now. "Your Darwin will be there and Einstein. He was Jewish, Einstein. Jews don't believe in Jesus, you know." He paused to consider. "The Brontë sisters, I'm sure, are in Hell." How did he know about *Wuthering Heights,* I wondered. "And Shakespeare. Not that it really matters to me, but I know you'd want to meet those people. I really don't give a shit about poetry."

"Then why do you want to go to Hell so badly?" I asked, as I swiveled back and then cast my line out into the middle of the pond.

He put his hand on top of my head, as if he were palming a basketball, but then his fingers began petting my hair as I counted five seconds, just enough time to let the lure sink.

"Because you wouldn't last a minute there on your own," he said, staring off with me over the water, at nothing in particular.

×◯

SUNDAY, JUNE 30, 6:00 P.M.
CHAPTER XIV: *Mutual Affinities of Organic Beings*

The natural system is the system that scientists use to classify organisms (it uses order, family, genus, species, etc.). Darwin thinks that these classifications are actually trying to come up with a "community of descent," which means that it tries to relate animals to each other according to their common ancestors. He thinks that we don't realize we have been trying to do this, but unconsciously we have. In trying to classify animals by their common characteristics, we have been coming up with a family tree of descent, like his Tree of Life. In it, we rank some animals as more related than others. Animals are not classified by their looks. The mouse and the shrew look very similar, but they are classified very differently. This is because external appearances, like hair and feathers, are brought on by the environment. So they aren't important in classification. What is important are the unimportant body parts, the ones we think don't matter. Body parts that were once useful and have been phased out are what show us ancestral links. Like "bastard wings" in birds that don't help in flight and a lobe of lung in snakes.

This means that animals can look alike because they live in the same environment, but that doesn't mean they are the same. It's the things we can't see that show how we are really related to one another.

There is a rare butterfly in South America—a *Leptalis*—that moves around in big flocks with another butterfly, the *Ithomia*. The *Leptalis* is so similar looking to the *Ithomia* that even a collector can be fooled. These butterflies look a lot alike, but they are so different in structure that they not only belong to different genera, but to different families. This happens in at least ten other kinds of butterflies. The mocked and the mockers always inhabit the same region, "the mockers are almost invariably rare insects, the mocked in almost every case abound in swarms." The mocked are a distinct species and the mockers are varieties, which means that it is the mocker who has changed to conform to the larger group. "The form which is imitated keeps the usual dress of the group to which it belongs, whilst the counterfeiters have changed their dress and do not resemble their nearest allies."

There is a big advantage to mimicking, because the mocked are usually considered distasteful to predators, while the rare mockers are tasty. And so by resembling the gross-tasting butterflies, the mockers can survive in their hostile environment. Darwin says that a lot of weaker creatures work like this: "they are reduced, like most weak creatures, to trickery and dissimulation."

Beth and I stepped into the Church an hour before the play started, arriving with my parents early so they could get their makeup and such done. We found an empty classroom on the north side of the complex, away from the bustle of actors and technicians. It was my old first-grade classroom, where Mrs. Brattle had taught me to count by fives and tens. Obsessively moving clumps of beads, clicking from left to right. Ten, twenty, thirty, forty. And later counting them one by one to check the miracle of math. It was always correct. Five groups of ten always checked out to fifty, ten groups of five, the astonishingly same number. The important clicking of math as I transported huge numbers with a single finger. Thirty-five, even fifty beads became manageable. The abacus, I remembered, with multicolored wooden beads. An antique. I had the sudden urge to see it and touch it again. But the abacus was gone. And so was the entire school. Closed down a few years ago, propelling me into the public school system. My parents, I remembered, closed up in their bedroom, discussing the evils of a secular fifth grade. The things they would teach me about science and the world.

"Beth, what does your uncle do at Lynxx?"

She was looking in a closet and didn't even turn around when she answered. "He makes some kind of mixing agent. A chemical that lets you mix other things together that normally wouldn't mix. It keeps them from separating."

I nodded, thinking of glow paint and Twinkies.

"What's this?" Beth was pointing to a flag on the wall, hanging next to the American flag.

"That's the Christian flag," I said.

She touched it. Something I had never done before, although I had once pledged to it every morning. "It's silky," she said, stretching it out to inspect the cross, in the upper left, where the fifty stars would have been. "I never knew there was a Christian flag."

"I don't think Methodists have one. Here." I held out my hand to her, closed around the flat, circular rock I had kept in my pocket ever since we returned from Kentucky. "I got this for you in Kentucky." I actually hadn't gotten it for her. I got it for me. But suddenly I felt the need to give it to her. I had been turning it over and over in my palm for days now, had resisted the urge to skip it across the Acawan River. I felt I had gotten what I needed from it. Beth needed it now, I decided.

She took it from my hand and held it up to the light. "What is it?"

"A blastoid fossil from the gift shop." I liked saying that word, as if I knew what it really was. I took pleasure in Beth's confusion at the flat coinlike rock. "They're extinct," I said, jumping down from the desktop I was sitting on and making my way over to the bookshelves.

"Thanks, Mel." She placed the stone in her left breast pocket. Its dark body showed through her translucent white blouse. "I'll keep it forever."

Coming from anyone else, I wouldn't have believed it. But I knew Beth would never say something like that just to say it. "Let's look it up," she said, "in those encyclopedias." She pointed high on the bookshelf to a set of *God's World* encyclopedias. "It should be in there."

"Okay." I pushed a desk over and stood on top of it, stretching every inch of my body up toward the top shelf, on tiptoe, feeling my calves cramp. Still too high. Taking one foot and placing it a step above, on one of the shelves, I lifted myself off the desk, leaving my other foot dangling in the air as I tapped the corner of the *B* volume with a single finger. Wiggling it out of its position between *A* and *C,* I felt myself tipping slightly back. But I was still holding tight to the shelves. It took a moment for me to realize that the entire bookshelf was coming out from the wall. Beth screamed, rushing forward and tackling the bookshelf back against the wall with a violent snap. At just that moment, I found the binding with my finger and pulled the book out and away from me, sending it into the air, its hundreds of paper wings flapping vainly before it hit the floor.

"Blastoid" was not in the encyclopedia. It should have been somewhere between "Babel, the Tower of" and "Boaz."

"Well, anyway," I said, closing the book abruptly around the wrinkled pages. "Blastoids are really important. They may even be related to us."

"You believe that?" Beth was again looking at the stone, turning it over in the light. "I can't see it."

"It isn't something you can see. People can't see everything, you know."

∝ ⊃○

As the airplane took off, the family tipped back in their seats, shaking their legs so the folding chairs also shook, signifying turbulence. There were parents and two children, a boy and a girl. Twins, supposedly.

The father was a good-looking man, with a neatly trimmed goatee and mustache, small shoulders. His knees were large and knobby, though, propped up and apart as they bounced. He was wearing a Hawaiian shirt. They all were. They were on vacation.

The woman was striking in no way. Her head was down, tiny wrists placed on her lap. She was a mom, a loving mother. She did not speak.

The children were rowdy, looking off to the sides, marveling at the shrinking landscape. They looked about thirteen or so but acted like they were six. Airplanes were exciting like that, I guess. I had never flown before.

Just as everyone expected, something went wrong. We were all expecting it by now, after the appropriate dialogue. "I really had a good time at church last night," the father yelled over engine noise. "That play was really moving. Changed my life."

The little boy nodded. "I'm so glad I accepted Jesus into my heart. I feel so free. I just wish Mommy and Jen had, too." He leaned over to his mother, who just looked down to inspect her nails. Jen was the one to speak.

"We're going to. We just didn't feel like it. Next Sunday we will. It's a big decision, you know, and we had our doubts."

The mother nodded; the father shook his head in concern. The stage lights flickered and the speakers roared, causing them all to look around. As they did this, their knees started going like crazy, their chairs lurching. A small front speaker crackled.

"Ladies and gentlemen, we've had some trouble taking off. Flight attendants, please prepare for an emergency landing."

A woman in a blue suit walked onto the stage, passed by the family, checked to see if their seat belts were on, and exited. The mother had her head in her hands, crying. The children looked stunned, facing forward, holding hands. The father was gathering his family in his arms just as the lights went out and they all four screamed. Those screams were abruptly lost in the sound of the engine, twisting metal. And then the light came up, so fast and so bright that I felt a pain in the back of my eyeballs. The first thing I saw was my mother.

She was standing in the back row of female angels, off to the side, posed with her hands pressed together in front of her. She was in a place where no one else would have noticed her, but I knew where she was standing, and when the lights came up, my eyes were already there. Her face was blank, devout, not even looking at the family as they walked across the stage, dazed.

Saint Peter was in the center of the angels, behind a golden podium. He had a blond beard, curly hair, and a beer belly that sat high, right below his sternum. He wore glasses. You could tell by his face that he had some bad news.

He informed them that they were indeed dead, and that this was their final judgment. The family huddled together, as if they knew what was coming next.

Saint Peter continued, "All of you had the opportunity last night to accept Christ into your lives, to be born again in His blood. At the United Church of the Holy Pentecost in Slow Rapids, Indiana, you heard the Message. You heard Christ knocking on the door of your hearts." He looked down to consult his book. "Two of you answered; two of you denied Him." He removed his glasses, rubbed the pad prints on his nose, as if this job were getting to be too much for him. The way my dad always did. He raised a weary arm toward stage left, my right, where a burst of flame rose up in return. Real fire, at first, that died down and relinquished to a steady stage fire. Silky fabric illuminated red and blown by powerful fans. I wondered how they got ahold of a real fire like that.

The demons looked more like shadows than like demons, as least the way my mother described the demons she had seen in real life. These ones wore all black, even their faces and eyes covered in a translucent black material that allowed them to see us, but no one could see their faces. They had black stage makeup on underneath, so not even the peachiness of their skin showed. I picked my father out of the gang by his tall stature, the fullness of his beard behind the veil. He was limping grotesquely as some of the other younger demons turned somersaults. They were moaning and screaming gibberish. Satan didn't come out this time, but the demons were scary enough without him. The family cringed. The mother began screaming hysterically as she hid behind her husband.

After about a minute of struggle, the demons grabbed ahold of the mother and daughter. My father was the one who got the little girl, Jen. She kicked and screamed, but he didn't let go. Another demon came and grabbed her legs. They both carried her off together, with the mother being dragged a few feet behind. The angels, my mother, were still staring straight ahead, their hands pressed together.

"I love you, Dad, Jason!" Jen called right before she disappeared behind the wall of fire.

"I love you, Jen!"

The mother just screamed, kicking hysterically, biting at the shadows that couldn't be bitten. When she was gone, too, the stage lights came up a bit. I hadn't noticed they had been turned down. Saint Peter stepped out from behind his podium to console the father and son, collapsed into each other's arms.

"The Lord only has the power to save a few from the tortures of Hell. He would love to be able to accept everyone in His kingdom, but that is not possible. Only those who seek Him may enter, and you two have done so." He parted his arms, stretching them out like Christ on the cross. "You may enter Christ's kingdom."

The lights brightened even more, which I didn't think was possible. I squinted, seeing the angels finally come to life—their hands parting, their arms outstretched now to stage right to show the way to Heaven. They were all smiling now, even my mother, smiling down to watch the father and son walk offstage and toward a doorway of light. The emergency exit. I watched these angels, their coordinated movements, all in sync as they raised their arms, looked to their right, lowered their arms, and faced forward. My mother was a bit behind on this final movement, and I saw the glitter of her cheeks shimmer a second after everyone else's, her face turning directly to the audience and taking on full light a second before the entire sanctuary went black. End of act 1.

This darkness following bright light was so intense that I couldn't even see my knees as I looked down at my lap. The darkness was familiar, reminded me of something. I could feel my pupils, exhausted by constant exercise, widening, trying to reach something in this huge sanctuary. But nothing came through. Before my eyes could fully adjust, the light came up a bit, allowing me a dim perception of objects: heads, a thousand or more heads, all floating above the pews, still. All staring forward, not knowing what to do. After a few seconds, a single head in front stirred, looking around and then slowly raising, getting up. From there, a few in that area followed suit, finally allowing everyone to rise and make their way to the restroom, outside for some air. It was just dark enough that the white dashes of glow tape on the carpet could still guide them to the exits. I turned to get up and almost stumbled over Beth. I had forgotten she was there.

She was still staring forward, toward the stage, not even looking at me when I stepped on her feet. Her eyes sparkled with tears that I could tell she was trying to hold back, her head lifted slightly. Behind us, a child was screaming, just having seen his mother dragged off to Hell. Someone was comforting him, trying to convince him that she was just acting, that his mother was backstage getting ready for another scene in act 2. I plugged an ear against the noise.

"Can you believe they got ahold of a flame thrower or whatever that was? Don't you have to have some kind of license for that?" I said, trying to prod Beth into her usual sarcasm. She shook her head in response, still staring forward, her hands folded on her lap, saying nothing. I knew then that my parents' plan, that God's plan, was working.

When I first invited her to the play, I had been really excited at the opportunity to get her saved. I knew I had made a promise to God, but that wasn't the only reason. I did want Beth to be saved, I wanted her to go to Heaven, but now I wasn't sure what any of this even meant. Now, there was nothing but doubt and confusion. The past few weeks had been the worst of my life; I didn't want Beth to have to go through all of that. But I couldn't tell my parents I had changed my mind, and I couldn't break my promise to God, so I agreed to bring her. It was easier than saying no. I also didn't want to sit through the damn thing by myself. After seeing it for the past five years, I had forgotten how terrible I had felt the first few times. I always cried throughout the play, even though I knew what was coming. I knew the plane would crash, the store owner would be shot in the burglary. These familiar people onstage, dying. The parents of my peers, Sunday school teachers, even my own parents falling limp onstage over and over. Death was so frightening, and something that was coming to us all. My body would be rotting underground, but that didn't matter if my soul was in Heaven.

Seeing the play three or four times a week, I went up to altar call every night, in tears, Pastor Lyle pacing on the stage in front of us, calling on us all to repent.

But now, for some reason, all I could see was the absurdity of it all: How Satan had forgotten to take off his watch; how the demons had accidentally ripped Mrs. Bell's Easter dress to reveal a black bra strap; and how Mr. Cashuba, while being beaten by the demons, gave his three-year-old in the audience a covert thumbs-up to ensure her that he was indeed okay. I recalled my father pulling at Mrs. Bell's dress, as if he had been thinking lustful thoughts when he discovered her alluring underwear, so properly concealed under the cotton floral print with a neat doily woven up to the neck. Beth, I knew, had seen none of this.

There was no transitional stage for me. I hadn't gradually become indifferent to all this. Somehow, suddenly, this was all I could see. I couldn't believe that I had to keep myself from laughing when Tessa Goodman died in a car accident and was dragged away by demons. I knew if Jared were here, he would be laughing, too. And Kyle, if she were still home, would be crying.

I had no idea what to say to Beth. During that ten-minute intermission, I sat motionless beside her, listening to her breathe. I cursed myself for bringing her here, screaming the worst profanities in my mind with my hands folded quietly on my lap. No one knew. I looked so decent, dressed up to look like everyone else, wearing one of Kyle's old skirts.

I watched the newcomers returning to their seats after the houselights blinked three times. There were over a thousand members in the Church, but I could always tell who was a newcomer and who wasn't. I could tell who belonged. Everyone who didn't belong was almost always with someone who did. They followed behind, usually a little disoriented by the electric guitars and the speaking in tongues. Many of these newcomers were Catholic and had no idea whether these elaborate marathon services were worship or blasphemy. They usually sat in the back, waiting for Pastor Lyle to break out the snakes. I knew I looked like I belonged.

Every newcomer at the play was brought by somebody, somebody who thought they needed to be saved. I watched the church members side-glancing these guests every time Satan and his demons came out of the wings to drag another unsuspecting sinner away. I never looked at Beth during the play. I tried not to think of her in that way, as a newcomer. I had hoped that she was too smart for this. I thought, if anything, she would talk some sense into me.

But there was a chance that it was all true. Of course I thought of it. Every day. Every hour, lately. I still prayed at night, deliberated about what kind of sin would send me to Hell and what kind would be overlooked. Making my peace with God after reading Darwin, asking to be forgiven, although God had already let me know that Darwin wasn't forgivable. All those signs He had given me—the sermons, the close calls. Could I only be forgiven for the same sin a certain number of times? And those sins that didn't count, the ones that I couldn't find in the Bible, could they eventually add up to a sin that did count? How many? All these people around me—the members, Pastor Lyle—they all seemed to know, but there was no way I was going to ask whether reading Darwin but not believing him was a sin; I didn't believe him. Whether saying "fuck" was worth more damnation points than just thinking it. Suddenly, I started saying it over and over in my head: *fuck, fuck, fuck.* I looked over to Pastor Lyle's wife, walking by, leading a gaggle of Catholics back to their seats. As she passed, she looked at Beth, still teary-eyed, and gave me a smile and a wink. Immediately, I had the urge to throw myself over Beth, to hide her. But instead I smiled back. *Fuck, fuck, fuck.* It really was funny, but it also made me want to cry.

The lights came down on act 2 just as the last of the audience members were returning to their seats. I watched the uneasy silhouettes around me shift and settle into the darkness, just to be jolted a few seconds later with a blinding flash of light that introduced the next scene. The choking at the restaurant scene. I had known that it was coming, but I could not brace myself against the shock of the flashbulb. I jumped with the rest of the audience.

The second act went on for over an hour, reenacting every type of sudden death that could fall upon us. There was a construction site accident, lots of car accidents, murder, a heart attack, another plane wreck, a suicide. The little boy behind us was relieved to see his mother returned from Hell, but as she held a revolver up to her temple, he began to whimper over our shoulders.

The people were good, bad, young, old—all that mattered was whether they were saved. The old lady who had choked on the potato was such a nice old lady, lots of character development to show how she'd given her money to charity and had lots of grandchildren who loved her. But none of these things, not even adopting three orphans from China, could make up for her lack of salvation. All of these people ended up before Saint Peter, before my mother— forced into indifference by her angel's costume. All of these people were dragged away by my father, forced into ferocity by his demon getup. My mother was so beautiful, my father just a shadow. No one could touch him.

By the end of the play, Satan's black-and-red face paint had run all down his face, making him look even more menacing than before. Every time he came out with his entourage of demons to take away one of the really bad sinners, he looked more haggard, tired from turning cartwheels and screaming. With a thick finger thrust out past the edge of the stage, he delivered the last line of the play. The swirled mess of his face leaning out past the reach of the stage lights, suddenly shadow. "I'm coming for *you* next!" And with this, the stage went black.

A spotlight snapped on somewhere in the back of the sanctuary. The next thing we saw was Pastor Lyle in his purple suit standing in a bright circle, center stage. From the middle of the sanctuary, I could tell that he had stage makeup on, a little too much, the way his eyes stared out at us, looking much bigger than they actually were.

The lights did not come up, so not to break the mood. There was just the little island that Pastor Lyle inhabited, completely separate from the dark sea of the audience. No one moved. The shiny fabric streamers, which were meant to represent Hell, still flickered, stage left, to the industrial fan's low hum. Pastor Lyle stood there facing us, his face blank, as if he had been suddenly shoved out onto stage and expected to move us all to revolution.

And then, without warning, he leaped upon us with his teeth-baring smile. "The world is a confusing place, my friends." His voice was low and serious, although he was grinning like the Cheshire cat. He didn't look confused at all but sort of amused at the thought that we were. Everything seemed to make perfect sense to him. I envied him for it. "You will hear many things from many different people about what is right and what is wrong." Pause. "You will hear some people tell you that there is no ultimate truth, that what is right is merely subjective." He walked with measured steps, stage right. "People will try to convince you that there is no God, that the world is bound to nothing but our own selfish desires, that there is nothing more than life and death. That there are no consequences in death." Longer pause. "Let me tell you, my brothers and sisters, that the only words you can trust from these people are the words that flood from their mouths when they have to stand *right here* at judgment and explain to God why they denied Him all their lives!" A few *amens*, head nods across the audience. The people—most defined only by vague shadows, others by the mere fact that they were in the way of the spotlight—looked so tiny in the huge room. Overhead the rented network of theater lights arched its black skeleton over the audience, taking up the place where the aluminum cross was supposed to be. Beyond that the high-domed ceiling of the sanctuary was almost invisible, the rafters receding into nothing. I could just see the huge wooden supports hanging straight down from the ceiling like stalactites, their blunted ends hovering thirty or more feet above.

"Oh, the things they will say *then,* in front of God, begging for their lives," Pastor Lyle said, still smiling. "You can almost hear it, can't you?" I thought of Darwin at his judgment, what he would have said to God. Would he have been surprised to find himself in an afterlife? He never said that God didn't exist. I had the feeling that he didn't see God the same way that we did. Was that bad? Somehow I couldn't see him begging for his life.

"You can see them begging God's forgiveness, can't you? Can't you hear all the excuses? Some of you, even, can hear *yourselves* saying those things." He walked back to center stage.

He was right. I knew exactly what I would say to God. Pastor Lyle paused to allow me, to allow all of us, to imagine that conversation with God. I would remind God how I had asked for His salvation at least five hundred times and how that had to count for something, and how reading Darwin was just a way of getting to know my enemy. I knew that and He knew it.

Very softly now, a single note chimed on the piano, swelling into another note, and another, and then a guitar chord. I don't know how long that first note lasted. I couldn't recall any silence being broken. It was as if the music had always been there. Somehow, the musicians had crept onto the stage unnoticed, using the shadows to perform their art so subtly that it seemed woven into the air, into Pastor Lyle's speech.

"Tonight all of you have witnessed your own judgment in your own minds. You have seen yourselves standing right here. Which way you will go is something only you and God know." He walked down the stage steps and to the main floor, the spotlight following him. "Jesus said, 'For judgment I have come into this world, so that the blind will see and those who see will become blind.'"

Suddenly aware of the air-conditioning, my whole body shivered once. What did that verse mean? Was it better to be blind during life and then see at death, or the other way around? My muscles tightened as Pastor Lyle walked a few steps down one of the aisles and pointed to a specific person. Not me. "Some of you have been living on the edge of sin, flirting with the Devil. Letting him take advantage of you in ways that you can justify to yourselves. Immorality, doubt. God knows your hearts more than you yourselves know them."

My heart. I had always imagined my heart like a file cabinet, occasionally opened and perused by God, ordering files and making new ones. "There is only one way to be sure that your heart is right with the Lord. There is only one way to be sure that you will spend eternity with God. The Lord is knocking on the door of your heart right now. Will you answer?"

My chest *was* pounding, but from what I couldn't be sure.

"If you choose to accept Jesus as your Savior, please come up to the altar right now and ask Him into your heart."

Pastor Lyle strolled up the aisle as the music crescendoed into full song. At first the spotlight had a hard time keeping up with him and lagged a bit, focusing on people in the audience, as if they were particularly guilty of sin. They just bowed their heads in the light, looking pensive. All around the sanctuary, I could see the uncertain shadows of people. I, too, pressed my feet to the floor, ready to get up and walk to the front. Behind me the little boy was speaking. "Dad, I want to go up and see Mom." A slight rustling behind me and then their silhouettes drifting down the aisle toward the altar. The father's frame was massive and lumbering but still seemed to be directed by this tiny child pulling his arm. In every aisle people were now standing up and walking to the front. People of all ages, holding hands, weeping as they walked. My eyes, too, were glazed over, blurry with tears. I could see my parents up front, praying with some people I didn't recognize, illuminated by the light that signaled Pastor Lyle's return from his stroll. Some of the called were on their knees; some were waving a gentle hand toward the ceiling. One man was on all fours. After the flow of sinners dwindled to a stop, Pastor Lyle turned and walked up another aisle, taking the light with him.

"God loves every one of you. He loves you so much that He gave His only begotten son to die for you. Now, are you going to deny Him *your* love? I want everyone who has not accepted Christ to be saved today. I want there to be a celebration in Heaven for all of you who want to start down the right path. I want there to be no doubt in your minds that you are headed to Heaven when you die. I am going to count to five, and if you have not yet come up to receive Him, this is your last chance." A long exhausted breath. "One."

I felt my heart leap out of my chest.

"If you have not been leading the life that Jesus wants you to live, *now* is your chance to turn your life around." He paused, midstep, to watch about ten more people filter to the front of the sanctuary, and then he turned around and walked back. I looked down at the floor, at the dashes of glow tape that outlined the aisle, leading to the altar: God telling me I should go.

"Two. If you feel any doubt, any doubt at all as to your standing with God, come up now." Another pause. Another group, mostly children. Some of them I knew. Again Pastor Lyle walked across the front, to the other side of the sanctuary, and then turned up another aisle. My aisle.

"Three. If you want to come up and something is stopping you. If you feel your feet fighting to touch the ground, I want you to come up right now. That is Satan trying to keep his grip on you. Don't let Satan win your soul today. Don't let him taint your heart with doubt. Come up right now." An elderly couple, holding on to each other, shuffled to the front, followed by the Catholics and Pastor Lyle's wife, herding them with a gentle smile. I clasped my hands together, sliding the cold sweat across my skin. My feet, still tapping at the ground, were now going numb as Pastor Lyle cleared the aisle's halfway mark and continued walking.

"Four. This may be your last chance at salvation. Come and lay yourself across Christ's altar. You don't know if you will make it home tonight. You may die in a car accident; there may be a fire in your home. If you are thinking to yourself that you can wait until next week, *I am telling you that there is no guarantee of next week!*"

He was close now, only three rows in front of me, the spotlight grazing the darkness just a few feet away. My mind felt like a snapped reel. I thought of everything I was going to do this week, all the potential danger. Death was everywhere and I had been treating it way too lightly. I thought of the millions of shells collecting one atop the other in Kentucky, the mass grave, the carbonic acid of dead animals draining down, carving out stone. The monsters that died in those passages, the ones that lived and then died anyway. Myself, a monster wandering the caves with no eyes, hair all over my body, forgetting English.

"Jesus said, 'If you were blind, you would not be guilty of sin; but now that you claim you can see, your guilt remains.' Give up your sins tonight, my brothers and sisters. Don't let them keep you from Heaven."

I had sinned; I knew I had sinned when I was reading Darwin. I wasn't blind. I knew exactly what I had been doing. But God was supposed to forgive me; He always forgives. I remembered standing up at the altar just a few weeks ago and opening myself up to Him, begging Him to clean me out, to take me over and make me forget everything. But He had passed me by. Everyone around me was filled, and all I could do was stand there, completely empty, a husk. Then I knew that asking forgiveness was not enough, that putting Darwin away, even burning him in the fireplace, wasn't enough. What did He want from me?

To my right, I was suddenly aware of a movement. I knew. It was Beth. He wanted Beth. God was going to get His half of our agreement. I had completely forgotten she was there. Pastor Lyle was standing right outside our row now, looking down at Beth, the spotlight haloing him and her and me. He smiled at her and reached a hand down. And she took it. She was standing up. She had her hand closed up in his, and he was helping her up! Without thinking, I reached over and grabbed her arm, pulling her out of Pastor Lyle's hand and back down so hard that my shoulder popped painfully. She turned to me with a look of shock on her face.

"Five!" Pastor Lyle's voice crackled into his mic. I knew he was staring down at me, but I didn't even look at him. I just locked eyes with Beth.

I didn't know what to say. I could feel my own face looking back at her like a mirror, just as stunned at what I had done. I could feel her shaking, the veins in her wrist pounding, fighting my instinctual grip. She tried to squirm loose, but still I kept my fingers tight around her wrist, holding her down long after the spotlight had left, long after I had recited the Sinner's Prayer with Pastor Lyle and his new converts.

∝ ⊃⊂

I knew that as long as Beth was with me, I would be okay. Riding home from the play, my parents did not say a word. My father did not even look in the rearview mirror, probably afraid of what he'd see sitting in his backseat. They wouldn't want to scare Beth by yelling at me. After the play I had held her hand, pushed her through the church hallways, holding her in front of me like a shield. A shield against all the church members who had seen what I had done, all staring in disbelief at their Bible Quiz Champion, the girl who was destined to do great works for God. And now I had broken my promise to Him. I had snatched a soul from His hands.

I comforted myself with the possibility that what I had done was so unthinkable that a lot of people weren't sure they had seen it right.

But my parents knew. I had seen them talking to Pastor Lyle in the hallway, their heads bowed, ashamed. Something he said seemed to console them. When they found me hiding behind Beth in the hallway, they just herded us out to the parking lot, not saying a word.

Beth hadn't said anything, either. She had let me steer her around the Church. Now she was sitting next to me in the backseat of the minivan, completely silent. I had no idea what she was thinking of me. Maybe she was grateful that I had saved her from Pastor Lyle, but then again she might have decided, like everyone else, that I was evil.

We dropped Beth at home. My parents tried to be cheery and say good-bye, but it ended up sounding sarcastic. They told Beth she was welcome to come to church anytime, and she thanked them politely before sliding the door shut. We stayed parked in her driveway, all three of us watching her walk up to her house and take the key from her back pocket. She struggled with the lock for a few seconds and then disappeared inside the house. Only after she had closed the door behind her did my father put the car into reverse and back out into the street.

I was expecting something the second Beth was out of sight. For my mother to wheel around in her seat and slap me across the face, for my father to break down in tears, or at least for one of them to start screaming. But nothing happened. Dad drove slowly the entire way home, retracing my bus route in the dark, taking extra care around the turns. When we finally pulled into the empty driveway, I was too afraid to get out of the car. Mom and Dad got out, closing their doors, causing the cab to go dark while I just sat inside, wondering if Jared was home. His car was still at the shop, which meant that he could either be trapped at home now or out with friends. Dad came around to the side door and opened it, holding his hand out to me. He was still wearing all black.

"C'mon, sweetheart," he said, in a soft voice. "Let's go inside."

For a second I considered the possibility that they didn't know what happened. That maybe the spotlight had missed me somehow, that I had remained outside its border, swimming in darkness, and that no one had seen anything, just Pastor Lyle extending his hand to someone and nothing else. Maybe Pastor Lyle had taken pity on me and not told them. I felt my throat expand in relief as I took my father's hand and let him help me out of the car. Everything was back to normal.

But once we were out of the car, he didn't let go of my hand. He squeezed it hard, leading me to the front door, as if there were a chance I would try to run away. Mom walked carefully behind us, her angel costume swishing against her legs. The pressure of my father's grip was crushing my fingers together, although he walked slowly, no hurry or anger in his steps.

We stopped at the front door, the three of us in the soft circle of porch light as my father awkwardly fumbled for the keys with his one hand. I watched him try to sift through the various keys, and then he dropped them. Still, without letting go of me, he bent down, sorting through them on the ground and finding the house key before picking them up again. With the key in the lock, he turned the latch and pushed the door open in one motion.

Leading me up the stairs and through the dark hallway, no one turned on any of the lights until I was ushered into my bedroom. My mother turned on the light behind us, and suddenly we were all three in my cramped little bedroom, with nothing else to look at but the worn paperback lounging on my pillow, facedown and perfectly halved, waiting for my return.

My mouth fell open, but nothing, not even breath, came out. Every part of my body wanted to disappear at the same time, just leap down my throat and hide in my belly. A series of events that had been waiting for me all this time was now set in motion. Adrenaline rushed to the outer reaches of my body, my fingertips and toes, making me wonder if I had left it out on purpose. Maybe all along I had wanted to get caught.

My mother squeezed around us and picked the book up to look at it.

"Darwin," she said, with no expression at all on her face. She turned it over in her hands, inspecting it as if it were a piece of fruit at the grocery store. "Isn't that the guy who thinks God is a monkey?"

My father did not loosen his grip on my hand as my mother flipped quickly through the pages, checking to see if there was really writing inside. She must have seen my notes, the stars in the margins. She looked up at me as if I had stabbed her in the chest.

"Where did you get this?"

"I got it from the library," I said, deciding that was the most neutral answer. No one to blame, no one to punish.

Mother inspected the binding. "There's no label here." She opened it to the back. "There's no due-date sticker."

"I stole it," I heard myself say. "I stole it from the library and peeled off the stickers."

She stared down at the front of the book, the picture of the ship rocking on rough water. The horror of it seemed to overwhelm her for a moment. "Why are you reading this?" The thought of me as a heathen was clearly more distressing than the possibility that I was a thief. With my father still holding me at his side, I could feel my fingers going prickly and numb.

"I don't know," I said. "I just wanted to."

My mother's eyes drifted over to my father's. I couldn't see his expression as he stood next to me but could guess by the way she looked at him and shrank back that he was on the verge of something. He was going to snap, I knew it. Just like Jared told me. He was going to revert to his former self and start throwing things, hitting me. I was going to see the man who had been hiding in him all these years, the man who had made my mother chew all her nails off. I tensed my body in expectation and jumped when I heard the doorbell ring.

My father and I were now sitting on the edge of the bed, my hand still crumpled in his fist. I listened to the whispering at the front door, my mother speaking to whoever was there for a few minutes. And then I heard two sets of feet walking up the front stairs. When I saw him walk in with his purple suit and his Bible under his arm, I immediately began to cry. With my parents I had felt a dry-eyed intensity, a defensiveness, but now, with Pastor Lyle standing in the doorway, inspecting me, I felt like I was going to melt with shame.

His blond hair was spiked dark with sweat, his skin streaked with orange foundation. He must have come directly from the play, not even bothering to go home to wash off his stage makeup. He looked around my room, nodding, as if the walls themselves confirmed everything he believed about me. His outlined eyes coasted over the cream wallpaper, along the floor, and rested for a moment on a pile of dirty laundry in front of my closet. A dirty pair of white panties sprawled out on top in an obscene pose that revealed the sweat-stained crotch. He pursed his lips at them and then looked away, into a bare corner. I felt my face turn hot and was sure my father could feel the temperature rising in my fingers.

"Melanie," Pastor Lyle said, in that caramel prayer voice of his. He walked over and sat next to me on the bed. The springs moaned under his weight, making all of my muscles tense. The mattress sloped into him, and I had to lean slightly away to keep from falling into him. He was so close I could see a dimple on his left earlobe, where I could only guess his ear had once been pierced. I focused on it a moment, wondering what this could mean. I was picturing a gold hoop there when my father finally let go of my hand, got up from the bed, and walked out of the room with my mother, closing the door behind them.

My hand ached as I worked my fingers back to life. I breathed in deep to compose myself and got a lungful of Pastor Lyle's musty human scent. I swallowed, wondering if I was shaking visibly or if it was just in my head.

After a few moments of silence as I tried to clench my body still, Pastor Lyle shifted, turning to face me.

"Melanie, I know you haven't been feeling like yourself lately. Your mom told me a lot about what has been going on with you for the past few weeks. And now she tells me you've been reading that Darwin stuff."

I could feel his small eyes burning my skin, just begging me to look at him, but I just stared at the carpet, at my toes, which seemed much farther away from me than they really were.

"Do you know why you were reading that? Do you know why you have been fighting at school and curious about"—he paused—"ungodly things?"

I considered for a moment asking him whether by ungodly things he meant Darwin or thongs but thought better of it. My mind was on a rampage, no longer accountable to God or my parents or anyone. But Pastor Lyle was different. With his muscled arms and his loose hair, with that ghostly dent in his ear, I felt accountable to him. Right then I wanted nothing more than to please him.

"Melanie," he coaxed. The way he said my name made it sound like a song. "Do you know why you've been doing these things?"

I shook my head and bit my tongue, not letting myself say anything. I could feel the heat of him filling the room. It was so hot in this little room. I could feel moisture collecting under my arms, along my spine, in the down of my upper lip.

"That's what I thought," he said. "Sometimes people can't control what they are doing. And it's not their fault. You don't need to feel guilty for what's been going on. God does not hold you accountable. You haven't sinned, Melanie."

I couldn't believe what I was hearing. I would not be punished. I had no idea how this happened, but I was willing to accept it. My entire body relaxed with the sound of the words I somehow always suspected were true. It wasn't my fault.

"You haven't sinned, Melanie," he said again, pushing my shoulders back onto the bed. I let him ease me onto the mattress, completely relaxed, wondering whose fault it was. If they weren't my sins, whose were they?

Pastor Lyle leaned over me and brushed back a few stray hairs clinging to my forehead. I breathed him in again, filling my lungs. And then I held it in. Staring up at the ceiling, I found the spots where I had written down all of the possible sins in glow paint. They refused to appear in the dark, were invisible in the light. No one would ever see them. They weren't my sins. They didn't belong to me.

"I'm going to help, Melanie. If you want to be in control again, just lie still, and I'll help you." It was just like in my dreams, him hovering over me, sitting on my bed, speaking softly. He put a hand on my arm and I closed my eyes.

"Jesus Lord," he said, those two words making a slight breeze that cooled my neck. "I am asking for your help to clean out this little girl. She has been a faithful servant for you all her life, but now she needs your help." His sweaty fingers, which completely circled my upper arm, squeezed for emphasis. I half opened my eyes to look at him. His eyes were squeezed shut, his head thrust over my body. I could see a drop of sweat hanging on the end of his chin, a second away from falling on my chest. I closed my eyes again.

"Lord Jesus," he continued. "This girl has been *possessed* by an evil spirit, and we ask your help in casting him out."

My eyes flew open. "I felt him, Father," he said. "I felt his strength tonight. I fought him tonight, Jesus. I fought him for the soul of a little girl, but he was very strong. He *used* Melanie to snatch her from my grip. I felt his strength, felt the strength that could never be the strength of a young girl. Please, Lord, *release* Melanie from this evil demon."

I tried to pull my arm away, but Pastor Lyle pinned it down to the mattress. My clothes were sticking to me, my hair sweaty and matted around my neck. I looked down and could see my skirt bunched up around my thighs. My bare legs shiny and white, lying there useless like two broken sticks.

The heat in the room was unbearable. I tried to shift, but again Pastor Lyle leaned into me with his weight to keep me still. "With the help of the Lord, I will cast thee out, evil spirit. The Lord has ordered you to leave."

There was nothing to do. If I fought, it would only make things worse. Just lie here, I told myself. Just lie still and take it. This will be over soon. I closed my eyes again, trying to think of something else, something to take my mind off the heat, Pastor Lyle breathing above me. My thoughts curled back to Darwin, to his butterflies. He never described how they looked, but now I imagined them as being white. A huge flock of white butterflies with orange lacy patterns cluttered my mind, obscuring everything.

Pastor Lyle's words had no meaning; they were far away. I began to count the butterflies, even though there were too many to count. But then I felt something slap my chest and I opened my eyes. Pastor Lyle's hand was holding me down by my chest, his fingers spread and tense like claws. His thumb and pinkie stretched out over each of my breasts possessively. "Release her heart. I command you to release her heart!"

Something in me panicked, and I tried to force myself up on my elbows. The heat, the pressure of his body on my chest. He threw me back on the bed, but I tried to get up again. With his eyes still closed, Pastor Lyle put his other hand on my chest and pushed me down. *"Release her!"* he cried, his face down close to me now, almost smothered in my neck. The orange foundation had turned to sludge on his cheeks, making his whole face look like melting clay. I kicked a leg and tried to roll onto my side.

"Get off me!" I tried to yell, but the pressure on my chest made it come out like a choking plea. I kicked both legs now, hitting Pastor Lyle on his side with my knees, loosening his grip. "Get your filthy fucking hands off me!" My hips bucked and for a moment I was free. All my limbs scrambled, not knowing how to coordinate an escape. But before I could get up, Pastor Lyle had swung his whole self on top of me, straddling my waist. I screamed and raised my arms to slap at his face. "Jared!" I yelled.

He forced my arms down again and moved his body up my torso to pin my elbows down with his knees. His hands free, he placed his sweaty palms on my forehead, slid his fingers around the back of my skull, and squeezed. "You no longer have any power over this girl," he said, breathing heavily. His sour breath was laced with mint. I stared down at his crotch, just inches from my face. The purple fabric stretched tight to reveal the black stitching of the seam. I started kicking again, my legs working as if they were running in place, my knees striking his back with as much force as I could gather.

"Help!" Pastor Lyle yelled, and immediately I heard my bedroom door swing open. In a second I could see my parents at the side of the bed. They had been waiting at the door, listening to all of this. Both had tears in their eyes and were staring down at me in disbelief.

"Hold her arms and legs," Pastor Lyle told them. "It's fighting us. It's using her body to fight us."

"No," I yelled, looking my father right in the eyes. "Make him stop. Make him get off me!"

"That's not your daughter," Pastor Lyle said. "We have to free her. That's not Melanie talking."

My mother bit her lower lip and shook her head. My father looked closely at me, studying my face.

"It is!" I yelled. "It's me!"

"Don't let him fool you," Pastor Lyle said, sliding another inch nearer my face. "This one is strong—I can feel it."

"Shut the fuck up!" I snapped my teeth in the direction of his crotch, making him jerk back.

My mother put a stunned hand over her mouth, her eyes flooded over with tears.

"Let me go! Dad!"

"That's not your daughter," Pastor Lyle said again.

"Stop saying that!" I began kneeing him again in the back. "You filthy fucking bastard! Get off me! Dad!"

I watched my father's face harden into determination.

"Hold her arms and legs."

With reluctance, as if they'd been asked to handle a large snake, my parents hesitated and then laid their hands on me, my father grabbing hold of my knees and my mother pulling her angel sleeves over her hands and pinning my wrists down. I stared up at the utter blankness of the ceiling, trying not to look at them. With Pastor Lyle still sitting on me, it was almost impossible to move. I knew the more I fought, the more they would be convinced of the demon inside me, but still I fought. I shook my head from side to side like a crazy person and arched my back. I could not see my father behind Pastor Lyle but could feel his hands shaking, wobbling my kneecaps back and forth. My mother, with her face turned to the side, stared at a spot on the wall until I was too tired to fight and Pastor Lyle had finished his prayer.

I looked out the windows but could see nothing. I had no idea what time it was and could not bring myself to turn around to look at the clock ticking behind me. To move, I had decided, was to acknowledge defeat. I stared down at my hands, which were holding each other on my lap, trying to act normal.

"You are back in control now, Melanie," Pastor Lyle said, sitting on my parents' couch with a cup of coffee sheltered between his hands. My parents, still in costume, sat on either side of him smiling brightly, like matching table lamps.

I was sitting opposite them on the edge of my mother's rocking chair, my skirt still twisted to the side, my back and neck burning from the heat of the fire in the fireplace. While I was alone with Pastor Lyle in the bedroom, my parents had started a fire. In June. The fire that was heating up the house to an unbearable temperature. This was the heat I had felt when he was sitting next to me, brushing my hair from my forehead.

My entire body felt like it had been pulled apart and jammed back together again. I had trouble just sitting there in our living room, in this civilized pose, when all I wanted to do was collapse on the floor. I wanted to lie down and go completely limp, so limp that no one could grab me or move me or force me to stand. I fingered the buttons on my blouse, finding that one near the bottom was missing.

"This is an important time for you," Pastor Lyle said to his hands. "Now that you are back in control, you are accountable for everything you do. And I think it's important that you begin with a clean slate." He reached down, set his mug onto the coffee table, and picked up Darwin, held it up for me to see. The *Beagle* on the cover, rocking back and forth, as he waved the book at me. "This false teaching contradicts the Word of God. It's filled with lies inspired by Satan, meant to trick us into believing a lot of things that aren't true." He leaned forward, his eyes squinting, focusing the beams of his stare right into my eyes. "Do you really believe that people come from monkeys, Melanie?" He paused, waiting for me to answer as I listened to the sound of water draining somewhere in the walls. My parents leaned forward, too, just slightly.

"No," I said.

"Do you believe that God created the world and made us all perfect, in His image?"

"Yes," I said, wiggling a finger through the orphaned buttonhole.

Pastor Lyle studied me for a moment. I met his stare, trying to look him right in the pupils. Finally, he nodded, which caused my parents to sigh and lean back against the couch. Pastor Lyle stood up and held the book out to me. "If you continue to possess this, the sin of it will be on your soul."

I stood up, reached across the coffee table, and took Darwin from him.

"Burn each page," Pastor Lyle told me. "Prove your faith to the Lord."

"Gladly," I said, turning to the fireplace and sitting down on the hearth. My eyebrows tightened in the heat, the hair on my arms tried to retreat back into my skin. I placed a hand on the rough brick, painted with black-and-white splotches to make it look older than it really was. I envisioned the Devil with his gold wristwatch on, traveling the world, burying artifacts, and restructuring carbon bonds to trick us into thinking the earth was older than it was. His last stop, this fireplace. Can of paint in hand, painting age spots on the bricks in the middle of the night. I laughed deep down in my throat, where no one could see or hear. Gladly. If this was all it took, then I would do it gladly. None of this mattered, I now knew. This exact moment I had been dreading, when all I had worked for seemed to be crashing down, this entire month that had changed everything I had once believed in—it all became nothing more than a speck, a thousandth of a tenth of an inch on an infinite measure of time. I glanced back at Pastor Lyle and my parents, the intensity in their faces so convinced of the gravity of this moment, as if I had the power to create or destroy God with my own hands. I opened to the first page, which read in huge letters: "THE THEORY THAT SHOOK THE WORLD." I ripped it out and threw it into the fire. This was easy. I watched the page shrivel and turn black, like the fast-forward of an animal decomposing. I did the same to the second page, the title page. I couldn't believe that this was all it took to convince them. They would never realize that the book didn't even matter anymore. I thought of Darwin's butterflies again, how not even scientists could tell an impostor without a microscope. I imagined the Church, the entire sanctuary filled with butterflies, white-and-orange butterflies that swarmed all the way up to the ceiling, their wings frantic but utterly silent. I turned to my parents and smiled as I ripped out another page, feeling laughter again flutter in my chest. There were only four hundred and ninety pages to go until my soul was clean.

Epilogue

After my parents dropped her off at her house that night of the play, I did not talk to Beth for two weeks, when she called to ask me why I hadn't called her. I didn't have an answer for this, other than telling her I had been busy with camp. I did not want to bring up the play or ask her if she forgave me for what I had done. When I went over to her house the next night, she didn't mention it, for which I was grateful. And when I told her that I had lost her dad's Darwin book, she shrugged and said he wouldn't miss it. She didn't think he even knew he owned it. She never mentioned going to church with me again. I never asked her about it, although my parents brought it up every now and then. When the play rolled around a year later, I told them Beth was on vacation in Florida, and even went without seeing or talking to her that entire week to make them believe it. I was in the play that year. My parents insisted that I try out. Pastor Lyle gave me the part of Jen, the little girl in the plane wreck who goes to Hell. My parents were so proud that they invited everyone they knew to come and see me.

Jared was gone by the end of the summer—moved to Indianapolis to work some job no one knew anything about. Before he left, he told me to never take a job that would risk my health. He coughed as he said this, whether for effect or because he was really sick, I couldn't tell. At first I wasn't sure I could make it without him, but after a while I stopped looking for his car in the driveway whenever I came home from school. And by the time the weather turned cold, I was used to being an only child, used to having all of my parents' attention on me. I had started to take pleasure in the fact that I had learned to elude them, even as I won yet another county title in the Bible Quiz Championship. They could have dissected me on the kitchen table, turned me inside out, and still would have known nothing about me at all.

Kyle came home again in November, toting Caitlyn, a twenty-pound belly, and two suitcases. We hadn't seen her in five months, since she'd left to marry Lance. She was seven months pregnant. I was in the ninth grade and at school when she arrived, but I remember hopping off the bus to see her standing in the front yard, looking like she was going to pop. Caitlyn was on a blanket in the grass, chewing on a rubber toy. The suitcases sat on the front stoop. Kyle told me she'd been knocking and ringing the doorbell for a good hour, but Mom had locked herself in the house and would not answer the door. Lifting Caitlyn up onto my hip, I walked to the door and fished in my pocket for the key. When I stepped inside, my mother was standing at the top of the stairs, staring down at me and Caitlyn. She started screaming at me, calling me a whore, a terrible mother, telling me to get out of her house, but I just stood there and took it. When she was finished, she retreated to her bedroom and slammed the door. I turned to see if Kyle had heard, but she was across the street, dipping her feet in the pond. I could see her on the old white dock my father had built twenty years before, lying on her back and letting her legs hang over the side. She was completely still, with her face turned up to the sun. Her belly bulged into the air like a balloon, and I would not have been surprised if, right then, she just floated away with the weightlessness of it.

Acknowledgments

I'd like to thank Nicholas Sparks and the University of Notre Dame for the financial support that made it possible to write this book. Without the fellowships awarded to me, I would never have had the time to even think of beginning such a project. Also, much gratitude to my first readers: Valerie Sayers, Steve Tomasula, and Corey Madsen. Their commentary and enthusiasm were vital to shaping the narrative in its early stages. Thank you to my editor, Jenna Johnson. I was so lucky to have an editor who shared my vision for my first novel. Her trust and input were invaluable when I was so close, yet so far. Many thanks to my agent, Alice Tasman. Her suggestions made me see my own story in completely different ways and sharpened my critical eye. Without her dedication, insight, and hard work, this book wouldn't have made it into print. Thank you, Jamison Davis, for sticking it to the Man and letting me make free copies at your work. And to Nate Gunsch, Director of Special Ops: Giddy up! Thank you, Susan Amster, Sara Branch, Erin DeWitt, and Susan Gerber for overseeing the infinite, tedious details that would have left me cross-eyed. To Dani Rado, whose tremendous support during the revision process spanned from the editorial to the domestic. If only everyone was so well-rounded. Thank you to the Shesko family—Greg, Marilyn, and Liz—for their love, generosity, and for introducing me to Thai food and the *New Yorker*—now *that's* salvation. Much love and thanks to my father, whose compassion in life has taught me compassion toward my characters, and whose faith in me has somehow survived alongside his faith in God. And finally, I am forever indebted to Anthony Walton, my mentor and friend, who taught me everything I know about reading, writing, and keeping my eye on the ball.